A *National Geographic Traveler* Book of
A Barnes & Noble "Discover Great New Writers" Pick
A WETA (PBS) Book of the Week
A *JVibe* "Scintillating Summer Read"

PRAISE FOR

A LONG, LONG TIME AGO
AND ESSENTIALLY TRUE

"Beautiful . . . For all the great literary love stories, it's sometimes hard to imagine a new one will come along and be as moving or full of feeling as a Romeo and Juliet, or a Elizabeth and Mr. Darcy, or a Daisy and Gatsby. But the relationship between Pigeon and Anielica . . . is the stuff of great romantic epics. And this debut novel is also full of humor . . . thanks to Brigid Pasulka's unforgettable writing . . . It really feels like a true-life fairy tale." — *Glamour*

"Engaging . . . [Pasulka's] sweet, generous novel offers hope that her appealing heroine and a nation too often brutalized frequently by the forces of history will both have better tomorrows."
— *Chicago Tribune*

"Transports us through the outer layers straight into the heart of Poland, brilliantly evoking the country's emotional landscape. Pasulka's narrative masterfully braids two stories."
— *National Geographic Traveler*

"Completely charming." — *Chicago Reader*

"With the effortless, accomplished grace of a gifted storyteller, Pasulka weaves together the two strands of her story, re-imagining half a century of Polish history through the legacy of one profound love affair — that of the Pigeon and Anielica — which readers won't soon forget." — BookBrowse

"*Essentially True* is warm and charming, and it brings together a matched pair of stories about old and new Poland together with careful craft."—*Philadelphia City Paper*

"The two stories [Pasulka] tells have a fairy tale quality . . . [and offer] an understanding of what the times during the war and after the fall of communism were like."—*Concord Insider*

"Reading *A Long, Long Time Ago and Essentially True* made me want to dig out all those brittle, yellowing photo albums my mom has stashed away in the attic and brush the dust off my own family's history."—*JVibe*

"Delicately written and nicely observed."—*The Onion*'s A. V. Club

"A heartwarming tale."—*Polish American Journal*

"[Pasulka's] novel's conclusion is brave and not simple, not easy, not pat—much like the people of Poland."—The Book Studio

"Pasulka's delightful debut...creates a world that's magical despite the absence of magical happenings, and where Poland's history is bound up in one family's story."—*Publishers Weekly*, starred review

"Consistently magical . . . This first-time novelist has an indisputable talent for a tale well-told . . . Like any good host, she makes us feel as if we've found a small piece of home."—*BookPage*

"Gripping . . . History is not dead—it is just fascinating to see it at work in the present."—*Times* (UK)

"A lively book which is part satire, part fairytale."—*Guardian* (UK)

"[Pasulka's] writing has an enjoyably peppery wit . . . while the portrait of a national character built on centuries of facing down colonisers rings essentially true."—*Financial Times* (UK)

"Moving and convincingly told."—*Metro* (UK)

"What Louis de Bernières did for Kefalonia, Brigid Pasulka does for Poland, weaving together the two strands of her story with a deftly magical touch into a witty, wise, and heartbreaking love story that will enchant you to the very end."— Bookhugger (UK)

"Brilliant . . . While the book has such a lovely comedic approach . . . it never loses sight of the painful truths of the families it gives us."
— Bookbag (UK)

"Pasulka is not just a gifted storyteller, but a natural comic . . . A well told and charming story that has an intoxicating mix of tragedy and humor, with a dusting of miracle, magic. and a lot of love."
— *Post* (Ireland)

"In this life-affirming novel of past and present, Brigid Pasulka twines the bright colors of fable with the subtler tones of disillusionment, survival, and rebirth — incarnating not only her characters and their lives, but Poland itself. Rarely does a novel succeed so well in evoking place and history, especially with a story as winning as this one. A marvelous debut."
— Nicole Mones, author of *The Last Chinese Chef* and *Lost in Translation*

"Funny and romantic like all the best true stories."
— Charlotte Mendelson, author of *When We Were Bad*

"Grand in scope, yet meticulous in detail, Brigid Pasulka's generous and affectionate novel finds universal truths in both its most-dramatic moments and its most-intimate observations. A compassionate, elegant, and moving debut."
— Adam Langer, author of *Crossing California*

"Two lives, a grandmother's and her granddaughter's, are knit together in a finely wrought tapestry that illuminates an inheritance of a less familiar kind. At once haunting and exquisitely vibrant, Pasulka's original tale is a treasure, transcending history, time, and place."— *Martha McPhee,* author of *Gorgeous Lies* and *L'America*

A LONG, LONG TIME AGO AND ESSENTIALLY TRUE

Brigid Pasulka

A LONG,
LONG
TIME AGO
AND
ESSENTIALLY
TRUE

Mariner Books
Houghton Mifflin Harcourt
BOSTON NEW YORK

First Mariner Books edition 2010

Copyright © 2009 by Brigid Pasulka

www.hmhbooks.com

Library of Congress Cataloging-in-Publication Data
Pasulka, Brigid.
  A long, long time ago and essentially true /
Brigid Pasulka.
     p. cm.
  ISBN 978-0-547-05507-7
  1. Young women — Poland — Fiction. 2. Grand-
parents — Fiction. 3. Krakow (Poland) — Fiction.
4. Poland—Fiction. I. Title.
  PS3616.A866L66 2009
  813'.6 — dc22   2008049494

ISBN 978-0-547-33628-2 (pbk.)

Book design by Melissa Lotfy

Printed in the United States of America

DOC 10 9 8 7 6 5 4 3

Some Polish names have been modified, and some
Polish words have been simplified or Anglicized
to make the pronunciation and meaning clearer
for the non-Polish-speaking reader.

For Anna and Anita,
without whom
my Krakow would not exist

Let me gaze once more on Krakow,
at her walls, where every brick and
every stone is dear to me.

—POPE JOHN PAUL II on the
Krakow Błonia, June 10, 1979

A LONG, LONG
TIME AGO AND
ESSENTIALLY TRUE

I

A Faraway Land

THE PIGEON WAS NOT one to sit around and pine, and so the day after he saw the beautiful Anielica Hetmańska up on Old Baldy Hill, he went to talk to her father.

The Pigeon's village was two hills and three valleys away, and he came upon her only by Providence, or "by chance," as some would start to say after the communists and their half-attempts at secularization. He happened to be visiting his older brother, Jakub, who was living at the old sheep camp and tending the Hetmański flock through the summer; she happened to be running an errand for the Fates and her father to drop off a bottle of his special herbal ovine fertility concoction. Ordinarily, of course, a maiden meeting with a bachelor alone—and over the matter of ovine procreation no less—would be considered *verboten* or *nilzya* or whatever the Polish equivalent was before the Nazis and the Soviets routed the language and appropriated all the words for forbiddenness. But the Pigeon's brother, Jakub, was a simpleton, a gentle simpleton, and the risk of Anielica twisting an ankle in the hike was greater than any danger posed by Jakub.

The Pigeon happened to be climbing up the side of the hill just as the sun was sliding down, and when he spotted his brother talking to the girl in front of the old sheep hut, he stopped flat in his shadow and ducked behind a tree to watch. The breeze was blowing from behind, and he couldn't make out a word of what they were saying, but he could see his brother talking and bulging his eyes. He was used to his brother's way of speaking by now, and he was only reminded of it when he saw him talking to strangers. Jakub spoke with a clenched jaw, his lips spreading and puckering around an impenetrable grate of teeth, which, along with the lack of pauses in his thoughts, created a low, buzzing monotone. The only inflection to his words came through his eyes, which bugged out when there was a word he wanted to stress, then quickly receded. It was very much like a radio left on and stuck at the edge of a station: annoying at first, but quite easy to ignore after the first twenty years or so.

If you were not used to talking to him, the common stance was to lean backward, one foot pointed to the side, looking for an end to the loop of monologue that never came, finally reaching in and snapping one of his sentences in half before muttering a quick good-bye and making an escape. But the girl was not like this at all. In fact, she seemed to be leaning in toward Jakub, her nodding chin following his every word, her parted lips anticipating what he would say next with what very closely resembled interest and pleasure.

She was absolutely stunning. She had strong legs and high cheekbones, a blood-and-milk complexion and Cupid's-bow lips, and the Pigeon was suddenly full of admiration for his brother for having the courage to stand there and have an ordinary conversation with such a beautiful creature. He crouched behind the pine tree, watching them for perhaps half an hour, and he started toward the hut only once she was on her way down the other side of the hill.

"Who was *that?*"

His brother stared wistfully at the empty crest of the hill long after she had disappeared.

". . . That, oh, that, that is the angel, she brought me medicine, for the sheep, not for me, and she also brought me some fresh bread, you know, she comes to visit me very often, she is the daughter of Pan Hetmański, she brought me herbs for his sheep, so they will have more sheep, and I didn't see you coming, how long were you watching . . ." Jakub breathed in deeply through his teeth.

"The angel? What do you mean, 'the angel'?" The Pigeon and the rest of the family were always vigilant for signs of his brother's simpleness turning into something more worrying.

"... if I knew you were there I would have introduced you, even though she came to see me, she comes to see me often, and 'the angel' is her *name*—Anielica—and she is Pan Hetmański's daughter, she is going to come again sometime soon, she said, maybe she will bring the herbs or bread or ..."

"She *is* very beautiful," the Pigeon said, and he brought the milk pail of Sunday dinner into the sheep hut and set it down on the bench. His brother followed.

"... maybe a book, sometimes she reads to me, yes, she is very beautiful, isn't she, more beautiful than mama, don't tell mama that, but do tell mama that I like the socks she knitted me, it is very cold up here this summer, not during the day but at night, and Pan Hetmański brought extra blankets up last week, he is very nice, and they have two dozen sheep, but it is strange that they do not live in a nicer house, it is just a hut over in Half-Village, nothing special, our house is much nicer, I think ..."

Sometimes the talking could go on forever.

The thing was to act, and the Pigeon knew just what to do.

Throughout history, from medieval workshops to loft rehabs in the E.U., we Poles have always been known by our *złote rączki*, our golden hands. The ability to fix wagons and computers, to construct Enigma machines and homemade wedding cakes, to erect village churches and American skyscrapers all without ever opening a book or applying for permits or drafting a blueprint. And since courting a beautiful girl by using a full range of body parts has only recently become acceptable, in the spring of 1939 the Pigeon made the solemn decision to court Anielica through his hands. Specifically, he vowed to turn her parents' modest hut into the envy of the twenty-seven other inhabitants of Half-Village, into a dwelling that would elicit hosannas-in-the-highest every time they passed.

Besides Jakub, the Pigeon had eight sisters, who had taught him the importance of a clean shirt and a shave, and so the next morning before dawn, he donned his church clothes, borrowed his father's wedding shoes, and made the long walk over two hills and three valleys to the Hetmański family door. He knocked and waited patiently on the modest path, overgrown with weeds and muddy with the run-off from the mountain, until Pan Hetmański finally appeared at the door.

"Excuse me for bothering you so early in the morning, Pan, but I was wondering if Pan wouldn't mind if I made some improvements to Pan's house. For free, of course."

"You want to make improvements to my house?"

"For free."

"And what did you say your name was?"

"Everyone calls me the Pigeon."

Pan Hetmański stood in his substantial nightshirt and rubbed his chin thoughtfully. "And exactly what improvements did you have in mind?"

"Well, take this path for one, it could be paved . . . and there could be a garden wall to keep out the Gypsies . . . and glass could be put in these windows . . . and a new tin roof, perhaps."

Pan Hetmański suppressed a smirk. "For free, you say." Another man might have been offended rather than amused, but Pan Hetmański was a highlander and not a farmer, and thus more concerned with enjoying his plot of land than with working it. Besides, there had been enough young men lurking around lately to make him aware of what the Pigeon was up to, that the request was not to work on the hut, but to work somewhere in the vicinity of his fifteen-year-old daughter, Anielica. At least this one had the decency to come to the door and offer something useful.

"And how do I know you will not make rubble of my house?"

"If you would like to see my work, I can take you to my parents' house. I did a complete *remont* last summer."

"And you will work for free."

"Yes, Pan."

"And would this have anything to do with my daughter?"

"I will leave that up to Pan. In time, of course."

"I'm not going to help you with any of the work."

"Of course not, Pan."

"And if you touch her I will throw you off the mountain and let the wild boars gnaw your bones."

"Of course, Pan."

"*And* if you make up *stories* about touching her, I will cut out your tongue and my wife will use it as a pincushion for her embroidery needles."

"That won't be necessary, Pan."

The others had been easily scared away by such talk, and as Pan Hetmański stood in the doorway scowling at the Pigeon, he regretted that he had not answered the door with a knife or an awl in his hand to appear more threatening.

"And when will you begin?"

"Now if you like. I brought a change of clothes."

"*Now?* Good God, you *are* an eager one. Why don't you preserve your enthusiasm until the weekend?" He smiled. "And whatever else might be propelling you."

"Friday evening then?"

"Saturday morning," Pan Hetmański countered, suppressing another smirk.

"We'll see if he shows up, the young buck," he mumbled to his wife after he had shut the door.

"I hope so. I do need a new pincushion."

The attention given to Anielica in the past year was not entirely unexpected. Some said that Pan Hetmański had even planned for it. He had always been known as a man with big dreams born into a small village, and though he occupied himself with the modest business of sheep, he had conferred his dreams on his children. His son he had named after the great medieval king, Władysław Jagiełło, which, despite the obvious bureaucratic snafus it caused, proved to be the perfect name for a partisan when the war came. By the time his daughter was born, he had raised his aspirations to even greater heights.

The angel herself had heard the entire conversation from the corner of the main room, where she was pretending to do her embroidery. "Who was that?" she asked her father as indifferently as she could manage.

"He calls himself the Pigeon. He says he is from one of the villages on the other side of the Napping Knight." The Napping Knight was the optimists' name for the Sleeping Knight, a rock formation and legend that is believed to wake in times of trouble to help the Polish people. After being thoroughly tuckered out by the Tatars,

5

Ottomans, Turks, Cossacks, Russians, Prussians, and Swedes, however, it hadn't risen in some time, and would, in the years of Nazi occupation, also come to be known as the Oversleeping Knight, and later, during the Soviets, the Blasted Malingering Knight.

"The Pigeon?"

"The Pigeon."

"Is that because of his nose or the way he walks?" Indeed the Pigeon was well-endowed of nose, and his feet turned in, causing his toes to kiss with each step.

"Hopefully, it is not because of the size of his pecker," Anielica's mother interjected, laughing roughly. She had, in the tradition of *górale* women, become weathered by the merciless wind and snow that pounded the Tatras.

"Fortunately, he didn't provide me with that information," Pan Hetmański said.

"And *why* is he going to work on the house again?" Anielica asked.

"Don't you see?" Her mother laughed. "Your father has sold you to the highest bidder."

"Sold? What are you talking about? Don't be ridiculous! This one is just like the others. He will give up before he even gets a chance to peep in the window."

"You can't see anything through the blasted greased paper anyway," Anielica's mother said, waving her arm in her daughter's direction. "But that doesn't mean that he can't picture it all in his mind from the yard."

Anielica went over to the window. She pulled back the edge of the greased paper and watched the figure disappear into the woods, the corners of her mouth creeping upward, cocking the bow that would eventually lodge the arrow securely in the Pigeon's heart.

2

Golden Hands

I RENA'S HANDS ARE WIDE and sturdy, the veins like hard roots
breaking through the soil. I watch them from a stool wedged
between the door and the old Singer sewing machine as she makes a
plum cake. First, they contort and contract as they set up the knead-
ing board and line the ingredients up in a row, then they hover inde-
cisively over the board for a moment, washing themselves in the
warm, yellow sunlight. They transform in midair, losing some of
their bulk, fluttering like wings, and when they gather enough momentum, they swoop down and pile the flour, pressing a well into
it. They grip the eggs like rocks and crack them on the side of the
board. They cup the glossy yolks as the whites trickle through a
mesh of fingers and into a bowl. They drop the yolks into the center of the hill of flour and knead the dough mercilessly into flakes
and lumps and finally a heavy ball, the heels pressing the dough into
the board, the tips of her fingers curling up around it, almost tickling it.

"I've never seen anyone make a cake as fast as you," I say.

"*Złote rączki*," Irena says. Golden hands.

It's said that all Poles have them, and that this is how you know
your place in life, by the ease of your hands, that whether you are
born to make cakes or butcher animals, cuddle children or paint pictures, drive nails or play jazz, your hands know it before you do. Long

7

before birth, the movements are choreographed into the tendons as they're formed.

"I think I was born without them," I say.

"Eh? Why don't you speak normal Polish instead of that damn *góralski* Polish. I practically have to turn my ears inside out, and I still don't understand a word you're saying." She smiles. Irena loves to tease me about being a *góralka*—a highlander—even though she was born in the mountains too.

I smile back.

Irena frowns. Over the past month, she has been trying to teach me to talk back to her like her daughter, Magda, does. Insolence is the only language she really understands.

"Anyway, all Poles have golden hands. Even *górale*. At least yours must be good at *góralskie* things—shearing sheep and plucking chickens and making cakes," she says.

I shake my head. "Nela always chased me away from the stove."

"Why was that?"

"She said she didn't want me to end up cooking for someone else."

"She's right."

Irena reaches up to the shelf above the sink and pulls down the butter mug. She swirls a knife in the water and sinks it into the damp butter. She drops a lump into the metal pan, rubbing it into pinwheels, massaging the excess into her dry skin. She picks up the ball of dough and starts pinching off pieces, flinging them into the pan.

"Irena?"

"Yes?"

"Do you remember my grandfather?"

"Only a little. But I have heard many, many stories about him. He was legendary. Killing Szwaby left and right, blowing up transports, and setting booby traps in the woods . . . bam! As accurate as a pigeon. That was during the war, when there were Nazis living in Wawel." Irena leans over and pretends to spit on the floor, as she does whenever she has to say anything distasteful. "But they say that even after he came to Krakow, he was still fighting the Soviets in secret. They say that Pigeon Street was named after him, and that he knew the pope." I know better than to ask which pope. In the two millennia of the Catholic Church, there has always, only, ever been one pope for us.

"So it was the Soviets who killed him?"

"Actually, when I was very little, I remember my parents thinking that he was not dead at all, that he had only been given a One-Way Ticket to the West. My mother used to say that he was probably cozied up in some sitting room in England, sipping tea with milk."

"Do you really think so?"

Irena frowns. She sloshes the whites into a wide bowl and beats them with a spring until they are stiff, white peaks. "Now? No. After so many years? If that were the case, he would have found some way to get in touch with your grandmother. The way he loved her . . . but as far as I know . . ." She looks up at me, leaving her hands unsupervised. "You never talked about this with your grandmother?"

"She barely talked about him at all."

"Why not?"

"She didn't like telling me stories with sad endings. She said she had lived all the sad endings herself so I wouldn't have to."

"Well, I have no problem telling sad endings, sad beginnings, or sad middles," Irena says.

I smile.

"You miss her, don't you?"

"Very much."

"It will get easier," she says with one sharp nod, and then turns back to her work. She swaps the spring for a wooden spoon and ladles the white foam onto the dough in the pan, then picks up a plum and begins tearing the flesh from the pit. The pieces of plum go into the pan along with more pinches of dough, and when she's finished, she slides the pan into the oven and bangs the door shut. She brushes the loose flour from the wooden board into the garbage pail, stows the board alongside the refrigerator, checks on the potatoes steaming for dinner, fills the kettle, lights the stove, pulls a stool out for herself and wedges it in the narrow aisle.

"Ah," she says, her body finally relaxing only as her backside hits the stool. "Baking for yourself is always better than baking for a husband. Remember I said that when you are chained to an ungrateful alcoholic who beats you and your screaming brats." She laughs, throwing her head back.

9

"Irena, why do you say I will marry an alcoholic?"

"I am only joking. You do have jokes up in the mountains, don't you?"

I study her face. She's about fifty, with short, wiry hair as black as a burnt log and dark circles stamped around her eyes no matter how much sleep she gets. She has dentures already, which are the wrong size, and when she smiles they distort her lips into a maniacal grin.

"You know, my father always told me that I would never get married, that I was born with one foot on the shelf."

Irena frowns again. "Phooh! Was that right before he declared himself the King of Persia and passed out in his own urine?"

The kettle shrieks, and she reaches over my head to pull two glasses down from the other shelf. From an empty can she keeps close to the sink, she plucks two tea bags, already brown and dried with use. Irena can squeeze five cups of tea out of a single tea bag, use a match for a week, butter two slices of bread with what others leave on the knife, and wash an entire sink full of dishes with half a liter of hot water. Her stinginess is her birthmark from the village, her impatience the blemish of the city, where she's lived since she was five years old.

"How many do you have now anyway? Twenty-one?"

"Twenty-two."

"On the shelf at twenty-two? Why, you have not even cracked the spine of your book yet."

"Some people in the village consider twenty-two to be on the shelf already."

"Some people still think that the sun revolves around the earth. What other *bzdury* did he pack into that head of yours?"

"I don't remember anymore."

"Good. Keep it that way."

It's a lie of course. When you're a child, every word embeds itself like a splinter. Even when the skin grows over, you can still feel it somewhere underneath. He told me that I would never be beautiful, that I would end up on the shelf, a *stara panna*, an old mushroom, that I had better take the first man who shows the slightest bit of interest. And to say the truth, I have never been the Anielica of the village, as they say where I am from. In pictures, my features always huddle in the middle of my face, and my hair is so blond, my eyebrows all but disappear. My thin lips cower under my nose, and no matter what my expression and the source of light, the shadows manage to find every bump, dent, and dimple. Ever since I can remember, everyone except Nela has called me Baba Yaga, after the old witch in the fairy tale.

Irena makes up plates, and we carry them into the living room, where we eat our dinner from the coffee table. Over the month I've been living with her, the table has gradually shed its formality, first losing the table linens, then the good china, then the colored napkins. Today Irena eats with her plate balanced on her knees. She is a solid but practical cook, and the menu never changes. *Kotlet schabowy*, potatoes with parsley, cucumbers and cream, *kompot*, and tea.

"Could you pass me the remote?" Irena says.

I can smell the plums melting into the meringue. Irena flips through all the commercials and settles on a retrospective. That's all they ever show on television these days, it seems — retrospectives and commercials. Back and forth, communism and capitalism, past and future, and all we can do in the present is stare at both with disbelief. First, all the familiar Solidarity leaders from the eighties parade by — Wałęsa, Popiełuszko, Walentynowicz, Lis, Gwiazda — followed immediately by the dancing chocolate bars and the clean-scrubbed village girls leading cows across meadows.

Irena mutes the television and sniffs at the air. She never uses a timer, but her cakes always come out perfectly browned. She stacks the dirty plates and carries them into the kitchen. There's the sound of a key scraping in the door, and my legs stiffen against the edge of the love seat.

Irena mutters something under her breath.

"What was that, *mamo*?"

Magda enters as she always does, on a raft of perfume and cigarette smoke, sweeping her arms as she walks, turning on the balls of her feet like a dancer bolted to a music box. Irena told me that it was once Magda's dream to become a ballerina, but her hips had grown out too far, and her splayed toes had rebelled against the taping of her feet. After that, she devoted herself to becoming a prosecutor, though at the moment, she is nearly failing out of her first year of law school.

"Speaking of old maids," Irena calls from the kitchen. "You know what they say, give away the milk for free and you can't sell the cow. Where did *you* sleep last night?"

"In paradise," Magda says, and sighs dramatically. She drops her bag exactly where she's standing and fingers her dark hair, which is shaped into the sleek pageboy that is popular among the university girls now. Part of me is annoyed by her, by her preening and the way that she treats Irena, and the other, fascinated by her secret girlish rituals — the bottles of makeup and nail polish in her room, the smell of spring after she's finished showering, the heeled shoes scattered by the door. Magda always looks like she's just stepped off the cover of an *Elle* or *Kobieta,* and I think half the reason she ignores me is because I trim my own hair and buy my clothes by the kilogram. Sometimes I catch her glancing at my rucksack and my lug-soled shoes and quickly averting her eyes, as if my belongings are giant boils or missing limbs; should she dwell on them for too long, my plainness might even be contagious.

"Put on some slippers," Irena chides her. "I don't need to wash these floors any more than I already do."

"They're new shoes. I'm trying to break them in."

"New shoes? With whose money?"

"Żaba bought them for me."

"That should tell you something when a boy's name is Frog."

"Sometimes frogs turn out to be princes."

"And sometimes they just sit on a lily pad and ribbit all their lives. Have you been smoking?"

I sit frozen on the edge of the love seat. My entire life, I knew only one house, and I moved around it without thinking. Now, suddenly I have to worry about where I put my toothbrush in the bathroom and when I can use the washing machine and how long I can leave an empty teacup on the table without feeling bad when someone else takes it away. Across the front hall, Irena yanks at the oven door and bangs the cake pan on top of the stove. She gets out plates and forks and serves up the cake.

"Where's my piece?" Magda asks.

"At the store. If you hurry, you can still buy one."

"You know, *mamo*, someday you're going to wish you treated me better."

"Oh, please. Don't be so dramatic. First it was lupus, then early-onset Parkinson's, then chronic fatigue . . . any excuse not to study. *Głupia gęś*," Irena says. Stupid goose.

"I wasn't going to worry you, but I'm having some tests done tomorrow."

"Really? While you're there, why don't you ask the doctor to fix your legs so they close?"

"Maybe it's you who needs to go out and get yourself a little something, *mamo*. Maybe that would put you in a better mood. I've seen the way that Pan Guzik gives you the eye when you go out to the courtyard to feed the cats. Or what about Stash? He always had a thing for you."

"*Głupia panienka*," Irena says. "I hope you don't think what you're getting from that frog-boy qualifies as a *little something*."

"You're right. I wouldn't call it *little* at all."

"*Bezczelna*," Irena mutters.

Their constant bickering makes me nervous, like a storm gathering beneath my feet. Sometimes I want to jump up and tell them to stop, stop before it's too late, but I know that between mothers and daughters it's never that simple. I sit on the love seat, keeping one eye on the kitchen and one on the television. There's some grainy footage of protesters being sprayed by fire hoses on the Rynek, and the way the camera bounces and tilts, I can imagine the person trying to keep it hidden under his coat, running away when the hoses turn on him. In the kitchen, Magda helps herself to a piece of cake from the pan, dribbling crumbs on the floor.

"Clean that up," Irena snaps.

Instead, Magda snatches a plate from the shelf and heads to her room. She looks over and sees me sitting in the living room in front of the mute television, and furrows her eyebrows at me. She bangs the door of her room shut behind her, and the plastic panel rattles in the frame.

"And don't bang the door," Irena calls after her. Irena comes into the living room carrying two plates of cake and sets one down on the coffee table in front of me.

"Bezczelna," she mutters. "Trying to tell that girl anything is like throwing beans against the wall."

She picks up the remote and turns up the volume, and for the rest of the afternoon, the monotone voice of the retrospective competes with the rock oompah of Goran Bregović coming from the other side of the flat.

3

The Non-Courtship

ANIELICA'S BROTHER, Władysław Jagiełło, took to the Pigeon right away, and in the tradition of great kings, he went out in the yard, rolled up his sleeves, and went to work building a wall. It was with the wall that the Pigeon had decided to begin, subtly, flirtatiously, on the outermost perimeter of her property. He said it was to keep out the wild boars and the Gypsies, but everyone else saw it for what it was—marking his territory against other would-be suitors. And Pan Hetmański agreed to make it the first project because, after suffering so many invasions from the Russians, Tatars, Ottomans, Turks, Cossacks, Prussians, and good God, even the Swedes, it is a primal instinct of all Poles everywhere to fence and wall in what belongs to us: our houses, our sheep barns, our communal garden plots, even our graves.

To build the wall, the Pigeon and Władysław Jagiełło mined the stones from higher up on the mountain, where the forest met the pasture and begat rocks the size of a man's head. The Pigeon and his golden hands felt for the right contours and shapes, instinctively finding each stone's siblings so that they fit together without chinking and would hold strong even against the butting of a ram's head or the kick of an angry Gypsy.

After the wall around the yard, the two young men went into the woods, felling trees, cutting and planing boards for a week straight.

The Hetmański family were dispersed among the neighbors' houses for three nights as the Pigeon and Władysław Jagiełło dug a proper cellar and built proper supports for a proper floor, no longer the straw and dirt the family had lived with for years, but planks so tight and smooth that they could be swept clean without the broom catching on splinters or trapping dust between the boards. At the end of the third evening, the Pigeon gathered the family and opened the door to the hut so they could inspect his work. He stood in front of the fireplace with his hands on his hips, nervously watching the fifteen-year-old Anielica run her hands across the smooth floorboards.

"It's beautiful," she said.

He grinned, his smile hiding under the shadow of his nose like a mustache. "And there is a cellar now too. I will show you later." He ate his dinner sitting on the wall with Władysław Jagiełło, as he always did, and when the sun was only a few glittering scraps of gold at the base of the trees, he led the family back to a pile of dead leaves behind the house. He brushed the leaves away to reveal a wooden panel with two rope handles, and the Pigeon and Władysław Jagiełło each grasped one and pulled hard to reveal a round hole with a wooden ladder. Władysław Jagiełło climbed down first, and the rest of the family followed.

"Why so secret?" Anielica asked.

"Just in case."

"In case of what?"

"Just in case," her father repeated.

Everyone else nodded in agreement, and when they returned to the surface, they replaced the cover and spread the leaves and dirt over it as naturally as possible. Pani Hetmańska was so moved by the work they had done that she broke from her usual hardness, first hugging her son and then the Pigeon, the dirt and grime from his face leaving an imprint on her cotton blouse not unlike the shroud of Torino. The Pigeon blushed and ducked his head in embarrassment. Then, without any ceremony, just as he had done every evening for the past several weeks, he gathered his tools, put on his vest, and set off to walk the two hills and three valleys back to his parents' house.

The transformation of the Hetmański hut that summer was nothing short of miraculous. May saw the windows replaced with clear glass and sturdy frames, as well as a pump and a pipe fitted to make a kitchen sink. June, the addition of two small rooms on either side of the main room. In July, the Pigeon took Pan Hetmański aside and had a Serious Conversation About Hygiene, a full eight years before the communist volunteers were dispersed throughout the mountains to have their own Serious Conversations About Hygiene with the górale. Unsuccessfully, if you remember. It wasn't that the górale were *against* hygiene per se; rather, they were simply against anyone *outside* their garden walls trying to make any suggestions about what went on *inside* their garden walls, and the communists eventually learned the valuable lesson that any subsequent policies enforced on the highlanders should neatly skip the discussion step. The Pigeon, though, after only a few months, had gained more respect in Pan Hetmański's eyes than the communists ever would, and the result was that one Friday, the Pigeon and Władysław Jagiełło took off down the mountain with a pallet of sheepskins and returned two days later bearing a white porcelain throne for Anielica and the rest of the family.

The Pigeon worked tirelessly every day that summer, stopping only for the midday meal, which he and Władysław Jagiełło ate outside, first on the wall and then on the bench they had constructed with the leftover floorboards. They grew as close as brothers. Władysław Jagiełło, who had always been a little soft, admired the strength of the slightly older Pigeon, and had by the fall been transformed along with the hut, his back now strong, his hands rough, his skin thick with sweat and sun, his will hardened. And the Pigeon enjoyed having a boy his age he could actually converse with, and not just interrupt.

Besides this friendship, the Pigeon never once asked for anything in return, barely even catching glimpses of Anielica, who mostly stayed in the house or disappeared into the woods. Pani Hetmańska, whose affections for the boy had grown, would try to send her out in the mornings with a pitcher of cold water or a hunk of bread and butter, but despite her looks, Anielica was painfully shy and could barely raise her eyes to look at him. Whenever the Pigeon saw her coming, he would grab his shirt, wipe his face with it, and quickly put it on. They never spoke beyond the most polite "Thank you kindly" and "You're most welcome," and Anielica always returned to the house with an empty tray and disappointment in her eyes.

The other residents of Half-Village observed the curious non-courtship with intense interest, and opinion polls were taken daily. Although results were subject to fluctuation, on average about five out of the twenty-seven other residents of Half-Village thought that the Pigeon did not talk because he had been stunned into silence by Anielica's beauty up close. Five thought that he was a coward, that he did not have the eggs to speak to her and had done all the work for nothing. Sixteen thought that he was an idiot and the only language he could speak was the language of work, the language of his hands.

But the Pigeon was not an idiot. As it turned out, he was more literate than all the inhabitants of Half-Village save the rare beauty he was building the house around. As the oldest son—besides Jakub, no one ever counted Jakub—he had attended primary school in his village for the first two years, but his parents could not afford the extravagance of shoes for long, especially at the rate his feet grew. So he had made a deal with one of the neighbor children whereby he would do the boy's chores each day if the boy brought home books for him to read and taught him everything he had learned at school.

And the Pigeon was no *głupek* about women either. He had learned something about them from his eight sisters, and if over the years he had absorbed only this one thing, it would stand as vindication that a boy does not suffer needlessly from growing up in a house with eight sisters. That thing was that a woman's heart is not bought by the currency of a man's emotion for her. A woman's heart is won over by her own feelings for herself when he just happens to be around, and as the hut slowly transformed itself into a three-room mansion around her, Anielica could not help but feel even more beautiful, even more worthy.

In some girls, this kind of pride might be applied to the exterior, caked on like layers of makeup, but with Anielica, the pride filled her heart from within, and when she looked around, she happened to look out the clear glass windows, past the newly laid stone path and into the yard, where the Pigeon and her brother were pounding together sheets of tin to make what would come to be known as The Best Roof Anyone Had Ever Seen This Side of the Oversleeping Knight. If you laugh at the name, you have never seen the roof. There he was, stooping over the sheets of tin, laughing at something her brother had said, the motions of his arm rippling through his back, the sunlight perching on his long nose.

Which brings up the theory of the twenty-seventh resident of Half-Village, that the Pigeon was not after Anielica's attentions at all, but Władysław Jagiełło's, and at that he had succeeded from the very first day. It was a bold position to take because everyone knows that Poland did not have air-conditioning, homeless people, good Mexican food, or homosexuals until after the communists left. The twenty-seventh resident should be commended for being ahead of his time. He was in fact wrong, though. The Pigeon's heart had always and would always answer only to Anielica, and after all the speculating around and about them, it was the angel herself who finally found the words to break the silence.

4

The Seven Good Years of Pani Bożena

THE NUMBER 8 TRAM scrapes along Królewska Street like a knife cutting along the radius of a tree stump, crossing the ring roads that divide the city, slowly revealing its age. At the very center is the main square—the Rynek—guarded by the centuries-old, stuccoed *kamienice* that once held the Nazi officers who were not quite important enough to live in Wawel Castle—here, I spit on the ground for Irena. Next come the idealistic, postwar blocks of flats, built with honest sweat by honest men, followed immediately by the sprawling *osiedla*, pinned together by dishonest men with the leftovers of graft and embezzlement in the fifties and sixties. After that appear the sturdier blocks, like Irena's, from the seventies, when Gierek was in charge and all the shelves were full, and then the crumbling projects built resentfully between the strikes of the eighties. Finally, there are the single-family houses with high gates, constructed only in the past few years with American dollars as crisp as dry leaves. I travel this route twice a day, past an endless and dizzying number of side streets and cars, rolling back time in the mornings, speeding toward the future in the afternoons.

Pani Bożena owns one entire corner *kamienica* on Bishop Square. It's only steps from the music school and a couple of consulates, a grand location heavy with trees, which is probably why the prostitutes favor it. The prostitutes on Bishop Square are considered the lowest in the hierarchy, the girls who are not allowed into the hotels or even the betting bars, the ones who cannot even find an *alfons* to exploit them. They cluster on the sidewalk in fake leather miniskirts and go-go boots, and they wear heavy evening makeup, which turns slick and orange by the morning. Irena told me that most of them are either Yugoslavian or from the village, and so I feel a strange kinship with them. We are sisters here, I want to tell them when I see them getting dropped off from the night before, outsiders in this city where only after three generations can you say that you are "from here." Instead I stand on Pani Bożena's front step and look up at the sky, pretending not to see them, sneaking glances at them out of the corner of my eye.

I wait for the trumpeter to play the *hejnał* from St. Mary's at eight o'clock sharp before ringing the doorbell. I stand there patiently, listening as the jangling *brrrng* echoes up and down the grand staircase. There are six flats in Pani Bożena's *kamienica*, but now they are all empty save her own.

"I could rent out the other flats of course," she always says, her eyelids bored with this idea. "But that life, to be a landlady," she says as she wiggles her ringed fingers in disapproval, "is not for me."

What she means is that it's beneath her, and that she has no need to rent out the other flats. Her late husband was exactly the type that Irena rails against every day, a crooked official in the city government, who lived just long enough to buy the building Pani Bożena lives in and a few others for only *grosze* right as they privatized. As a result, Pani Bożena is a woman with echoing staircases and large banknotes, which in the beginning I would take to the outdoor markets, causing the women behind me in line to mutter and curse me with their eyes as the vendors ran from stall to stall to find change. To say the truth, I don't know where all the small bills go when I bring them back to her. She must diligently take them back to the bank every week to exchange them for large, crisp denominations. After all, without the five-hundred-thousand-złotych bills, without the empty *kamienica* and the silk bathrobes, without a village girl to do her shopping, cooking, and dusting, she would just be another pensioner instead of the Grande Dame of Bishop Square.

It takes Pani Bożena a long time to answer the door, and when she finally appears, she's wearing a pink dressing gown with feathers that coil around her bosom and wrists.

"Must you ring the bell so loudly? You'll wake the dead. Not that I'm anywhere near death, of course." She stands in the open doorway and lifts the hem of her dressing gown. "Have you ever seen legs like that on a pensioner?"

A woman and a child are passing by on the sidewalk, and the mother gives Pani Bożena a strange look.

"Well . . . have you?"

"No." I want to add that no other pensioner has ever lifted her robe to show me.

"Of course you haven't. These are the legs of Olivia de Havilland. Have I ever told you that people used to tell me I looked like her?"

I look at the line of foundation along her jaw, the feathering lipstick, the purple eye shadow sliding down to her crows'-feet. I shake my head and follow her in.

The building is a fortress, a *matryoshka* doll of doors, each successive pair smaller than the last, and Pani Bożena carefully opens each set, choosing from the giant key ring that she jangles rhythmically as she ascends the stairs.

"I thought you were going to fix that bell, by the way."

"It's not any better?" In fact, I spent the first two weeks experimenting with the doorbell, wrapping different pieces of material around the clapper—wool yarn, then cotton, then a bit of satin clipped from an old pair of her underwear. First she would complain that it was too loud, then too quiet, and finally I realized that even if I managed to fix the doorbell, she would still open the door complaining about something. It might as well be the doorbell.

At the door of the flat, she squints at the ring of keys and chooses the right one. She has bad eyesight but refuses to wear glasses. I hang my coat and my rucksack on one of the hooks by the door, and she leads the way to her bedroom. She sits down in front of her dressing table, on the green velvet stool, whose surface has been crushed into half-moons over the years. She straightens her back and neck as if there's someone watching her.

"Could you just give my face a little touch-up, Baba Yaga?" she asks. She smirks like a child whenever she says my name, her smile distributed evenly between her eyes and her mouth, her white, translucent curls framing her face like the papery skin of garlic. She looks a little like Shirley Temple, actually. The age only begins to settle in her face when she's displeased or when she does her own makeup. I unscrew the cap on the cold cream, unfold a tissue, and go to work.

"And could you do my hair like Elizabeth Taylor today?" she asks.

"From *Cleopatra, Father of the Bride,* or *Cat on a Hot Roof*?" I think this is part of the reason she keeps me on, because I know all the old movies.

"From *Dynasty*."

"That's Joan Collins."

"Oh. Then Joan Collins. In that scene right before she has the fight with Krystle in the studio. When her hair is all piled on her head."

"Okay."

I stand between her and the mirror so she will not notice that all I'm doing is taking the makeup off. I rub the cold cream into her face and tell her to close her eyes as I run my fingertips across her eyelids and sweep a dry brush across her cheeks. I take out a wig and wrestle with it, but she grows impatient and it sits lopsided on her head for the rest of the day.

Pani Bożena is in her late sixties, the same age Nela would be, but to say the truth, Nela was much more beautiful. She could have easily passed for a Hollywood starlet. She had long blond hair that she would twirl into pin curlers at night and brush out into soft waves in the morning. She wore filmy blouses and brightly colored skirts that she managed to sew from the leftover material from her clients and the relief packages, and a detachable fur collar that she rotated among her sweaters and coat three seasons of the year. There were always shortages, but even if she was only going to the church or the market or her job at the post office in Pisarowice, she wore eye makeup and red lipstick. Like pornography, they told us in scouts, but to me she was beautiful, and as she stood behind the counter at the post office, I always thought she should be conducting television interviews and giving out autographs instead of wrapping and stamping packages. The only thing missing was a Clark Gable or a Marcello Mastroianni at her side, smiling a picket-fence smile, fetching packages from the back room, and making change.

"A little more rouge," Pani Bożena says. "Don't you dare make me look washed out."

I sweep the brush across her cheeks again. "There," I say, and step back.

She squints at her image in the mirror. "That's better. That's fine, just fine."

And then she gets dressed while I start the chores. Dusting is always at the top of the list. Her flat is constructed almost entirely of knickknacks: crystal dishes, silver frames, lace doilies, candle holders, statuettes of children and animals, throw blankets, candy dishes, snow globes, wooden inlaid boxes, old Soviet pins, crosses and icons. If they were all removed from their places at the same time, I'm convinced that the entire *kamienica* would collapse in on itself, so I pick them up one by one, starting at the candy dish on the high shelf in the kitchen on Monday, ending up on Friday at the picture of the pope in the bedroom. After the dusting, Pani Bożena likes for me to sweep the stairs. Sometimes there's washing to be done or lacework to be soaked in salt, but I spend most of the morning out shopping for *obiad*.

I'm a terrible cook, and not in the endearing way that girls my age insist they are so that they appear liberated. When I first started working for Pani Bożena, it made me unbelievably anxious. She would start to rattle off exotic dishes and ingredients — hollandaise, béarnaise, pesto, pâté, crêpes, caviar, soufflé, paella, lingonberries — things that she and the other government wives were apparently eating while the rest of us were staring at bottles of vinegar on the shelves. For a full three hours every morning, I would rush around as if my life depended on it, first to one of the bookstores on the Rynek to memorize a recipe, then to the market at Nowy Kleparz, then to some of the specialty stores in the old town. I would measure everything meticulously, time everything exactly, and dirty every pot and pan in the kitchen. I would do my level best. And then for the rest of the day I would have to listen to Pani Bożena complain about the burnt garbage I was feeding her.

And then one miraculous day, I was walking down Dominican Street when I found a bright red sign blooming out of one of the pastel *kamienice*. Hipermarket Europa. I still take a breath when I step inside. How dazzling, how sterile the displays are! I can wander around with a green plastic basket on my arm and pick up anything at all from the shelves. Hipermarket Europa offers five kinds of pickles, six types of kefir, and milk in cardboard cartons. They have separate departments for baked goods, meat, and alcohol, all three set back along the side and disguised to look like village huts. The middle aisle is one long freezer with packets of already-prepared food shipped from every corner of the world: Chinese stir-fry, American hamburgers, quiche lorraine. Oh, I wish Nela could see it. The first time, I spent over an hour browsing and bought only a plastic-wrapped package of pierogi. When I handed the cashier one of Pani Bożena's five-hundred-thousand-złotych bills, she didn't even flinch, and when I was finished, I had an extra hour or so to wander around the Błonia. I've been back every day since.

Maybe I should do one of those television commercials. *Hipermarket Europa has changed my life.* And then I wander across a meadow in my full skirt and embroidered blouse, leading a cow.

"Your cooking certainly has improved," Pani Bożena says. "This is the second-best duck Peking I've ever had. And what is this? A chocolate éclair?"

"With a touch of espresso."

"Very nice. The *best* duck Peking I ever had, of course, was on Sylwester the year I was in Łódź making the movie. That was in, let's see, 1951 . . ."

I listen. This is mostly what I'm paid for. Company. A grande dame shouldn't have to eat alone. A grande dame should always have someone on hand to listen to her stories. A grande dame cannot be invisible. So I hear about shopping at the Pewex and attending parties with the other government wives. Mostly, she likes to tell stories about the seven years immediately after the war, the seven years when she sang at the Old Theater and one of the cabarets, the seven years when she was a small celebrity, even being called up to the studios in Łódź to make a film. Łódź! Imagine! Over here, under this magic mushroom is where Wajda found his ashes and diamonds, across that stone bridge is where Kieślowski and Véronique began their double lives. When Irena first arranged the job with Pani

Bożena, I couldn't believe my good fortune. I thought I was going to hear firsthand about the fairyland I always imagined, where enchanted elves and their golden projectors spin the thin filament of light that weaves together cinema audiences throughout the world.

". . . and that was the same party when Andrzej Wajda made a toast with a glass of wine and actually drank it to the bottom in one gulp. Imagine! So very Russian, so very gauche . . . so when he offered me a part in one of his films, I absolutely refused."

"Refused Wajda?"

"Yes. Refused him. I told him that no good film could ever come from such a rude, rude man. Picasso didn't burp up his masterpieces after all."

"And you don't regret it?"

"Absolutely not. What has he done since then, I ask you."

I tick them off on my fingers. "*Kanal. Generation. Ashes and Diamonds. The Wedding. Man of Marble. Man of Marble* was one of my grandmother's favorites. She told me how the audiences would get up from their seats at the end and sing the anthem . . ."

Pani Bożena looks at me disapprovingly, as if I have shouted out during Mass, and I instantly silence myself. She holds out her glass for more wine. "A flash in the pan," she says. "Color of the month. Nothing that will endure, certainly. But the food that Sylwester was spectacular. For appetizers they had miniature blintzes with red caviar and deviled quail eggs and . . ."

And that is the problem with Pani Bożena's stories. They are exactly like her flat, made entirely of knickknacks, of the banalities, the day-to-day pettiness and drudgery that happen in any job, so that she might as well be talking about cobblering or sheep raising or factory work. I have heard about Piotr the Chauffeur, who had terrible scars on his face, and Piotr the Stagehand, who had shabby shoes. I know what kind of car she was picked up in when she was in Łódź, the brand of chocolates delivered to her dressing room, and how much her lipstick cost. I know how one of the piano players at the cabaret used to intentionally play a wrong note on one of her songs, and how the studio seamstress in Łódź was jealous of her and tried to sew her costumes too tight.

I clear the plates and go into the kitchen to start the water for Pani Bożena's coffee.

"You're not making that same sludge again, are you?" Pani Bożena calls from the table.

"I bought some Tchibo today. Is that all right?"

"Ground or instant?"

"Ground."

"Oh, it will have to do, I suppose. As long as it's not that awful Nescafé you used to buy. You could run a car on it, that awful Nescafé."

It depresses me to listen to her talk sometimes. It makes me miss Nela horribly. Pani Bożena and Nela would have never gotten along. Nela could take even ordinary things—sheep, tea, books, old routines—and turn them around and around in her hands until they became entirely new and grand and brilliant.

"Did I ever tell you about the coffee they used to serve at the cabaret?"

"No."

"Pure Colombian, dark roasted, finely ground. Oh, they did everything right there . . ."

"She wasn't always like that," Stash says when I get to the club. He has a gray mustache and a ponytail tied at the nape of his neck, and his shirtsleeves are always rolled halfway up his forearms. He looks a little like Peter Fonda, in the right light. "I tell you, her *skleroza* has a hold of her now, but there was a time when she was really something."

"I know—the voice of a bird, the body of an angel. She tells me every day."

"Not only," he says, and he starts pulling down chairs. The room is long like a tomb, with a concrete floor and a clutter of microphone stands, speakers, and wires at the far end. It's filled to brimming with mismatched furniture—a big wicker chaise, some short stools, intricately carved dining room chairs, benches, picnic tables, and tiny metal café tables that barely fit two drinks and an ashtray. Every evening, I imagine it will require a miracle of transformation to turn it into a club before the first customers arrive, and every evening I'm surprised to find that the only difference between day and night at Stash's is turning over the chairs and swapping the fluorescent overhead lights for candles.

"You know, we used to call her Bożena, Patron Saint of the Black-listed."

"The musicians?"

"Musicians, painters, writers, journalists. Even a gram of creativity in the old days was enough to immunize you against steady employment. She was the one who kept us all afloat back then."

"Pani Bożena?"

Stash takes a seat at the bar, the only piece of furniture in the place that's worth anything. It's solid oak with a glossy finish that I can't resist running my hand over every time I pass. He reaches over the bar with one of his long arms and pours himself an Okocim from the tap. "Sure. If you needed a job, she was the one to go to. If you needed someone to stay with in Warsaw or Zakopane, she always had a sympathetic friend. If you only needed a drink and some company, she kept an open tab at Pod Gruszką for all of us."

"Really?"

He takes a drink of the beer, and the foam clings to his mustache. "Her husband, well, God rest his soul now, but when he was on this earth, he was just like the other bureaucrats, only out for himself . . . but his head was full of love for Bożena, and somehow, she always managed to convince him that each favor was the last one he would ever have to do. I'm surprised he didn't get into more trouble for it." Stash takes another drink. "I'm surprised Irena hasn't told you all this."

"She's too busy railing at the politicians and Magda."

Stash laughs.

Irena is how I got this job too. To get anything done in the new Poland, you have to know someone who knows someone who knows someone who can *załatwić* it for you. Stash and Irena apparently go back to the seventies. Just friends, Irena told me. No *bara-bara*.

Stash takes another drink. "And how is she?"

I smile. This is really the only topic of conversation he cares about, and he tries to hide his interest by scraping at an imaginary spot on the bar with his fingernail.

"She's fine."

"Is Magda still giving her problems?"

"Her exam is in a month. Irena doesn't think she'll pass."

Stash sighs deeply. I take this as a slight against Magda, and somehow it gives me a small nudge of satisfaction.

"If only she knew what her mother gave up for her."

"What do you mean?"

But we are cut short by the shouts of two of the other musicians coming in. They have known each other for so long that when they greet each other, their voices blend together just like their instruments when they play. Stash pours them drinks, and I busy myself lighting all the candles, mashing new ones into the old drippings, sometimes laying a new wick into the whole melted mess. Some people believe that in the drippings, you can see the future.

After a drink, they begin to practice. I had never heard Dixieland jazz before I started working here, had never met a musician in fact, unless you count Pan Romantowski and his fiddle. I guess I imagined them to be slightly above the rest of us, like saints or angels, holding their instruments in the air like chalices, a golden aura surrounding them. But Stash and his friends grip their instruments like forks and knives. They sweat. They laugh and mess around with each other when they are playing, like boys playing football. Most of the time I can't tell the line between when they are warming up and actually performing; the tables just start to fill up and the breaks between pouring drinks become shorter and shorter.

The other bar girl, Kinga, usually makes it in at about seven-thirty, but she's late tonight. She's tiny, with bright-raspberry-colored hair and gestures like a child's. Her hands flutter at her sides when she's excited, and her upper lip folds down to cover her teeth when she smiles.

"How was little Franek today?" I ask. Kinga babysits a toddler on Queen Jadwiga Street during the day.

"Sad." She pouts. "I told him I was leaving for Italy soon. We practiced how to say *ciao-ciao*."

Since I met her, Kinga has been telling me that she is leaving soon. She wants to go to Rome to work as an au pair, but really anywhere will do. She said that in *liceum*, she tried to go to France to study, then made plans to move to Sweden with Martin, the Swedish tourist she was head-over-backside in love with. For a while she was even convinced that she would win the green card lottery to America. But nothing ever panned out.

"Have you heard from the agency?"

"They're still trying to match me with a family."

"How much longer do you think it will take?"

"Any time now." She puts her hands on her hips and turns around to inventory the bottles on the shelves behind us. "If only it wasn't for that stupid Swedish whore who elbowed her way in, I would be somewhere in Lapland with Martin by now," she says, sighing.

Stash blows his trumpet, a few quick blasts signaling the break. He never bothers to put on the stereo, so there is only the din of voices surging in front of the bar.

"A *setka*," someone shouts, and as I grab for a shot glass, three others fall over on the drying rack. Kinga springs into motion beside me. She's been working here for three years now, and her hands are swift and nimble compared to mine, which fumble and bang against the tap and the edge of the bar.

"Are you okay?" she says as her hands dance at the tap, deftly avoiding collisions with mine. "That looks like it hurt."

"A beer," someone says.

"Small or large."

"Large."

"Three thousand."

"And one for me."

"Three thousand." I grope around in the pocket of my apron for the change.

"Small Żywiec."

"No Żywiec," Kinga snaps. "Only Okocim."

"Okocim then."

"Two thousand."

"Could I please have an orange juice, please?"

I look up. It's a boy about my age with shaggy hair the color of dishwater.

"Orange juice and what?"

"Just orange juice . . . and nothing."

"Two thousand."

"Pardon me, but I . . . I'm playing tonight . . . I'm the clarinet . . . the clarinetist."

"You are?"

"I am. I just started. Honest."

"Come on," a voice shouts from behind, "stop flirting and start pouring."

"Wait your turn, Janek!" Kinga shouts back at him. She reaches over me. "He is. He just started."

I overfill the glass of orange juice and it splashes all over my hand.

"Pale chickens," I mutter, and he smiles.

I wipe off the glass and hand it to him.

"Thank you," he says.

"You're welcome." He smiles at me again before disappearing into the crowd.

"Thank you!" Janek roars. "You're welcome! What kind of place is this turning into? Before you know it, there will be lace tablecloths and two-night tourists."

"If it helps, we will always be rude to you," Kinga says.

"I thought the other one was supposed to be the witch." Janek laughs loudly, as if he's the funniest man in the world.

I watch the boy through the second and third sets. I try to watch Stash and the others too, but my eyes go right back to the *klarnecista*, everyone else disappearing around him. He reminds me of a messier version of Steve Dallas from *The Sweet Smell of Success*, his black T-shirt tired and fading, his pants three centimeters short and shiny from too much ironing. I can tell that he's a year or two younger than me, and yet he's so confident, with his lips clamped around the mouthpiece, his face damp, his hips swaying slightly with the music. Even surrounded by these legends.

Kinga catches me. "He's cute, isn't he?"

"What do you mean?"

"The *klarnecista*. Don't pretend. Your tongue is hanging out of your mouth."

"You don't know his name?"

"Sure I do," she says.

"What is it?"

"*Klarnecista*." She laughs, revealing two crooked front teeth turning outward like butterfly wings. She quickly closes her lips around them.

"When did he start?"

"Last Friday, but his regular day is going to be Wed-nes-day," and she singsongs it and taps out the syllables on my arm. "And he's really good. Stash says that he's a natural, that if he keeps at it, he'll be one of the best in a few years."

"You're not interested in him?"

Kinga laughs again. "He's *Polish*," she says, as if it should be obvious to me. "Besides, in another few weeks, I'll be long gone. *Ciaociao* for now."

I look back toward the stage.

"You should talk to him."

"Right. Just go up and talk to him."

"Look, it doesn't have to be about the massacre at Katyń."

"About what?"

"Just ask him what he likes to do on the weekends, and hopefully he'll get the idea."

I've never been out on a date with a boy. The few boys in the village were like brothers to me, and I never got to know the girls at *liceum* well enough to meet their brothers or their cousins.

After the third set, there's no encore or waiting around, only the scraping of chairs, the hollow *clomp* of empty glasses on the tables, a rush for the door. It's almost eleven, and most people are hurrying to catch the last buses and trams. I start washing the glasses at the bar as Kinga weaves between the tables with a tray on her narrow hip, collecting the strays. The two large picnic tables along the wall are still not making any move to get up. They are foreigners — Englishmen mostly — most of them graying and paunchy. English teachers and small businessmen who either live nearby or can afford the taxi fare. They keep chatting, undisturbed by the exodus, a few Polish girls surrounding them, also sure of their rides home. Some of them lean on the shoulders of the men, some sit on their laps. They're the same girls every week, but they seem to get passed around the group, until the gossip surrounds each of them like a cloud of gnats.

"Could I please have another orange juice, please?"

My cheeks suddenly feel warm. "Sure." I pour the orange juice and pass it to him. He stands at the bar and drinks it while I finish washing the glasses. I can feel his eyes on my face, and I suddenly wish I had put some lip balm on, had washed my hair today, had worn my blue Italia '82 zip-up that I always get complimented on.

"So, are you from here?" he finally asks.

"No." I shake my head. "The village." When I first arrived, I said Half-Village, but soon I realized that people in the city always talk about the village as if there's only one, as if they're all interchangeable. No one ever bothers to ask which one.

"Which one?"

I look up at him. "It's called Half-Village. Near Osiek. Past Nowy Targ."

"Half-Village? That's funny."

"And you are from Krakow?"

"Huta, actually."

"Oh." No one ever admits to being from Huta. Huta is a poured-concrete wart on the eastern side of the city, a bunch of *osiedla* and a steelworks built in the fifties, the communist antidote to Krakow's universities and theaters.

We are both silent. *Amnesia of love,* Nela used to call it when it happened in films. My mind races for something else to say, but it is completely, utterly, maddeningly blank. I keep my head down, washing the glasses, and the silence prickles around us. He gulps down his juice, reaches over and places the empty glass in the sink.

"Last bus," he says, picking up his case from the stool. *"Na razie."*

"Na razie."

He walks out the door, his shoulders hunched a little, glancing back at me as he leaves. As he climbs the stairs out of the dugout to street level, I can only see his pant legs through the front window. They are about three centimeters too short, and I watch as his ankles make their way across the top of the window in the direction of the bus stop.

"Well?" Kinga comes back to the bar with the tray of empty glasses. "And what?"

"And nothing."

She slaps her tiny palm on her forehead. *"Oj!* Nothing?"

"Nothing."

"Not even his name?"

"Nothing."

But it doesn't feel like nothing. Each day I'm here, the vision of the city that Nela promised me has been steadily shrinking and receding, overtaken by the daily routines and obligations I lug like a stone from Irena's to Pani Bożena's to Stash's and back again. But tonight, for the first time since I arrived under the dull, gray canopy of the train station, I feel the strike of flint against that stone, a small spark of possibility, and it's just enough to illuminate the fairy-tale city Nela used to tell me about—the delicate filigree of streets, the shining cornices of the buildings, the streetlights that stretch all the way up Królewska like formations of fireflies, leading the way back to Irena's.

5

Czesław

THE APPARENT SILENCE of the Pigeon on the matter of their daughter concerned Anielica's parents. The bill of goodwill they had racked up with him over the summer entitled him to ask for just about anything, and they were in agreement with the rest of the inhabitants of Half-Village that the transformation of the Hetmański hut was certainly worth a second-born female child, even one as beautiful as Anielica. But as the summer wore on and he made no decisive overtures, they began to worry that he would *not* ask for anything in return, that perhaps he had decided against it once he had observed her up close, that perhaps the rumors started by the twenty-seventh resident of Half-Village that he was really after the company of Władysław Jagiełło were true.

So Pan and Pani Hetmańska decided to act, inventing more excuses to send Anielica out into the yard and finding more reasons to call Władysław Jagiełło in, for surely there was not a harder-working young man or a more dependable future husband than the Pigeon in all of the surrounding villages. When this question was added to the polls, their neighbors were in complete agreement.

While the Hetmańskis and the other inhabitants of Half-Village all agreed about the Pigeon, the Pigeon's family was divided on the matter of Anielica, nine to one—no one ever counted Jakub's vote. The Pigeon's father and sisters were very much in favor of the match, so much that they had absolved the Pigeon of his chores and obliga-tions all summer. The Pigeon's mother was against. She had nothing against Anielica or the Hetmańskis personally. They were two hills and three valleys away after all, and she knew only what her son had told her about them. But like most village mothers, she had always wished for him to become a priest, servicing the parish twenty me-ters from her door.

She had been planting this idea in his mind since he was a baby, and though he considered it for a short while, by the age of thirteen he had taken to joking with his mother that his nose was too much of a protrusion to lie prostrate before the altar for his ordination.

"If it is too large to lie prostrate in front of the altar, then it is also too large to kiss a girl without inflicting a concussion."

"Sometimes out of great suffering comes great love," the Pigeon answered.

"You read too much," his mother snapped.

The Pigeon had, in fact, given a great deal of thought to this even-tuality, of his nose meeting hers. His nose, which was as crooked and knotted as an oak growing toward a shifting hole in the canopy, and hers, which was as straight as a pine, long and aristocratic, setting off her high cheekbones and long eyelashes. Without that nose, she would have only been a pretty village girl, blooming as briefly as the edelweiss on the forest floor; with it, her face was elevated to that of a grand and legendary beauty who would be absorbed into the folk-lore of the surrounding villages. "Well, she certainly wasn't the An-ielica of the village" and "Who do you think you are, young lady? Anielica Hetmańska?" are just a few of the sayings that can still be heard today in that region.

The Pigeon, undeterred by anything, was certainly not cowed by olfactory challenges. After all, countless generations of Poles have managed to procreate despite their noses. No, his hesitation ran deeper. The Pigeon was no longer thinking like a boy, but rather like a man — that is, with his brain finally outpacing his pecker by a few steps. Even after Anielica began leaving notes for him — crumpled into knotholes, buried in piles of stones — he still feared making a misstep. So he waited and worked, waited and worked, until there was no chance whatsoever that the sincerity of his intentions could be misinterpreted.

Finally, near the end of July, it was again time to act. And though he was not one to ask permission, for the second time, he put on his best permission-asking clothes, borrowed his father's wedding shoes, and appeared in front of the Hetmański door (which he had carved), glancing nervously at the windows (which he had built), his shoes tapping against the stone pathway (which he had laid). His face was scrubbed pink, the thickets of hair slicked down with lard as best he could across his forehead.

"What the devil! Who is *that?*" Pani Hetmańska called from the kitchen sink (which the Pigeon had installed).

"It's the Pigeon!" Anielica shouted excitedly, pulling back the interior shutters (which the Pigeon had made) to get a better look.

Pan Hetmański, who had begun to think of the Pigeon as a second son, and only wished that he had been around at the birth to name him more grandly, opened the door and greeted him heartily. "Pigeon! What brings you here on a Sunday?"

"Please, Pan Hetmański, my Christian name is Czesław."

"*Czesław?*" the entire household behind Pan Hetmański echoed, and the Pigeon heard tittering from behind the door.

"On such an occasion, I wish to speak as a man and not as a bird, especially one that indiscriminately leaves its mark everywhere."

"I understand," Pan Hetmański said, suppressing a smirk, "Czesław." There was more tittering behind him.

The Pigeon cleared his throat. "I would very much appreciate it if Pan would permit me to escort Pan's daughter to church this morning. In full view of Pan and his wife, of course."

Pan Hetmański closed the door halfway and pretended to hem and haw over it, while behind him, his wife and daughter clucked and tsked at him. When the silence stretched too long, they even heaved a pillow and then a cabbage at his legs from behind, hoping to speed his answer.

"I will permit it," Pan Hetmański finally agreed. "With the escort of Władysław Jagiełło."

Later, at the wedding feast, some would say that Pan Hetmański had been naive for leaving the seventeen-year-old Władysław Jagiełło in charge of his most valuable possession — his daughter's reputation. After months of impatient observation of the flickering relationship, however, Pan Hetmański had decided that what it needed was fewer logs and more fanning. He had also been lately concerned with his son's refusal to attend Mass, his insistence that he could pray better sitting beneath the branches of a pine tree in the woods than on a pine bench in a dark church. And although Pan Hetmański had shown measured patience for this too, allowing Władysław Jagiełło to escort the Pigeon and Anielica to Mass presented itself as the perfect solution. It was a way to cook two roasts on one fire. To eat his mutton and have the wool too.

"Thank you, Pan, thank you kindly," the Pigeon said. "I will wait outside until Panna Anielica and Władysław Jagiełło are ready."

"Pigeon ... eh ... Czesław?"

"Pan?"

"Normally I give permission to take my daughter for a walk after only the building of a wall and a stone pathway." He smiled. "For future reference."

"But, Pan, I knew after the first week that a walk was not the only thing I would request," the Pigeon said, smiling, "and winter will be here soon."

6

For Sale

EVERY FRIDAY AFTERNOON, Pani Bożena gives me two crisp twenty-dollar bills. At the end of my first week, it seemed like a fortune, and I almost stared a hole through her hands as she held it out to me. In the village, we were never as poor as our neighbors, and if we needed money, it always seemed to appear. But other than her job at the post office and paying for tickets to the cinema in Osiek, I hardly ever saw Nela touch a złoty. Mostly, we traded things. Nela would do Pani Konopnicka's mending in exchange for a constant supply of fresh eggs, milk, and butter, she would sew and embroider the linens for the church instead of donating money at *kolęda*, and then once a year, during the slaughtering season, she would make Pani Walczak a good dress and get three sheep in return. Three sheep. Nela was a very good seamstress.

So when Pani Bożena recognized my surprise on that first Friday, a smile of satisfaction crept across her face, and since then, every Friday afternoon, she slips into the role of benevolent mistress, a variation on the grande dame.

"Are you sure that is enough?" she asks.

"Yes, Pani Bożena, more than generous."

She smiles at me. "And why don't you leave a little early today? Go on, you deserve it."

"Are you sure there is nothing more for me to do?"

"No, no. I will be fine on my own for the weekend. It's good for me to rough it once in a while."

"Are you sure?"

"Yes, sure. Go on. Enjoy the sunshine while you are young. Not that I am old of course. Have you ever seen teeth like this on a pensioner?" She grins at me. "All my own."

I shake my head dutifully. "No, never."

She always holds on to the bills until the scene is finished. She presents to me as if they are the winnings from the Toto Lotek, and I, in turn, take them from her as if they are a ticking bomb.

There's so much for sale now. The display windows that line my path home look like Pani Bożena's house on a larger and more tasteful scale, as if the whole city might one day collapse in on itself in a heap of Adidas shoes, VCRs, Fuji film, lipstick, chessboards, watches, sunglasses, cigarettes, Wrigley's gum, and Lion bars. Most of the people on the street are carrying home pay packets in their shoes, the pessimists limping along, the optimists with an extra spring in their step, and I know they all feel the temptation too. By the Monday after my first pay packet, so much money had trickled through my fingers that I could only contribute a small lump of yellow cheese to Irena's refrigerator, and all that week I ate my *kanapki* in embarrassment, using half-slices of ham and cutting the cheese thinner than I used to at home.

Since then I'm careful not to spend. I skirt past the mannequins in the windows on Szczepański Square. I hold my breath along Shoemaker's Street, where the smells of kebobs and French fries mingle in the air. I tiptoe past the German drugstore with its giant photos of flawless faces and backsides and its salesgirls in lab coats and neatly tied hair. I exchange only one of Pani Bożena's banknotes each Friday, and I make sure that I wait until I pass the gauntlet of stores and kiosks on the Rynek to do it. The other banknote goes immediately under the mattress, along with the money I earn from Stash's. It's said that there are so many American dollars stuffed under mattresses in Poland that we could bankrupt America in one big spending spree, and sometimes it seems like that's exactly what's happening as I walk past the line stretching down the block in front of the Adidas store.

But in a month, I've managed to save almost a hundred dollars.

Enough to rent a room from a *babcia* on a pension, but not enough for my own flat and my own groceries, not even the smallest *garsoniera* in Huta.

I cross Aleje carefully in the middle of a crowd and I go to my usual *kantor*, a hut run by a woman and her husband on the Square of the Invalids. For some reason, it's closed, and instead of crossing back over Aleje, I find another one across Freedom Park. The woman behind the glass has seen all the hiding places, and she doesn't even flinch when she sees me tuck the wad of złote into my bra. After half a block, though, the corners are already poking at my chest, and I duck into a narrow passageway to readjust. It's just an ordinary passageway, papered with handbills and death notices; hundreds connect streets and courtyards throughout the city. But halfway down this one, there's a red metal door and a small red sign, hardly noticeable. Kino Mikro. The only other evidence of a cinema is a piece of white copier paper with the month's schedule tabled out in tiny print.

I read the schedule while I stand there and adjust the złote in my bra. There are none of the American blockbusters playing at Kino Kijów or Wanda or Uciecha, none of the action films or the romantic comedies with the Happy End. Instead, the schedule is starkly similar to the death notices a few feet away. All the forgotten films: small, old, independent, and international. Later today, I can see Roberto Benigni trip over himself a hundred times and still get the girl. If I come tomorrow, I can see Gregory Peck and Audrey Hepburn riding a Vespa through the streets of Rzym. Next week, I can see German and French films completely absent of Nazi soldiers, Indian musicals with costumes fluttering across the screen like flags, South American films where every scene opens up on someone else's bed, and the old Soviet war films, which haven't played even in Osiek since the communists were voted out of office three years ago.

The first film I ever saw was a Soviet war film, one of the hundreds of films with the same basic plot that were played over and over in youth centers across Eastern Europe in those days. I don't remember the name. *Victory at Something Something*. A small group of blond-haired, blue-eyed Russian Komsomols doing their summer training in the woods are forced to become partisans and end up defeating an entire German company with a rock, some twine, and a single Kalashnikov. Something like that. The plot wasn't important. But I remember the feeling I had that day, after the Komsomols killed the last Nazi and the audience started to applaud. Not because the Russians had won, of course, but because the Germans had lost. And I remember the acute longing I felt stepping out of the youth center, disappointed to go home.

For the next ten years, Nela and I went almost every Sunday afternoon. When her arthritis got the best of her, I would make the weekly trip to Osiek alone, returning in the afternoon to narrate my version of the film, picking out the actors from a film encyclopedia that had come in one of the relief packages and the glossy tabloids that had started appearing in kiosks before the communists' seats were even cold. After *liceum,* I even had a job there.

The cinema in Osiek was one of the miracles of my childhood. There, I could climb out of my life for two precious hours and press my nose up against the bedrooms and offices and courtyards of complete strangers, strangers whose faces were not scuffed and squashed by life, who got angry quickly and articulately, leaving perfect treads as they stalked off. Mothers who did not die. Fathers who did not fight with grandmothers or drink until they fell down or build stone walls down the middle of their living rooms, exiling their daughters to live on the other side. Daughters who felt like they belonged.

I open the door cautiously and step inside, then follow the signs down a dark hallway and into a dimly lit room with the same faux wood paneling and plastic chandeliers as the youth center in Osiek. But here there's no proper counter, no glass shield, no mouse hole to hand the ticket through. There's only one girl, sitting on a folding chair to the side.

"Would you like to buy a ticket?" the girl asks. "The first film just started. It is still the special matinee price, and you can stay for the later shows."

"How much?"

"Six thousand złotych."

Only six thousand złotych. I succumb.

I stay for the matinee. And the second film. And the third. The silhouettes around me become familiar friends. The rickety rows of seats and the creaky parquet magnify every shift and sneeze and sigh so that when one person moves, we all move; when one person is moved, we are all moved. During the intermissions, we eavesdrop on the conversations from the park below, rising through the open window, sifting past the red velvet curtains.

In the end, Henryk and Anna decide to move to Stockholm and stay in love. Alfredo remembers Toto before he dies. Roberto Benigni stumbles and still gets the girl. And the entire time, I can almost feel Nela sitting beside me, the warmth of her body, the soft, accidental brush of her fur collar. After three films, my *dupa* is half-asleep and my eyes are bleary, but I don't want to leave. I sit anchored in my seat until the room clears out and the ticket girl pokes her head in.

"That was the last one," she says.

"I was just leaving."

I don't want to leave.

It's warm out tonight, so I walk back to Irena's instead of taking the tram. I love the afterglow of films, the nimbus of hope and idealism that follows you out from the cinema. The world opens wide, dreams seem close enough to touch, and anything is possible. I think about the *klarnecista* at Stash's. Tadeusz. Kinga asked around for me. It's a name from another century. An epic name. Nela used to read the story to me even before we had to memorize parts of it for school, and she would tear up as she read about Pan Tadeusz and Zosia and the love affair that survived brutal warfare, feuding families, and twelve chapters of iambic pentameter.

When I get to the Street of Kazimierz the Great, I look up and check the living room window to see what Irena is doing. I already know the code — if the window is dark, she's either sleeping or has a migraine; if it's dimly lit, she's reading one of her news magazines; if it's brightly lit, she's reading the smaller print of the satirical newspaper she likes; if it's flickering, I'm sure to find her inside watching television. Tonight it's flickering, and indeed, Irena is sitting in the living room watching her retrospectives.

I stand in the doorway of the living room. Magda's light is on across the hall, and she's listening to Elektryczne Gitary on her tape player. It's the funny song you hear all over these days, the one about the guy on the bus with the leaf in his hair who no one bothers to tell.

"What are you watching?" I ask Irena.

"A documentary about Katyń."

"Is that a battle?"

She looks up at me, startled. "You have never heard of Katyń?"

I shrug.

"The massacre in Katyń Forest? The Soviet brutality at Katyń?" She keeps saying it in different ways, hoping to loosen my memory.

I shake my head.

"Don't they teach you anything in the mountains? That is like saying you have never heard of Wałęsa."

"Is that the electrician?" I laugh.

"Now I don't know whether you are kidding or not, I really don't. How can you not have heard of Katyń?"

"I told you, Nela never told those stories."

"But this is not just another sad story. This is our past. Without this, we have nothing. I can't believe you have never heard of it."

"If everyone knows so much about it, why do they need to make a documentary?"

She looks at me, blinking, watching in disbelief as I plunge into an entirely new gorge of ignorance. "My naive little *góralka*. There is an enormous difference between *knowing* about something and having the freedom to *speak* about it. Phooh!" She swats her hand in my direction and turns her attention back to the television.

I sit down in the armchair next to the door. I look up at the painting above the television set. The canvas is bigger than anything else in the room, and bright blue, standing out among the browns and oranges of the rest of the furniture. Two perfectly white figures flit and dodge between the blue shadows, one in the shape of a woman, the second one smaller, the figure repeated more, as if it holds more energy.

"Where have you been tonight anyway?" Irena asks, her eyes still on the television.

"At a film."

She squints at me through her glasses, which she holds at the corner because she's broken one of the earpieces and considers it a waste to buy a new pair. "One?"

"Three, actually."

"With someone else?"

"By myself."

Irena shakes her head. In Irena's Krakow, there are no theaters, cinemas, restaurants, or cafés and no temptations to visit any of them. In Irena's Krakow, there are nothing but trams and vegetable stalls, post offices, blocks of flats, and the occasional milk bar.

"I know, I know. I'm a *głupia panienka* for spending all my money." I've heard Irena give the speech to Magda: you can only eat one meal at a time, you can only sleep in one bed, you can only soil one pair of underwear . . .

"For your information, I wasn't about to say that at all. After all, if you can't spend a few złote at the cinema when you are young, what is youth for? *Głupstwa są najpiękniesze.*" The stupid things you do in life are the most beautiful.

"That's not what you say to Magda."

"You are not Magda. Magda needs to learn responsibility. You need to learn the beauty of stupidities." The music in the other room stops. "You work, work, work all week long, and for what? To sit around with old women and to go to the cinema alone. You don't go out, you don't go chasing after boys . . ."

"Neither do you."

"That's different. I'm old. My book is already closed."

"You're not old. You're fifty."

"Fifty-two," she says.

Magda emerges from her room dressed to go out. She stands in front of the hall mirror, picking and preening.

"You're going out now?" Irena says. "The trams are about to stop running."

"The taxis haven't."

"I can tell from how you're dressed that you're going out with that *alfons.*" That pimp.

Magda doesn't say anything.

"What's the matter? Cat got your tongue? Why don't you shake that *dupa* of yours and see if a sentence falls out?"

Magda pulls at her eyelids and checks her teeth for lipstick. "If you're looking at my *dupa*, you must have noticed my new pants then. That *alfons* bought them for me. The sweater too. Nice, no?" She pivots around on the balls of her feet.

"Oh, the pants are fine. It's your head that needs help. Have you forgotten your exam is in less than a month?"

"All work and no play . . ."

"All play and no work . . ."

Magda comes to the doorway and poses against the frame, fluffing her hair with her fingers and curling her lips seductively. "*Mamo*, loan me a stówka."

"A stówka? Who do you think I am? The Vatican? I just gave you money on Monday. And I only gave you that because you told me you would answer the tourist letters this week."

"I had to pay the doctor for more tests."

"Maybe you should have gone to the psychiatrist instead."

"And I had to buy a book for school."

"Don't bother. You're flunking out," Irena says. "Maybe you should just quit and start charging for that *dupa* of yours."

"Maybe I will."

"By the pound. You'll make more."

"And since you were just looking at my *dupa*, you can be my first customer." She holds out her hand. "Stówka, please."

"You think your *dupa* is worth a *stówka*? Why aren't you studying tonight?"

"I studied all day."

"It doesn't do any good to study all day if you go out at night and get knocked up." Irena shakes her head. "You'll never be a prosecutor. I don't even know why I waste my breath."

As soon as Irena says it, I can see Magda's face harden, the bones rising to the surface, her dark eyebrows leveling. She grabs her jacket and her purse and slams the front door behind her, her heels leaving a trail of echoes down the concrete stairwell.

I get up from the armchair. "I think I'm going to go to bed."

"Trust me, Baba Yaga, it's for her own good."

"Pardon?"

"I know you think I'm being harsh, but I'm only trying to motivate her."

"I didn't say anything, Irena."

"You didn't have to. I can see it in your eyes. But I'm telling you, it is the only thing that works on her. Mark my words, no matter what time that girl comes home tonight, she will make it a point to get up early tomorrow and study harder than she has in a month. Just to prove me wrong." She's distracted by the television, by the black-and-white images of forests and officers flashing across the screen. "Mark my words," she says.

7

You Do Not Have to Talk First About the Massacre at Katyń

ANIELICA WAS FILLED with such excitement for the walk that she dressed for Mass faster than she ever had, and her mother reached over and mussed her hair so she would have to take the time to fix it and not seem so eager. When she finally appeared behind her brother in the doorway, a breeze blew through the Pigeon's chest that felt a little like longing, even though he was standing only a few moments and a few meters away from her. He stood up from the bench awkwardly, with none of the grace that he had when he was splitting logs or piling stones, and he absentmindedly wiped his hand across his hair, trying to smooth it. The lard had melted in the sun, and he came up with a palm full of it, then turned around and stooped over until he found a convenient plant to wipe it on.

Anielica smiled at him and he bobbed his head slightly in acknowledgment.

"Hey, Czesław," Władysław Jagiełło said, laughing.

"Be quiet, brother," Anielica reprimanded him. "You are no one to joke about names."

They set off down the mountain to Pisarowice, the village in the valley that cradled the church. Usually, it was easiest to hike straight

48

down one of the rocky gutters carved by the spring melt, but Władysław Jagiełło led them on a path that terraced across the mountain, losing only several meters in elevation before doubling back in the other direction. It was the least efficient way down, but the Pigeon was grateful both for the extra time with Anielica and for the easy path. He was not used to the shoes, and he could feel the imprints of his father's feet pressing uncomfortably against his little toe and the ball of his foot each time they met even the slightest loss of elevation. He let Anielica walk ahead on the narrow path, and as he watched her skirts ripple from behind, he fingered the stack of her notes in his back pocket as if they were a tarot deck foretelling his future.

Władysław Jagiełło walked well ahead of them on the path, giving them their privacy by absorbing himself in the patterns of the leaves, the tiny flowers underfoot, the birdsongs piercing the foliage. But Anielica and the Pigeon still did not talk, in part because of shyness, but mostly because everything that needed to be decided between them had already been decided in the privacy of their separate hearts.

Anyone in Poland will tell you that magical things can happen in the forest. You could be walking along an overgrown path and suddenly find yourself facing Baba Yaga and her hut built on chicken feet, or be surrounded by singing fairies or talking ravens or carnivorous ogres. Indeed, that afternoon, as they made their way down the mountain, zigzagging back and forth in The Most Inefficient Descent Ever Made from Half-Village to Pisarowice, something magical did happen. The birds began to sing, not birdsong, but children's songs about spirits in the forest, star-crossed lovers, and long-dead kings. The Pigeon, who had been daydreaming about noses again, did not notice when Anielica stopped in her tracks, and he bumped into her from behind, instinctively reaching out to catch her and ending up with a handful of her ample bosom. He apologized profusely, the first coherent words he had spoken to her, but she only stared off into the distance, her face a collage of fear and confusion. He followed her gaze along the path ahead, where he saw the figure of a girl filling out a white blouse and a flowered skirt, her dark curly hair piled into a messy bun.

"Pale chickens!" Anielica whispered, the strongest language she'd ever used.

But Władysław Jagiełło walked fearlessly to the girl on the path and enfolded her in his arms. It was only then that Anielica recognized her as a Jewish girl from one of the neighboring shtetls. Anielica did not remember her name, but knew she was a year or two older and had a brother. She was far up the path, but she recognized Anielica too, and had just raised her hand to wave when Władysław Jagiełło, in the tradition of great kings, hoisted her over his shoulder and ran off into the woods.

Anielica and the Pigeon looked at each other. They waited in silence, expecting them to reappear at any moment, but the minutes stretched, and the Pigeon shifted his weight, his feet suffocating inside the shoes.

"What are we to do?" Anielica finally asked.

"We'll have to wait. We can't show up at the church unchaperoned." The Pigeon began collecting fern branches and spreading them on a nearby log, seed-side down so they would not dirty their clothes.

Anielica sat on the nest of ferns, and the Pigeon sat beside her, loosening the ties on his shoes. The stack of notes in his pocket pressed against his backside, and he felt them again for reassurance. Anielica blushed.

He'd found the first one folded carefully into a crack in the handle of his hatchet, and the second one stuck to the bucket of pine tar he was using to coat the rope chinking. He had found one nearly every day for the next month, and he was disappointed on the rare days when there was not one waiting for him somewhere in his work. He loved those notes. They were not common love notes in that they did not seek to net or pin down any emotion. Instead, they were simple secrets, small ones at first, things her parents and her brother might have known, circling closer to her heart toward the bottom of the stack. He had memorized them all.

I AM MISSING MY SECOND MOLAR
ON THE LEFT SIDE, BOTTOM.

I LOVE TO READ.

ONCE I WAKE UP, I CAN'T FALL BACK ASLEEP.

50

I HAVE NEVER BEEN TO THE CITY.

I LIKE TO HELP MY FATHER
MAKE BLACKBERRY HOOCH.

I HAVE NAMES FOR OUR SHEEP.

I DO NOT LIKE MY NAME.

WHEN I WAS LITTLE,
I WANTED TO BE A GYPSY.

WHEN I WANT TO BE ALONE,
I WALK TO THE OLD SHEEP CAMP.

I CRY WHEN FATHER KILLS THE SHEEP.

I HATED OUR OLD HUT.

SOMETIMES I READ BOOKS THAT
MY PARENTS WOULD NOT LIKE.

WHEN I AM A MOTHER, I DO NOT WANT
TO BE AS HARSH AS MY OWN.

I LOVE TO WATCH YOU WORK.

They were small pieces of her mind, discrete packages of thought, but once passed to another person, they became half-conversations, torn down the middle, waiting patiently to be completed. In the coming years, the Resistance would use a similar method to identify partners and cooperators in the underground, memorizing half-dialogues or tearing postcards with scenes of their beloved but non-existent nation down the middle, the halves rejoined upon meeting.

The Pigeon took a deep breath. He was sweating, and his heart was beating through the top of his head and the soles of his feet. There was so much to consider. So many acts of consequence had preempted the first words, and now it seemed impossible to find the words that would equal the weight of the action already taken, of the emotions already felt. When you meet a girl for the first time, at the market or in a clearing or after Mass, there is no consequence at all to the first words. They can be as light and transparent as asking about the path or the weather or the health of a mutual acquaintance. As they say now, "You do not have to talk first about the massacre at Katyń." But this was still a year before Katyń, and sitting on the log next to Anielica, the Pigeon suddenly felt the burden of her unrivaled beauty, a summer's worth of work on the house, the approval of the Hetmańskis, his friendship with Władysław Jagiełło, and the pocketful of secrets. He silently cursed himself for not speaking to her the first time he had seen her up on Old Baldy Hill. Then he swallowed his nerves, took a deep breath, and began.

"So you are missing your second molar on the bottom left side?"

She nodded.

"Really? I am missing one too. Right here," he said, pulling back one side of his lip until she saw the gaping hole.

She blushed and smiled. The silence of the woods once again threatened to close in on them, and they both shifted uncomfortably on the log.

"And here is another one that is about to go." The Pigeon pulled back the other side of his mouth, exposing a black and rotting root. "My mother says it is from not cleaning them," he said, then quickly added, "but I do. I clean them every day. I don't want you to think that I don't."

Suddenly, there was a noise that sounded like a hoot owl deep in the forest. They both froze, their awkwardness transforming to alertness, then realization about the source of the noise. The Pigeon blushed and looked down at his shoes, and when he looked up, Anielica was smiling the smile that sealed his fate, not the fate his mother had planned for him, but an equally mystical one. In the end, their bond would be the only thing in Half-Village that would withstand the Nazis, the communists, the capitalists, and more immediately, the fall and rise of Władysław Jagiełło, which would begin that very morning.

8

Vampire, Whore, Nightmare, Witch, Piranha, Frog-Face, Villain, Devil, Sonofabitch, Shithead, Hooligan, and Halfdead

WHEN I WAKE UP, Magda is still sleeping. Irena is banging pots in the kitchen, making food for the cats. There are twelve of them who live in the courtyard, but I only recognize Hooligan and Halfdead, Halfdead because she's so thin and mangy, Hooligan because he has a small white kerchief of fur pointing upward to his chin. The others are sleek and black, and Irena is constantly fretting about cults kidnapping them for sacrifices. That and whether they have been infected with feline AIDS, which has also been on the news a lot lately. This started happening after the communists left, Irena tells me. There were no cults or AIDS in Krakow before then, she says, no crime, no beggars, and a fine fire department.

"But I thought you protested against the communists."

"Phooh. That was before I found out that capitalists are just communists without the polyester."

She's in her house slippers, standing over a handful of sloppy livers and kidneys cooking in the pan. She throws in a lump of damp noodles, cold from the refrigerator, and the mixture hisses and spits at her as she pats it with a large aluminum spoon. I squeeze past her to the refrigerator and start pulling out ingredients for our *kanapki*. Irena tells me not to buy any groceries now, but I still buy them, so the refrigerator is full to bursting with yellow and white cheese, ham and yogurt.

"Did you hear Magda come in last night?"

"No."

"It must have been three or four in the morning."

"I didn't hear."

"How couldn't you? She was banging and tripping all the way to her room."

"I guess I slept through it."

"I don't see how." Irena shuts off the stove and divides the mixture onto four old margarine-tub lids. "Oh, and don't forget to move your things into the living room today. I made space for you in the wardrobe."

"Okay."

"If you want, you can have the love seat."

"I'll be fine with the ottoman."

"And buzz me in when I come back, will you?"

"Uh-huh."

She takes the food out to the courtyard as she does every morning. I hear the entrance door bang down below and watch from the open window as she crosses the courtyard to the trash shed, setting the food down near the unraveling chainlink fence.

"*Ch-ch-ch-ch-ch-ch-ch-ch-ch-ch* . . . Vam-pire," she singsongs, and her voice floats up four stories. "*Ch-ch-ch-ch-ch-ch-ch-ch-ch-ch. . .* Who-ore."

And Vampire, Whore, Nightmare, Witch, Piranha, Frog-Face, Villain, Devil, Sonofabitch, Shithead, Hooligan, and Halfdead appear one by one in a tight island at her feet, their black fur glinting like a deep cask of wine. It's a touching scene without the soundtrack, without Irena swearing at the cats as she sets down the food, without her muttering to herself as she returns to the flat.

"Those *pieprzone* cats. I spend all my money on those *pieprzone* cats. The Piekarskis, the Brzezińskis, they are able to spend their money on new furniture and *remont*. You know the Brzezińskis. The

54

kindly, white-haired man from upstairs. Their daughter just married a Dutch pathologist or philanthropist or philatelist or something like that. Redid their entire flat with the proceeds. And I can't even get mine to get out of bed." She looks around the kitchen in the unmerciful morning light, at the small section of buckling tile just beneath the window, at the chipped porcelain sink that hangs loosely in the countertop and the matted brown carpeting in the front hall. "Sucking me dry, they are." But I don't know if she's talking about Magda or the cats or both.

She fishes a half-burnt match out of the can next to the sink and filches a blue droplet of fire from the hot-water heater. She lights the stove and clangs the kettle onto the burner, then stops to listen. The only sound in the flat is the knife against the wooden cutting board as I slice the cheese.

"Shhhh . . ." Irena says, and holds a finger to her lips. I stop. Irena furrows her brow for a moment, listening, then shakes her head.

"That *głupia panienka*," she says, and begins buttering the bread. "She could sleep through the Purges."

I finish making the *kanapki*, and Irena drops a tea bag into my glass. We sit down on the rickety stools in the alley of the kitchen.

"She's never going to pass those damn exams. And she'll probably fail the last-chance exams in September too. Lazy, lazy, lazy, and once again, lazy. I don't know why I even care anymore. She'll end up a shop girl, a bar girl, a cigarette girl, or some other kind of girl." She takes a bite of her *kanapka* and half of it disappears.

"But Irena, I am a bar girl."

"You are starting out as a bar girl," she says with her mouth full, "not ending up as one. That's the difference." Irena stares at the wall between the kitchen and Magda's bedroom as she finishes her breakfast. She picks up her plate, brushes the crumbs into the garbage pail and drops it into the sink with a clatter, then stops to listen again. Nothing. She goes into the hallway and stands next to Magda's door, pressing her ear against the translucent plastic panel, resting her fingertips on the handle of the door. She wanders back into the kitchen, opens up the refrigerator and closes it again. The kettle starts whistling softly and I pour the water into the glasses. There's a loud noise from Magda's room.

"See?" I say. "She's getting up now."

Irena shakes her head. "No, she does that in her sleep sometimes. Hits the wall with her hand."

"Oh."

I spoon sugar into the glasses—three for Irena, one and a half for me—and stir.

"That's it," Irena says. She charges out of the kitchen and barges into Magda's room. I hear her yanking open the curtains and rummaging around in the large wall cabinet, which is used as a catchall for the entire flat.

"Mmmmm . . ." The flimsy daybed beneath Magda lets out a similar groan.

"Oh, stop your moaning," Irena hisses. Her voice is muffled by the wall. "That Frog who was breathing heavy down your neck last night isn't here now."

"Mmm. Too bad."

"Get up. You need to study. You've lost half the day already."

"What time is it?"

"Noon."

"No, it's not. It's eight-fifteen."

"If you knew, why did you ask?"

"I don't feel well, *mamusiu*. I think there is something wrong with my glands. They're all swollen."

"You have a hangover, *hipochondryk*. Either that or syphilis."

"Is there any breakfast left, *mamusiu*?"

"At the store. Get a job and you can buy it." I hear her opening and slamming the cabinets in a constant rhythm, like a magician spinning plates, keeping them aloft. "You're twenty years old. I shouldn't have to do this. Look at Baba Yaga. I don't have to wake *her* up."

"She's two years older. In two years I'll be as responsible as her, I swear."

Irena's voice suddenly becomes low, and the wall between us tamps the words into flat murmurs that I can't quite make out.

"Okay. *Okay*," Magda says loudly, and the bed groans again. "I'm getting up. Stop harassing me."

She wanders into the kitchen wearing a pair of tap pants and a tight T-shirt. She goes right past me to the refrigerator, and Irena traipses behind her, stopping at the doorway. I try to make myself as small as possible.

"And don't waste half the morning on your nails," Irena says.

I stuff a *kanapka* in my mouth, but it sticks in my throat, and I wash it down with a mouthful of tea.

Irena turns to me. "Are you almost ready?"

"Ready for what?" Magda asks.

I swallow. "Yes, ready for what?"

"After breakfast, we're going out," she says. "You and me." She turns to Magda. "That's what you do when you work hard all week. You get to go out."

Magda smirks. "Where can you go out at eight-thirty on a Saturday morning?"

"None of your business, little daughter. *Out.* Just like you tell me."

"But I wanted to do some washing this morning," I say.

Irena gives me a stern look. "Tomorrow. This is my last morning of freedom before the tourists. We're going out."

She turns to Magda. "See, you'll have the whole flat to yourself, so there's no excuse not to study today."

Magda smirks again. "Yes, *mamo.* Anything else?"

"Yes. There will be guests starting tonight, so no more walking around half-naked."

"Yes, *mamo.* And you too. No scandals while you are out. Baba Yaga, watch her. Don't let her shake any bushes."

"Bezczelna," Irena says. But I look up just in time to witness the hint of a smile crossing her lips, like a cloud passing briefly over the sun, and all of a sudden, I become aware of a pinching in my chest that feels a lot like jealousy.

Królewska Street is split down the middle by the early morning sun coming up over the buildings, one set of tram tracks exposed by sunlight, the other hidden in shadows. The sidewalks are still empty except for the occasional *babcia* going to market or to pray the rosary. It takes a while to make our way to the Rynek because Irena stops and leaves food for cats in four or five courtyards, calling up on the *domofony* of the locked ones, where sympathetic grandmothers buzz her in. Instead of going straight down Królewska, Irena takes me down side streets, across parks, through passageways and courtyards. She crosses in front of trams and against the light. This is her city. What Nela and I used to talk about around the iron stove in the village was just a postcard of what Irena knows.

"Where are we going exactly?" I know from the *kamienice* that we are in the old town, but I don't recognize anything in particular.

"There is a nice little café under the Sukiennice."

"You know, Irena," I say, wagging a finger at her. "You can only eat one meal at a time, you can only sleep in one bed, you can only blow your nose into one tissue . . ."

But she doesn't laugh. There's something else on her mind.

We cross a street and suddenly, we're in Szczepański Square. According to Nela, there used to be a bustling open market here, but now it's only a parking lot with stores on three sides. Irena crosses the parking lot, ducking around the gates, and I follow her. She stops in front of a store called Cotton Club, which at this time of the morning is quiet, inhabited only by bored mannequins on their tiptoes, craning their necks to see the other side of the square.

"Well, I'll be damned," she said.

"What is it?"

"This is where Spatif was."

"What's Spatif?"

"The actors' bar. I heard it had closed . . . but a jeans store? We used to meet up here after the shows."

"Who's we?"

"All the troublemakers."

"Who were the troublemakers?"

"Well, let's see . . . there was Dorota and Sławek, both actors, married, then divorced . . . Krystyna, a journalist, terminally unemployed. She used to write for *Tygodnik* until she wrote one too many articles on the triumvirate."

"The triumvirate?"

"The pope, Wałęsa, and Miłosz. 'Seventy-nine, 'eighty, and 'eighty-one. That was a happy story; your grandmother should have told you that one. And then there was Marcin, a playwright, and Seweryn, another writer, who together started one literary magazine after another. The police would take their printing press and throw them in jail for a while, and then they would get another press and start another one, and the police would find that one too ... eventually, they gave both of them One-Way Tickets and no one really heard from them again. And then Stash, of course, who had to watch all the mediocre trumpet players in the city get their accolades and their flats on the Rynek while he played for free with his friends ..."

She continues flipping through her old acquaintances as we walk on to the Rynek. Everyone she mentions is an artist, a writer, a singer, a musician, or a journalist, all of them alternately tolerated, ignored, harassed, blacklisted, and exiled throughout the seventies and eighties. The streets are coming alive now, the shadows shortening. We pass several shopkeepers raising gates and opening locks.

"Right there. See that sign?"

"The green one?"

Irena points to a corner *kamienica*. "That's Pod Gruszką—Under the Pear. That used to be the journalists' club."

"And now?"

"Oh, it still is, but no one sits around like they did in the old days. I guess these days there is so much inflation, corruption, crime, and homelessness to report on, there is no time anymore. In the old days, though, some of them would stay here drinking until the morning hours. In protest."

"Protest?"

"Of course. When someone is telling you what to do all the time, anything you do of your own volition becomes a protest, doesn't it?"

I think of Magda, but I don't have the nerve to say it. We walk on to the Sukiennice, around the side to one of the cafés. Irena takes a menu from another table and sits down without waiting for the hostess. She opens it and flinches at the prices.

"Well, it is only once a year," she says, more to herself than to me. "And there will be tourists tonight."

About two weeks ago, Irena warned me about the tourists. I've seen them proliferating in the old town since the beginning of May, the Italians with their sweaters tied around their shoulders and the Americans with their giant water bottles, towering rucksacks, and famously large backsides. I've seen enough movies and enough episodes of *Dynasty* at Pani Bożena's to know about their culture and their habits, but I still can't imagine that by tonight, I will be sharing the same bathroom with one of them.

Irena has been taking tourists into her flat since the summer after her ex-husband, Wiktor, died and left the third room—my room—vacant. She says it pays twice as much as her cafeteria job ever did and leaves her winters free to read and look after the cats and her elderly neighbors. Three years ago, it was mostly fellow Poles, Slovaks, and Hungarians but, especially last summer, she says, the Westerners began streaming in, hopping from Berlin to Prague to Warsaw to Krakow to Budapest on overnight trains as if from exhibit to exhibit in a grand concrete zoo.

"By the time they get here, they don't even know what country they are in anymore," Irena complains. "They get off the train saying *Guten Tag* and get back on saying *da svidanya*. And then they talk about the 'Iron Curtain' and 'Eastern Europe' as if we are all one country. Imagine confusing us with the East Germans, the Czechs, and the Hungarians! The only things an East German, a Czech, a Pole, and a Hungarian ever agreed on was that the Czechs have the best television dramas, the Slovaks have the most mixed-up language, and Gorbachev's birthmark is the work of a pigeon."

I laugh.

"But I don't care. I just smile and take their money anyway." She laughs. "I sound like a prostitute, don't I?"

I shake my head.

"It's okay, sometimes I *feel* like a prostitute standing there at the train station," Irena says. "Excuse," she says in English, imitating herself. "You want rent room? One night—one hundred thousand złotych. Very chip. Very chip and very near for center." She laughs, and for a split second, I can imagine her as she was ten years ago, sitting with Stash and her other friends, telling stories, her face animated.

The waitress comes. I order a coffee and Irena, an ice cream.

"Irena?"

"Yes?"

"How did you know all the artists and journalists and actors? I thought you said you used to work in a cafeteria."

She hesitates. "Everyone knew everyone in the old days. Or at least all the communists knew all the other communists, and all the troublemakers knew all the other troublemakers."

"And you were a troublemaker too?"

"The worst kind." She smiles. "I was a painter."

"That painting above the television?"

She nods. "And there are some others in the wardrobe in Magda's room. But it wasn't so much about the paintings in those days. It was the protests."

"At the Church of the Ark?"

"You heard about them?"

"A little from my grandmother."

"I thought she didn't tell sad stories."

"I think she thought there was a happy ending somewhere out there."

"Did she tell you about the protests at Wawel too?"

"A little."

"Those were the marches everyone came out for. Devout and atheists alike would all fill the courtyard for Mass and afterward, process all the way up Grodzka Street, flooding onto the Rynek. The police would cut off the exits and turn on the hoses, even in winter, and sometimes they even sprayed blue dye. Those who couldn't scrub it off had to call in sick to work the following morning." She smiles. "Ah, I was never so dedicated a churchgoer as when the priests were railing against the communists. Now they only pass the plate, but there was a time when what they said mattered, when people hung on their every word, when we were all working toward the same goal. Now it is just every man for himself. That *facet* from Harvard. I tell you, he can take his shock economics and . . ."

"Is that why you quit protesting?"

"No. I would have kept going if for nothing else than to throw things at the *pieprzona* police, but I wanted Magda to be able to get into university, and she couldn't do that if her mother was a trouble-maker. So when Magda was about ten, Pani Bożena got me the job in the cafeteria and a Party membership."

"Is that when you stopped going out with the other trouble-makers?"

She laughs. "Yes. And then, irony of ironies, those very people ended up turning the whole system on its head so that Party memberships didn't even matter anymore."

The waitress brings our order, and Irena lets her ice cream sit in front of her.

"Did I ever tell you about how they would throw leaflets from the top floor of the galleria? Or dig up the concrete pavement squares and throw them from the roofs onto the police cars?"

"From the roofs?"

She nods.

"Didn't they get in trouble?"

"They caught Stash a few times. Took him to Mogilskie Street and kept him there for a few days. God only knows what happened."

She knots her eyebrows just like Magda does.

"Don't tell him that I told you, of course."

"No, of course not."

Irena's ice cream has melted in the dish, and she starts to eat, carefully cleaning the sides of the bowl with her spoon, silent until she's finished. She can't stand to wait for the waitress, so we leave the payment on the table.

"There is one more thing I want to show you," she says.

The pigeons are beginning to gather around the flower stalls, and Irena stares at a young boy feeding them birdseed out of a paper cone. They swarm, and the little boy, only a toddler, throws up his hands as if he's drowning in birds. His mother and older sister look on and laugh. Irena smiles. I've never seen her so relaxed.

We walk to Floriańska Street, at the top of the Rynek. The late-morning sky is stretched thin overhead and the sun is beating through to my bare hands and scalp. Ten years ago, when there were no boutiques and everyone was rationed one new pair of shoes a year, Irena and I might not have looked out of place on Floriańska Street, but now the street is lined with façades of clean, light stone, polished chrome and glass, and with my secondhand jacket and Irena's fake-leather, patchwork purse, we look like two refugees from the past.

There is one exception to the shops and boutiques, as out of place as we are. Halfway down Floriańska, right next to the Vero Moda shop, there's a wall of tinted windows, the giant red silhouette of a painted bird spanning one of them, its wings outstretched. Feniks. I know this club already. Kinga calls it the Old Folks Home.

Irena cups her hands around her eyes and peers into the darkened window, then steps back. She stands there in silence for a few minutes, then shakes her head roughly as if she's freeing it from something.

"This was the third point," she says.

"Of what?"

"Of the Bermuda Triangle. Spatif, Pod Gruszką, and Feniks."

"The Bermuda Triangle?"

"We always said that between these three places, it was so easy to disappear."

"You mean, get arrested?"

She shakes her head. "Internal exile. Inside yourself."

I watch her reflection in the glass, wishing that I could go into her thoughts and recover all the stories in her head. Thanks to Nela's careful editing, when I arrived in Krakow, my vision of the city was simple and pristine. Nela never talked about the Nazis or the Soviets, never mentioned the food or shoe shortages, the cramped flats, or the curfews. Never the knock in the middle of the night or the screams from the basement of the police station on Mogilskie Street. I grew up knowing the placement of every cobblestone on Grodzka Street but never hearing about the riot police standing along the side with their truncheons and shields. She would describe the families sitting around their tables in grand, stuccoed *kamienica* without mentioning the empty chairs left by wars, mass graves, camps, or arrests. Sitting on top of Old Baldy Hill, I could easily convince myself that I could just make out the spires of St. Mary's Church over the horizon, when it was probably only a mirage created by the pleading, desperate prayers wafting up from the pews, competing with the smoke from Huta.

"And you and Stash?" I ask. "What happened between you two?"

"I have to go. The train will be here from Warsaw."

"You don't want to tell me?"

"I would, but I have to go."

I smile. "Thank you for the *głupstwa,* Irena."

"That was not *głupstwa.* That was only ice cream. I will show you *głupstwa* another time, when I don't have a train to meet."

I watch her disappear into the swelling crowd of tourists and shoppers. I don't have to be at Stash's until later, but I don't want to go home and be alone with Magda, so instead I walk to the Błonia. I come here sometimes after doing Pani Bożena's shopping or when I want to escape the city. There's a tangle of tram tracks, crosswalks, bike paths, and begging Gypsies to navigate, but as soon as I cross onto the grass, onto that vast, open field, the rumble of the traffic starts to fade, replaced by the shouts of children running around and the occasional bark of a dog. I find a spot in the middle, take my jacket off and tie it around my waist. I look across the rooftops and spires of the city and try to see all the endings concealed behind the windows, but it is too much to imagine.

I lie back in the grass. The sun is bright, and when I close my eyes, I see pink instead of darkness. The grass pricks at my skin. A bug crawls on my arm. I hear the clanking of a tram bell in the distance. And before I know it, I drift off back to the village, back to my grandmother's side of our little wooden house, back to the bench in front of the iron stove.

9

The Simultaneous Fall, Conversion, and Betrothal of Władysław Jagiełło

S o, YOU LIKE to read then?"

Having finished the discussion about their teeth, the Pigeon methodically went on to the next half-conversation in his pocket, just as when he had finished with the side rooms, he had gone on to hammering out the roof, and when he had finished the roof, he had gone on to replacing the chinking between the logs with knotted rope and pinesap.

"I adore reading."

"Me too."

"I don't remember you from the primary school."

"I only went for the first two years. But my friend went for the last two, and he came home and brought me books and taught me everything he learned."

"What was his name?"

"Bartek."

"Bartek Wet-Pants?"

"I'll tell him you said so."

"Oh, no. Don't do that. Please don't tell him I said that." Anielica feigned anxiety, but inside, she breathed a sigh of relief. She had already decided that in her future husband, she could tolerate just about anything—impotence, accordion playing, garlic breath—but try as she might, she could not picture herself with an *analfabeta*, an illiterate.

She smiled again at the Pigeon, and he was suddenly struck with a near-fatal case of *amnezja miłości*. Amnesia of love. A worldwide epidemic. Silence took over. The Pigeon desperately searched his memory for the next note in the stack, for anything in fact, but his entire mind was deserted, and the only thing he could see was Anielica's smile. It was a wonderful smile. She still had all her front teeth, and the bow-curve of her top lip was so pronounced that you could see it even when it was stretched into a wide smile.

"At least you still have all your front teeth," he said.

She laughed. "And you have yours."

"I do."

"Me too."

"I know."

Mercifully, they were saved by the reappearance of Władysław Jagiełło and the girl, who came tripping back down the path with leaves sticking out of her hair that would have given the impression of a virgin's wreath had it not been for the row of mismatched buttons down her blouse and the fact that her skirt was now on backward.

"Shall we continue walking?" Władysław Jagiełło asked.

The Pigeon cleared his throat, and the girl looked down at her blouse and began hastily straightening her clothes. The Pigeon looked away politely, pretending to track the sun through the trees.

"We should hurry. Mass has probably already started."

They took one of the gullies the rest of the way down, and the Pigeon led the way, extending one arm behind him for Anielica to grab when her church shoes slipped on the patches of loose rocks. The girl—Marysia—followed Anielica, and Władysław Jagiełło walked behind her, picking the leaves out of her hair as they went, leaning down and whispering endearments in her ear.

Anielica and her family had been going to the church in Pisarowice since she was born. It was built so close to the edge of the forest that as they descended into the valley, they heard the congregation singing and caught glimpses of the brown steeple through the trees. Still, it was a surprise when the clearing opened up at the last moment, and a disappointment on this particular day. Anielica made a quick, silent Act of Contrition at the thought that she wished to continue her walk with the Pigeon instead of entering the church.

She was not alone in her transgressing for long. Perhaps it is the devil at work, perhaps merely the high emotions of the Mass, the vibrations of song, or the muskiness of the incense. Perhaps it is the proximity of so many well-scrubbed and well-heeled members of the opposite sex, or simply the vise of goodness and purity squeezing in from all sides, but there have been and always will be a greater number of lascivious thoughts produced during the few hours of religious services than during all the other hours in the week. And it was exactly this phenomenon that gripped the eighteen-year-old Władysław Jagiełło as he stopped at the edge of the clearing and marveled at the sight of the wooden steeple rising into the sky. Putting his hands on Marysia's hips in front of him, he spun her around and kissed her full on the mouth, firmly gripped her rump, and finished with a playful but audible slap. Anielica turned around just in time to see the finale, causing her to lose her place in the Act of Contrition and start again from the beginning, with even more vigor than before.

"Stop it, Władek." Marysia slapped him hard on the arm. She was the only one Anielica had ever heard not call her brother by his full name. "You'll scandalize me right in front of your church."

"Why should you care?" he said. "Besides, they're all inside thinking of their own sins."

All but one. Pani Plotka always knelt outside the church doors in the dirt because, as she said, she wanted to leave the front pews for those who needed them. Pani Plotka had claimed no sin on her conscience for the past twenty years, leaving her hands free to throw the first stone while the rest of the congregation used theirs to beat their chests. *My fault, my fault, my very great fault. And so I beg holiest Mary, always a virgin, and all the angels and saints, and you, my brothers and sisters, to pray for me . . .*

Pani Plotka had witnessed everything, and gave her entire attention over to the scene in the clearing as Marysia pouted at Władysław Jagiełło, as Władysław Jagiełło tried to soothe Marysia, as Anielica grew impatient with both of them, and as the Pigeon reminded Anielica that it would be an even greater scandal if they appeared, late, in the back of the church without their chaperone. Finally, Władysław Jagiełło's charm won Marysia over, and after a kiss on the cheek, Marysia, whose shtetl was in the direction of the Pigeon's village, went skipping back into the woods. Pani Plotka's head was now hung deep in prayer, and as the three hurried past her, they failed to notice her eyes rolling to the corners, gathering all the evidence she would need.

Anielica took her place in the pew next to her mother, breathing a sigh of relief when her mother did not even seem to register her presence in her peripheral vision. The priest was already at the "Hosanna in the Highest," and Anielica began to sing loudly to make up for the half of the Mass she had already missed. Over her own voice, though, she heard her mother's clear pitch rising beside her in song.

> Holy, holy, holy Lord
> Why give us this daughter of dishonor?
> Heaven and earth are full of fingers pointing.
> Shame in the highest.
> Blessed is He who comes and saves me from my shame,
> Shame in the highest.

That was not the end. Far from it. *Our Father, Who art in heaven, hallowed be Thy name* became *Our Daughter, who art in mortal sin, hath sullied our good name.* For the "Lamb of God," Pani Hetmańska simply changed all the pronouns to "her" and enunciated this one word with as much violence as possible. *Lamb of God, Who takes away the sins of the world, have mercy on HER. Lamb of God, Who takes away the sins of the world, have mercy on HER. Lamb of God, Who takes away the sins of the world* ... Anielica did not dare go to Communion, and her mother, to make it more obvious, made her stand up, scoot out of the pew, and wait behind her while the priest traveled up and down the aisle. By the final blessing, she had more than made her point, and Anielica dreaded the walk home.

But Anielica's savior that day turned out to be none other than old Pani Plotka, who, after Mass, explained the exact nature of the shame, or *wstyd,* to a few of the matriarchs of the surrounding villages. She pretended to be shouting for the benefit of Pani Gruba, who was going deaf, but she only applied the volume discriminately to the most shocking phrases. Soon, everyone from Half-Village,

Pisarowice, and the other two villages that shared the church were listening to the story of how THAT HETMAŃSKI BOY was practically RAPING a girl, a JEWISH girl, right IN FRONT OF THE CHURCH, only a quarter of an hour before, and that he had forced his sister to look on as if it were some kind of ORGY. As she told the story, the people flowing out of the church doors circled around her, listening with far greater attention than they had given to the homily just half an hour before. Pani Plotka described Władysław Jagiełło as a PERPETRATOR, Marysia as a JEWISH WOMAN OF SULLIED CONSCIENCE (BUT AREN'T THEY ALL), and the entire incident as THE GREATEST SCANDAL THAT HAD EVER OCCURRED in the history of the villages. ALTHOUGH, HERE COME PAN AND PANI HETMAŃSKA WHO WILL HAVE A PERFECTLY GOOD EXPLANATION FOR THE ABOMINABLE BEHAVIOR OF THEIR CHILDREN, AND PERHAPS WE SHOULD LET THEM DELIVER IT NOW. Toward the end, Pani Plotka's volume control had gone kaput.

All eyes turned to Pan and Pani Hetmańska for an answer, and they in turn looked to their children, who were cowed at the edge of the crowd. Pani Plotka, showing herself to be a more-than-competent prosecutor, judge, jury, and firing squad, allowed for the dramatic pause. Anielica's face was positively stricken with *wstyd*, and Władysław Jagiełło only looked sheepishly at the ground. It was finally the Pigeon who stepped up, who faced one hundred pairs of eyes and answered for the family, of which he was already—spiritually, if not biologically and bureaucratically—a part.

"I will explain," he began, and Pan Hetmański breathed a sigh of relief and nudged his wife as if recording his score in some ongoing, unspoken argument. "Władysław Jagiełło *did* kiss a girl in front of the church this morning." Pan Hetmański's eyes bulged in alarm, and his wife nudged him back, an invisible hash mark to tie the game. "But it was only a kiss, and furthermore the girl is not just any girl, but his *fiancée*." Władysław Jagiełło looked up, startled, and he started pinching the Pigeon from behind.

"Well, I for one haven't heard about any engagement," Pani Plotka disputed, and a murmur rippled through the congregation.

"You wouldn't have," Pan Hetmański said, taking over for the Pigeon, who was otherwise occupied in fending off the blitzkrieg of pinching at his back. "Władysław Jagiełło and . . ."

"Marysia," Anielica interjected.

". . . Marysia were privately betrothed, and we have only been waiting for her conversion and to finish the work on the house in order to announce a date for the wedding and the reception."

"Manure," Pani Plotka hissed, and now the crowd turned their disapproval on her for using such strong language in front of the church doors. "A reception at the *groom's* house and not the bride's?"

"How can a Jewish family host a Christian wedding?" the Pigeon offered, and the crowd began to murmur.

"But she will convert, of course."

"That's what he said."

"Indeed, they have been working on a complete *remont* of the house. Everyone knows that."

"And there is no other reason to put in so much work except in anticipation of a wedding."

The entire yard filled with the chatter of relief, like a summer storm clearing the air. The villagers were, for the most part, content with the answers that the Hetmański family had provided, and were too chuffed at the prospect of a *wesele* and of viewing the improvements to the Hetmański house to hear the rest of Pani Plotka's exhortations against the scandalous union of a Christian and a Christ-crucifier, too chuffed indeed to notice the groom, whose face had grown as pale and fragile as the shell of an egg. It would remain like that the entire winter, the color only returning to it seven months later, when his cheek felt the breath of his first child, a dark little girl who could have been easily mistaken for a Gypsy.

10

The Festival of Virgins

AFTER THE MORNING out with Irena, I start to hear more stories like Irena's, stories that Nela left out. On the street. From strangers. And it seems they have been here all along. All I had to do was stand in the middle of the street or under one of the bus shelters, wiggle an imaginary dial, and tune in to the conversations passing by. For about a week, I do just this, and I start to hear the people around me all talking about the old days. The War. The Trains. The Secret Police. The Shortages.

"Young people today don't know a thing about suffering," I hear an old woman tell her friend while I am waiting at the tram stop. "All this 'pizza' and 'kebob' now. They would be appalled to see what we ate during the war. Remember the winter of 'forty-four, when everyone was so hungry, we thought about eating each other?" And for some reason they both laugh.

I click the imaginary dial off. To say the truth, I don't want to hear their stories. They are just another terrible burden I don't need. I say a silent prayer of gratitude to Nela for her editing and walk to work instead.

It's been a month since Tadeusz started playing at Stash's, and I've memorized all the private details and intimate gestures that fool me into thinking I know him. I notice if his blond stubble is clean shaven, and I picture him in front of his corroded bathroom mirror, razor in hand, carefully moving the blade up his outstretched neck, giving it one final flick as he comes to his chin. I notice that he wears the same faded black T-shirt every Wednesday and that every other Wednesday, it has the look of cardboard from being freshly washed and hung outside. I know that if the final set ends right around eleven, he will rush out to catch his bus, but if it ends before, he can take a little time to chat. I know that he is shy because he varies his greetings to me in a predictable pattern. *Co słychać?* one time, then *Jak leci?* then *Jak tam?* then back to *Co słychać?*

"Stop dreaming and just ask him out," Kinga says.

"Ask him out?"

"It's the New Poland. Anything is possible."

"I can't ask him out."

"Why not? Ask him to come with us on Saturday. It would be the most appropriate first date ever."

It's Kinga's last week in Poland and she's particularly cheerful. Stash has given us both Saturday off so we can celebrate her send-off. The city is relaunching the Festival of Virgins this year, and Kinga wants me to meet her and a few of her old classmates from *liceum* there.

When the music stops after the third set and the grand exodus begins, I can feel his eyes on me from across the room. I can feel him stretching out the time as he packs up his clarinet and says goodbye to Stash and the other band members. By the time he makes his way back to the bar, the place has almost completely cleared out.

"Jak leci?" he asks.

"Good. Orange juice?"

"Thanks."

He stands there and drinks it while I wash the glasses.

"So, do you work every night?" he asks.

"I'm off Fridays and Sundays usually. But this weekend, Saturday too. It's Kinga's last weekend, so we're going to the Festival of Virgins."

"Oh," he says.

"She's moving to Italy," I tell him, because it's better than silence.

"Really?"

"To be an au pair."

"Oh." He nods. There's still a little juice in his glass.

"And you? Do you work somewhere else?"

"You mean other than here?"

"Yes."

"I can't. I have to stay home and watch my sisters while my parents work."

"Oh."

"But my other sister can babysit too sometimes. If I ever need a night off."

The moment squats in front of us, staring us in the face, but neither of us seems to be able to force the words out, and more moments stack up until the first one is smothered at the bottom of the pile. He drinks the last of his orange juice and reaches over and puts his glass in the sink. He taps at his watch, an old aluminum thing with a worn leather strap.

"The bus?" I say.

"The bus."

"See you next Wednesday."

"*Na razie.*"

Sometimes I'm so frustrated I could cry.

Magda is hardly in the flat anymore. When she is, she goes straight to her room and stays there until morning, when she hears everyone leave. Except for her music and the cigarette smoke that trickles out from under the door, it's almost as if she doesn't live with us anymore, and sometimes when Irena talks about her daughter, the tourists assume that she means me, and neither Irena nor I correct them.

There's an older American couple staying tonight, and they're sitting and talking with Irena when I get home. Since my bed is now the foldout ottoman in the corner of the living room, I have to sit with them and be polite until they decide to go to bed. There used to be jokes about how all the furniture in Poland folds out into beds at night. There's one joke where a group of cousins comes to visit, and when it's time to get ready for bed, they fold out all the furniture except for the one, big, double-sized Western bed, which none of the cousins wants to sleep on because they don't know how to unfold it. So one of them ends up sleeping on the floor. It's a very funny joke if you tell it right.

"Jezus Maria," Irena says as the American couple heads off to the guest room. "I thought they were going to keep talking forever. Blah, blah, blah."

"Irena, I didn't know you spoke English that well. I'm impressed."

"Don't be. Blah, blah, blah is all I hear."

I laugh.

"Seriously," Irena says. "I only understand about ten percent."

"Seriously?"

Irena taps her forehead. "It is one of the tricks of the trade." She explains as we make up our beds. "Number one, of course, the rule above all other rules, is to smile. Especially if they are American or Japanese. I make sure I grin like an idiot and don't stop."

I grin at her.

"More."

"Like this?"

"More. Until your face is paralyzed. Then you know it's enough. Now say, 'Excuse. You will tea or coffee?'"

"What does that mean?"

"You didn't learn English in school?"

"Russian."

"Well, that's useless now." She tries to teach me a few more phrases in English: "Flat very near for center," "No, is not much far," and "What day you go away?"

"It's such a rudimentary language," I say. "Like cavemen."

She nods. "And then on the tram, I just ask them about America or Japan or wherever they are from so they will talk and talk and not realize how far it is from the center."

I laugh.

"And, of course, I nod a lot. But it is not so much the nodding as it is the forehead. If you always nod like an idiot, they will suspect something. The trick is that when they talk about something complicated, they will tend to use their hands. So when I notice them using their hands, I squint and wrinkle my forehead as if I am trying hard, but don't quite understand. Then slowly, slowly, I release my forehead and begin to nod because the chances are that they saw me squint and are trying to clarify what they said in the first place."

"And if they ask you a question you don't understand?"

"I say, 'Oh, before I forget!' and then I tell them about Wawel Castle. Or the salt mines. Something that I've nearly memorized I've said it so many times before. And then I ask them about their job or their family or America again and just let them go on about themselves."

"And they never catch on?"

"They think I'm the best conversationalist they've ever met!"

She goes over to the dresser underneath the television and opens a drawer, stuffed full of letters.

"Look. All from tourists. They send Christmas cards and pictures. Some of them even invite me to America."

"Why don't you go?"

"Why would I leave here?"

"You could work."

"I can work here."

"You could marry a rich American."

"And which awful American man would you have me marry?"

"Pani Bożena likes John Forsythe."

"She can have him. Too old."

"What about Jerry Springer?"

"Who's that?"

"The *facet* on television who makes the fat people angry."

"Springer . . . that sounds German." She wrinkles her nose and pretends to spit on the ground.

"Then why not just go to Hollywood, New York City, and the Grand Canyon and come back?"

"Why don't *you* go?"

"Maybe I will," I say.

She pulls a handful of letters from the drawer and tosses them in my lap. *"Proszę bardzo,"* she says, and laughs.

"What's so funny?"

"What's so funny? The only person less likely than me to get a visa is *you*."

It's true. They never give visas to unmarried women, but they never, ever, *ever* give visas to *young* unmarried women from the village, especially ones who haven't been to university and have no family in America.

"Phooh! Who needs that America anyway," she says. "I only wish I knew enough English to write back. I tried to get Magda to help, but that girl is as lazy as a donkey."

"Stubborn as a donkey?"

"That too. No, I guess they will just have to think that we Poles are rude because we never answer our letters. Unless you want to learn how to write English."

"Irena, why don't you learn?"

"Ach, I am too old to learn anything. You'll see when you are my age."

On Saturday night, I wait for Kinga on the bridge near the Jubilat department store. The banks of the Wisła are rolling with people, and orphaned flower wreaths float at the edge of the water, waiting to be fished out by their rightful suitors. There's a stage set up opposite the castle, the scaffolding glowing red and orange, and a band sings covers of American songs. Apparently, everyone in the city arranged to meet each other on the same bridge, and people press in on me from all sides, spilling beer and shouting conversations. I stand in one place with my back against the railing, hoping that Kinga will find me. Soon enough, I see her raspberry hair moving toward me. She reaches out to me through the crowd on the bridge, miming drowning.

"Ugh! There are so many people! I am so ready to leave this damn country. Look at this *bałagan*."

"Where are your *liceum* friends?"

"I don't see them. But they said they were also supposed to meet some of their university friends. At the dragon, I think. Let's go check there."

It takes us half an hour to struggle along the banks to the dragon statue behind Wawel.

"There they are!" Kinga pulls me through the crowd by the arm.

There are two girls, Ola and Gosia, and Gosia's boyfriend, Paweł. They all kiss on the cheeks, one, two, three. Ola seems nice, but Gosia seems like a bit of a *lalunia*. The three girls all went to *liceum* together, but Kinga is meeting Gosia's boyfriend for the first time, so they work out their common acquaintances and degrees of separation while I wait to the side and grin like an idiot, nodding my head, furrowing and relaxing my brow.

"And are you from Krakow?" Ola asks me.

"The village."

"Oh," Gosia says.

"This is Baba Yaga. We work together at the jazz club."

"Baba Yaga?"

"It's just a nickname."

"And in the village, did you live in a chicken-feet house?" Gosia asks. Her boyfriend laughs and looks at her admiringly. Gosia is wearing one of the plastic three-thousand-złotych flower wreaths we saw for sale on the way over.

"So. What did we miss already?" Kinga asks.

"Ola lost her *wianek*," Gosia says. "Oh, wait, that's old news."

Ola hits her on the arm. "You're one to talk."

"Maybe we should get out of this crowd and go find some beers?" Kinga asks.

"Actually, Monika and Grażyna are here too. One of their friends from university is as drunk as a pig, so they just took her to the bathroom. They should be back in a minute."

"It's pretty early for that," Kinga says.

"I know. They said she's been drinking since noon."

"Is everyone in this country an alcoholic?" Kinga says.

"Oh, loosen up."

We stand there listening to the band on the other side of the river. I recognize some of the songs as ones that one of the girls at *liceum* used to play on her tape recorder during the breaks. All around us, people wander by, boys snatching the *wianki* from the girls' heads and making jokes about the lack of virgins at the festival. Some of the younger kids climb all over the dragon statue. Ola smiles at me. I smile back at her. To say the truth, I would rather be at Stash's tending bar, or at home with Irena watching television.

"There they are."

"It's about time! Where have you *been?*"

"We had to go all the way to the hotel to find a bathroom. She's a mess. She can't even walk."

"Maybe somebody should take her home?"

"Not me. It's my last night out."

Monika and Grażyna are supporting the girl in the middle. She has her head down, and her hair is covering her face.

"Magda?"

Her head bobs up. "Baba Yaga?"

"You two know each other?" Kinga asks.

"This is Magda," I say. "The cousin I told you about. The one I'm living with."

"*Kurwa*," Magda slurs, looking up at me. "It's Baba Yaga."

"Here, let's put her down," Monika says, and they sit her on the concrete, propped against the dragon statue.

"*Kurwa*," Magda says again. "It's Baba Yaga."

"What do you want to do?" someone asks.

"Grażyna and I can take her home by taxi," Monika says, "and then just walk back."

"Speak for yourself," Grażyna says. "You're the one who let her get this messed up."

"She had a bad day."

"I'm sure she'll thank you tomorrow for making it better."

"Okay, well, *I* can take her then," Monika says.

"There's no way you'll make it back here. Doesn't she live all the way up Królewska?"

"And then how are we going to meet in this crowd?"

"We could just leave her here and take turns watching her."

"We'd spend the whole night coming back and forth through the crowd."

"*Kurwa*," Magda mutters again from the ground.

"I'll take her home," I say, and everyone turns to look at me.

"No, no," Kinga says. "It's my last night to celebrate. I want you to stay." But I can tell that no one else really cares, and there was only the customary insisting and counter-insisting to go through.

"Really, it's okay. I'll take her home."

"Are you sure?"

"She's my cousin," I say.

"I'm happy to go if you want to stay here," Monika says.

"Really, it's okay."

"Are you sure?"

"Sure."

"Come back if you can," Kinga says.

"Okay." But we all know there is no way to meet again in this crowd. They help me get Magda to the taxi stand in front of Jubilat and put her in the backseat. The driver barely glances back.

"It should only cost about eight thousand," Monika says. She hands me two thousand złotych and nudges Grażyna to do the same.

"I'm not leaving for Rome until Friday," Kinga says, kissing me on the cheeks — one, two, the Italian way. "I'll still see you at Stash's this week."

"Okay. *Na razie.*"

"*Ciao-ciao.*"

"*Hej.*"

As the taxi pulls away, Magda leans into the corner and lets her head tip back against the seat. I reach over her and open the window. It smells like my father used to — stale beer, vomit, and smoke. Stash won't let anyone get this legless at his place. When he sees someone in a bad way, he flicks at his neck from across the room, which is the signal for us to start pouring him one-quarter beer and three-quarters Sprite. They can't even taste the difference usually.

"Fucking Żaba. Fucking Ruda Zdzira."

All the way up Królewska, Magda's eyes flutter open and closed as she babbles about frogs and red whores and the airplanes circling in her head. I finally make out that her boyfriend, Żaba, has left her for a girl she calls Ruda Zdzira, Red-Haired Whore.

"And my fucking exam is on Monday. They couldn't even wait until that was over. My fucking exam. Oh, I am going to fail, fail, fail, and once again, fail."

"You don't know that."

"Yes I do."

The taxi drops us off. I get her into the courtyard and up the stairs.

"My fucking exam. I am so going to fail."

"Shhh . . ."

Irena and the tourists are already in bed, and I lead Magda to her room. I've never been in her bedroom before. I've had the thought to go in there when she and Irena were both out, but I was always afraid that she would come home while I was in there, or would somehow know. I guess I imagined that it would be a *bałagan,* clothes flung everywhere, cups of tea left to mold over. Instead, I'm surprised at how neat it is. Her lipstick and nail polish are lined up like ammunition, the outfit she wore yesterday folded neatly on the chair.

"That *skurwysyn*. I can't believe it. That *skurwysyn*."

"Here, get into bed. Do you want some water?"

She nods her head vigorously.

I get the water from the kitchen. I make her take off her shoes and I put the blanket over her, just like my mother used to do for my father. She probably didn't know why she did it for him either.

"Baba Yaga?"

"Yes?"

She's silent.

"Magda?"

"I forgot."

I get to the door.

"Oh, I remember now. I'm so going to fucking fail."

"You don't know that."

"No. My mother is fucking right. I'm never going to be a fucking prosecutor."

"How does she know?"

There's no answer.

"Magda?"

Still no answer. I close the door softly behind me.

On Sunday morning, through the haze of sleep, I hear Irena shower and leave to take the tourists back to the station. I fall back asleep for a little while, and when I get up, I tiptoe into the kitchen and make my breakfast as quietly as possible, making sure the knife doesn't touch the board and the kettle comes off the burner before it whistles. Magda's door opens suddenly, and I jump.

"You're up." And not only is she awake, but she's showered and dressed with a duffel bag in her hand.

"Hey, thanks for bringing me home last night." She leans against the door frame of the kitchen.

"It was nothing."

"Sorry you were the one to get stuck. Monika told me."

"No problem."

I expect the conversation to end there, but she stays, hovering in the doorway. "I was really a mess."

I shrug.

She ducks her head and fixes her bangs. "I told you everything, didn't I?"

"Less or more."

She stares at me while I sip at my tea. "You're not going to tell my mother, are you?"

"It's none of my business."

"Thanks. I don't think I can stand to hear another 'I told you so' right now."

I motion to her duffel bag. "Are you going somewhere?"

"Monika said I could stay with her for a while. But don't tell my mother. Let her think that I'm at Żaba's. Serves her right. She thinks I didn't study, well, let her think that. Maybe if I'd spent a little less time studying, Ruda Zdzira wouldn't have been able to get her teeth into him."

I don't know why she's telling me these things. For the first time, she seems ordinary, pitiable even. Her face is pale and puffy, and the line of her bangs is uneven.

"Promise you won't say anything?"

"Promise."

"Okay." And she nods her head like she's closing the lid on a box.

Irena returns just as I'm finishing my tea. She's breathing heavily, a carrier bag in each hand.

"Is that *głupia panienka* awake yet? I heard her come in at dawn last night."

"She stepped out."

"Out? But the exam is tomorrow. Who does she think she is?"

"To *study*. She went out to *study*, I think. To the library."

"Well, it's about time—the damn exam is tomorrow. And if she doesn't pass, you know what I'm going to say? You know what I'm going to say?"

"You tried your best, *kochana*?"

Irena laughs. "No. I'm going to say 'I told you so. Next time you listen to me, because I told you so.'"

II

The Difference Between
Matrimony and the Nazis

WHEN MARYSIA'S PARENTS found out about the wedding, they were not overjoyed at the match. They had planned for Marysia to marry one of the boys in the shtetl, and had no intention of attending either the ceremony or the reception. Everything fell to Pan and Pani Hetmańska, who were only too happy to arrange the day that would free their name from the scandal that began in the churchyard.

The Hetmańskis were not wealthy — no *górale* besides the ones in Zakopane were truly wealthy in those days — but they were at least not as abjectly poor as the rest. Pan Hetmański had managed his flock prudently, and his sheep were known in the surrounding villages as particularly fertile. It was said that he had a special tincture of herbs that he fed to the ewes, but that he wisely withheld the concoction from his own wife, because in the end, it was their limited offspring that kept them half a *grosz* above the traditional village penury.

The relative status of the Hetmańskis naturally raised the expectations for the *wesele*, and all the old sayings came to roost on the family's shoulders. *A guest in the house is like God in the house. Go into debt but show your best. You can't serve* barszcz *from a castle.* Heaped on top of the usual sayings were the scandal in the front of the church and the prospect of half-Jewish grandchildren, both of which had to be made up for. There were also the rumors that the Germans were about to invade, possibly making this the last celebration in the surrounding villages at least until the following spring.

Pan Hetmański, Władysław Jagiełło, and the Pigeon made three trips past the Sleeping Knight that August, selling and trading everything they could and bringing it all back in the form of food: cages of wild ducklings, strings of dried fish, sacks of flour, salt and sugar, lumps of yeast, jugs of oil and cow's milk. In the two weeks before the wedding, they stripped the garden, collecting every green tomato, every finger carrot, every plum-sized beet, every new potato, and Pani Hetmańska, Marysia, Anielica, and a few of the neighbor women worked feverishly, bonding over the steaming pots, the piles of peelings, the jars of preserves. It seemed like there was enough food to last for a year.

The rumors of the German invasion had been buzzing since the spring, but they did not cause a panic. There were always rumors about everything, especially the Germans, and they only gathered as much weight and truth as people allowed. Pan Cywilski, who lived next to the church in Pisarowice, had a shortwave radio, which he had made from discarded parts from the last war, and which he kept on his windowsill as a service to the community. It was tuned to the BBC mostly, but that was fifty years before the foreign English teachers with their poor hygiene and their defaulted student loans moved into every hamlet, suddenly becoming nice and middle-class. At that time, only a few people in the entire region could decipher the squawks emanating from Pan Cywilski's radio. He himself claimed to speak English like a native, but every report he gave contradicted the one before, and the *górale* found it hard to believe that the great statesmen of the world could be so inconsistent and nonsensical from day to day.

The Pigeon had mysteriously disappeared a few days before the wedding, and it was only as Pan Hetmański struggled under the weight of a heavy jug that he realized how much he had taken him for granted.

"Where is that blasted boy?" he asked his wife, his grumbling masking his concern. "You don't think he's having second thoughts about our Anielica, do you?"

"Of course not, you stupid goose. He's probably just helping his own family. He does have his own parents and sisters, you know." And Jakub, but nobody ever counted Jakub.

He tried to observe Anielica for clues. She did not mention the Pigeon at all, but every so often as she was rolling dough or embroidering the wedding sheets, a smile would alight briefly on her lips. Pan Hetmański did not know if the smile concealed a past secret or a future one, but he was satisfied that she didn't seem bothered by the Pigeon's absence.

The day before the wedding, he reappeared to help set up the yard. The neighbors of Half-Village had loaned mismatched tables, benches and stools, all their rough linen panels, cutlery, pitchers, dishes, glasses, and pots, even though it meant that the night before, they had to eat dinner with their hands while sitting cross-legged on the grass in the main clearing. The Hetmański *wesele* was very much a communal effort, the first push of cooperation and solidarity that would get them through the war and the next fifty years.

On the day of the wedding, Władysław Jagiełło was only eighteen, but the dryness of his lips and the dark circles penciled in around his eyes made him look ten years older. Marysia, by contrast, looked flush and fresh faced, but it was not clear whether it was from the excitement of the day or her morning sickness, which in the month before the wedding had already killed a patch of wildflowers on the side of her parents' hut. At any rate, she was the only one naive enough to fully enjoy the day. In the intervening month, everyone in the surrounding villages had discovered the exact nature of the engagement, though no one said a thing. Everyone in the mountains knows that weddings, weather, and history are the three things that cannot be reversed, and so as the wedding preparations culminated, as the days grew shorter and the breezes picked up strength, as the rumors of the Nazi invasion gathered, Half-Village came to be dominated by a distinct atmosphere of resignation.

"What's the difference between matrimony and the Nazis?"

"In the end, they say the Nazis put you out of your misery."

Every man in the surrounding villages claimed to have invented this joke, and they repeated it to the young Władysław Jagiełło at every opportunity, laughing at the way it made his face blanch.

Still, it is doubtful that Władysław Jagiełło could have chosen better even if he had chosen more cautiously. Marysia was a rare optimist in a country that decades later would be declared Most Pessimistic by a commission of the European Union—one of the few unanimous decisions made in Brussels that year—and Marysia's optimism would become invaluable as the wife of a king-cum-cold-footed-groom-cum-partisan-cum-migrant in a country stuck smack in the middle of half a century of war both hot and cold.

12

Alexis, Blake, Krystle, Sammy Jo, and Magda

O N MONDAY MORNING, there are no tourists. I eat my *ka-napki* and watch Irena neglect hers. I have never seen her this nervous. She takes a sip of her tea and puts it down. She goes into the front hall, straightens the line of slippers, and comes back. She opens the refrigerator, closes it, and sits back down.

"How long will it be before she hears?" I ask.

"Hears about what?" Irena says.

"The exam. Whether she passed."

"Phooh," Irena says. "For all I know she didn't even go."

"She wouldn't do that."

"Ach, she'd do it just to spite me. Never mind that she's the one who wanted to become a prosecutor in the first place. Anyway, that doesn't concern me. Let her arrange herself. She made her bed, now she can sleep in it."

Pani Bożena wants me to do her hair like Brigitte Bardot, and I have to do it over a few times because she isn't satisfied. I wash a load of laundry and hang it out to dry. I wander around between the freezers in Hipermarket Europa to escape the clinging heat. A lot of foreigners come to Hipermarket Europa, and I think the cashiers and the girls standing sentry at the ends of the aisles sometimes mistake the jeans, trainers, and athletic jackets I buy at the secondhand shop for firsthand. So I try to play foreigner. I walk slowly, as if I'm on vacation and have nowhere else to be. I squint up at the signs in Polish as if I'm having trouble deciphering them. I pick up the boxes of frozen dinners and the bottles of wine, and I either frown or nod my head at the quality while taking a furtive glance at the price. As I go from the bakery hut to the butcher hut to the wine hut to the cashier, the voices of the salespeople traipse after me with "Thank you, Pani" and "As Pani judges" and "If I can be of service," and when I answer them, I try to press the mountains out of the words until my accent is as flat and smooth as the bluestone on the Rynek. I even add a French accent sometimes and stumble on my words, and when I do, the cashier smiles more and counts the change slowly into my hand.

I end up buying a package of Spanish seafood stew for *obiad,* which Pani Bożena says reminds her of the singer who used to play the part of Don Pasquale at the opera.

"He asked me to marry him," she says, "or would have if I weren't already married. Anyway, it was his dream when he retired to go back and live in Katowice with his mother." She wrinkles her nose.

"And Katowice is . . . bad?"

"Horrible. Unlivable." And then she begins to list the other men who wanted to marry her, along with a detailed list of their faults.

"So how did you know that your husband was the right one?"

She takes a long drink from her wineglass. "It was just after the war. There was nothing left in Warsaw for me. He and his brother were coming to Krakow to make a fresh start. And he loved me so. He would have done anything for me."

I wait for her to say more, but instead she turns her attention to the last two shrimp she's been saving on the plate. "My compliments. The fourth-best paella I've ever had. I hope you've had time to make dessert. I feel a sweet tooth coming on."

"Crème caramel."

"That will do." She holds out her glass for more wine.

While Pani Bożena is napping after *obiad,* I crumple the boxes and bags carefully and quietly, and I sneak the evidence down to the trash cans in the courtyard. Her naps are becoming longer and longer, and if she doesn't wake up in time to watch *Dynasty,* I have strict instructions to watch it for her and report what happened that day. For a while, I did just that. I told her about Blake being released from jail and being nearly run off the road on the way home. I told her about Krystle escaping from the mental hospital in Switzerland, but only after she'd been hypnotized by the evil doctor, which compelled her to call her location in to the bad guys anytime she saw a ceiling fan. I told her about Alexis collaborating with the sinister worldwide economic network run out of a cellar somewhere in California, and Sammy Jo, who is modeling jeans and sleeping with as many men as she can in order to get back at her family.

But the past few weeks, I've become so deathly bored with the Carringtons that I've been flipping instead to the classic films on Channel Four. After all, how can Linda Evans compete with Ingrid Bergman or Maja Komorowska? How can John Forsythe hold a candle to Marcello Mastroianni or Daniel Olbrychski or Bogusław Linda? Once in a while, they show something American or French or Italian, but mostly, they show all the great Polish directors: Zanussi, Kieślowski, Łoziński, Wajda, Holland, and Polański, even if he did do what they say with that young American girl. At least now he can forgo the humiliation of having to line up in front of the consulate on Stolarska Street and beg for a visa.

Today, somehow, Pani Bożena manages to go without a nap after *obiad*, and she crinkles up her nose and tries to reconcile what's on the screen with the stories I've invented.

"And John? I thought you said last week that the bad men finally ran him off the road for good. But he looks fine . . ."

"That's his twin."

"And Sammy Jo? Why isn't she modeling and sleeping around anymore?"

"Alexis's worldwide economic network shaved her head. She's embarrassed."

"Shaved her head?"

"No one has hair that blond. It's a wig."

"Oh, poor Sammy Jo."

My mind has been wandering to Magda the entire day. I think of her sitting under the spires and gargoyles of the law school, hunching over her exam, sweating, struggling against the thoughts in her mind, grasping for the dream just above her head, the dream of a Big Life.

I used to want a Big Life too. When I was a little girl, I'd try to see it by climbing anything I could. I'd hike up Old Baldy Hill to the old sheep camp, cling to the roof of the barn like Spider-Man, and sit up in a pine tree for hours, pressing my fingers into the pinesap, letting my mind wander for hundreds of kilometers before reeling it back in. At different times I dreamed of becoming a fire watcher, an airplane pilot, a soaring eagle, a guardian angel. Anything that would allow me to see far and wide.

"And what about the *homoseksualny* son?"

"What?"

"The *pedał*. Where is his boyfriend?"

"Oh. He met Edyta Górniak when she was on tour in the U.S. Now he's straight."

"I knew it! That Edyta Górniak. So *elegancka*. You know, I used to turn many a *pedał* straight in my day too."

But I know now there will be no Big Life for me. Even when I try to picture myself five years from now, I can't see past the Carringtons' beach house, past my days at Pani Bożena's, my nights at Stash's, my Friday afternoons at Mikro, and my weekends watching Irena and Magda bicker back and forth. At least when I was in the village I could imagine something on the horizon. Here in the city, the dreams that once swelled inside me now feel like nothing more than a dried-up little kernel rattling around, and the only thing I can see is the crumb trail of obligations leading me from one day to the next.

On Wednesday afternoon, I run into Kinga at the Square of the Invalids, also on her way to Stash's.

"Did you get Magda home okay on Saturday?" she asks.

"Yes, but she was a mess."

"When is her exam again?"

"It was Monday. I don't think she has much of a chance, though."

"Poor thing."

"Poor thing?"

"It's not her. It's the system. They make the first-year exams impossible in order to free up spots for the tuition-paying students. And that's everywhere, not just the law school. The only ones who have a chance in this *pieprzony* capitalism are the rich and the very well connected."

"Well, it's not like Magda really tried," I say. "You saw her on Saturday. Her mother says she's been like that all year."

"Try or no try, it wouldn't have mattered anyway," Kinga philosophizes. "It's all going to shit in the end. I'm telling you, Baba Yaga, the best option is to get out while you can."

"Who would pour the drinks then?"

"Speaking of which, did Stash find someone to replace me yet?"

"He told me he had the sign in the window for only an afternoon, and ten girls applied. But I haven't seen anyone yet." It's like that all over now. Ten girls for every job. Unemployment is . . . well, unemployment is a sad story my grandmother wouldn't want me to tell, and if I did, Irena would make me mention that there was no unemployment before capitalism. And here, I would have to spit on the ground.

We knock on the window a few times and Stash comes out of the office, rubbing his eyes. He can't stand doing any of the paperwork or the inventory.

"Is there a new girl coming in?" we ask him.

"She already came in."

"When?"

"On Saturday. While you two were off at your festival."

"And?"

"Jacek caught her stealing from the *kasa*. Imagine. The first night."

"So is there another one?"

He shrugs. "I don't know. I think I'm going to wait until I find someone I can trust."

"I'm sorry, Stash."

"*Małe piwo,*" he says. Small beer. "There are worse things. How was the *wianki* festival?"

"It was fine."

"Anyone fish your *wianki* out of the river?"

I shake my head.

"Don't worry, someone will." He winks at me, and I wonder how much he knows.

The heat creeps down from the street and in through the make-shift screen door that Stash built himself. By the end of the first set, Kinga and I are both sweating, and I try to keep my face dry with a few crumpled tissues. I'm much faster behind the bar than when I first started. Kinga and I have worked out an implicit choreography in our movements, and I will miss it, and her, when she's gone.

"I'll be back for the holidays," she says. "Or maybe you can come and visit me in Rome."

"That would be fun," I say, but to say the truth, Rome might as well be Mars.

She and Stash go into the office between the second and third sets, and she trades her apron for her last pay packet. When we say goodbye, we are full of kisses and *ciao-ciao*s, and for the rest of the night, I start to think that maybe she has it right. Maybe the only way is to leave. Even if she comes back someday, maybe by then the country will be booming, and she'll have a suitcase full of foreign currency and another language.

"Co słychać?" After the third set, he catches me off guard. His cheeks are pink, and the edge of his hair is damp.

"Not much," I say.

"How was the Festival of Virgins?"

"Fun. Crowded."

"Hmm," he says, and then he just stands there.

"Orange juice?"

He shakes his head. It's a few minutes before eleven, and he taps at his watch, the same old aluminum watch that he'll probably wear until he's a pensioner.

"The bus?" I ask.

"The bus."

"Na razie."

"Na razie."

I'm resigned. Resigned to the shelf, destined to be an old mush-room, to let my *wianek* disintegrate as it floats on down the Wisła, past Jubilat and out of town, never to be rescued. But as he reaches the door, he turns around, his sloping shoulders framed in the door-way.

"Listen," he says, suddenly very serious. "Listen . . . I was wondering if you wanted to meet for coffee sometime. I mean, coffee, tea, beer, whatever you wanted. Well, maybe not beer. I'm sure you're sick of pouring it all day, and I don't really drink much. But maybe we can meet somewhere on the Rynek some day."

"Okay," I say.

"Okay?"

"That would be great."

He smiles triumphantly, his misty pink complexion glowing in the low light. He must drink kefir and juice all day long. "How about Sunday then? I'm free on Sunday. In the afternoon, that is."

"Sunday's fine."

"Meet at Adaś?"

"Okay," I say again. I feel like a grinning *dupek*.

"At three?"

"Great."

"Great." He turns away quickly and bumps into a square man who is also on his way out. *"Przepraszam,"* he tells the man sheepishly. The screen door sticks and wobbles in the heat, and Tadeusz is careful not to look back at me as he ducks outside.

"Did he do it?" Stash comes up behind me and drops two more glasses into the sink.

"You knew?"

"I'm just glad you were finally able to put him out of his misery. He's a nice boy."

"Shy."

"Yes, shy, nervous. But you don't want the smoothest one in the room either, Baba Yaga. Ask Irena. Strike that. Don't ask Irena."

Up on the street, there's finally a cool breeze picking up. On the way home, I replay the conversation with Tadeusz over and over in my mind, substituting wittier things I could have said, thinking about what I'm going to wear on Sunday and what Nela would think of him. The only advice she ever gave me was never to marry a "But." That was just after we saw the film *He Doesn't Hit Me, He Doesn't Drink, But* . . . and I guess she had enough faith in me to know I would avoid the first two. She herself never settled. Even though my grandfather died so long ago, I would sometimes catch her standing at the clothesline or in front of the stove, still as a statue, the loneliness surfacing in her eyes. When I asked her what was wrong, she would simply smile at me and reach up and touch the soft fur of her collar, soothing whatever sad thought had come to mind.

She hardly ever talked about him directly, as if even touching him with her voice was too much sadness to bear. Growing up, I only knew that his name was Czesław, that most people called him the Pigeon, that he was a carpenter, that he had a crooked nose like mine and wore jodhpurs and a forage cap during the war. And that he wasn't a "But," because with only his memory and the one sepia photo she kept under her pillow, Nela had adamantly refused almost every man in the surrounding villages. The married ones she sent back to their wives, of course, with a slap on the face and twice as many Hail Marys as the priest would give them. The single ones she would allow to hover a safe distance away. They would chop our wood, they would butcher our chickens, they would turn over our garden, but that was the closest they would ever come to Nela's heart. After my father left, the only man who ever set foot in our house was Uncle Jakub, and that was only because he was my grandfather's brother and a half-wit, and she felt sorry for him.

Magda has been gone for three days, and the tourists are out, so the flat feels enormous with only Irena and me. When I come in, she's watching television, or rather, she's lying on the love seat with her eyes closed and her knees hugged to her chest while the television happens to be on.

"What are you watching?"

"It's stuck on the station."

She picks up the remote and slaps it against her palm, stretches her arm out, and presses hard on the buttons. Nothing happens, and neither of us gets up to change the channel. It's a contest called *Mister Poland,* and at the moment, the contestants are giving interviews in front of a fake meadow, smiling coyly at the interviewer and trying too hard to be funny. Irena leans her head back on the arm of the love seat and closes her eyes again.

"Guess what, Irena," I say.

"Unless you won the Toto Lotek, save it for tomorrow."

"What's the matter?"

"I have my damn period again. I must be the oldest woman on earth with her period still. *Cholera jasna.*"

"Can I get you anything? Tea maybe?"

"How about a new daughter? That *głupia gęś* failed her exams. And she knew she would. That's why she hasn't been home. Pani Kulikowska told me. She probably doesn't even care. She's probably shacked up with that little boy as we speak, forgetting that she ever wanted to be a prosecutor in the first place."

It's on the tip of my tongue to tell her about Magda, about Żaba and Ruda Zdzira, that she was just preoccupied for the exam, and she will surely pass the last-chance exams in September. But I don't say it. I swallow the truth, and it sits as a lump in my throat. Because the more important truth is that I'm relieved that Magda has failed the exam. I'm the responsible daughter, and Magda, the prodigal one. I am the one that Irena prefers, maybe not the star, but the understudy who always comes through. Nela would be ashamed of me for even thinking this.

Irena sighs. "Two years lost," she laments. "She can't even get into a new program for next year now. Two years lost because of a stupid boy."

She cocks one eye open. "What were you going to tell me?"

"What?"

"You came in and said 'Guess what?'"

"Oh. Tadeusz asked me out. The *klarnecista* I told you about."

"That's great," she says, completely without enthusiasm.

"We're meeting on Sunday."

She doesn't answer. She watches the young men on the screen with their highlighted hair, strutting down the runway in tight swimming costumes and tank tops.

"You know what?" she says.

I lean forward. "What?"

"I should have voted for the damn communists. This crap would have never happened under the damn communists."

I don't know if she means Magda or *Mister Poland*. Maybe it's all the same.

13

The War After the War to End All Wars

ON THE DAY of the wedding, as the Hetmański family reached the church in Pisarowice, there was an unsettling buzz in the clearing, and Pani Hetmańska began to perspire at the possibility that her son and his bride had caused yet another scandal. But as they approached, the drone separated itself into distinct words. *The Germans. Have crossed. The border.*

Those who had marched in the previous war had already done the calculations. It would take a full week and five days to reach the Tatras, they had decided, and that was only if the Polish army failed to stop or stall them. There was no immediate panic. In fact, Father Adamczyk seemed to stretch out the wedding Mass as a way of thumbing his nose at the Germans, and the villagers' minds wandered, not to war, but to the prospect of the *wesele* afterward, where they would be able to scrutinize both Marysia's bump and the *remont* of the Hetmański house.

After the Mass, Pan Cywilski unfolded the camera he had built from an old bellows and a baking powder tin and took some pictures of the bride and groom, the Hetmańskis, and the maidens in their flower crowns, of whom he was especially fond. Władysław Jagiełło and Marysia, subdued by the scandal they had caused in the same clearing a month before, smacked a chaste kiss, and everyone applauded, except for Pani Plotka. She was in attendance only because she couldn't bear to hear about anything that happened in the villages secondhand, but she stood back at the edge of the clearing as if waiting for the condemnatory lightning to fell all those who celebrated the depraved pair. Later, when the German Blitz struck, Pani Plotka would consider herself vindicated, and until her death she would continue to blame the Great War, the Holocaust, and the Soviet occupation on the audacity and immorality of the Pagan and the Jewess, as she made it a point to refer to them.

Meanwhile, the other couple to come out of that particular Sunday had begun to court in the open. For a month straight, the Pigeon had been a fixture on the bench he had built in the yard of the Hetmański house, already waiting with the morning birds when Anielica woke up. After breakfast, they would hike up Old Baldy Hill to spell Władysław Jagiełło, who was spending nights at the sheep camp. Jakub had been there since April without a break, and for a few weeks he returned to his parents' house while the Hetmański family took it in turns: the Pigeon and Anielica during the day, Pan Hetmański in the late afternoon and evenings, and Władysław Jagiełło at night, which turned out to be exactly what he needed to calm his nerves before the wedding. The Pigeon and Anielica, too, cherished the weeks on Old Baldy Hill. They would spend the entire morning and half the afternoon in the surrounding pastures, talking and reading to each other, or one watching over the flock while the other napped.

In the afternoons, Pan Hetmański would hike up the mountain to relieve them, and as he stood among his flock, he counted his sheep with a wagging finger and spread their wool, examining their sides for injuries. After the shame of his son, certain villagers whispered behind his shoulders that he should not be letting his daughter out of the house in only the company of an eligible bachelor and a flock of sheep, but it was precisely the sheep that formed the first line of defense of his daughter's reputation. Anyone who has ever tended sheep for an afternoon knows that they cannot be left alone for a moment without falling off a cliff or wandering off, and in this way, they were better chaperones than Władysław Jagiełło had been.

The second line of defense, of course, was the villagers themselves, and Pan Hetmański put his faith in the web of gossip that drew them all together. He knew full well that they would report any indecency they saw the instant after it happened, and he made a great show of speaking with the neighbors in hushed voices when the Pigeon and Anielica were around, glancing frequently at the couple even if the conversation happened to be about the Germans or the lack of rain. In truth, though—and Pan Hetmański would take this to his grave—he trusted the Pigeon more than even his own son.

After the *ślub*, the bride rode up the mountain to the *wesele* on a wooden stool carried between Władysław Jagiełło and the Pigeon. The family followed, then the maidens, holding on to their *wianki* for dear life with one hand, swatting the men away from their skirts with the other. The view that met them when they reached Half-Village did not disappoint. The house looked beautiful in the afternoon light, and the neighbors led each other on tours of the interior, peeking first into one side room and then the other. They took turns opening the pump in the kitchen and dumping water down the porcelain toilet, which had been set behind the house in its own cabinet for hygienic reasons and not incorporated into the main rooms, as had been rumored the pitiable city folk had been forced to do with theirs.

Out in the yard, rough linen panels that had hung as fly screens all summer long were draped over the tables, anchored on the ends with jugs of homemade *bimber* and berry wine. Inside the perimeter of the stone wall, Pan Hetmański and Władysław Jagiełło had stuck a ring of torches into the ground, the ends coated in pine tar that would be set afire once the sun set behind the mountain. The feast that materialized on the tables, even on that day, was referred to as The Best Celebration Anyone in Half-Village Could Remember, which is amazing, really, considering that superlatives are always reserved for the distant past. There was clay-baked duckling and pine-smoked lamb, deviled eggs, new potatoes smothered in butter and chives, mushrooms filled with ground mutton and cheese, pierogi stuffed with everything you could think of, fresh pastries brimming with fruit and sweet cheese, fresh bread and wedges of *oszczypek* warmed to melting in the open fire.

The *górale* ate and drank past when their hunger was sated. They ate and drank until all the old grudges were blunted and turned into songs, until the unspoken gossip bloomed between them as bawdy jokes, until they forgot the words to the songs and the punch lines to the jokes. They ate and drank until they did not notice the empty jugs drunk by the youngest of the boys or the missing crowns on the heads of some of the maidens. The *górale* could have easily drained all the wine at Cana, but in Half-Village, there was always more. There were toasts to the bride, toasts to the groom, toasts to both fathers-in-law, the absence of one hardly noticed, toasts to the Pigeon, Władysław Jagiełło, the priest, Marshal Piłsudski, Jesus, and Winston Churchill.

Finally, when the men's toasts had degenerated into hailing certain women's body parts, and when several men had stripped off their shirts to defend the honor of those body parts, the Pigeon gathered up Anielica, her brother, and his new bride, and the party of four sneaked off into the woods.

"Where are we going?" Marysia asked.

"Shh . . . you'll see."

They walked roughly west, the moon splashing light at their feet. Władysław Jagiełło and the Pigeon started out carrying Marysia on the wooden stool, but they were not as sober as on the way from the church, and after they dropped her twice she elected to walk, hiking her skirt up and tucking the hem into the waistband of her undergarments so it bloomed above her knees. They laughed most of the way, retelling some of the bawdy jokes they had heard that night and sharing scraps of gossip, oblivious to the small crowd gathering behind them: the giggling maidens who'd followed them out of curiosity, the men who'd followed the maidens for obvious reasons, the younger boys who'd followed the men, hoping that they were about to uncover a new stash of *bimber*, and the dogs who'd followed the small crowd to escape the rowdiness of the party at the house.

When they finally reached the clearing, the four abruptly stopped and became aware of the rustling behind them. The Pigeon, who looked like a schoolboy in his suit and shoes, was suddenly as flushed and formal as the day he'd asked Pan Hetmański to take his daughter for a walk.

"Państwo Władysław Jagiełło Hetmańcy . . ." He cleared his throat. "May I present to you on the occasion of your wedding, this small token of our support." He dug two pinesap torches into the ground and lit them. They flickered and spat at first, but eventually their steady flames revealed the secret of his absence, the secret of Anielica's smile during the few days before the wedding. It was a marriage bed, built in the deepest recesses of the forest. The Pigeon had wandered the woods for an entire day until he'd found the right spot — flat ground, well drained, with four trees growing in a perfect square.

He had cleared the brush and pegged the cross braces directly to the trunks, then fitted six strong, squared branches across. He had bent smaller, greener branches into a headboard and footboard, and Anielica had helped him wind vines around the frame and decorate it with flowers and fresh leaves. They'd stuffed two sheets with pine needles for a mattress and covered it with sheepskins. Anielica had herself collected the down and feathers from every chicken and goose in the five surrounding villages, and she had sewn and stuffed a long pillow and *pierzyna* that lofted like clouds, covered in linens that she had salted, embroidered, and ironed.

"It is, of course, our intention," the Pigeon continued, "to help you build a roof over this bed, a bedroom under that roof, and a house around that bedroom."

The clearing was silent. They were all — the maidens, the young men, the boys, the dogs, and Władysław Jagiełło — stupefied by the magnanimousness of the gesture. To this day, rooms of grandmothers and grandfathers in the area can still be quieted by the mere mention of the marriage bed. It was only Marysia — young, simple, optimistic, grateful Marysia — who was able to speak.

"And this bed?" she said cautiously. "This entire bed is all for me?"

Władysław Jagiełło and Anielica laughed, but the Pigeon and the rest of the crowd understood her well. They had all grown up with feet in their faces and blankets that never stretched wide enough to cover everyone.

"Yes," the Pigeon finally said. "It is all for you."

"And me," Władysław Jagiełło shouted, grabbing his bride and flinging her onto the bed, tickling her until she squealed. "Don't forget about me."

The maidens who still possessed their *wianki* blushed and averted their eyes. The young boys strained to catch a glimpse, and the young men looked to the forest canopy, for all of a sudden, Marysia's squeals were drowned out by the buzzing of planes overhead.

They had not counted on the planes. When the men of the village had declared that it would take almost two weeks for the Germans to arrive, they had calculated it in boot strides and blisters, and not thrust, lift, and yaw. Some of the villagers did not even realize what the drone in the distance was.

"The torches!" the Pigeon shouted. He upended the two torches, snuffing them out in the dirt, and he bolted in the direction of the Hetmański house. Anielica went after him.

"Stay here," he said. "All of you but Władysław Jagiełło." He had never before given Anielica any kind of command, and the gravity of it frightened her.

"Be careful," she said.

"We'll be back. Just stay here."

The War After the War to End All Wars had begun.

14

Pan Tadeusz

I KEEP REPEATING the conversation with Tadeusz in my mind, reaching out to touch it to make sure it doesn't disappear. Still, it's almost a surprise when I spot him waiting for me at the statue of Mickiewicz in the middle of the Rynek. It's the last week in June, but it's been windy and rainy all week. Tadeusz is wearing only a blue dress shirt and the same black pants he wears to the club. As I walk toward him, my heart begins to pound erratically, like Pani Bożena's old washing machine when it starts to spin, and I stop under the arches of the Sukiennice to watch him. He's turning in place, looking for me, and I wait until he's looking in the other direction. He spots me when I'm only a few meters away, and I pretend to have just noticed him.

"So should we go to Jama Michalika then?" he asks abruptly, as if he's already had the first few minutes of the conversation in his own head.

"Sure. Why not?"

As we walk down Floriańska Street, Tadeusz tells me all about Jama Michalika. He tells me about Young Poland and the bohemians drinking absinthe and discussing literature, the artists who left their sketches in payment for their drinks, and the Little Green Balloon Cabaret that was founded there. It gives us something to talk about, and I just listen and nod as if I hadn't heard it a thousand times before from Nela, as if I didn't seek out Jama Michalika on my second day in Krakow, as if I haven't stood outside the window every time I pass, daring myself to go in.

He holds the door for me, and we pass the old *babcia* at the *garderoba* counter.

"*Dzień dobry*, Pani."

"Good day. Is it still cold out there?" The *babcia* places two tags on the counter.

"Yes."

"They say it will rain later," Tadeusz adds.

She turns my coat over in her hands before she hangs it up, and she looks at it with approval. It's a short, light trench coat with a wide collar and a belt like Katharine Hepburn used to wear. Nela made it for herself back in the seventies, but it's coming back in style again.

"You should have a coat yourself, little son," she says as she withdraws the second tag.

"I'm not cold, Pani," he insists.

I can tell by the way Tadeusz's head swings around that, for all his talking, he has never been to Jama Michalika either. It's dim except for the colored light skipping across the stained glass overhead, and as our eyes adjust, the sketches and murals emerge from the dark like the eyes of animals in the forest. The waiter's white apron reaches almost to his feet, and he smirks slightly as Tadeusz pulls out one of the oversized, Alice-in-Magicland chairs for me.

"Tea?" the waiter asks.

I nod.

"The same," Tadeusz says.

"Anything else?" But he has already sized us up, and he doesn't even bother setting down the menus.

Tadeusz clears his throat. "Did you want anything else?" he asks.

"No, no," I say, calculating how much the tea alone must cost here.

"No," Tadeusz tells the waiter, as if he's translating for me.

We settle in, and there's a stretch of silence. I smile and he smiles.

"You have a nice smile," he says.

"Thanks," I say.

Silence.

"I've never had a cavity," he offers.

"Really?"

He puts his hand to his mouth. He has a habit of clearing his throat and covering his mouth before he talks, as if he has a horribly contagious disease. "Fortunately. With nine of us, we can't exactly afford to take everyone to the dentist."

"Oh."

There's another long silence. The tea comes, attended by silver spoons and lumps of sugar, slices of lemon, petite wafer cookies, and the bill, and Tadeusz ineptly negotiates the tea service and the payment.

"So what's that like?" I ask once the waiter goes away. "With so many sisters."

As he speaks, the image in my mind slowly fills in, though not exactly where I'd drawn the lines. He's nineteen and the oldest, and they all live in a three-room flat in an *osiedle* in Huta. He finished *liceum* last year and has been busy taking care of his sisters while his parents run the *lombard* they started a few years ago.

"But they're having a hard time of it. A lot of people selling and no one buying, not even to reclaim their own things. And there are so many *lombardy* now."

It's true. There's practically one on every block here.

"And what about you?" he asks. "Any brothers and sisters?"

"Just me."

"And your parents? What do they do?"

"Nothing. I mean, my mother passed away."

"When?"

"When I was six."

"Of what?"

"Cancer."

"I'm so sorry. And your father?"

"He left right after."

"*Boże.*"

I shrug.

"So who raised you?"

"My grandmother. Nela. She only passed away this year. Just after Easter. It was always her idea that I come to Krakow. She spent a couple of years here after the war, and she always talked about it." It occurs to me just then that I haven't really talked about her to anyone since I came here. Not even Irena.

"What was she like?"

"What do you mean?"

"I mean, what was she like? Was she plump? Did she bake?"

I look up at Tadeusz and his eyes pull me forward. "She was amazing, really. Beautiful. Everyone said she could have been a Hollywood starlet. She had long, blond hair like Veronica Lake, and all the men in the villages around us were crazy about her."

"Veronica who?"

"Veronica Lake. You know, the American film star."

Tadeusz shrugs.

"But she turned out to be a postmistress. And a seamstress. That's what she did in Krakow right after the war too. She and my Great-Aunt Marysia sewed uniforms during the day and costumes for the Old Theater at night. On the black. She said that's how it was right after the war, everyone working on the black, that there was so much black that at night the entire country disappeared."

Tadeusz smiles, and I think of his perfect teeth with no cavities. I worry that I'm boring him, but once I start talking about Nela, it feels like I can't stop.

"She was a very good seamstress too. She had clients even in New York, and the material would come by post, beautiful material that you couldn't even get in the Pewex stores then. She used to sew a dress for this woman in our village once a year and the woman paid her three sheep for it."

Tadeusz laughs.

I blush.

We sip at our tea. We talk some more about the village, about Huta, about Kinga going to Rome to be an au pair and all of our classmates who want to leave the country. The waiter impatiently clears our cups, and I have the terrible sinking feeling that the afternoon is ending before it has picked up any momentum, that it can easily be clipped short at any time now, the ends neatly tucked away.

"Maybe we should go?" Tadeusz finally asks, and I can feel the disappointment in my stomach.

He waits until I stand before he does, and as we leave, both of us take one last look at the room. We retrieve my coat from the *garderoba,* and Tadeusz leaves a thousand złotych in the *babcia's* metal tray.

"Now, wear your jacket next time, little son," she admonishes him.

"I'm not cold, Pani," he says again.

We stand out on the street. The wind is still gusting, and the clouds creep lower and lower, daring me.

"Well," he says.

"Do you have to go home?"

He clears his throat. "Not necessarily."

"Do you want to take a walk around the Planty?"

"Sure." Sure. As easy as that.

We walk through the city gate and past the old fortress to the Planty, the belt of trees and grass that girdles the old town. Most people call it the Strafing Zone these days because of all the birds that roost in the trees overhead. There are a few other couples walking the same loop as we are, some older, dressed in elegant trench coats, some our age, in warm-up jackets. Tadeusz jams his hands into his pockets. From time to time, he glances at me shyly, but we don't talk much.

"So, when did you start playing the clarinet?" I ask.

And this is the question, the question that wedges itself into the small cracks of his politeness and splits him wide open, making him forget to cover his mouth or clear his throat. His hands come out of his pockets waving and gesticulating, and he has to talk quickly in order to keep up with them. Another couple passing by turns to look. He learned to play only two and a half years ago, he tells me, on a clarinet that had been left in the shop. A friend of his father's knows a friend who has a friend who knows Stash, and Stash agreed to let him play there once a week as a favor.

"A favor? Stash says you're the most promising young *klarnecista* in Krakow."

He tries to hide his smile, but I can tell that he's pleased. "No."

"Really. So he doesn't pay you?"

He shrugs. "Only in orange juice."

"You should ask him to pay you."

"Oh, I couldn't. It's an honor just to play with them."

"Why not? He pays the others, and you're just as good."

"Don't flatter—"

"I'm not flattering."

"Do you really think so?"

"Why not?"

He stops in the middle of the path and turns to face me. "You know, you're right. You're right. I *will* ask him. What have I got to lose?" He looks like a madman, his cheeks pink with excitement, his shaggy hair blown straight by the wind, his exhilaration forming a protective shield around him. Around us.

"I *will* talk to him," Tadeusz repeats.

"You should," I say.

"I will." He laughs nervously.

"You should."

"So what about you then?"

"What about me?"

"What about you? What do you want to be when you grow up?" He smiles.

We're facing each other in the middle of the path, the other couples diverting around us.

"A rich and famous bar girl," I say, laughing.

He doesn't laugh. "Seriously."

"Seriously?" I ask. His face has the same intense expression he gets whenever he plays. "I don't know."

He stares at me, expectantly.

"Come on, let's walk down to the university," I say.

His hands are jammed in his pockets again, and he kicks at imaginary stones. "Actually, I should be getting home. The clouds look like they're about to open up."

"Me too." But it's a lie. I don't really want it to end.

We walk toward the Square of the Invalids, where he can catch a bus to Huta.

"So that's what you want to be, a *klarnecista*? As a job, I mean?"

"If I can. It's a long shot, but I was thinking that I would just stay at Stash's for a while and get some experience so I can play in some other clubs, and then eventually form my own group—my friend Konrad is a trumpet player—and then start to book my own engagements, first here in Krakow, and then maybe in Warsaw and Katowice . . ."

106

I keep him talking about it as long as I can, all the way up Królewska Street, past the twenty-four-hour store, and into Irena's courtyard. The wind has picked up again, and the clouds swell overhead.

"I'm sorry, I've been talking your ear off this entire time."

"That's okay."

He walks me to the entrance door.

"Thank you," he says. "This afternoon was very nice."

"It was."

"Maybe we could meet again sometime."

"Yes."

I feel like we're in one of those Russian period movies with dance cards and elbow-length gloves, and all I want to do is grab him by the shoulders and pull him toward me, feel his clarinet lips pressing against mine, feel the warmth of his exuberance leaching into my skin. Instead he gives me a quick peck on the lips and hurries off.

"Na razie," he calls over his shoulder.

"Pa."

Irena is in the living room, watching television. There's a special on the pope with the same pictures that they always show: the young boy in his short pants, the handsome young man skiing in the Tatras, the young priest saying Mass on an upturned canoe. Irena looks up at me and grumbles. She's been in a foul mood all week.

"Cześć, Irena." There's a noise somewhere in the flat. "Is Magda back?"

Irena shakes her head. "Tourists. Germans." She pretends to spit on the ground.

I hear the rain start just then, fat drops flattening against the balcony, and I picture Tadeusz in his dress shirt, seeking cover under a tree or an awning.

"And how was your date?" Irena asks, without taking her eyes off the television.

"It was good."

"Don't worry. You can teach him how to kiss."

"What do you mean?"

"I mean, who does that boy think he is? An assassin? It's like he's got a poison dart in his mouth or something."

"You were *spying* on us?"

"It's my window. Besides, what else do we old ladies have to do but watch puritanical young people bungle up a simple thing like kissing?"

"Watch your retrospectives on the pope and pray your rosary, same as the other old ladies."

She smiles, pleased at my progress. "Oh, I'm already going to hell anyway."

"Don't say that, Irena."

"What? I don't mind," she says. "That's where all the interesting people are anyway."

The pope is looking over the crowd in St. Peter's Square. "If I make mistakes in Italian," he says, "correct me." The crowd laughs and applauds.

"Irena?"

"Yes?"

"Do you ever think you'll go back to painting?"

She looks over at me, a little surprised. "Phooh. There's no time for painting in the New Poland. No one cares about those things anymore. Not even me."

"Is there anything else then?"

She looks at me, confused. "What do you mean?"

"I mean, do you have some kind of dream? About the future."

She studies the flashing pictures of the Vatican: the pope jogging in his private garden, staring at the papers on his desk, kneeling at his private shrine to the Virgin Mary, standing next to a white car, falling, the circle of people shrinking around him.

"Irena?"

She clears her throat and closes her eyes reverently. "My dream . . ." she says.

I wait.

"A truck."

"A truck?"

Suddenly, her eyes pop open. "Yes, a truck. A big truck. From the city. It will park in the courtyard and throw every one of those stray, mangy *pieprzone* cats in the back, and the driver will come and *re-mont* my kitchen, install CNN, and ask Magda to marry him. Yes. That is my dream." And she laughs long and hard.

15

The Sturm Before the Calm

No one spent the first night of bombing in his own bed. Safety was somewhere else — someone else's barn, someone else's cellar, someone else's village. In the end, there were about thirty from the *wesele* who gathered at the marriage bed in the forest rather than face the vulnerability of their own homes. The children were tucked and retucked under the giant *pierzyna,* and still they kept poking their heads out to hear the kettle drums and the cymbals in the distance, to see the flashes of pink dawn in the sky long before the sun rose. The women huddled in a few groups around the bed, their voices billowing with confidence when reassuring the children, creaking with doubt when turning to each other. The men sat with their backs against the trees, keeping to the perimeter, guarding their families, against what they did not yet know.

The Pigeon and Władysław Jagiełło had run back to extinguish the torches in the yard, and had returned with some of the guests and every blanket and linen in Half-Village before disappearing once again. Up in the pastures it was cold overnight, but the wedding bed, hidden deep in the virgin woods, was well insulated by layers of foliage and detritus. Besides, that first night, no one would sleep long enough to let the cold settle inside.

The bombing continued all night long. It was impossible to tell how far away they fell, for the great booms ricocheted off the peaks and were swallowed whole by the valleys. In between there were hushed whispers and coughs, the shifting of bodies against pine needles and leaves, and the occasional squawk of a child as he answered back to his dreams. The animals, startled by the noise, began sending out reconnaissance, and watched the Half-Villagers from a safe distance away. Anielica and Marysia, newly sisters, gave up a blanket to Pani Hetmańska and one of the other women from the village, and huddled instead under one of the linen sheets.

The second time the Pigeon and Władysław Jagiełło left, they were gone for the rest of the night, returning only in the morning with buckets of cold pierogi and mutton and stories from the night before. They had first gone up to Old Baldy Hill to check on Jakub, then down to Pisarowice and on to Marysia's shtetl and the Pigeon's village. Several houses in Osiek had been hit, they said. The men had rushed out of the houses as soon as they had heard the drone of the bombers, snatching rocks and throwing them at the traitorous streetlamps. But they had not been swift enough, and several women and children had been killed, the gaping holes left in the ground testaments to the town's grief.

That much could be confirmed. The rest was all panicked speculation. Some said they had seen German paratroopers landing at dawn in the pastures beyond Osiek, and at that very moment, they crouched, waiting for darkness to fall again. Some in the other villages were packing their belongings onto carts. Some were already on the road, headed for the cities, where they deemed it would be safer.

The partygoers, who only a few hours before had been dancing the *zbójnickiego*, singing *"Ej, ty baco, baco nas,"* and toasting their wives' body parts, sat in cold silence around the marriage bed as they listened and ate, interrupted only by the occasional fretting of the youngest children, who couldn't yet read the hush, and who only wanted to go home to their own toys, their own pet chickens and lambs. In fact, children usually have the right instincts in crises, and the Pigeon too began to urge the wedding guests to go back to their homes and make preparations during the daylight, sticking to the woods and taking as much of the leftover food as they could carry.

The Pigeon himself stayed long enough to help clear the Hetmański yard of the tables and benches and then, after a brief conference with Pan Hetmański and Władysław Jagiełło, he returned home to his mother, father, and sisters, promising to come and find the family at the marriage bed the next morning.

The work did not stop all day. Pani Hetmańska and Anielica properly packed the rest of the leftovers, which had been hastily stowed under weighted baskets and cloths. They wrapped the bread in paper and stored the onions and dried mushrooms in the rafters. They pickled or soured the remaining cucumbers and cabbage, and salted the meat, laying it out in the sun to dry. Pan Hetmański and Władysław Jagiełło spent the morning digging holes for the potatoes and for three large, empty barrels, which they packed with food — salted meat, flour, and cheese in one, carrots and beets nestled in sand in another, alcohol, oil, and preserves in the third. They sealed the lids, covering them in dirt, scattering the leaves and rocks so that nothing would be suspected.

Pan Hetmański went off into the woods that morning and dug another hole for their valuables, but he refused to tell anyone in the family where it was for fear that the knowledge would leave them prey to the Germans. Everyone else seemed to be doing the same, and when the men of each household would see each other through the trees, they would politely avert their eyes and walk in the other direction. After the war, some would go back and dig randomly for the belongings of their own families or others, leaving the woods a minefield of sudden holes and twisted ankles.

"Why don't we just put everything in the cellar?" Anielica asked.

Her brother and her father exchanged knowing glances. "What cellar?"

"The cellar that the Pigeon built."

"No one knows about the cellar, Anielica. And no one *can* know about the cellar. You must never tell anyone. Hold it in like a mouthful of water."

The one valuable the Hetmańskis kept above ground was the picture of the Black Madonna of Częstochowa that hung in the main room. Every night, before they went to the marriage bed in the woods, either Anielica or her mother would lean it against the garden wall for protection. Indeed, it guarded the house faithfully until the middle of November, when two drunken Germans used it for target practice. It was then retired to the wall of the main room, where all who entered could see the bullet holes piercing the smooth forehead of the mother, ripping open the chest of the preternaturally calm child on her lap. "*Bóg zapłać*," Pani Hetmańska whispered each time she passed the defaced picture. God will pay you back.

For the first two weeks, the Hetmańskis and Marysia spent nights at the marriage bed, days preparing for the worst. Marysia cried and cried about her own family, but Władysław Jagiełło would not let her go back to the shtetl, assuring her that they had surely escaped and would be reunited soon.

The Pigeon went back to his own family every night, returning before dawn, and when Anielica opened her eyes in the morning, there he was, just as he had promised, smiling at her from a stump at the edge of the clearing. She would slide out from under the edge of the enormous *pierzyna*, careful not to wake her parents or her brother and his bride, who slept on sheepskins several meters away. Those first few weeks, Anielica slept in her clothes, as everyone did, and kept a clip on her cuff to sweep her hair up. She was even more beautiful this way, and the Pigeon told her so every morning on their early walk through the woods, unchaperoned by brothers or gossip or sheep. This was not the time for Pan Hetmański to impose restrictions on their courtship, and even if he had wanted to, it was too late. Without ever putting his hands on Anielica, the Pigeon had already made his way into the deepest recesses of her heart. It was only a matter of waiting—for the bombs to stop falling and for the bride to age a few more years—before he initiated a proper betrothal.

The couple made their way back to the marriage bed each morning when they heard Pan Hetmański's voice, and the entire family would walk back to the house together, have breakfast, and discuss the Pigeon's reconnaissance from the night before. The Pigeon never showed up empty-handed, always bringing matches or tea or news for stockpiling. Pan Cywilski had taken his radio off the windowsill for fear of confiscation, but he remained open for business as a one-man bureau of information.

Most of the Polish stations had been knocked out in the first few days, and the entire valley relied on the BBC and Pan Cywilski, whose English was once again called into question as he related the atrocities of the Germans through the Pigeon: the executions in the market squares, the Trains, the ripping apart of families, the roundups of Jews and Poles and Jewish Poles and Polish Jews and Gypsies and professors and officers and priests. All of Poland was on the move. The Germans were forcing migrations to the center of the country with thirty kilograms of belongings per family and five minutes to pack. Those left in the cities were escaping to the villages, those in the villages were fleeing to the cities, and the Germans were strafing all the roads in between, killing everything that moved, looting everything that didn't, absolved by their own chaplains and the Polish priests who valued this world over the next.

"Surely Pan Cywilski is exaggerating."

"But Father Adamczyk told me the same information. He also wanted me to tell everyone that Mass would be conducted as usual until the Germans dragged him from the altar."

Which would be only a matter of months.

"Surely the British will intervene. After all, they must honor the treaty."

But hundreds of kilometers away, instead of bombs, the British dropped leaflets, urging the Germans to reconsider. Instead of machine-gun fire, there was applause in the House of Commons as leaders of the three parties gave speeches about honor and exhortations to act. The French, feeling the deepest *fraternité* with Poland, occupied a dozen abandoned villages on the German border before quickly pulling back.

"I am telling you, it is up to *us*," the Pigeon concluded solemnly after each report.

"But what can we possibly do?" Anielica asked. "We must wait for the Americans."

"The Americans? The Americans haven't a care in the world. Why would they become involved? No, it is up to us."

16

The Beauty of Stupidities

By THE END OF JULY, Tadeusz and I have fallen into a routine. He meets me after Pani Bożena's on Fridays and we go to Mikro together. On Sundays, we meet at a milk bar near Nowy Kleparz. Our conversations are always the same. Always about the future—his future as a *klarnecista*—as if every time we mention it, we are incubating the idea with the warmth of our breath. And then afterward, he walks me back to Irena's, where he continues to assassinate me with small pecks on the lips. Like Chinese water torture, Irena adds.

It's been almost a month since Magda left, and Irena grows increasingly agitated with each passing day.

"I can't believe that *głupia panienka* is shacking up with that Frog. Who knows, she could even be married or knocked up by now. At twenty. Well, that's a fine life for you. And after everything I've tried to do for her."

"Irena, you don't know that she's pregnant. Or even with Żaba for that matter."

"If she isn't with that little boy, then why doesn't she come home?"

"Maybe she's afraid."

"Afraid of *what?*"

"Maybe of what you would say about her failing her exam?"

"Afraid? Magda has never been afraid of anything in her life, certainly not of my opinion. She would do better to have some fear of something. Of having a dead-end future, for example."

We are silent for a minute. She looks up at me from the love seat. "What? Say it."

"It's not my business."

"Say it."

"I don't know. Do you think that maybe it's possible that you are too hard on her sometimes?"

Irena laughs. "Of course I'm hard on her! If I wasn't, she wouldn't have gotten this far. Let me tell you, she would have never even made it through primary school or *liceum* without me pushing her constantly."

"But maybe for the exam you were on her head too much sometimes?"

"Maybe the problem was that I wasn't on her head enough. Phooh! Maybe that's why your entire generation is so damn apathetic," she continues, "because you don't have anyone trying to push you in the opposite direction."

"We're not all apathetic."

"Yes, you are. At least half of you. The other half are too busy squandering all their freedom on the moment."

"Well, maybe that's not apathy. Maybe we're just paralyzed by too many choices."

"That's ridiculous," Irena says. "There's no such thing as too many choices. You just pick one and live with it."

She sits back on the love seat and turns on the television. "I don't care anymore anyway. It's her life, let her mess it up."

"Except you do care."

"No, I don't."

"Then why do you sit here grumbling about it every night?"

"And who taught you to talk back to me?"

"You did."

"Yes. I did. And if you remember that was only after weeks of pushing you until you pushed back. And that is *exactly* what I'm trying to do for Magda."

A man with white hair fanning out of his nostrils appears in the doorway.

"Excuse. Excuse. Sorry. You half *Tee? Kamillentee?*"

115

"Yes, yes." Irena smiles broadly. "I make you. I bring you to room. To *Zimmer*. Your wife too want?"

"*Ja, ja*. Wife too. *Danke*. You will door close?"

"Yes. Door close," Irena says.

The old man smiles and closes the door on his own beaming face.

"Damn brownshirts," Irena mutters.

I get up from the chair, click my heels together, and give the Nazi salute. "I'll get it," I say, but Irena doesn't even crack a smile.

"That's okay." She pulls herself up off the love seat.

"Irena, really, sit. I'll get it."

"No, you won't." She pushes past me.

"What was that for?" I follow her into the kitchen. She lights the stove and bangs the kettle on the burner.

"I said I'll get it."

"But why did you just push me?"

"Today it's tea. Tomorrow it's ironing their sheets. Next year you will be standing at the station waiting for the trains."

"What's wrong with that?"

"Everything."

"But you do that."

"I was built for it."

"Maybe I was built for it too."

"No. I've already raised one permanent bar girl, I won't be responsible for another." She purses her lips together like a child refusing to swallow.

"Irena, I know you're upset about Magda, but . . ."

"Magda. You. Your whole generation. You have freedoms we only dreamed about. The whole world is open to you, and what are you doing with it? You go to the same mediocre jobs every day and sit around my living room."

"Maybe this is the life I want."

"Then you suffer from a lack of imagination."

The kettle whistles, and Irena arranges two glasses of hot water on an aluminum tray along with two new tea bags, the sugar bowl, a saucer, and two spoons. She carries the tray to the door of the guest room and knocks gently.

"Oh, *danke*, thank you."

"Pleasure my."

"Wait, wait, my wife, she have *Fragen*. Tourist *Fragen*."

Irena invites them into the living room, and a minute later, they are caught up in the rat-a-tat-tat of English, of Auschwitz and St. Mary's Church, tram routes, restaurants and cafés. Irena is smiling at the Germans so widely, it looks as if her face just might split. They stay for half an hour while I sit politely on the love seat, and when they leave, we immediately make up the ottoman and the love seat and get into bed. Irena shifts and clears her throat a few times as she always does right before she falls asleep. She's never talked to me the way she has tonight, and I guess I'm waiting for her to smooth things over, just as my mother did when there was an argument in the house.

"You know something, don't you?"

I shift on the ottoman. "What do you mean?"

"You know something about Magda." Her eyes are leveled at me in the darkness.

"What makes you say that?"

She doesn't say anything. She lets her eyes do all the work.

"Okay," I say quietly. "She's not at Żaba's. She's not even with him anymore."

"What else?"

"They broke up a couple of days before the exam. He cheated on her with one of her friends, and she was really upset, and she knew she was going to fail. That's why she hasn't been home."

"And all this time, I've been worried sick. Where is she then?"

"Please don't tell her I told you. I swore I wouldn't say anything."

"I don't care what you swore. Where is she?"

"At her friend's. At Monika's."

"Monika, the one who also studies law?"

"Yes."

Irena turns over to face the wall. "*Głupia gęś.*"

"What?"

"I just called you a *głupia gęś*. Don't you understand? She only told you because she thought you would tell me. And instead, you've let an entire month go by."

"I'm sorry, Irena."

She doesn't answer.

"I said I'm sorry, Irena."

I press my back against the wall and feel the pressure of it against my whole body. I want to feel enclosed again, protected, safe, as I was in the village. I wrap the blanket tightly around me, and I try to comfort myself by thinking about Tadeusz, but the loneliness that has opened up inside me is bigger than one person can fill. I try to soothe myself by listening to the breathing of the flat—the wheel of the electric meter, the creaking of the floor above, Irena shifting and sighing a few meters away—but it only makes me feel more alone, as if from here to the love seat is the greatest distance in the world.

She's already gone when I get up in the morning. Stash can tell something is wrong as soon as I walk in the door that afternoon.

"What's eating you?" he asks.

"Do you happen to know a *babcia* with a room for rent?"

"What happened?"

"I don't know. I think I might have to move."

I tell him everything, and he just listens. When Stash listens, you can tell that he's really listening to you and not just making faces.

When I'm finished, he smiles calmly. "Did she actually tell you to leave?"

"No."

"Listen, I'm sure she said some things she regrets now. I'm sure by the time you get home, everything will be in the past for her. You know she does everything as quickly and efficiently as possible, and that includes getting angry and getting over it."

I hope he's right. As I'm walking home that night, I prepare what I'm going to say. *I'm sorry, Irena. I should have told you. If you don't want me to live here anymore, I will understand.* I try to follow the trail of ifs in my mind if I have to move out, but I can't bring myself to imagine Irena's absence, just like I could have never imagined her presence in my life a few months ago.

I see the glow in the window from the Street of Kazimierz the Great, and I imagine her sitting on the love seat reading one of her news magazines. My heart starts to beat faster. The conversation I have been methodically laying out in my head all the way home starts to cramp and knot together. When I come in, though, the living room door is closed, and I hear low voices.

"Baba Yaga, is that you?" Irena calls when she hears the front door open. "Baba Yaga, *chodź tu.*"

I hang up my rucksack, change into my house slippers, and open the door of the living room. Magda is there. She's sitting next to Irena on the love seat, her eyes swollen from crying, her head resting on Irena's shoulder while Irena strokes her hair.

"*Cześć.*"

"*Cześć.*"

I stand there for a minute in the doorway, not knowing what to do. I've never seen them *not* arguing.

"Come. Sit," Irena says.

"I don't want to interrupt."

"It's okay," she says.

"I think I'm going to bed anyway," Magda says. "*Dobranoc.*" I stand aside to let her pass.

"*Dobranoc,*" Irena answers.

I sit down in the armchair by the door, but Irena has already started changing into her pajamas, so I stand up and start preparing the ottoman.

"And how was Stash's tonight?" she asks.

"Fine." I try to remember everything that I had rehearsed on the way home, but only one thing surfaces. "Irena, I'll move out if you want me to."

"Why in the world would I want you to move out?"

"I just thought you might."

"Well, don't think then." She snaps a sheet over her head and lets it drift down onto the love seat.

"But, Irena, I feel terrible that I lied to you."

"Good. But you also told me the truth. Magda and I had a long talk today. A long talk. And I talked to Monika's mother too. And do you know what she was doing the entire time she was gone? The entire time that I was not getting on her head?"

"What?"

"Studying."

"Studying?"

"Every day. The whole day."

"For what?"

119

"For the last-chance exams in September."

"You really think she has a chance to pass after she's failed them once?"

Irena turns around and gives me a strange look. She pulls the duvet from the wardrobe and tosses it on top of the sheet. "Well, maybe it will be my biggest stupidity of all to believe she can."

"I'm really sorry I lied to you, Irena. And if you ever want me to move out, you can just tell me."

Irena stops her motion and puts her hands on her hips. "Baba Yaga, did your grandmother ever tell you about the day she fought off a Nazi *skurwysyn* who was trying to rape my mother?"

"No."

"Did she ever tell you about how your grandfather shot the Soviet *skurwysyn* who was trying to burn down the house with my parents and me inside?"

"No."

"Well, you're not going anywhere." She turns out the light and gets into bed. I can just make out her silhouette across the room, and this time, she's facing me.

17

Life As If

THE FIRST WINTER was relatively easy, considering what the BBC and Pan Cywilski had predicted. The sheep were all safe in the barn, and there was money to be made selling potatoes and canned produce and wool to the cities. The Germans, who had set up permanent camp in Osiek, were deterred by the snow from coming up the mountain, and on their occasional visits, they plodded and cursed so much that it was impossible not to hear them coming.

The Pigeon and Władysław Jagiełło eventually brought back word of the destruction of Marysia's entire shtetl, and all the neighbors watched Marysia carefully, expecting her to throw herself into a well of despair. Instead, the Jewish-Gentile child growing inside her seemed to preserve her optimism, and she took on the preternatural calmness of the Madonna, despite the brutal tragedy that had surely befallen her parents and her brother. The inhabitants of Half-Village and Pisarowice were too full of pity for the girl by then to call her a Christ-crucifier or count the months backward to the wedding, which amounted to a scandalous six, and once word was out that a baby had been born, even with the Germans in Wawel, even with the vultures circling overhead, the neighbors in Half-Village and Pisarowice came to shower Marysia with attention and gifts.

The Lukasiewicz family from Pisarowice brought six jars of mashed sweet carrots, and the Bojdas, a chicken, which they had the foresight not to boil and mash, and which continued to provide consistent egg production for the next couple of years. The Romantowski son brought his fiddle around at sunset one evening and played a lullaby that put the Hetmański baby straight to sleep. Even Pan Cywilski came over one afternoon and fitted the wooden cradle with a crank and a motor that would keep the little one rocking for a good twenty minutes while her mother attended to other things.

The child turned out to be a girl, a fat pullet of a baby with a full head of dark, curly hair and a calm countenance just like her mother's. When she held her, Marysia looked very much like the portraits of the Black Madonna that had leaned against all the fences and walls only six months before. The color came back into Władysław Jagiełło's cheeks, and he became as good a father as ever lived, starting with the naming of his daughter. In the spirit of his father's progenitory ambition, several girls' names had been suggested, including Queen Jadwiga (though that was immediately rejected as nominal incest), Marie Curie, Kopernika, and Chopina. But Władysław Jagiełło, who without the constant comparisons to his namesake would have been considered a good and successful man, had already decided. He named her Irena. Not Saint Irena or Queen Irena or Irena the Great. Just Irena. And when people found out—even Pan Hetmański—there was surprisingly very little fuss, just as there was very little fuss about anything anymore.

By the summer of 1940, everyone was already jaded by the war. After Hitler had paraded through Warsaw, after the shtetls had been emptied, the radios confiscated, the books burned, the schools shut, Wawel Castle commandeered, the professors shot, and the generals exiled, what else could the Nazis possibly do? What else?

Not satisfied to let the rhetorical question hang in the air, the villagers watched their tea leaves and candle drippings carefully for the answer. They went trooping off to astrologers, palm readers, crystal gazers, psychics, necromancers, and magicians. Pani Plotka put out a sign advertising herself as a fortune-teller, leaning it against her front gate next to her picture of the Black Madonna of Częstochowa, and the other women clucked their tongues and rolled their eyes at her. Right before sneaking around to the back door.

As it turned out, Pani Plotka could accurately conjure up all the gossip from Half-Village to Osiek. If she told you that your husband was cheating on you or that your neighbor was stealing eggs from your coop, you were sure to find the offender a few days later, midsnatch, red faced and apologetic if he knew what was good for him. But like the underground newspapers, radio stations, and strangers passing through, she was woefully inaccurate about the end of the war. The first rumored date of peace was December twelfth, after a group of pilgrims had been to Częstochowa and seen the number twelve etched into the cloak of the real Black Madonna, and over the next five years, rumors of the end of the war resurfaced every few months. The Germans capitulated and left Poland in control of Libya. Hitler was shot in a dispute with one of his generals, then killed in a duel with Stalin. The Jews in Auschwitz rose up and threw the camp *Kommandanten* into the ovens. The Polish officers thought to be dead had really been away planning a coup against Hans Frank and the rest of the Szwaby sipping their schnapps in Wawel Castle.

When they began, all of the rumors sounded credible, substantiated by the BBC or Nostradamus, and all of the rumors were optimistic at their core. Even later on, after their homes had been looted, their food rationed, their children forced into Baudienst, their daughters and sisters raped, their priests taken away, the *górale* always somehow cultivated enough hope to maintain a relatively normal life.

Życie. Or at least *życie na niby.* Life as if.

They sheared the sheep. They cooked the meals. They went to the market in Osiek and bought ersatz coffee, ersatz honey, and ersatz bread. They read the death notices and the flyers papering the message poles, pretending not to understand the ones written in German. They sent their youngest children off to the primary school every morning until it closed. They went to the church every Sunday until it closed. They visited their friends and greeted their acquaintances. When they happened to see a German, they merely treated it as an inconvenience, pointedly ignoring him and still giving him a wide berth, just as one would a demented old man or a rabid dog.

But behind their ersatz life beat the heart of the Resistance. There were no snitches in Half-Village or Pisarowice because everyone was involved. The Pigeon, Władysław Jagiełło, Pan Wzwolenski, and the oldest Epler boy were scattered around the countryside fighting for the Home Army, setting ambushes and booby traps in the woods, shepherding new recruits through the mountains, doing reconnaissance, and running newspapers, and all of the villagers kept the secret and accommodated the partisans sent back to bunk in the village. The newly *remont*ed Hetmański house became the headquarters of the Resistance in Half-Village. Pani Hetmańska, Anielica, and Marysia began to tutor the children in the mornings, organize a theater for them in the afternoons, and sew uniforms at night.

Of course, they had to take precautions. Once in a while, German soldiers would venture up the mountain to Half-Village and find the youngest Epler boy leaning against a tree, his foot pressing a hidden black button that Pan Cywilski had wired to a lightbulb hidden in a mouse hole in the Hetmański house. As soon as it flashed, the children would scatter from their lessons. The boys would escape out the window and busy themselves chopping wood or digging in the gardens, and as a result, there were half-started holes and half-stacks of firewood everywhere. The girls would hide the books in the secret compartment in the wardrobe that the Pigeon had built, and pick up a less-threatening implement—an embroidery ring, a rolling pin, or a whisk. By the time the Germans reached the front door, they would not be able to see the traces of Sienkiewicz on their lips, the tracks of Mickiewicz galloping through their minds. Or the tiny lightbulb rolling around loose in the apron pocket of the older woman.

In the evenings, for both the company and the conservation of the kerosene, the women and children of Half-Village would gather at the Hetmański house, the oldest children leaving one by one to put the youngest to bed. The later it became, the more frank the conversation, and they could pass an entire evening talking and sewing: sometimes miniature costumes for the theater, sometimes uniforms for the Home Army, either retailoring stolen German uniforms with Polish insignias or sewing them from scratch. Someone always sat with an unfinished duvet cover in her lap to throw the uniforms and forage caps in if an unexpected visitor arrived, but after a few encounters with the partisans, the Germans were reluctant to venture into the woods at all, and after the initial plundering of the village, which yielded pitifully few valuables, it was a waste of breath climbing up from the valley.

So the Half-Villagers continued to work together and share one another's secrets. All but one: the cellar under the Hetmański house. Only the Hetmańskis and the floorboards knew.

18

The Cellar Under the Sheep

To say the truth, I expect to wake up the next morning and find the entire night before gone, evaporated. I expect that Magda will sleep until noon, Irena will continue to grouse about her, and nothing will change. When I get up, though, the light in Magda's room is already on, and Irena is sitting in the kitchen, smiling and drinking her tea, the dark circles almost gone from around her eyes.

"It's the seventh sign," Irena says. "I think the land is about to fall into the sea."

And this is exactly what I expect—for the land to fall into the sea and the truce to end. But each day, they surprise me, and each other too. Magda is up studying before I leave each morning, and Irena makes her tea and pretends she doesn't smell the cigarettes when she knows Magda is smoking out her window. Stash agrees to hire Magda for a few nights a week to replace Kinga, and she arranges to work two more nights at the wine bar in the Corner of St. Thomas the Disbeliever.

"*Niesamowite*" becomes Irena's mantra. Unbelievable. "She's going to have two jobs! And study! I see it with my own eyes, and still! Never in my life! Do you know she even went to the store last night without being asked? I have never been prouder. We should celebrate."

"Celebrate?"

"Yes, go out."

"But you've already been out once this year."

"Don't be smart. We'll go to Piwnica. The three of us."

"I'll believe *that* when I see it."

But the entire week, Irena insists. Piwnica, or "Cellar," is what her generation calls the Cellar Under the Sheep. Mine calls it Barany, or "Sheep," as in "Let's go to the Sheep," and usually that means the disco or the cinema on the first floor. When Irena's generation says Piwnica, there's no doubt that they mean the Cabaret. Nela used to talk about it all the time, and it's one of the monologues Irena repeats to the guests all summer, though they usually only listen politely and then go out to one of the Western bars on St. Anne's Street.

"Seven o'clock on Saturday," she tells me. "We'll meet on the Rynek under the statue of Mickiewicz. My old friend Jósef still works the door. I'm sure he will let us in for free."

"But Magda and I are both working that night."

"I already called Stash and took care of it."

I meet Tadeusz at Mikro on Friday. *Sami Swoi* is playing, and on the way back to Irena's, we quote lines back to each other, just like Nela and I used to do on the bus ride home from the cinema in Osiek. We recount the neighbors' arguments over the cow, the cat, the eggs, and the pots until we can't laugh anymore.

"I finally talked to Stash," Tadeusz says suddenly.

"And?"

"And he said yes."

"He'll pay you?"

Tadeusz nods.

"That's fantastic! How did you do that?"

"I told him I had another offer to play during the week."

"Very sly."

"I did."

"Have another offer?"

"From U Moniaka. Someone from there was over at Stash's and heard me play."

"U Moniaka?" U Moniaka is a club with matching chairs and two-night tourists just off the Rynek.

"And Stash said he didn't want to lose me."

"That's terrific! You see?"

He smiles and reaches for my hand. "It's not much."

"It's not the money that matters."

"Thank you."

"I didn't do anything."

He squeezes my hand. "Yes, you did."

And indeed, I feel like it's almost as much my victory as his. We hold hands the entire walk home, all the way to Irena's, lapsing into a comfortable silence. I imagine Tadeusz ten years from now, the *klarnecista* everyone comes to see, maybe even on tour or running his own club. And I can see myself sitting in the audience watching him, doing paperwork in the back office, pouring drinks, or working the crowd as I weave through the tables.

We stand under the yellow light of Irena's entranceway and he kisses me, not just the peck of an assassin, but long enough so I can feel the warmth of his lips against mine. And as I walk up the stairs, something is percolating inside me, maybe the first vapors of love, maybe just the future finally showing itself.

On Saturday, Stash gets the niece of the trombonist and her friend to cover the bar for the night. I help him set up and then head over to the Rynek. The wooden benches around Adaś are already packed with teenagers horsing around — kicking at each other's sneakers, stealing each other's hats or backpacks and ransoming them back for attention. I wonder if they even read *Pan Tadeusz* anymore in school or if they know that the first statue of Mickiewicz was pulled down by the Nazis during the war.

I wait the customary fifteen minutes, the *kwadrans akademicki,* but at quarter after seven, there's no sign of either of them. I stare between the glowing arches of the Sukiennice expecting to see Irena first, rushing through at her usual speed, gripping a plastic bag full of empty margarine tubs and milk bottles. Instead, Magda emerges through the middle archway, her toes pointed, her long legs leading as if with every step she's testing the water. Everyone else is wearing short sleeves tonight, but Magda is wearing a sweater, and has a light scarf tied around her neck. Since she returned, we haven't really said anything beyond polite exchanges in the hallway, and I start to get a little nervous.

"*Cześć.*"

"*Cześć.*"

"Let me guess. She's not here?"

"I'm sure she'll be here. She's been talking about it all week."

Magda laughs. "And she's been talking about going to Paris since Martial Law."

"You think she's not coming?"

"Has she ever been to Paris?"

"But she seemed so definite about it."

"Ha!" Magda pulls out a cigarette and lights it. "If you want, we can wait a little longer, but she isn't coming. One hundred percent."

"You really think she won't?"

"For sure she won't."

I look up at the clock tower rising behind the pale, yellow Sukiennice, like a smokestack rising behind an ocean liner, lanterns swaying along its length. Magda stands there smoking. It makes her look terribly sophisticated the way she cocks her hand to the side and the smoke trails off behind her, like Audrey Hepburn or Claudia Cardinale.

"Magda, I'm sorry I told her."

She shrugs.

"You know how she is. I cracked."

She smiles slightly. "I was angry at first, but it's probably for the best anyway. We haven't gotten along this well in years."

"Why's that?"

She takes a long drag from the cigarette. "I don't know. One day, I was doing whatever she told me, and then the next, I was saying no just to say no, and she was saying yes just to say yes. You never did that to your mother?"

"We never got that far."

"I'm sorry. I forgot."

"It's okay."

We stand there for a few minutes watching the clock tower and looking for Irena. People are hurrying to make their appointments.

"It's twenty-five past," Magda finally says. She scuffs the end of the cigarette gently against the bluestone and puts the butt back into her pocket. "Come on. I think the doorman will recognize me anyway."

He does recognize her. He's a little older than Irena, stocky, with white hair in the shape of a horseshoe around his head, and he nearly shouts for joy as he takes Magda's hand and kisses it. "Magda! And where is my Irenka?" he asks.

"In Paris. Where else?"

"She never comes out anymore," he says. "No one has seen her out in such a long time."

"No one but the cats."

"I've heard that. Well, I'm honored that she has sent her beautiful daughter in her place." Magda does a little curtsy. "Is this your friend?" he asks.

Magda hesitates. "Our cousin from the village. Baba Yaga."

He smiles. "Pleased to meet you, Baba Yaga. Please don't eat me. I promise you I am pure of heart."

Magda laughs loudly. I manage a polite smile.

"Well, the show is supposed to start in five minutes," he says, "but they never start on time. Go have a drink first, and come and get me if you have trouble finding a seat."

"*Dzięki.*"

"Anything for Irenka." And he takes a deep bow.

The Cellar Under the Sheep is someone's vision of the afterlife. At the bottom of the main staircase, there's a choice to turn either right or left. To the right is the heavy oak door leading to the Cabaret. To the left is the long stone tunnel to the disco, glowing with red lights and smoke and decadence, the music thumping right through to your bones. A line of people stretches down the tunnel, waiting to get past the bouncer. We go to the right, and when the oak door closes behind us, we're quickly drawn into a maze of smaller stone rooms and archways, echoing with laughter and the tinkling of glasses, all of it presided over by a man in a white suit with wispy white hair and a silver whistle that hangs over his large belly.

"That's Piotr Skrzynecki," Magda says. "He's the director."

"I've seen pictures," I say, "but that was back when he didn't have such a beer belly."

"It's cancer."

"He doesn't look sick."

"They say he's so charismatic that he and the tumor have just learned to live with each other."

Magda hands me a vodka and orange juice, and I take it. The doorman has somehow sent word to the bar, and the bartender waves our money away. By my second drink, I'm starting to relax, or maybe it just seems that way because Magda is becoming more uptight. I don't think it's the alcohol, but simply holding a drink that makes her feel more self-possessed. She looks out over my head and begins to narrate the parade of people walking. These are the daughters of a famous actor. That one is a poster artist with his own gallery on St. John's Street. That one is a novelist back to visit after emigrating to Sweden twenty years before.

"Jewish," she adds.

Finally, Piotr Skrzynecki blows his silver whistle and everyone heads into the main room, which is even more beautiful than either Nela or Irena described it. It's all white, like in a dream. The ceiling is draped in white sheets, softening the corners of the room and diffusing the outlines of the beams into soft grays. And then there are children's toys and farm implements and kitchen tools all suspended precariously from the ceiling, all painted white.

I would give anything for Nela to be alive for one more night and see the Cabaret, or even to be able to go home and describe it to her afterward. I would tell her that I've found the repository of all happy endings, the secret passageway between dozing and dreaming, the vault of unrequited freedom, the precious catacombs of the Polish soul. All these years they have been resting beneath the stones of the Rynek, deep in a cellar, behind an oak door, only coming to life on Saturday nights on a humble, creaky stage just twice the size of the grand piano wedged next to it.

There are probably three hundred of us to witness it, packed into this cellar together on folding chairs, on sills and stones jutting from the wall, on railings, even on the corners of the stage. Magda and I find places on a back windowsill, thigh to thigh with three other girls. When everyone is in place, it starts, with no introduction or warning. The lights go out and Gypsy jazz begins to whine, followed by the proud, wistful folk songs I've not heard since I sat on Nela's lap as a child. There are Wałęsa imitations, satires of life both in the New Poland and the Old, too many Russian jokes to count, an imitation of an American politician playing his saxophone and talking about his underwear, and more songs, more songs, one after the other, crescendoing and crashing over us. The music has me by the shoulders, the nostalgia by the throat, the laughter by the stomach. I try desperately to ingest it all, to swallow it whole and hold it in, to let it vibrate in my belly and blaze from my fingertips, and it feels like one of the greatest disappointments of my life when the lights come back on, when the singers and actors take their final bows and tramp across the piano lid to the exit.

We clap until our hands itch, desperately trying to clap them back into existence, but the stage remains empty and forlorn. We shuffle around for a few minutes afterward, but without the performers we are like lost sheep, following the crowd to the heavy oak door. After sitting so tightly together for a few hours, after breathing the same air and being caressed by the same music, it seems as if there should be more ceremony in our leaving each other.

Instead, the Boney M song blasting from the disco engulfs us, and we reluctantly head up the stairs. Out on the street, a warm breeze has picked up. I look over at Magda buttoning her sweater and adjusting her scarf around her neck like an old woman, and I suddenly feel connected to her, like survivors after dodging fate in a spectacular accident. I can tell by her silence that she must feel it too. And as we walk home under the streetlights, I feel the same connection to everyone we pass, as if we all fit together like stones in a wall, as if everything in sight is merely an extension of myself, a piece of the same soul. The lights, the trees, the storefronts, the kiosks, the teenagers, the Gypsies, the grandmothers and grandfathers. And so, when I turn to Magda, it seems completely natural, as if we've always been close and chatty, as if she never ignored me and I was never jealous of her.

"So have you talked to him?"

She looks puzzled. "Who?"

"Żaba."

"Only to tell him off."

"That must have been awful. How did you find out?"

She hesitates. "I went over to her house one night and I ran into them coming down the stairwell."

"*Boże.*"

"You know, the worst part was that they didn't even try to make excuses or deny anything or apologize."

She is silent for a minute. We are walking along Karmelicka toward the neon Biprostal sign in the distance.

"I'll never forget it. You know, they both just looked at me like I was so stupid, so naive. Like it was my fault because I should have known."

Silence again, as if the sentences are individual telegraphs, and I have to wait for the next one to come across the wires.

"The irony is that when they first met, they couldn't stand each other, and I tried so hard to make them get along, to get them to like each other."

"And how long were you with him?"

"Seven months. But her . . . eight fucking years. She was my best friend. *Best.*"

We continue talking the rest of the way home. It could be the Cabaret. It could be the free drinks or the bottle of vodka we pull out of the cabinet once we get home. It could be that Magda feels the same isolation I feel, that we are both locked inside ourselves, waiting for anything—a tiny bird, a blown leaf, a question—to bridge the moat.

We sit up in the kitchen and talk until three in the morning. I tell her about the village, about my mother and father, Nela and the neighbors, and she in turn tells me about her father, about Żaba, about her fear of failing the last-chance exams in September. The bond between Irena and me developed slowly, *krok* by *krok*, pushed along simply by the torque of the hands of the clock, but my friendship with Magda is forged in that one night, that single flash of light searing us into the hypotenuse of the triangle we three are to become, the triangle in which it will be so easy to get lost.

19

Confessions

IN THE SECOND YEAR of the war, the Pigeon and Władysław Jagiełło stopped by just once every week or two, bringing supplies when times were good, asking for them when they weren't. Whenever they stayed overnight, they slept hidden in the barn; otherwise, they spent their nights in bunkers dug in the woods or in other barns in other villages. In turn, they would send their compatriots in the Home Army to spend nights in Half-Village, always passing along the same battered half-postcard of the Tatra landscape with a crude line drawing of a pigeon on the back in heavy pencil. After several months, the landscape faded and blistered with water damage, and the pencil drawing was constantly changing as it wore away and was redrawn. The piece of card became so mangled that the man carrying it usually had no idea of its value, had no idea that it was, in fact, a golden ticket that would buy him a good night's sleep, a soft bed of hay, a warm meal, a change of clothes, and a glimpse of the most beautiful girl the mountains had ever borne.

In the first year of the war, the Hetmańskis had taken the risk of sharing dinner in the house with the guests—they were always called guests, never strangers or soldiers or partisans or even visitors. They would sit around the great larch table the Pigeon had built and share the news and any new jokes about the Führer they had heard, their voices always full of hope and incremental victories. Then one of the guests would compliment the table, and Anielica would en-thusiastically point out everything in the house that the Pigeon's golden hands had built, as if in doing so she could conjure up the rest of his body. Kind words would flow about the Pigeon from all around the table, and Anielica would luxuriate in them until Pan Hetmański announced that it was time for bed. He would take the guests out to the barn, where they would look skeptically at the thin space between the hay and the wall, inching their way along side-ways until they came to a corner cave, perfect sleeping quarters for one or two men.

The Pigeon continued to send partisans to be billeted throughout the war, but after the first year, the gatherings became less joyous, the food more meager. No one exchanged names anymore, and the great larch table fell silent save for the clinking of silverware against the plates. Eventually the guests stopped appearing at all, and the card would simply be slid under the door. Most had heard of Anielica's beauty by then, however, and would try to sneak a look at her pale arm and moonlit face as she left the dinner pail inside the barn door.

One day as she was leaving the pail, a hand reached out and snatched her arm. It was unfamiliar and rough, though for some rea-son she did not flinch.

"It's me," he said, confirming what her extremities already knew.

"It's you."

He pulled her inside the barn and held her tightly against his chest. He smelled of the forest, of pinesap and dried leaves, damp mushrooms, feathers, fur, and mold. He kissed her briefly on the lips, then drew back. Even in the war, as every other social barrier came crashing down, this one stayed up.

"When we are married," the Pigeon would sometimes begin, but propriety kept him from even finishing the sentence.

"I've missed you," she said.

"It hasn't been safe to come." Her eyes adjusted to the light, and she watched him as he reached into his pack, hoping for a *laska* of sausage or a jar of jam. Pan Hetmański said that in Zakopane you could still find these things. But instead of food, the Pigeon pulled forth something metal, something that gleamed even in the scraps of moonlight slipping between the cracks in the barn, and Anielica suddenly recognized it as the ciborium from the church.

"Father Adamczyk. He's been taken away."

"For what?"

"For refusing to hear confessions."

"The Nazis have moved into Pisarowice?"

"They are turning the church into a munitions warehouse. I need you to keep this in the house. In the wardrobe, under a clean cloth. Stack only worthless junk in front of it. Reverence it every day."

"But if they are turning it into a munitions warehouse, weren't there guards around the church? How did you manage to get it out?"

"There were guards, yes . . . of course there were guards. But they were all drunk of course. Yes, they were drunk, as Germans frequently are, so we sneaked up behind them, tied them up, and blindfolded them." He could not look her in the eye when he said it, and when he gave her the ciborium, his hands were trembling.

"Your hands are trembling."

"It is from holding the Blessed Sacrament."

She knew that it was not the complete truth, but she took the ciborium from him and put it in the wardrobe as he had asked, and the Blessed Sacrament was doled out in sixteenths and thirty-seconds, only on holy days, for the next three years.

20

The Difference Between Matrimony and Pierogi Ruskie

I TELL PANI BOŻENA that I've been to the Cabaret over the weekend.

"Oh, now it is nothing like what it used to be in the old days," she says as I follow her up the stairs. "Now it is only gimmicks and slapstick, a couple of catchy tunes."

"I thought it was amazing."

"It will never be how it used to be."

Today, she wants me to make her look like Gina Lollobrigida. She sits down on the dressing stool and pulls a jangle of cords and metal out of one of the drawers. I curl, tease, pin, and poke at the wig, but it never looks quite right. She puts on a white dress, strides around the living room like she's hurdling invisible obstacles, and talks with a flirtatious lilt to her voice. Although this sort of thing is nothing new, there's been something different about her in the past month, as if the film stars are slowly eclipsing her own personality so that when the time comes, she might very well die as Shirley MacLaine or Elizabeth Taylor or Katharine Hepburn instead of Pani Bożena.

I escape for a couple of hours and bring back a package of Indian curry and flatbread from Hipermarket Europa. We eat dinner in silence, and the entire afternoon, I feel like I'm suffocating. At the end of the day, I breathe a sigh of relief as I step out onto the street.

Irena's flat, on the other hand, has come to life since the night of the Cabaret, the days stretching into one long, uninterrupted conversation as the three of us come and go, as we call back and forth from different rooms of the flat, picking up a train of thought and putting it back down, an hour later turning it over and picking it up again.

"*Mamo*, what are you cooking?" Magda calls from her room.

"Pierogi."

"*Ruskie?*"

"You can smell it already? I've barely let the onions hit the pan."

"I'm hungry."

There's another pause, and then from the kitchen: "Do you know what that smell really is?"

"The cats?"

"Marriage."

"*Marriage?*"

"Oh, *Boże*, here we go again with the man-hating."

"Marriage," Irena continues. "You spend an hour making dinner, you sweat, you work your *dupa* off . . ." I hear the cabinets banging open, the garbage pail as she replaces it under the sink. ". . . and then two hours later, your husband goes to the shitter and you're left having to think of another meal. Whenever I didn't know what to make, I made pierogi *ruskie*."

"The 'shitter,' *mamo?*" I can hear Magda laughing from her room.

"You go ahead and laugh," Irena says, "but you'll see how it is. Both of you. And then I will have the last laugh."

There's a loud clatter in the kitchen, something metal falling to the floor.

"Do you want help in there?" I ask.

"Are you kidding?" Magda calls. "If you help her, it will ruin everything; then she can't complain anymore."

"You're damn right," Irena answers. "I have to build up years of gratefulness and guilt if I want one of you to be around in my old age. Like money in the bank. That's what my own mother did. She was no idiot."

In August, the tourists come thick and fast through Irena's flat, Mikro plays a string of beach films, and the crowd at Stash's dwindles in favor of the outdoor cafés that are replicating themselves daily on the Rynek. But the Englishmen continue to come. They nod and smile when they see me, but there's an implicit understanding between us that I am not like the girls who hover around them at the table and laugh at everything they say. Magda won't even go near them. She says she's allergic to the Colonizers, as she calls them, and pulls one sleeve up to her shoulder to show me the microscopic red bumps she calls hives. Now that Magda is working with me a few nights a week, our conversations carry over from Irena's to Stash's and back, which makes the days run together even more.

At the end of the second set, Tadeusz comes back to the bar. His face is flushed, and he untucks his black T-shirt, fanning himself with the hem. I have his glass of orange juice ready, and half of it disappears in the first gulp. Usually, in the break after the second set, Magda takes over while we duck to a side table and talk about how he's played so far that night. He keeps an inventory in his head—one column of the notes that bleated too much or turned to foam on the reed, the other of the ones that rang as clear and true as Stash's trumpet next to him. He fingers them like rosary beads and asks me over and over what I thought of this part or that part.

On this particular night, though, he jumps up from the stool and disappears into Stash's office. He comes out with a jacket rolled up into a ball.

"Where are you going?"

He laughs. "That's when you know you have a girlfriend. 'Where are you going? Where are you going?'"

"Very funny." But I can't help smiling. Girlfriend. He called me his girlfriend.

Tadeusz takes my hand, leads me to an empty table in the corner, and hands me the jacket. There is something with corners inside, and I unroll the bundle carefully.

"Someone brought it into the pawn shop and never came back to reclaim it. My father said I could take it."

"What is it?"

"Look for yourself."

I take it out of the jacket and run my hand along the pebbled black plastic, the rounded edges, the chrome trim. I press my fingertips into the black rubber padding around the eyepiece and the handgrip. I fiddle with the lens cap and flip the little screen out to the side.

"I have a few extra tapes for it too. There's a place over in Huta that just opened up where you can get them if you need more."

"But what is it?"

"What do you mean? It's a video camera."

"I know it's a video camera, but for what?"

"I thought that since you're so obsessed with films, maybe you could start to make some of your own."

The camera stares up at me, like a child the stork brought, its one eye looking at me in complete submission.

"Here," Tadeusz says, and he takes the camera in his hands. "You just press this." A green light comes on, and he points it at me.

I put my hand over the lens.

"Don't do that," he says.

"I don't want it to break." I laugh, and I snatch it back from him. I point the camera at him, and his face appears, flushed and smiling, in the little screen.

"As simple as that?"

"As simple as that."

I press the stop button and hold it in my lap. "It's beautiful, Tadeusz. Thank you."

"Try it out," he says. "Play around with it."

"I will."

"You could take a few shots of the club, practice on Magda."

"I will."

Stash blows one long, loud note from his trumpet. "Okay. I'll see you after." Tadeusz leans over to give me a kiss on the cheek, presses his hands against the chair, and catapults off. I take the camera back to the bar and find a clean dishtowel to wrap it in.

"What's that?" Magda asks.

"It's a video camera. Tadeusz gave it to me."

"I didn't think he was that wild."

I slap her arm. "Not like that. It was just something lying around his parents' pawn shop. He thought I might like to play around with it."

Magda snatches it from the dishtowel. "*Fajne*," she says. She takes off the lens cap and points it at me, but I cover the lens with my hand.

"Come on," Magda says.

"No."

"Just one little shot."

"No."

"Fine, then I will film your boyfriend." She finds the zoom key and points it at the stage. "Oh, Tadeusz." She sighs and starts making kissing noises into the microphone.

"Give me that," I say. I take it from her and turn it off, wrap it up in the towel, and tie it tightly.

"Any idea what you'll film?"

I shrug. "It's just for laughs. He always says I'm obsessed with films."

"Are you?" And it suddenly dawns on me how little we know of each other, how the years we were only distant cousins tower over the small pile of days we have actually been friends.

When I get home, I put the camera on the high shelf in my room, but it stares back at me in the dark and I can't sleep. I stuff it in my rucksack and leave it there, and when Pani Bożena goes for her nap after *obiad* the next day, I take it out again and unwrap it. I don't watch *Dynasty;* I don't watch the film on Channel Four. I just sit there holding the camera, staring at it, running my fingers along the edges.

"What are you doing?"

I jump. Pani Bożena is up early from her nap. This morning, she wanted to be Liz Taylor in *Cleopatra*, so she made me fashion a copper wire into a tiara with a rattlesnake striking from the middle of her forehead. She must have slept in it.

"Nothing. Just taking a break."

"What is that?"

"A video camera someone gave me."

"For what?"

For what. Exactly. I lie. "I thought I could start recording *Dynasty* for you in the afternoons so you can watch it when you wake up from your nap."

"You can do that?"

"I think so. There's an electronics shop over on Long Street. I can ask there if I need special cords or something."

Pani Bożena hustles me out of the house with a five-hundred-thousand-złotych note, and the next afternoon, the camera dutifully records Sammy Jo and the rest of them, the tape whining and hissing at me as if I am the worst traitor in the world.

When I get home, Magda is working at the wine bar, the tourists are locked in their room for the night, and Irena is reading a news-magazine in the living room.

"What's the matter?" she asks without looking up.

"Nothing."

"What kind of nothing?"

"Nothing. I'm fine."

"You're not fine. The past few days you've hardly said a word."

"I have a lot on my mind."

"Is it the *klarnecista*?"

"Not exactly."

"Then what exactly?"

When I try to tell her, though, it comes out a jumble of Tadeusz, Magda, the camera, *Dynasty*, law school, Kinga, Italy, Pani Bożena, and a clarinet. As I'm talking, she scrunches up her forehead like she does with the tourists, only it never relaxes into understanding. In fact, the more I talk, the more her face contorts.

"Oh, before I forget. Have you seen the news about the forest fire near Katowice? They say it is the worst fire in decades, and two fire-men have died already . . ."

"Irena, I already know all your tourist tricks."

"That wasn't a tourist trick. I thought you'd really want to know."

"I'm going to go wash up."

I go out into the hall and flip on the light.

"Baba Yaga," she calls.

"Yes?" I come back and lean against the door frame.

"Paris."

"*Co?*"

"I've always wanted to go to Paris. Ride the Métro and walk along the Seine and visit the Musée d'Orsay. That's my dream."

"Really?"

"Really."

21

And What Are We to Do?

Y THE FOURTH YEAR of the war, Irena had grown from a fat pullet to a gangly, grubby child of three. Marysia and Anielica would sit in front of the stove mending the uniforms they had sewn three years before, watching Irena playing in the shadows of the kerosene lamp and daring to hope out loud for the future.

"Maybe after the war, we can move to Brook-leen, and little Irenka can learn English and marry a *biznesmen*," Marysia would say.

"Or Krakow," Anielica would offer. "It is said that in Krakow all the women are princesses and all the men are broad and handsome."

"What's Brook-leen?" little Irena asked. "Do they have villages there?"

Irena loved to play in the dirt like a Gypsy girl, and Pani Hetmańska tried to keep her in the house during the middle of the day, scrubbing her down each evening to keep her complexion light. No one else was worried. Marysia, with her dark, curly hair tucked under a scarf, had lived openly among them throughout the entire war with no incident, and for the most part, Half-Village remained a forgotten mouse hole in the Lebensraum. Many other villages had splintered, of course, turned on each other at the slightest provocation and divided along ragged lines: Poles vs. Poles, Jews vs. Jews, Poles vs. Jews, Polish nationalists vs. Polish communists, Poles vs.

Ukrainians, Ukrainians vs. Everybody, and as usual, Everybody vs. the Gypsies. All of Zakopane was awash in jam and honey and real coffee, and in the fourth year of the war, no other evidence was needed to prove that the town fathers were in collusion with the Gestapo.

That was simply not how it was in Half-Village or Pisarowice. Though they disagreed on just about everything before and after the war, during the war, the villagers were as loyal to one another as the mountain itself, as constant as the snow. No one snitched that the youngest Epler boy, who was nearing two meters tall, had been thirteen for three birthdays straight. No one said anything about where the newspapers came from or who slept in the Hetmański barn. No one reported the stills of *bimber* that had been set up deep in the woods where the old marriage bed stood. No one spoke of the Pigeon's brother, Jakub, who had been hiding out in the sheep camp on Old Baldy Hill the entire war, refusing to go into service for either the Vaterland or Mother Poland. And no one ever spoke of the primary school or the children's theater in the Hetmański house, or missed one of their evening performances.

The costumes, props, and refreshments had diminished as the shortages spread, and by the fourth year, the grand productions they had envisioned were whittled down to a few of the children standing in front of the room once every few weeks, reciting Mickiewicz, Asnyk, Sienkiewicz, Reymont, Orzeszkowa, or Miłosz. But no one would think of canceling the performances, for with so many books in the country confiscated, all the schools closed, all the churches turned into bunkers or munitions storage, all the cinemas devoid of Polish films, this was the only way to immortalize the Polish spirit. Better than immortalize, in fact, because as the sixteen-, fifteen-, even fourteen-year-olds joined the Resistance or were forced into Baudienst, Pan Tadeusz and Zosia, Lygia and Marcus Vinicius, Justyna and Jan Bohaterowicz grew younger and younger with each performance.

This was true not only in the literature but throughout the country. With the shortages of food, fuel, and doctors, each winter the average age of the population crept downward with the thermometer. Suddenly, the youth were in charge of everything. The same generation who had at the beginning of the war asked, "And what are we to do?" began answering their own question, bravely, decisively, relentlessly. The Pigeon and Władysław Jagiełło were now in charge of several cells in the area, and Anielica and Marysia had taken over many of the men's chores as the younger men had left the village and Pan Hetmański began to show his age. They sheared the sheep, broke up the clumps of dirt in the garden, repaired the roof, and chopped the wood. They only drew the line at doing the slaughtering.

They had put it off as long as they could, but when Pan Hetmański could not bear to watch his neighbors eat one more bowl of cabbage-and-potato soup, one more loaf of ersatz bread spread with ersatz honey, washed down with ersatz coffee, he began to sacrifice his flock. It worked out to about once a month, so the dwindling flock became a sort of calendar. Since the meat was divided evenly among all the remaining Half-Villagers, it was not much. After an indulgent pot of mutton stew, each family would spread the rest of its ration throughout the month, making head cheese, boiling the bones for soup, spreading the marrow on the ersatz bread. Every few months, Pan Hetmański would take the sheepskins, along with the products of Pani Hetmańska's knitting and Anielica and Marysia's sewing, to Zakopane, where he would trade for wheat flour and kerosene. Traveling there had always meant two days of walking, but it was becoming an increasingly risky trip.

"If they are going to kill an old man for trading for food, well, let that be on their consciences if they have any," he would say boldly. But the war had turned Pani Hetmańska into a worrier, and she pleaded with him to let her accompany him on his trip, even if it meant leaving Anielica and Marysia behind on their own with Irenka for a few days.

At first Pan Hetmański absolutely refused, but his memory of the threats he encountered on his last trip prevailed, and it was surely safer to travel in a pair, especially with his wife, who had the strength of a man. Besides, the Germans had not been up the mountain to Half-Village since the summer, and there were rumors that Hitler was already making plans to withdraw from Poland altogether.

Finally, after listening to all three women for several days insist that Everything Would Be Okay, Pan Hetmański relented. They would be gone for only five days after all, and he would make sure that the Pigeon and Władysław Jagiełło could stop by at least once while making their rounds in the area.

"And you will promise me that neither of you will leave the village for any reason whatsoever?"

"Not for any reason."

"And you will not run the theater while I am gone?"

"But what will the children do with themselves all day?"

"They will finish all those half-dug holes and half-chopped piles of wood," Pan Hetmański said. "And you will promise to go to the cellar if the Germans come?"

They all glanced sideways at one another whenever the cellar was mentioned. "Yes," Anielica promised.

The day before they left, Pan Hetmański even quizzed little Irenka.

"And if you see a man in uniform who is not *tata* or Uncle Pigeon?"

"I *shut* the door."

"And if you hear a big bang from outside?"

"I *shut* the door."

"And if *mama* and Ciocia Anielica disappear?"

"I *shut* the door."

"And if *babcia* brings you a little treat, perhaps a little piece of bread with strawberry jam on it?" Pani Hetmańska asked.

"I *shut* the door."

They laughed. In the third year, laughter was rare indeed, and you had to snatch it up and collar it before it had a chance to sneak away. Satisfied, Pan and Pani Hetmańska set off through the snow to Zakopane.

22

And What Are We to Do?

SEPTEMBER COMES ALMOST as a surprise. The sidewalks and tram cars empty of tourists and fill with students in their first-day outfits—starched white shirts and black pinafores and suits, the littler ones with flowers for the teachers. Irena declares the end of the tourist season in five different languages. *Koniec. Kanyets. Fin. Fertig.* Finish. I move back into the third room, the room for tourists, alcoholic fathers in exile, and cousins from the village.

It's my third September not returning to school, and I can only faintly feel the imprint of the nine-month calendar beneath the New Year's to Christmas slog everyone else follows. I never thought seriously about going to university. That would have meant leaving Nela, and neither of us would have survived that. "When I am gone . . ." was how all the conversations about my future started. "But only when you are gone" was how they ended. It seemed like a long way away, and in the end, it sneaked up on us. I wasn't even there for her when she died. I came home from my job at the cinema in Osiek and Pani Wzwolenska was sitting at the larch table, Nela's body laid neatly on the bed.

Magda is taking her last-chance exams, so all week she hasn't been in to Stash's. Tonight, Stash is closed in his office on the phone, so I pull down the chairs and set up everything by myself. I'm just making the rounds to light the candles when who walks in the door but Kinga.

"What are you doing here? You're supposed to be in Rome!"

She holds up one tiny hand. "I don't even want to talk about it. Those *mafia bastardi*. They can *vafanculo*."

"But what happened?" I ask again, and of course she does want to talk about it. She tells me all about the *mafia bastardi* nanny agency, how they first sent her to be a nanny for a man who didn't even have any children, and then after she walked out, they reassigned her to a family where she was expected to cover up the mother's affairs, and the eight-year-old girl treated her like a servant.

"In the end, I think I was fired by the eight-year-old. And then the summer jobs all dried up and the agency thought I was too much trouble after that."

"So what are you going to do now?"

"England," she says, without any hesitation. "I have a friend in London who thinks she can get me a job, and anyway, learning English is much more useful than that *mafia bastardi* language."

Stash comes out of the office. "I thought I heard your voice. What are you doing here? What happened?"

"That *mafia bastardi* nanny agency, that's what happened." She goes into Stash's office and retells the story, and when she comes out, she's wearing her old apron. She surveys the bar area and moves a few things around, then takes her place beside me. "There," she says, and crosses her arms in satisfaction, and it's as if she never left.

Tadeusz and I make our usual plan to go to Mikro on Friday afternoon. There's a French comedy about a butcher in an apartment block, and the cinema is packed. As we walk home, I try to tell him about the main actor and the other films he was in, but Tadeusz has a case of the *głupawka*—the goofiness—today, and he can't stop laughing and making silly jokes, leaning his head on my shoulder and calling me madame.

"And vat deed you feelm so far, Madame Director?" he says, with a French accent even worse than the one I use at Hipermarket Europa.

"What do you mean?"

"Zee camera, Madame Director, zee camera!"

148

"Oh. That." To say the truth, I have not stopped thinking about the camera since he gave it to me. I carry it in my rucksack everywhere I go. It hangs down from the hook in Pani Bożena's front hall like a pendulum as I go about the dusting, it whispers to me through the music from its place behind the door in Stash's office, and it becomes a dead weight pulling at my shoulders as I trudge home at the end of the day.

"So, you have feelmed nussing?"

"I haven't had time."

"No time, Madame Director?"

"What am I supposed to do? Not go to work?"

"But how will you ever apply to Łódź, Madame Director?"

"Stop it, Tadeusz."

"Stop what?"

"Stop your *głupawka*."

"This is no *głupawka*. I'm being serious."

"You haven't said anything serious all afternoon."

"Now I have. Why not apply to Łódź?" And I notice that the accent is gone.

"Don't be ridiculous."

"I'm not being ridiculous. You probably know more about films than the professors." He stops in front of me on the sidewalk, blocking my way. "What was that you said to me once . . . why not?"

"I'll tell you why not. Because it's so unrealistic, I don't even know where to begin. Do you know how many places there are at Łódź each year?"

"How many?"

"Not many. And to get one, you have to know someone who knows someone who knows someone who can *załatwić* a place for you."

"Who told you that?"

"No one has to tell me that. I just know."

"I just know. I just know," he says, and pinches me playfully on the arm, but I'm annoyed with him tonight, and when we get to Irena's door, I'm the one who gives him a peck on the cheek before wriggling out of his grasp.

On Monday, Magda gets the news that she failed her last-chance exams, but surprisingly, the land doesn't fall into the sea. She won't talk about it at Stash's because, she says, "The world is small and has many ears," but on our walk home, she tells me all about it—how they weeded the class down to half of the size so they could accept more paying students, how a few students' parents hired the professors themselves for extra "tutoring."

"And what are you going to do now?"

We're passing the stretch of shops between Aleje and the Street of Kazimierz the Great: the bookmaker's storefront, the photographer's shop with the pope's graduation photo in the window, the second-hand store, the computer firm, the sex-video shop started by the family who used to be royalty back in the fifteenth century.

"What do you mean?"

"For a profession."

"Well, I'm going to be a prosecutor, of course."

"But how?"

She starts counting the steps off on her fingers. "First, I talked to Stash, and he said that he'll keep me on even though Kinga's come back, because who knows how long she'll be around anyway? So I'll work there and at the wine bar this year, keep studying, reapply completely in the spring, and start my first year over from zero next fall. And if worse comes to worst and I fail again, hopefully I'll have saved up enough money to become one of the paying students. It's not what I want, but if that's the only way . . ."

"You would do all that just to become a prosecutor?"

"There's nothing else I want to be."

"Nothing?"

"Nothing."

Even inside the flat, the natural forces are remarkably calm. Irena doesn't say anything about the exams either to Magda or to me, and the truce declared in July remains.

"Are you okay?" I ask Irena.

"Fine."

"Are you sure?"

"What am I to do? It's her life. She'll sort it out."

Meanwhile, my mind is preoccupied by a single syllable. Łódź. Łódź, Łódź, Łódź, Łódź. The word sounds like a chugging train, an American rap song, a washing machine on spin, an utter impossibility.

On Wednesday, I find myself eating with a sullen and tipsy Brigitte Bardot, who's complaining about the dry *boeuf bourguignon*. Under the table, I can feel my fingers anxiously bending and straightening, contorting and contracting, hovering around the space inside myself that I can feel opening up, demanding to be filled by something grand.

"Pani Bożena?"

She raises her eyes to look across the table at me.

"I was wondering . . . you know the video camera . . . well . . . I thought maybe you could advise me on . . . well, I was thinking of making a film, of filming something . . . you know, for fun, nothing serious . . . I thought, you have been to the film studios in Łódź and have met all those people, and you know what it takes to make a film . . ."

Brigitte Bardot laughs, throwing her head back in a way that almost frightens me. "Imagine!" she says.

"I know. It's silly. Never mind."

But her face lights up behind the cloud of red wine. "Imagine! All this time you have been working up the nerve."

"The nerve to do what?"

"Why, to ask me to star in your film."

"But I don't have a film in mind."

"Come, come," she says. "No need to be shy. You only had to ask. Who would you like me to play? Véronique? Holly Golightly? Queen Elizabeth?"

As I look across at her, with her falling wig and her face flushed with wine, I hear a sound in my mind, like pieces clicking into place. "Maybe you could just play yourself."

"Myself?"

"Yourself."

She takes another drink and pats her lips with her napkin as she considers this. "I suppose I could do that. Yes. I could do that. All right then. We start tomorrow. Bright and early. I'll make up a list of things that need extra attention around the flat before then."

When I ring the bell the next morning, she meets me in her best robe and a pair of pink, feathered mules, her makeup even more pronounced than usual, her hair tied Gypsy-style in a long silk scarf.

"Welcome to my humble residence," she says, bowing deeply.

I follow her up the stairs of the *kamienica*, and she keeps glancing back at me, smiling, as if the camera is already rolling. She's moved the furniture around since I left yesterday, rearranged some of the knickknacks, and draped scarves over the lamps to make the lighting more subtle. She sits down at her dressing table, but she is impatient today, and she gets up before I can finish removing the streaks of purple and red from her skin.

"Don't you want me to touch it up for you?"

"No, no, it's fine. Let's get started."

She rises from the velvet seat with as much grace as she can muster in the mules. First she wants to be filmed sitting in bed performing a very feminine stretch and yawn, ringing a tiny silver bell that she's pulled off one of the knickknacks in the living room. Then I film her eating breakfast in bed from a silver tray and drinking her tea from her best china teacups. I follow her as she sashays across the room, though she makes me stop the camera when she goes to sit down because she has figured out that she can't do it gracefully in the mules. I film her reclined on the chaise in the corner, her legs crossed and cocked, reading a "screenplay," which is no more than a phone book, the cover wrapped in plain white paper and tilted at a careful angle. I film her talking to the dial tone and calling it "darling" and "*kochana*," pretending that there's a director or producer on the other end, or another member of the faux beau monde. She positions herself for every shot and tells me where to stand. She even seems to have memorized witty quips for each scene. The entire morning we occupy ourselves with this charade, and when it's time for *obiad*, we have to settle for *kanapki*, which we eat off the china and crystal Pani Bożena set the table with the night before.

"Shut the camera off," she says.

"Why?"

"Do you think I want to be seen eating *kanapki*?"

"No one will see this, I promise you." But I do as she asks and leave it sitting on the chair across the room. While we were filming, Pani Bożena was gregarious and dynamic, but now, a long stretch of silence passes, the clinking of silver and crystal like a metronome, shuffling the time along. She drinks nearly an entire bottle of wine with her *kanapki* and quickly grows impatient with me filling her glass halfway. Finally, she reaches over to help herself, leaving the bottle next to her plate.

"I never told you about the second film, did I?"

"I didn't know there was a second one."

Pani Bożena folds her arms across her chest and leans back, her perfect posture sinking into the chair. "It was several years after the first one. After all, there are certain responsibilities associated with being a government official's wife, you know."

"Of course."

"Anyway, I was to play Catherine the Great," she says, flourishing her hand. "It was all very spontaneous, all very rush-rush. That's how great films are made, you know."

I nod as if I do know, and dribble what's left in the wine bottle into my glass.

"As it turned out, there was another actress who wanted the part. My part. I had my suspicions that she was . . . how shall I put this delicately . . . having sex with the director. She had no talent. She didn't even look like Catherine the Great. Just a young, plain, unripe face." She finishes the last of her wine and goes to pour more, but the bottle is empty.

"So the director took the part back from me . . . *stole* the part back from me." Pani Bożena takes a deep breath, the miniature accordion on the bridge of her nose stretching to take more air into the bellows. Her eyes glaze in the dim light cast by the covered lamps, but she doesn't move to wipe them. "That *buc*," she hisses.

The word surprises me. I've never heard her use anything like it, and it makes me feel that for once, I'm truly in the presence of Pani Bożena—not Katharine Hepburn, not Elizabeth Taylor, not even the Grande Dame of Bishop Square. My only regret is that the camera is sitting on the other side of the room, its single eye closed, asleep.

"Let me see it."

"See what?"

"What you filmed this morning."

I get the camera and flip open the screen on the side. I press the black buttons until there is a miniature Pani Bożena sitting up in her bed, and I hand her the camera.

Her pupils jump and dart as she watches the screen. I can see the images settling into her face, and suddenly she looks forlorn. She hands the camera back to me without a word. She's slumped a little in her chair, and she stares at something across the room.

"I'm sure you would have been a wonderful Catherine the Great," I say.

She looks up, startled. She quickly straightens up in her chair, an invisible string pulling her chin to the ceiling. "Well, of *course* I would have been."

She takes a long nap that afternoon, and I sit on the chaise with the camera in my lap, listening to her snoring on the other side of the wall. I think about how exhausting it must be to act out the life you wish you had, detail by detail, a life that was either thrown away or taken away or drifted away on its own, a life that there's no chance of ever getting back. And I was the one who brought that life right up to her face, who allowed her to rub it between her fingers, fog it with her breath, and realize that it wasn't hers. When I hear her stirring, I wrap the camera up in the dish towel and pack it in my rucksack. But she doesn't get up. She sleeps all afternoon, and when it's time to go, I let myself out. I take the camera home and stow it in a drawer, vowing never to bring it back again.

When I return the next morning, Pani Bożena answers the door in a simple cotton housedress, her garlic curls smashed against her head, one pink curler sticking out from her forehead like a unicorn's horn. As I follow her up the stairs, she says nothing about the day before.

"What if I do your hair like Marilyn Monroe today?" I ask. "Or Judy Garland?"

She stops on the landing, turns around, and squints at me. "Take a good look at me. Do I look *anything* like Marilyn Monroe to you?"

She unlocks her door, and we don't talk again until *obiad*.

23

Everything Will Be Okay

WHEN THE PIGEON came through the front door of the Hetmański house, the contents of the wardrobe were all over the floor. The ciborium was open, spilling the hosts like an open wound. Marysia was half-naked, her hands tied behind her back, and Marysia's brother was on his knees, the pistol of the German officer cracking against his skull, opening up a wound the same pinkish-red color as the thread they had used to embroider the Polish eagle on the forage caps. Marysia's father lay prostrate on the wooden floor, his white beard flattened against the boards, a German lackey in only his shorts pressing a bare foot into his back.

The officer looked up at the Pigeon, but before he could level his gun, the Pigeon whipped the rucksack from his shoulders and hurled it dead at his groin. Marysia's brother, weak though he was, was quick to snatch the pistol, and began opening up a Polish eagle on the side of the officer's head, making him shout in pain. The lackey reached for his gun, which, unfortunately for him, was still in its holster, slung over the back of a chair along with his jacket and his pants, and the Pigeon took the opportunity to beat him until he lay immobile on the floor. He took the lackey's gun from the holster and pointed it at the officer, who had begun to fight back against Marysia's brother.

"*Hände hoch!*" he shouted at the officer. "*Hände hoch* and on your knees!" The officer did as he was told.

"You will pay for this," the officer said calmly, the barrel of the pistol aimed at his head. "You have committed high treason against the Reich. You are *finished*. And so are the swine you have been hiding."

"Funny, that is exactly what we call you." The Pigeon delivered another kick to the officer's groin, and the officer bit down on his lip to hold the pain in.

It was only then that the Pigeon looked over and noticed Anielica huddled under the great larch table, naked, tied to the leg of it, the leg that he himself had carved. Her eyes stared back at him, flat and shallow like a sheep's, just before the knife draws across its throat. It was her skin, though, that frightened him the most, the pink expanse of it. He had never seen more than an envelope's worth of it at any time, and now here it was, exposed to him like an open wound, like a pink, damp lamb squirming out of its mother. He was ashamed. Ashamed for himself. Ashamed for her.

"Pi-geon," she whispered. Two dry puffs of air.

He held up one hand as if to protect his eyes from the pink glare, but he held the gun steady. He yanked the lackey to his knees next to the officer and walked behind them. He stared at the backs of their heads, memorizing the cowlicks in their hair, the divot where the skull met the neck.

"Which one?" he asked, training his gun first on one, then the other. "Which one?"

Anielica began to cry.

"Which one, damn it, *which one?*"

He walked around the two until he stood in front of them, and he aimed his gun at the forehead of the officer, who was kneeling there in his undershorts, his jacket buttoned almost to the top. The officer squared his shoulders and set his jaw as if he were dying nobly for the Vaterland.

"This one?"

Anielica hugged the leg of the table more tightly and hid her face behind her hair, which was loose and ragged.

"Or this one?" He pointed the gun at the lackey, who began to plead for his life. "*Bitte, bitte . . . Ich bitte Sie . . .*"

Anielica was silent except for the sobs surfacing violently, one by one from her throat, like a drowning man struggling to bob above the water.

The officer smirked. *"Vielleicht hat es ihr gefallen."* Maybe she liked it. The bullet caught him right in his Aryan overbite, sending bits of perfectly squared teeth flying. Anielica screamed. The officer writhed on his back, one of his feet pushing vainly against the floor. The bloody hole below his eyes gave him the visage of a character in the comic pages. Marysia sobbed softly while her brother worked feebly at the knots binding her hands. Marysia's father took one of the blankets from the bed and covered Anielica, and she shuddered visibly.

"O Gott," the lackey was shouting. *"Mein Gott."*

The Pigeon stepped back. He held the gun outstretched in front of him, steadying his elbow with the other hand. He opened another hole in the officer's groin, and the blood bloomed against his white undershorts.

"Vater unser, der Du bist im Himmel . . . ," the lackey recited.

"You think the Father is listening?" the Pigeon shouted. "You think anyone is listening to you, you fucking Kraut?"

". . . geheiligt werde Dein Name, Dein Reich komme . . ."

"Shut up," he said, leveling the gun at the lackey's head.

". . . Dein Wille geschehe, wie im Himmel so auch auf Erden . . ."

The Pigeon shot him, not as he had shot the officer, but mercifully, between the eyes. By then the officer had also bled out, and there was absolute silence in the house except for a high-pitched squeak coming from below, coming from the cellar.

"I *shut* the door. I *shut* the door. I *shut* the door. I *shut* the door." No one made a move to go and console her.

Marysia's father and brother lit a fire deep in the woods to soften the ground, stripped the bodies, and buried them. They scrubbed the floor and burned the rags, along with the uniforms and the clothes Anielica had been wearing. The sweet smoke rose high above the house, the only sign of life in the empty village. The Pigeon, meanwhile, tried to comfort Anielica, but she shook when he touched her, and finally, he left Marysia and her mother to do it. They dressed her and led her down to the cellar, where the rest of the women and children of the village waited. They had been shown the secret entrance by Marysia when they heard the shot that killed the youngest Epler boy. They would have all been safely concealed had Anielica not gone back for the ciborium, had Marysia, her brother, and father not run outside when they heard Anielica's screams.

They spent the entire night in the cellar, unsure of their fate. Whole villages had been turned to ash over incidents just like this. Or turned on each other. That night no one slept. There was not enough room for anyone to lie down, so they sat and waited, all nineteen of them, knees drawn to their chests, taking turns to stretch their legs. When one person whispered, everyone heard. When one person coughed, everyone felt the recoil. And when Anielica cried, they all felt the sobs in the depth of their gut, and they all pressed against her to console her. Though the Pigeon tried himself to calm her, he only managed to make her sob louder, as if in his face she could see the faces of the Germans, as if in his tarnished hands she could see the violence that had been done to her.

He let the women take over and sat along the perimeter with Pan Lubicz, the oldest of the villagers, who had lived in Half-Village since he was born.

"I'm sorry," he said to the old man.

"For what?"

"For not telling anyone about the cellar. About Marysia's family. And now the entire village is in danger because of us."

Pan Lubicz turned to the Pigeon with kindness in his eyes and patted him on the knee. "What makes you think we did not know? Everyone in this room knew."

And Pani Wzwolenska, who had once been a teacher and had hearing like a bat, looked up from across the cellar and smiled.

24

Załatwić

I DON'T EVEN have to look outside to know that winter's coming. A dense cloud has been collecting in my lungs, breaking free and rattling about in the mornings, settling and thickening in the afternoons. Irena insists that it's a head cold from constantly drinking cold noncarbonated water at the bar, but when I begin drinking the prescribed tea, the weight in my chest only becomes heavier, pulling my voice lower and lower.

I'm not used to the coal they use here in the city. Wood smoke stings your nose and the back of your throat, but it doesn't settle inside you the way coal does. During the first two weeks of October, the sidewalks are blocked with mountains of the stuff, which men in coveralls feed into the bowels of the buildings, leaving swirls of black dust on the sidewalk. And by the middle of the month, nearly all of the old, stuccoed *kamienice* from the Rynek to Aleje are steadily belching out thick, dark smoke. A false dusk precedes the real one, and I watch it fall through the dugout window at Stash's, first like snow in a photo negative, then like a hood, until I'm staring at my own glossy reflection in the window.

I've been working as a bar girl for six months now, with no end in sight. At least Magda can partition her past from her present from her future. At least she can say "When I failed my law school exams" and "When I take the entrance exam again in the spring." For me, time is as wide and boundless as the Błonia, stretching in all directions. As I watch Tadeusz play, I wonder how long you have to do something before you become it. How long does he have to play the *klarnet* before he really is a *klarnecista*? How long can I stand behind this bar and say that I'm not a bar girl?

I half listen as Kinga tells Magda about her friend in London who is trying to find a spot for her at a language school there.

"I thought you were going there to work, not study."

"That's how it works. The school gets you a student visa, you go there in the morning just to sign in, and then you leave and you're off to work."

"And where will you work?"

"I don't know. Probably a bar."

"But you can do that here."

"But I can learn English there. And make a lot more money."

"That's how they start," Magda says. "They convince everyone that they need to learn English, they come over here under the innocuous title of 'native speakers,' settle in and establish outposts they call language schools, and then before you know it, they've bought up half the Rynek and we're drinking milk in our tea. Mark my words, that's exactly what happened in India."

"You're paranoid," Kinga says. "And hypocritical. You already know English a lot better than I do."

"My mother made me go to lessons when I was too young to know any better."

"Your mother was a smart woman. You should take your English and get out while you can. This country is sinking fast."

"Only because people like you are leaving. If everyone our age would only stay . . ."

"Listen, I love Poland, but not enough to sacrifice myself and be poor all my life."

"Being poor here is better than doing slave labor for the Colonizers," Magda says, waving her hand in the direction of the table of Englishmen. "Besides, Polish boys are much better looking."

"You have me there."

And they both laugh.

The break comes. When I leave them, they are taking an inventory of the boys that hang around the club from week to week. Magda seems to have made a full recovery after Żaba. I meet Tadeusz with his orange juice at a table off to the side.

"How's everything?" Tadeusz asks.

"Fine. You?"

He shrugs.

"Do you want to go to Mikro on Friday? They're playing *Take It Easy*."

"I'll have to let you know."

We sit in silence, listening to the shouts and laughter in the room.

"You know, I've been thinking," I say. "Irena knows a lot of people at the Cabaret. I was thinking that maybe I could ask her to *załatwić* an audition for you."

Tadeusz runs his finger around the rim of his glass.

"Tadeusz, did you hear what I said? An audition at the Cabaret. With Piotr Skrzynecki."

"I heard you. I'm thinking about it."

"What's there to think about?"

"I just don't want you to inconvenience yourself. Or Irena. You know, for Irena to have to call in any favors if she is going to need them for Magda."

"It can't hurt to try. Can you imagine? Playing for the Cabaret? You would be famous. *Famous*."

Tadeusz covers his mouth. He clears his throat and leans back in his chair. "That would be great. Really great."

"You don't sound very excited about it."

"I just don't want to put you or Irena through any trouble."

"It's no trouble."

"I'll think about it."

Something bothers me about the expression on his face and the timbre of his voice. I try to convince myself that I'm just imagining things, but after the third set, he leaves right away, picking up his clarinet case and winding his homemade scarf around his neck like a bobbin.

"Where are you going?" I call after him.

"I'm going to miss the bus," he says. "Sorry. Call me tomorrow."

As we walk home, Magda is talking about one of the boys at the bar. I'm still thinking about Tadeusz, and when I get home, I go immediately to the living room.

"Irena, I need a favor."

"Mmm . . ." she says. She's watching another documentary, this time on the city of Lwów.

"Irena, I was thinking."

"Mm-hmm?"

"Since you know a few people at the Cabaret . . ."

"Mmm . . ."

"Do you think you could get Tadeusz an audition with Piotr Skrzynecki?"

She laughs loudly and mutes the television.

"What does that mean?" I ask.

"It means that it is a very big favor you are asking me to *załatwić*, a very big bargaining chip that I have indeed, and living in the new and improved Poland, I will have to think of some way to make sure that I profit from it."

"Name your price."

"You can't afford it."

"Try me."

Irena thinks for a minute. She gets up from the love seat, goes to the dresser underneath the television, and pulls open the bottom drawer.

"Answer the letters. These stupid, *pieprzone* letters," she says. "They all send them thinking they are doing something nice, but every single one is like a damn pebble in my shoe. You get Magda to answer these letters in English for me, and I will talk to someone at the Cabaret about your *klarnecista*."

"Why can't you answer them yourself?"

"With my English?"

"You seem to speak well enough to make them follow you home from the train station in the first place."

"Yes, but *writing* that infernal language . . . it's like they throw all the letters up in the air and transcribe them the way they land on the floor. No, Magda will have to do it. I've been asking her since the summer, but she says she is too busy. Isn't that irony? For years she has been too lazy to write them. Now she is too busy." She adjusts her glasses on the bridge of her nose and holds the broken part delicately between her fingers. "So. Do we have a deal?"

I go to Magda's room and tell her, and she laughs. "She's talking *bzdury*. When I tried to help her, she still didn't want to do it. She just blames it on me because she feels guilty about it. We'll call her bluff and Tadeusz will have his audition."

On Sunday, Magda and I hurry through dinner. As soon as we're finished, we get up and clear the dishes from the coffee table.

"Relax," Irena says. "Where do any of us have to be today?" It's sleeting outside, and we can hear the pinging of the ice against the metal railing of the balcony. Irena eats the last bite of *surowka* straight from the serving bowl and lays the fork down. Magda adds it to the stack of dishes in her hands and heads off to the kitchen.

"We're answering your letters today," she calls. "You told Baba Yaga you wanted to answer your letters, so we're answering your letters."

Irena puts her feet up on the love seat and stretches out as much as she can, her head propped against the armrest. "Not today. Another day, but not today."

"Oh, no you don't." Magda tosses a dishcloth to me, and I wipe off the coffee table.

Irena shields her face with her hands. "I don't feel well. Another day. I have my period. The weather is terrible. Another day."

I go into my room and bring back the plastic bag of pens and paper, envelopes and stamps that I have collected over the past week. When I come back, Magda is already shuffling through the pile of letters in her lap. "Come on, *mamo*, we're all going to work on them until they get done."

"And do you want me to write these letters in Polish or Russian?" Irena asks. "I'm bilingual, you know."

Magda puts the letters on the table and sets two in front of her mother. "Here. These are the two that can be answered in Polish.

The rest, you will dictate to me and I will translate into English. While we are doing that, Baba Yaga will copy the addresses onto the envelopes."

Irena rubs at her eyes. "But it's so dreary today. The barometer is low and I have cramps. I can't. Not today. It will only be bad news."

"*Mamo*, I'm serious. This one time I will do them. If not today, then I will never listen to you complain about them again."

Irena smiles slightly, her hands still over her eyes. "*Głupia panienka.*"

There are about forty letters—Christmas cards mostly, some from two or three years before, some with handwritten letters tucked inside. I wonder if these people will even remember Irena, but I know that if she doesn't write them, they will continue to squat in her mind. Magda digs into the pile. She hands me the envelope to copy the address, then smooths the letter flat on her lap.

"Okay. Betty and Walt Lyons from Green Lakes, Minnesota," she translates. "Dear Irena . . . *coś tam, coś tam* . . . had a wonderful time . . . *coś tam, coś tam* . . . come see us in Minnesota . . . *coś tam, coś tam* . . ."

"Where's Minnesota?" I ask.

"Near California. Everything is near California," Magda says authoritatively. "Except New York. Okay, *mamo*, what do you want to write back to them?"

"I don't know. I don't even remember who they are."

"I don't believe you, Irena," I say. "You remember all the guests. How old they are, what their children do for a living . . ."

"I told you, I'm not in the mood today."

"*Drogi* Betty *i* Walt . . ." Magda looks up at her mother.

Irena lifts her hand up like a visor and squints at Magda. "Dear Betty and Walt. I don't remember you, but I remember that you are from that country that forced those terrible soap operas and those greasy hamburgers on us."

Magda shakes her head and laughs. She begins writing. Irena waves her hand limply, conducting an imaginary, apathetic orchestra. "Things are terrible here in Poland. There is so much poverty and unemployment, and the filthy capitalist pigs in your country who wanted this revolution are doing nothing to help the people. Once the communists fell, you left us like manure in the pasture." Irena smiles. "Write, little daughter, write."

164

"Dear Betty and Walt," Magda translates back to us. "Sorry that I haven't written to you in so long, but that doesn't mean I haven't thought of you often. In fact, I remember your visit to Krakow as if it were yesterday. Things are difficult at the moment in Poland. There are many challenges; however, the Polish people are strong and will overcome these in time."

Irena clears her throat and continues. "It is sleeting outside today, and I feel like crap. My daughter, Magda, has failed out of law school and is now working at a bar." She laughs at her own pessimism.

"Don't forget to tell them about the cousin who came to visit and won't go away," I add.

"Yes, yes, good idea," Irena agrees. "Add that." We are all laughing.

Magda clears her throat and reads back to us what she wrote. "I still have my health, thank God. And Magda is working toward someday becoming a prosecutor, as she has always dreamed. A beloved cousin from the village has come to stay, who has brought us much happiness."

"I don't know whether to thank you or throw up," I say.

"My friend says that's how it is in America," Magda insists. "'How are you? How can I help you? God bless you. Have a nice day.'"

Irena continues. "There is no way in hell I could ever afford the airplane ticket to Minnesota, and even if I could, I'd go someplace more interesting like New York or California. Besides, your damn consulate won't give anyone a visa, and they treat us like dogs, making us line up outside for days in the rain."

"Thank you for your kind invitation," Magda reads back. "I hope that someday I will be able to visit America. Greetings to your children. Your friend, Irena."

Magda lines the letter up on the coffee table with the envelope I've addressed tucked beneath it. She and Irena write two more in the same way, which she lays down on the table next to the first. She stands up to survey the three letters.

"What about the rest of them?" I ask.

"It's all systematic," she says. And sure enough, she's thought everything out for maximum efficiency. While I address the envelopes, she reads the rest of the letters to Irena, and Irena decides whether to answer with version one, two, or three.

"Version zero."

"There is no version zero."

"Exactly," Irena says, crumpling the letter. "He was a *babiarz* . . . from Holland. Only interested in my *dupa*."

"Your *dupa*?" Magda and I look at each other and break up laughing.

"Go ahead and laugh, but believe it or not, there are a few men walking on this earth who at one point were interested in my *dupa*."

We start copying the letters, changing the names and the states, subtracting children, adding pets. Magda supervises and proofreads them after we're done. The work goes quickly, disappearing behind Irena's stories about the guests: the Italian who fell hopelessly in love with both her and Magda on the same weekend; the American man who lost his home in a fire and was touring the world with his insurance money; the Swiss woman who woke up every morning and stood on her head; the American couple who stacked their luggage behind the guest room door because they thought that Irena would come in during the night and rob them.

"They were in their seventies, I think. All wrinkly. Even if I had wanted their money, I would have been too scared to open the door and catch them in the act!" She laughs. "But the money seems to be the first thing they think of in America."

"Right," Magda says. "As if no one thinks of money here."

"Out of desperation," Irena says. "It is a different thing."

The pile of unanswered letters on the table has dwindled. I check the drawers beneath the television and find another short stack.

"We missed a few," I say, handing them to Irena.

She opens one. We sit in silence, listening to the storm outside as she looks over the paper. She frowns and hands it back to me.

It's not from one of the tourists. *Dear Irena*, it says in Polish, in the same uniform handwriting seared into all of our fingertips from the primary grades. *I am sorry to hear about your husband's death.*

Magda reaches for the letter. I hand it to her, and she reads it, wrinkling her brow in the same way as her mother. Irena shuffles through the rest of the stack. Magda finishes the letter and leans back in the armchair.

"I'll go and post these," I say, gathering up the finished letters, and neither of them protests that it's Sunday evening or that it's storming outside. It's only when I pull the door shut behind me, only when I'm standing in the corridor that I hear them start to talk.

Outside, the icy rain buffets my cheeks. I didn't bother to take an umbrella, and I can't go back now. The kiosks and the shop windows are dark, and the streets and sidewalks are nearly empty except for an occasional silhouette slouching under the awnings or the tram shelters. I run with the letters under my coat and stuff them into the red box hanging on the wall outside the post office. I run to the cluster of three phone booths a little farther down. They have just begun replacing the old blue communist phone booths across the city with new, bright yellow ones, the color of school buses and taxicabs in the American films. I slip into one of them, pull the door shut behind me, and sit down on the ribbed metal floor.

Sometimes it feels as if Irena and Magda were meant to be my real family, as if I was really meant to grow up there in the flat on the Street of Kazimierz the Great, as if I am meant to die in Krakow, buried in Rakowicki Cemetery, with Irena stacked below me and Magda above. Sometimes it seems as if the first six years I spent in Half-Village listening to my mother die and my father stumble and fall on the other side of the wall were a terrible mistake, and the fifteen I spent with Nela were nothing but a dream. Sometimes it feels as if I was dropped by the stork into the wrong house, or the city walls were misdrawn by a few hundred kilometers and I simply ended up on the wrong side. Tonight, though, I feel the distance between us—the kilometers stretching from the village to the city, the space between being a daughter and a cousin, the cavernous years of my absence.

I sit in the phone booth listening for the sounds of the city on a Sunday night—the sleet pinging against the metal, the occasional rumble of a tram or a car passing by, my own breathing. I watch the glass fog up and feel the cold metal seeping through to my backside. I rewrap my scarf so it covers my nose, breathing brief pockets of warmth into it, which quickly dissipate. I pull my coat tightly around me. I tuck my hands into the warmth under my arms. I sit there for an hour or so, waiting for the storm to pass, and when I return, neither of them asks where I've been.

25

Not Life

WHEN PAN AND PANI Hetmańska returned to the house in Half-Village, they were pleasantly surprised to see Władysław Jagiełło and the Pigeon, and they whooped and laughed as little Irenka ran into the side room shouting, "I *shut* the door. I *shut* the door." Pan Hetmański reached into his sack like Święty Mikołaj and rifled around for a treat for the "little Gypsy," as he called her. As he searched, the silence in the house stretched thin, and little Irenka was still cowering behind the door.

"*Cyganka,* why are you acting like that? Come here and get your treat."

"I *shut* the door. I *shut* the door." And she slammed the door to the side room so hard it bounced against the frame.

"Why is she behaving like that? And why is this rug here?" He bent over, grimacing from his stiff back, and picked up the rug. He peered at the stains on the floor in the dim light of the kerosene lamp, and he looked up, alarmed.

"*Barszcz,*" Władysław Jagiełło suggested.

"Oh, I am such a klutz," Marysia said, forcing a laugh. "You know me. I dropped a whole pot on the floor. The whole pot of *barszcz.*"

"What's going on here?" Pan Hetmański demanded, straightening to his full height, his sheepskin coat and his flap hat giving him the shape of a bear. "What is going on?"

"We should go for a walk," the Pigeon said softly, and Anielica went into the side room, her mother and Marysia following.

By the time the Pigeon and Pan Hetmański returned from their walk, Anielica was already sound asleep in the bed with her mother, and Pan Hetmański pulled a stool over to the side. He stayed there all night, the weight of his head balanced on his hand, his knife at his side, watching his angel sleep as she always did, on her back, her hands folded like a corpse, her chest rising and falling ever so slightly, up and down. Though he'd spent two days trudging through the snow under packs and skins, his eyes refused to close, kept open by the image of the officer and lackey he'd never seen, their bodies decomposing under the forest a few hundred meters away.

Pan Hetmański had demanded to hear all the details, but the Pigeon had refused to give voice to any but two: that his daughter had been pure in every way that was her choice, and that the Pigeon still had every intention of marrying her as soon as the war was over and the marriage could be sanctified by an honest priest and a proper *wesele*. The words gave Pan Hetmański sporadic comfort, and he must have whispered them enough times throughout the night for them to sink into Anielica's subconscious. For when she awoke, the puffiness around her eyes was gone and she smiled slightly at her father sitting on the stool next to her bed before she noticed the knife on the floor and remembered why.

The world had once again changed overnight. Władysław Jagiełło and the Pigeon split their duties so that there was always one of them around. Miraculously, or maybe because there were already so many Germans deserting by then, no one came to Half-Village to investigate the disappearance of the officer and the lackey. Marysia's brother, Berek, left the cellar for good and joined up with the People's Army, who were very tolerant of Jews as long as they pretended not to be Jewish. For the next three years, flouting the laws of eugenics, he turned out to be an even better shot than the Pigeon, and after killing as many Germans as he could, turned his gun on the Ukrainians in the east. He knew already, as the rest of the world eventually found out in Nuremberg, that as long as you are fighting the enemy, it doesn't really matter which enemy because you can go all the way to the wealthy suburbs of Argentina and back, and you will still never be able to find the rat who rounded up your neighbors, who shot your girlfriend, who clipped short your education, and who forced you to spend four years in a dirt cellar with your parents.

With the extra space left behind, Anielica, Marysia, and Irenka spent more and more time in the cellar with Marysia's parents, sharing stories, playing little games with Irenka and praying for the future, for as it turned out, they all had the same God. Though Marysia and Anielica had always been sisters-in-law, bound by the brother and husband in between, after the Germans arrived — and that came to mean that one horrible day and not the entire war — they became sisters as close as had ever lived. One never went outside the house without the other. They did the chores together, taught the children together, and most nights, slept in the same bed together. What one embroidered, the other could pick up where the first left off, and it was as if the design had been rendered by one hand. When one of their men was in Half-Village, the other was as happy as if it had been hers. They both had two mothers, two fathers, and shared one child, little Irenka, who would come to Anielica's lap just as easily as she would go to Marysia's.

In fact, after the Germans came, the entire village drew closer than they ever had been. One family's sorrow became everyone's sorrow. One family's risk became everyone's risk. They all began to pitch in and help Marysia's parents. They brought food, dumped chamber pots, refilled lamps, and kept them in papers and books. That winter, they even scrounged eight teacups and eight bits of candles so Marysia's parents could light a menorah. And so no one would go hungry, Pani Hetmańska organized the women and the children to dig deep into the forest and preserve and salt whatever it brought forth — berries and greens, mushrooms and roots, once in a while a pheasant or a wild boar that happened to slip into a trap. Each family worked according to their ability and the food was then distributed to each family according to their need. Pure socialism before the communists had a chance to make a *bałagan* of it. Pure socialism in spite of the fact that their stomachs remained in a constant state of half-emptiness, or half-fullness in the case of Marysia, who clung to her optimism no matter what. The bitter divide of other towns and villages were close at their ears, but the Half-Villagers continued to stick together.

By the spring of 1944, the last of the Hetmański sheep had been slaughtered. Both Pani Wzwolenska and Pani Kierzkowska's daughters had been widowed. That winter had been the most miserable one in memory, and though they had survived, there was no more kerosene, shoes, meat, or laughter. By the spring of 1944, the subsistence of the villagers could no longer be called Life, or even Life As If, but at least it was Not Death, and for that they were still grateful.

26

All Souls

I DON'T SEE Tadeusz for a week. He doesn't meet me at Mikro on Friday, and he doesn't come to Stash's. Finally, on Thursday, on my way back from Hipermarket Europa, I call him from the teachers' dormitory at the end of Pani Bożena's street. The receptionist at the front desk is friendly, and even though she knows I don't live there, she looks the other way as I close myself into one of the booths.

"Hello?" A little girl answers the phone.

"Hello, this is Baba Yaga. Could I please speak to Tadeusz?" There's giggling on the other end. Whenever I call Tadeusz, the phone passes through three or four of his sisters before he finally answers.

"Hello?"

"Tadeusz?"

"Baba Yaga?" There's a scream in the background behind him, followed by more giggling.

"You didn't come to Mikro on Friday. Or Stash's. I was worried."

"I had to babysit. I talked to Stash about it."

"Can you see a film tomorrow? I think *Miś* is playing."

"I don't know, Baba Yaga. My parents are really counting on me to babysit. They're really in trouble with the shop, and my father can't seem to find another job," he says.

"I'm sorry," I say. "I didn't realize it was so serious."

There's a long pause. "Hold on," he says. "Just a second." He puts his hand over the phone, and there's a long conference that involves five or six people. I look out onto the empty street, powdered with snow, and roll the phone cord between my fingers.

"Okay, I can meet you tomorrow. Five o'clock?"

"Okay. Five o'clock."

"*Na razie.*"

When we meet at the Square of the Invalids on Friday afternoon, the dusk is already drifting down through the branches of the trees. At this time of year, it seems that the sky is always dark or getting dark or emerging from the dark. We watch *Miś*, but Tadeusz doesn't laugh as much as Nela used to, and it doesn't seem as funny as before. Afterward, we walk through Freedom Park, shivering in the cold.

"I talked to Irena about the Cabaret," I tell Tadeusz, "and she said she'll ask for you."

Tadeusz stuffs his hands into his pockets, and his feet scrape the pavement as he walks.

"She said she thinks she might be able to arrange an audition. From there you'll have to prove yourself of course, but at least you'll get the chance."

We stop on the sidewalk in front of the bookmaker's. His face is impassive, his hair blowing in blond drifts around his face.

"Imagine," I say, but I can already feel that something is terribly wrong. "Playing for Piotr Skrzynecki. Can you imagine?"

Tadeusz clears his throat, covering his mouth with his fist. "Baba Yaga, I want to tell you something," he says. "I have been thinking about joining the army."

"The army?"

"The army."

"But . . ."

"I have to help out my parents."

"Well, is army pay that good anyway?"

"Not at first, but at least it's something if I volunteer. And after that, I would have a better chance at getting a spot in the police academy."

"I didn't know you wanted to be a policeman."

He shrugs.

"But what about your clarinet?"

He shrugs again. He can't look me in the eye.

"Tadeusz, you are so close. So close."

"Look, if I don't volunteer for the army now, I'll have to do my mandatory service anyway."

"Why don't you just try to *załatwić* a medical excuse for yourself? Everyone does it these days. I'm sure Stash knows someone who could help you."

"Baba Yaga, try and understand. I have to help my parents," he says. "My sisters."

I feel a dark cloud suddenly enveloping both of us. I try to picture Tadeusz in the army, his long hair shaved into a crew cut, his paunch tightened, his face clean shaven. I try to imagine him as one of the boys I've seen on the Rynek at the end of their military service: drunk, whooping and hollering, swinging their capes around and climbing flagpoles, the police just looking on and smiling, fondly remembering the end of their service and the cape stored away in a trunk somewhere.

"Hey," he says, reaching for my hand. "We can still see each other."

To say the truth, it hadn't even crossed my mind. All I can picture is the blank spot on the stage at Stash's. "But Tadeusz, don't quit now. You are so close."

"I'm still thinking about it, okay?" he says. "I just wanted to tell you before you and Irena go through the trouble of setting up an audition with Piotr Skrzynecki."

"Why don't you just play for him, meet with him and see? Surely your parents wouldn't want you to miss this."

"You act like it's life or death," he says. "There will be other chances. Besides, the army's not so bad. It's just a lot of sitting around. And there's an army orchestra. I can play for the orchestra to keep in practice, and then maybe I can try again when I come out."

"But you'll lose your momentum."

We're standing in front of Irena's door already.

"I have to go," he says. He leans over to give me a peck on the cheek, then changes his mind and kisses me full on the mouth. It's a wet, awkward kiss, and I feel his tongue filling up my mouth, flopping around like a half-asleep fish pulled from one of the tanks in the market. It feels desperate, the kind of desperation that only surfaces near the end, when it's too late.

"I'll see you on Wednesday," he says.

He walks away, and I'm left standing there, protesting and arguing with myself about why he can't go to the army, why he must continue, why if he wants to become a *klarnecista*, he should become a *klarnecista*. And for the first time, it dawns on me that maybe my protesting has very little to do with Tadeusz and his clarinet at all.

I sleep uneasily that night, and the next morning, I get up while it's still dark and take the video camera down from the shelf. I don't turn on the light, and I sit in the middle of the floor, fiddling with the tape and playing the clips of Tadeusz and Pani Bożena over and over in the little screen. Irena bursts into my room without knocking.

"Come on. Hup, hup. Let's go."

"Irena! Don't you knock? What if I had been changing?" Indeed, I feel as if she's caught me naked, as if I'm doing something illicit.

"*Please.* There's nothing I haven't seen in this lifetime. Come on. Hup, hup. No time to waste." She reaches over the daybed to open the window shade. There's a steady rain beating against the windows.

"Where are you going?"

"Shhh . . . I don't want to wake Magda."

"Where are you going?" I whisper.

"*We,*" she says, "are going to Malina today."

"Where?"

"Malina. It's All Souls Day. I have to visit the cemetery where Magda's father is buried."

"I thought you didn't celebrate holy days. I thought you said you wanted to go to hell, where all the interesting people are."

"I'll go to hell when I die. Today we are going to Malina."

"Why don't you take Magda?"

"She has enough to worry about."

"But it's Saturday. I have to work tonight."

"We'll be back in time."

"And I didn't even know your husband."

"*Ex*-husband," she corrects me. "And consider yourself one of the lucky ones. That *skurwysyn*. Come on. Enough excuses. Let's go. Hup, hup."

We take a tram to the PKS station. The rain has stopped for now, but the streets are flooded, the water swirling around the tires of the cars and crashing like waves against the curb. Irena walks a few feet ahead of me. I hadn't even thought of going back to the village to visit Nela's grave or my mother's. Nela had arranged for simple crosses for them both, side by side outside the church in Pisarowice.

"*Chodź,* snail," Irena says. She's carrying a bouquet of chrysanthemums wrapped in tissue, but when I ask about them, she insists that she pulled them from the vacant lot opposite the flat.

"You really think I would go out and *buy* flowers for that dead *skurwysyn?*"

She pushes our way to the front of the line, and we take a seat on the bus near the back. The aisle is overflowing with bags of flowers, candles, brooms, dustpans, and pruning shears, and the driver can only make it halfway up the aisle on his final check. He takes his time buckling himself in, flipping his mirrors and visors, stopping to talk to one of the other drivers out the window, and waiting for a few more passengers to get on. But no one gets impatient. We all have the same itinerary today.

The engine idles in the low gears as we thread the narrow streets and low viaducts of the old town, and as we reach the wide *aleje,* it grumbles and groans through the rest of the gears. Irena stares out the window. I watch her expressions open and close and wonder what is running through her mind.

"Irena?"

"Yes?"

"Tell me about your husband."

"*Ex*-husband. Wiktor." She doesn't even bother to look at me. "And there's nothing interesting to tell."

"There must be something."

"We met in the Bermuda Triangle. *Koniec.* Finish. It was doomed from the start."

I wait for her to continue, but she doesn't, so I try again. "At Feniks?"

She looks over at me. "Pod Gruszką."

"Was that back when you were a painter?"

"That was back when I was a *głupia panienka,* that's what I was."

Again there is silence.

"And then?"

She looks at me and laughs. "You're not going to leave me alone until I tell you, are you?"

"You're the one who made me come. At least you can entertain me."

She smiles. "Very well." She readjusts herself so she's facing me. "It was 1972. We met in January, married in June, and Magda came in November. I remember when we were dating, my father—your Great-Uncle Władysław Jagiełło—hated him. I was still living with my parents, so even though I was already thirty-two, we still had to sneak around."

"Irena, June to November is only six months."

"So they teach you math in the village, do they?" She laughs. "Yes, Magda was a few months premature, as many Polish babies are. Anyway, I ask you to imagine: I was thirty-two, painting and scraping by, living with my parents, already on the shelf, and this handsome man walked on the scene, trying very hard to impress me. He *did* impress me. With the people I normally associated with, it wasn't hard to impress me then, and he was a manager at the Cracovia Hotel and knew many, many important people. He would take me to the best restaurants, the best cafés. We would go out dancing and all the girls would stare at him. And then he would take me home by taxi. By taxi! In those days—can you imagine? And then he would say good night very sweetly, and I would be in the flat by midnight."

"That sounds nice."

"It was."

"But?"

She laughs at my persistence. "But later, when we were married, he admitted that after he would drop me off, he'd go back to the parties and get as drunk as a pig."

"You never found out?"

She shook her head. "Like I said, I was a *głupia panienka*. Worse than Magda, truth be told. At least she will admit to being a *głupia panienka* sometimes. I always thought I was above that."

She pauses. I wait patiently, and to my surprise, she continues.

"And so we were married." She shakes her head and flicks her neck as Nela always did when talking about my father. "Without the vodka, he really would have been something. Instead, he became a terrible drunk. Terrible. He would come home late every night from work, stinking drunk. Every night. Even when Magda was only a little brat. *Terrible,* you know?"

"Yes, I know."

"Yes, you know."

She looks out the window again, as if she's looking for someone else to tell the story for her. The tightly wrapped streets of the city have unraveled, and we're driving through open fields now, anchored down in places by unfinished A-frame houses, piles of concrete blocks, and half-sheets of corrugated steel. Every once in a while, there's a block flat rising ten or twenty stories out of the ground, as if the block flats in the city went to seed and were blown out to the countryside by a stiff gust of wind.

"So I decided to divorce him. Oh, my parents were happily married until my father died, and my mother was terribly upset when she found out that I had asked for a divorce. Divorces were not common in those days. In those days, you just shut your mouth and slept with someone else as discreetly as you could. And my mother, even though she lived with us and saw what he did, she was an eternal optimist. She kept saying that it would get better, that he would stop drinking. But I asked for a divorce anyway, and eventually I got one." Irena's eyes are darker now, the years stamped around them in the purple ink of passports. For a moment, I think that's the end.

"But then he refused to leave."

"What do you mean?"

"He said he would not leave the flat. Simply refused. And in Poland at that time, you could not force the man to leave. The woman could move out, but you could not force the man to leave. That was when he started staying in the third room — your room. Every night drunk. And I would look at him and wish I had never met him, that I had just gone on with my painting and my *głupstwa.*"

"But then there would be no Magda."

"Exactly. So I became very determined. Very determined that it would not all be a waste. So I started looking for a new flat for him. For Wiktor."

"How?"

"The truth was, I didn't know how it was going to happen. But I started visiting the housing office. I would go every Friday. *Every* Friday. They were so *sick* of seeing my face there, but I kept going back, and each Friday they would tell me the same thing: 'Your name is on the list. There are no flats available. Come back in a few months.' So I would return the very next Friday. And the next. Every Friday I did this. Every Friday for five years."

"Five years?"

"Five. And then, finally, one Friday they told me they had good news for me and showed me a flat."

"So he moved?"

She shakes her head. "No. He refused. And then two more, but he refused those as well."

"Just refused?"

She nods. "And then they showed me a *garsoniera* on Rydla Street."

"So he moved to Rydla Street?"

"No, no. He refused to move there too."

"And then?"

"And then we had another six years of living together, so I decided to make the best of it. It was in the middle of Martial Law. Magda was ten. I had to think about her going to *liceum* and university. So I quit painting, broke all my ties, and Pani Bożena got me the job in the cafeteria."

The bus is quiet. The other passengers are snoozing, and the rain has stopped.

"Why didn't you move to the *garsoniera*?"

"My mother was still alive at that time, and we couldn't fit the three of us in a tiny *garsoniera*."

"So when . . ."

"When did he die? Right after the elections. Three years ago. I remember telling someone that it was time for the country's freedom and mine too."

"He died from drinking?"

"No, no, not from drinking. His liver was made of iron. No, it was his heart. Apparently he'd had a hole in his heart all his life, but no one had ever found it. I had the police break the lock on his door when I realized that there hadn't been any food missing from the refrigerator in two days." Her eyes glisten with tears, and I can't tell if it's the sadness of those years squeezing her like milkweed or pure relief bubbling up from within.

"I remember telling a friend at the time that I was surprised he even had a heart at all." She laughs.

"But you visit his grave every year?"

"No. This is the first time."

"Oh."

"I don't know why."

"Because of the letters?"

She doesn't answer. She turns back toward the window. *Koniec.* Finish.

After another half an hour, the bus stops appear more frequently, picking up and dropping off. The bus comes alive with people grabbing for bags, digging in their purses for change, applying lipstick, finger-combing their hair. We get off with a small crowd of people headed for the same cemetery. From the bus stop, we walk single file along the muddy path on the shoulder, plodding along blindly until we see a few cars parked by the side of the road and the unmistakable cold granite fingers grasping skyward.

"Irena, maybe I'll wait for you here," I say.

"Don't be silly. This will only take a minute. I don't even have two minutes for that *skurwysyn*. Come on."

A thin mist crawls around and tugs at the tree trunks, like a small child trying to stand. We continue along the path, the mud sucking at our heels, the brown leaves clumping together on the ground and in the trees like mange. As we approach the gates of the cemetery, Irena walks more slowly than usual, even allowing an older woman to cut ahead of us.

"Irena," I say again, "maybe I'll just wait here for you."

"Don't be silly. You came this far, another twenty steps won't kill you." We step carefully on the narrow wooden planks that someone has thought to lay between the gravestones, and mud oozes from the edges. Irena pulls me along by the sleeve of my coat like I'm a child, and I let her. The gravestones here are more elaborate than the simple crosses in the cemetery in Pisarowice, some of them the size of small beds hovering half a meter above the ground, some of them demarcated by a tiny iron fence. Soggy flowers crown the headstones, and candles cover every surface, a few still flickering defiantly against the fog and the spittle of rain. Suddenly, Irena turns and touches my sleeve.

"Baba Yaga," she says, "maybe you can wait here for me."

I nod. I watch as Irena makes her way to a small gravestone near the back fence of the cemetery, and it is only then that I notice she has worn her best wool skirt. She gathers it under her and squats on one of the wooden planks next to a simple headstone, brushes it off with a few crumpled tissues and carefully sets down a few candles. She shakes the bouquet of chrysanthemums and sets them upright in a metal vase already filled with rainwater, fluffing them to make them look bigger than they are. She doesn't stop to bow her head or fold her hands; I don't see her lips forming around either a prayer or a curse. When she's finished, she simply gathers her skirt, stands up, and navigates her way back along the wobbly boards, her eyes cast downward.

As she reaches me, she draws a tissue from her pocket and presses it against her lips. *"Skurwysyn,"* she whispers. Son of a bitch.

On the way home, Irena stares out the window, her jaw set like stone. It's almost dark by the time we reach the city. The streets and the trams are packed with people traveling to and from Rakowicki Cemetery, and as we drive over the bridge by Jubilat, we see the thousands of flickering candles floating down the river. I leave Irena on the bus and get off at the Square of the Invalids. Magda and Kinga have already set up the chairs and are sitting at the bar, Magda with her cigarette, Stash and Kinga drinking beers.

"And where have you been?" Magda asks.

"What do you mean?"

"Where did you and *mama* sneak off to this morning?"

"She wanted me to go somewhere with her."

"Secret, secret. Where?"

"To Malina."

"What for?"

"To visit your father's grave."

"Boże." Kinga brings her hand to her chest, her fingertips just touching her sternum. On someone with a larger chest, it might appear vulgar, but on Kinga, it's a sincere gesture, like a child making a pledge.

"Why would she go there?" Magda asks. "She can barely take a tram to the other side of town, and all of a sudden, she takes a two-hour bus to Malina? She's never gone before. Why would she go and open up that chapter again? And why would she take you? You didn't even know him."

Stash looks up at me too, impatient for the answer.

"I don't know," I say. But it's a lie. I didn't know this morning, but now I know exactly why. She wasn't answering to the faint knock of nostalgia or reopening a chapter. Today was for closing something off. *Koniec*. Finish. And just like the people suffering on the retrospectives and the grandmothers and grandfathers at the tram stops who talk about the war as if it ended only a few weeks ago, Irena needed a witness.

27

The Soviets Will Keep You Warm

THEY KNEW THE SOVIETS were on their way because the Germans suddenly took to the woods. They were careless, leaving tracks in the snow and starting fires with wet wood that smoked and crackled from kilometers away. Many of them were actually Hungarians and Ukrainians who had deserted or been left behind, and they gladly gave up their weapons in exchange for their lives and a bit of food to sustain them.

There were several days of passing bands of soldiers before there came a terrifying calm.

"The Soviets will be here any moment, and they will burn everything. We must pack immediately and cross the border to Czechoslovakia."

"Nonsense. It will be safer in Krakow."

"You are foolish to go anywhere. We will be prey to desperate Germans. We should stay put and allow ourselves to be liberated by the Soviets."

"Liberated? They will steal the food we don't have, rape the youngest of our daughters, and make us call each other comrade."

"What is wrong with expressing brotherhood?"

"Brotherhood? Why doesn't anyone ever say sisterhood?"

As they say, three Poles, four opinions, and frightened as they were, for the first time in years, at least there was a choice, and they savored the taste of it, rolling it around in their mouths like the bouquet of a fine swig of *bimber*. Władysław Jagiełło and the Pigeon, like many in the Home Army, had been released to return to Half-Village and guard their families and neighbors, and the men kept watch for three nights straight before they heard the mortar shells through the wet dawn of the third morning. There was only time to gather the women, the children, and the ciborium and pack everyone into the cellar.

"What about the food?" Anielica asked.

"We will leave half of it up here for them to find. Otherwise, they will come looking for it. Give me your hair clips too."

Marysia and Anielica dutifully handed them over, their hair tumbling over their shoulders. The Pigeon smiled at the future that was just over the ridge, the future in which he would see her hair long and loose every night if he wanted to.

"They will think they have found the last of it."

"But this *is* the last of it," Anielica said. It was true. They had nothing left to lose, and so things could only get better from there. The turn in fortune was only weeks away. Months at the most. And that was not the necromancers or the politicians talking this time. It was a man who had traversed the forest tree by tree for five years, who had eaten everything remotely edible, who had endured twenty disappointing rumored ends to the war, who had fought valiantly with dynamite and guns and newsprint when that was all they had. They must only survive the ending.

Anielica's face became suddenly serious. She grabbed the Pigeon's hand and kissed him on the mouth. Not one of the villagers flinched. In their minds, the Pigeon and Anielica had already been married long ago, if not by official union, then at least by the separation they had endured.

"Please stay down here this time," she whispered.

They both knew that he couldn't. Old Pan Lubicz was now bedridden, and his wife, with the luxury of a long life already lived and the burden of old bones, insisted that if they were to die, they would die together, in their own house, in their own beds, and not as rats in a cellar.

"Don't worry," the Pigeon told Anielica, "I will be fine. They will be fine. I will keep watch from the Lubicz outhouse tonight, and in the morning, after eight hours of mortar fire, they will be persuaded to let us move them to safety before anything happens. And tomorrow night, we will all be snuggled in together in this very cellar."

Anielica put her hand on his cheek. "Are you lying?"

"I lie," he conceded, and he searched her eyes for absolution. "I have lied."

"But are you lying now?"

He covered her hand with his and pressed it into his cheek so that he could feel the hardness of her fingers against the bone of his jaw. "I don't know yet," he said.

Outside, the moon was full, casting shadows that soaked into the snow like blood. The Pigeon crept through the village, past the boulder that marked the Epler boy's grave, making sure to turn, loop, and double back through the snow, blending his steps into the general foot traffic. There wasn't a flicker of light anywhere in the village, not even from the Lubicz house. Pani Lubicz had refused to allow anyone to stay behind with her and her husband.

"If we are to die, it will not be with the blood of youth on our hands."

She had thrown the Pigeon out of her house earlier in the evening, had barely accepted the German Luger he had left with her, one of the many he had liberated from the fleeing conscripts the week before.

He reached the side of the Lubicz house and quietly trampled the snow in front of the outhouse. He rubbed a handful of snow into the hinges, and they opened silently. He felt for the board and replaced it over the opening. In the winter, the smell was not terrible. There was always a surplus of ashes in the winter, which were generously thrown down the holes to curb both the stench and the treacherous stalagmites. He pulled the door shut and sat down on the board. The moon trickled in through the crack, a rivulet of light sliding down his crooked nose. It had been a long time since the Pigeon had been able to sit and do nothing. Since the war had started, he was always on the move—digging bunkers or giving commands, carrying supplies, doing reconnaissance, setting traps. Even now as he sat in the outhouse, his legs, his back, and his hands felt restless, felt that they should be doing something—lifting or chopping or hammering or hauling.

His mind too was unsettled, and he occupied it by listening for the sounds of his adopted village—the creaking of the trees, the grunting of the wild boars in the distance, the susurration of the wind muffled by snow, the stubborn old woman shuffling around in her house two walls away. He would allow his mind to alight briefly on each sound before calling it back to perch inside the outhouse, where he became aware of his own breathing and the occasional groaning of the wood. Under different circumstances—that is, not sitting in an outhouse in the middle of a Polish winter waiting for the invasion of the most brutal army in the world—it might have been picturesque.

There were no mortars. They came on foot, in the blackest cavern of the night, tramping up the hill from Pisarowice, cursing in Russian. The Pigeon felt for the icy metal of the pistol in the pocket of his field coat. He caressed the barrel as he had Anielica's fingers, fit his hand against the handle as if against the palm of her hand. Anything for Anielica, his mind repeated, his mantra since they had met.

"*Chort vazmi,* there's no cocking path here."

"Cocking peasants."

"Look who's cocking talking, Dima."

"I'm looking straight cocking at him, Sasch. Where'd you say you were from again, ten kilometers east of the last outhouse in the Union?"

"Shut your cocking mouth or I'll show you the next cocking outhouse myself."

"*Goluboy.*"

"You're the cocking fag."

"Would you both shut it? You're so loud even the cocking Frogs in Versailles can hear you."

There were only three of them—apparently, that was all Half-Village merited—and as the Pigeon slipped outside, he heard one final creak from the house next door as Pani Lubicz got up from her chair. He positioned himself behind the outhouse, and he drew an imaginary line in his mind. If they had been Germans, the line might have been at the breaking down of the door, but they were Soviets, and he could not spare them the latitude. Though the German monster had once managed to gobble up Europe and pick its teeth with the bones, they were only frightened little boys now, some as young as fourteen, and they were organized and disciplined, even in retreat.

The Soviet Army, on the other hand, was really hundreds, thousands of separate armies, each with carte blanche — or *biała karta,* if you happened to be the victim of it — to invent and implement the most original brutalities ever inflicted, as long as they did not slander the names of Uncle Stalin or Grandfather Lenin, which could only be done through weakness and capitulation. There seemed to be an endless supply of Soviet soldiers, as if they had been cultivated on some great collective farm in Ukraine, and no matter where they were or what shortages existed, they always managed to find the alcohol. There had been stories among the partisans of a Russian squad that had drained a perfume shop in Budapest, of a recipe that called for spreading boot black on bread and letting the spirits soak in before scraping off the dried polish and consuming the bread. This band of three did not seem steady in their steps either, and they continued to stumble and jostle each other even as they reached the flat clearing.

"Awright you cocking peasants, where the cock are you? Come out, come out wherever ya cocking are!"

"Shhhh . . ."

The one calling for silence eventually prevailed, and he crept forward, leading the others with flutters of his hand. The Wzwolenski house was the nearest to the path, and they began there. The Pigeon watched from behind the outhouse, his heart racing. He had hoped that the soldiers would be wary of the emptiness of the village, be suspicious of an ambush, but instead the quiet seemed to embolden them. He wondered how many houses it would take before they figured out that the war and the Germans had drained all their valuables, that there wasn't even any alcohol left. They hadn't had alcohol in Half-Village for two years. Any wheat, potatoes, or berries were eaten, not distilled, and no one had the time or the energy to make the *bimber* anymore, so they just went without.

"Found it!"

The three men emerged from the Wzwolenski house with a brown bottle. One took a swig and passed it to the others. Two rounds and it was gone. Apparently Pan Wzwolenski's mother had not been ill the past two Sundays for nothing.

"There's got to be some more around here somewhere."

"Come out, come out wherever you cocking are."

"It wasn't funny the first time. Shut it."

"There's nobody left here anyway. Nobody in the whole cocking village."

"Shut it." The leader dismissed the other two soldiers with a wave of his hand, in the manner of short, mustachioed dictators from secondary republics.

The Hetmański house was next, and when they kicked in the door, the awful crack of the hinges was like knuckles breaking. The Pigeon flinched. His stomach churned as he listened to the sounds of dishes crashing, of wood splintering, of glass smashing and showering the floor. He imagined the rest of the village huddled together in the cellar listening to the crash of destruction, to the thump of boots over their heads, and he prayed that they would keep still, that Irenka especially would not cry out. When they emerged from the house, the leader was holding the twig broom, the broom that the Pigeon had bound, the broom that Anielica had used to sweep the floor, the floor that he had hewn from the trunks of the trees, the trees that had once protected the house from wind and enemies.

"Nothing. Cocking nothing! A couple of potatoes and a hair clip."

"Cocking peasants. Probably buried everything before we cocking got here."

The flame started small, no bigger than an insect held squirming between two fingers. Absolutely harmless until it multiplied in the thicket of the twig broom.

"I'll take that hair clip if you don't want it."

"I told you he was *goluboy*."

"*Goluboy*, nothing. It's for my *dyevushka*, Marina, back in Sokol."

"Go ahead. Take the cocking hair clip. Whenever I see my *dyevushka* back home, her hair won't be up for long anyway."

"You don't have a cocking *dyevushka*. Who would cocking go out with you?"

"Ah, just shut it you two. I'm sick of you."

The individual flames swelled into a globe of fire the size of a human head, hair smoking wildly. The Pigeon was not worried about the villagers in the cellar. He and Władysław Jagiełło had quietly discussed this eventuality and had decided that once they smelled the smoke, they would have time to evacuate and could spend the rest of the night by the old marriage bed, where they had heaped half the blankets and *pierzyna*s in the village, just in case.

"Let's go, Dima. Come on."

The man held the broom in his hands for a moment longer, memorizing the flames, illuminating his face. He had fair skin, fine features, and a long nose, like the aristocratic young nihilists in Turgenev's novels.

"*Halt*," the Pigeon shouted suddenly. "*Hör auf.* This is property of the Third Reich you are destroying. I must request that you cease and desist." The Pigeon said it once in German and then in German-accented Russian, pulling the soft Russian sounds up from the back of his throat, making them sound more guttural, more Teutonic. After five years of fighting, he and everyone else were fluent in the language of war.

But the Russians only snickered.

"Did you hear that? This is the property of the Third Reich."

"What cocking Third Reich?"

The Pigeon tried to change his voice slightly. "We have you surrounded."

The Russians howled with laughter. "Well, you'll have a front-row seat for the bonfire then."

"I said, *cease* and *desist. Tepyer.*"

The officer grabbed the broom by the handle and poked it head-first through the broken muntins. There was a faint glow inside the house, and suddenly, it seemed alive, as if it was more than a house, more than wood and stone. The hard work of his golden hands, his courtship, his friendship with Władysław Jagiełło, his adopted home, all of their deprivations during the war when all they really had was the house. It was all going up in smoke at the hands of a few drunken Russians. The Pigeon raised his gun and shot the officer in the chest. He fell in a heap in the snow.

"Shit, it *is* the cocking Germans. You crazy cocking goats," one of them shouted, taking cover behind the boulder in the middle of the clearing. The other one ran for the path down the mountain. "Don't you know you've lost the whole cocking war? Dima, where are you going? Dima!"

"He's over there," the Pigeon shouted to no one but himself. He ran through the backyards, clockwise around the lone Russian in the center of the clearing.

"Cover me," the Pigeon shouted, and ran again.

"Got it," he answered himself from the other side of the clearing.

The Russian hesitated for a moment behind the boulder, then ran after the other soldier down the path to Pisarowice. The Pigeon fired two bullets into the treetops. It was an extravagant gesture. In the fifth year of the war, it was one body, one bullet, and the Germans had even been skimping on this rule for a while already.

Meanwhile, the flames were spreading quickly, and the Hetmański house blazed a supernatural orange. The Pigeon took the cover off the outhouse hole and used it as a shovel to scoop snow onto the fire.

"Władysław Jagiełło," he shouted to the floor, "get up here!" He was soon joined by Władysław Jagiełło, Pan Hetmański, and Marysia's father, who managed to put out the fire. Miraculously, the only permanent damage was a charred spot on the wall in the exact shape of Poland in the fifteenth century, when it was the largest state in Europe. This, of course, was immediately hailed as a sign that the palm readers and fortune-tellers had never been able to match. The war, at least for Half-Village, was finally over. And though everyone in the cellar had heard clearly what had happened, they would all participate enthusiastically in the cover-up, and they would never utter a word out loud about the fact that the Pigeon had killed in order to protect the house and not Pan and Pani Lubicz.

28

And the Puppy Too

AFTER ALL SOULS DAY, Irena begins flinging open all the other stuffed drawers of her past, dusting her memories off and weeding them out in earnest. She starts calling her old friends and arranging meetings with them under the guise of helping to *załatwić* a second chance for Magda at the university.

"Ironic, isn't it?" she tells me. "These are the same friends I stopped meeting with in order to give Magda a better chance in the first place."

The phone calls she makes are in her usual style—blunt, brusque, and brutally efficient—but when she returns in the evenings from cafés in the old town and parties on the outskirts, she's flushed with memories and renewed acquaintance. She doesn't have time to watch the news or the retrospectives anymore, and when I ask her what she thinks about the Little Constitution that was just passed, she only wants to talk about whichever old friend she saw the night before.

Tadeusz has been avoiding me for the past two weeks. On Friday afternoons, he's too busy helping his parents clear out the shop, and on Sunday afternoons he has to watch his sisters. At Stash's he joins the line for the toilets during the breaks, and after the third set, he stays near the stage and talks to the other musicians until the last minute.

"Tadeusz," I call after him, his orange juice sitting abandoned on the bar.

"I have to go. The bus."

"Wait."

"Sorry. I can't. I'll call you tomorrow."

But he doesn't. In fact, he stops coming to the bar altogether, and when I come in each evening and Stash asks me how I'm doing, he seems more serious than usual and puts his entire face behind the question.

Eventually I break down and ask.

"He didn't tell you?" Stash asks.

"No."

"He quit to join the army. He said you two had talked about it."

"Not exactly."

"I'm sorry, Baba Yaga. I would have told you sooner. I thought you knew."

I spend the rest of the night rehearsing imaginary conversations in my head, and every little interruption annoys me.

"Do you know anything about that one?" Magda asks me.

"No."

"What about that one?"

"No."

"How about that tall one over there? He's cute." This is exactly the side of Magda that her mother fears, the side that could knock out the more logical, rational twin.

"Magda, I don't know anything about any of them. If you didn't notice, the only boy I ever talked to here was Tadeusz."

"Where is he anyway?"

"I think he broke up with me, okay?"

"You think?"

"He's been avoiding me for two weeks, and Stash just told me he quit."

"He didn't tell you?"

"No."

"That *kretyn*."

But I'm not ready to hear that either. "Where's Kinga anyway? Last time I checked, she still worked here, but she's been sitting with those Englishmen all night long."

One Englishman in particular is trying to help her learn English. He's fat and middle-aged, with skin the color of mayonnaise and curly red hair. His name is Ronan, and he's been teaching English at the Agricultural Institute since before the changes. In the beginning, Kinga offered to do a language swap, exchanging Polish conversation for English, but he said he'd already given up on Polish, said he'd lived here for five years already with only ten or so words and done just fine.

"Go ahead. Take a break if you want," Magda says. "I'll cover."

"She just shouldn't be taking advantage like that. I'm tired of it."

"You're just upset about Tadeusz," Magda says. "Don't worry. You know what they say . . . men are like trams. There's always another one to run you over." She laughs.

"I'm really not in the mood, Magda."

"All right. All right. But if you're so angry at him, why don't you just go and tell him off?"

"I can't do that."

"Why not? He shouldn't get away with this. Make him suffer as much as you. Better than taking it out on me."

The more I think about it, the more I can't let go of the idea. I know that if I call, there's a good chance that one of his sisters will pick up and he won't take the call. We've always met on the Rynek, and I don't know exactly where he lives in Huta, but I tell Stash I have to return something important to him, and he finally gives me the address from Tadeusz's *dowód osobisty*. It turns out to be on the farthest side of Huta, and it takes an hour and a half to get there on the bus. The whole time, I'm rehearsing in my head, clipping and adding words here and there, rearranging them for maximum effect. I ask several people on the bus and on the street for directions, and finally I find the right *osiedle*.

It's much different from the center, more like a concrete village than the city. Unsupervised children run around the vast courtyard, freeze-dried laundry flaps stiffly on the line, broken benches guard the entrance door. The lock is broken, and I go right up. I find the number of his apartment, and I stand against the wall of the corridor and take a few deep breaths. I can hear voices inside, his sisters shouting over one another and Tadeusz telling them to be quiet.

The neighbor lady comes home, and we both stand in silence while she searches for her keys. She looks at me suspiciously and opens her door just enough to squeeze through, as if I'm going to charge into her flat and rob her blind. I don't hear her moving around inside, and I imagine her watching me through the peephole.

I stand there for another five minutes, my heart beating through to the wall.

I can't do it.

"Did you do it?" Magda asks me when I get to Stash's later.

"Uh-huh." I'm too ashamed to tell her otherwise.

"How did it go? What did you say?"

"I don't want to talk about it."

"I remember going to tell off Żaba. I really gave him a piece of my mind. That sure felt good."

"Yeah. It did."

"Serves that bastard right."

"Yeah."

When we get home that night, Irena is waiting up for us. She's still half-dressed from going out with her friends, a soft gray turtleneck over her pajama pants. She tells us that her friend Krystyna has an older brother whose wife has a friend in the administrative offices of the law school, and who has been able to wipe Magda's whole miserable first year off her transcript and *załatwić* a seat for her in the entrance exam in the spring.

"You're joking, *mamo*."

"Not at all, little daughter."

"You actually found someone to do all that?"

Irena nods.

"Oh, *mamusiu*!" She throws her arms around her neck and kisses her.

"Get off me, you *wariatko*!" Irena says. But when she grins, she shows all her teeth. "And for this one, a spot in the entrance exam for the geography department."

"The what?"

"The geography department."

"Me?"

194

"Why not?"

"*Why?*"

"It's the easiest one to get into. They may even accept a village girl from a village *liceum*. But you will still have your *magister* from Jagiellonian when you graduate."

"Irena, I'm not taking the geography exam."

"Too bad. I've already gone through the trouble to *załatwić* it. You will go. If nothing else, you will keep Magda on track with her studying, and it will get your mind off that *klarnecista* assassin."

"Magda, you told her?"

"I'm sorry. I cracked. You know how she is."

"Eh," Irena says, waving her hand dismissively. "*Srał go pies.*" Let the dog piss on him. "And the puppy too," she adds.

And that is how, all of a sudden, I give over all my free time to preparing for an entrance exam for a subject I care nothing about. I learn about the Bedouins, fault lines, Pangaea, and something called ozone. I have to study for the Polish history section too, and I work to tease apart the battles and kings and treaties that are all clumped together in my mind. But Magda and Irena are happy, and to say the truth, even I am happy in a way. Happy to shake the routines that have been clumping my days together since May, happy to think of Nela beaming down on me with pride. With any luck, next fall I'll be able to say I'm a university student, filling exam booklets, lugging textbooks around, meeting classmates in cafés in the afternoons. Not a Big Life, but an easy life. No one is fighting. No one is dying. There are no walls. Irena, Magda, and I banter freely back and forth across the flat when we're together and save up stories for each other when we're not.

"Did you tell *mamo* about New Year's Eve yet?" Magda shouts from her room.

"What about New Year's Eve?" Irena is making pierogi *ruskie* again, spooning the potatoes and cheese out in little half-moons, pressing out circles of dough with a drinking glass.

"Stash is closing the club and having a private party. He wanted us to invite you."

Irena stops. Stopping her motion is like poking a stick into a wheel, and the glass bangs against the wooden board.

"Well?" Magda calls. "What do you think?"

"I think you should go and have a good time." Her hands pick up where she left off, swiping a fingertip of water around the edges of the dough, pinching the pockets shut, and pitching them into the boiling water.

"*Mamo*, I mean, what about *you?*"

"I already have plans." She lights another burner on the stove, bangs a pan on top of it, and throws a lump of bacon grease into it. She plucks a slotted spoon from the pipe above the sink, and when the pierogi are done, she fishes them out of the pot of boiling water and throws them into the pan. They hiss and pop at her, and she placates them with her spoon.

"Irena, he really wants you to come."

"Come on, *mamo*, it will be fun."

"I said I have plans already."

"Plans with the cats?"

"This isn't a deposition, Pani Prosecutor."

"I'm just trying to help you get some."

"*Bezczelna.*" But now when she says it, it sounds innocuous.

Magda and I tell Stash that we're working on her.

"Do you think she'll come?"

"I don't know."

He sits down on one of the stools. "Jezus Maria, I haven't seen her in . . . years."

"What about when she talked you into giving me a job? Or giving us a night off to go to the Cabaret?"

"Oh," he says. "You know her. They were two-minute phone calls, and I could tell she couldn't wait to hang up. We made plans to meet for coffee the first time, but she canceled." He smooths his hair back into his ponytail, and I notice that his fingers are permanently crooked and spaced for the keys on his trumpet. "Do you really think she'll come?"

"We'll make her come. We'll drag her here," Magda says.

"I'll believe it when I see it."

Suddenly, though, the party begins to grow in scope. The next morning he goes to the *hurtownia* to buy more liquor, even though the closet is already full, and he spends almost the entire evening circulating in the crowd and inviting more people. He comes in early a few mornings that week, to scrub the floors and clean out his office, and from his circle of friends he collects as many white tablecloths as he can, which we starch and iron on one of the picnic tables. He gives us a hundred thousand złotych to go to the market and buy proper white candles, and we scatter them around the tables in little white teacups that he bought for the bar but has never used. We loop white Christmas lights across the ceiling, and when Stash turns out the fluorescents and plugs in the cord, we all take in a breath.

"Stash, it's beautiful."

And he looks around, his hands on his hips, satisfied.

29

Life Has Become Better, Comrades; Life Has Become More Cheerful

THE RUSSIAN SQUAD that came to investigate the following morning was sober and well organized, kept in reserve for just these occasions. They were led by a young, bright-eyed lieutenant who spoke in Mickiewicz's Polish, and whose eyes took a silent inventory of the village before lowering his polished pistol. The body of the Soviet soldier had been cleaned and laid to rest on a platform of snow in the middle of the clearing, and all the villagers were gathered around, dressed in their folk costumes, which they dug out of their wardrobes twice a year for the festivals. The Romantowski son was squawking out the Soviet national anthem on his fiddle, which he had learned the night before from the Pigeon's humming it over and over while they worked.

They had been up half the night preparing the clearing, decking it out with every bit of red in the village: handkerchiefs and flyers that the People's Army had disseminated, scraps of material, red scarves, jackets and skirts tied to sticks and stuck into the snow. They had opened the last jars of raspberry preserves, which they had been saving for Easter, and used them to paint Soviet slogans in the snow. Workers of the World Unite. Destroy Fascists on the Sea and in the

Mountains. Toward the Bright Future. Life Has Become . . . But they ran out of preserves.

"*Tovarish*," the Pigeon said, taking the young lieutenant warmly by the shoulders. Comrade. The soldier at the lieutenant's side jabbed the Pigeon's rib cage with the barrel of his gun, but the young lieutenant held up a gloved hand, and the soldier stepped back.

"Welcome, Soviet liberators," the Pigeon began again.

The lieutenant eyed him warily. "We are here to investigate the attack on one of our advance teams last night, which resulted in the death of one of our comrades."

The Pigeon's eyes were drawn to the back of the group, where he recognized one of the men from the night before.

"Of course, comrade." The Pigeon let his voice rise and sink into the exaggerated valleys of the *górale* dialect. "Until last night, the Germans still had a tight grip on the village, and your men, your brave nephews of Josef Stalin, came in and liberated the village — a German platoon of twenty-five perhaps. Yours suffered only one casualty and took the lives of five or six Szwaby in return."

"Five or six?" The young lieutenant raised an eyebrow. One of the men in the group produced a notebook and the stub of a pencil and began taking notes.

"Yes, comrade," the Pigeon replied.

"And the bodies of these five or six?"

"The Germans managed to drag them away, off into the woods. That direction." And the Pigeon pointed. The lieutenant flicked his chin, and two of the party went over to investigate the spot where that morning Pani Wzwolenska had sacrificed the last of her chickens and the children had taken turns dragging each other by the feet through the snow.

"There's blood," one of the Russians called. "And snow pack."

The lieutenant walked over to the snow bier on which the body of Turgenev's nihilist lay. "And you, an able-bodied young man, you have been sitting in this village the entire war?"

"Oh, no, comrade. I have been away fighting with the People's Army. I just came back to the area a few days ago to protect my family from the desperate German exodus, and to welcome the Soviet liberators, of course."

"The People's Army?"

"I have the papers." Which was a surprise to everyone, but sure enough, the Pigeon reached into his jacket and produced a set of papers that he had fought for the communist People's Army and not the Polish Home Army.

"And where did your cell operate?"

"In the area of Kielce mostly."

"And you had direct combat with the Germans?"

"Yes."

"And your name?"

"Larch."

"Larch."

"Like the tree."

"Like the tree." The lieutenant smirked a little at the simpleton before him. The soldiers returned from investigating the path. They held a whispered conference with the lieutenant, and the lieutenant returned to the Pigeon.

"There will be a call to the cities in a few weeks. Go to Krakow and register as a freedom fighter so that you may get the benefits and recognition you deserve."

"Yes, comrade."

"Poland will become a great socialist nation. When socialism takes hold, there will be no poverty, even here in the mountains. There will be electricity in every house and all the children will be educated. Each will work according to his ability; each will draw according to his need."

"Yes, comrade. Long live Stalin. Long live Lenin."

"Long live Stalin. Long live Lenin."

When the soldiers departed down the path, they took the body with them, but the villagers left the platform and the decorations in the clearing in case another squad returned. Act as if.

Over the next few weeks, the reports flowed through the Pigeon and Pan Cywilski one after another, the liberated cities and camps stacking up like firewood. Dresden. Cologne. Gdańsk. Nuremberg. The Ruhr. Buchenwald. Bergen-Belsen. Berlin. Venice. Dachau.

Mussolini hanged. Hitler dead. Göring, not far behind.

It was over. They should have been relieved. Still, in the light of the moon one evening, as Anielica and the Pigeon went for their evening walk, she began to weep uncontrollably.

"What is it? What is it?" He tried to comfort her, but since the Night of the Barszcz, which is how they referred to that awful night now—by the stain it had left—she flinched whenever he tried to take her into his arms.

"All I see is red. Red, red, red, and once again red. First the Germans, now the Soviets. What about Poland? What about Poland?"

He took his handkerchief out and tried to dab at her eyes, but she took it from him and did it herself. "Look over there," he said, "and tell me what you see."

She stared out at the clearing, at the pieces of cloth frozen into stiff shapes.

"The Epler boy's grave. And red. Only red."

"That is what the Soviets see," the Pigeon said gently. "Now look at the snow. Look at the snow of our beloved Tatras."

She looked around again, and this time it was red and white, white and red, only the eagle missing. "You're right," she said. "I see it now. I see it."

And for the first time since the Night of the Barszcz, she wrapped her arms around him and hugged him tight.

In the spring, they planted the garden and repaired the house. The Pigeon dissolved his cell in the Home Army and traveled back and forth between the Hetmańskis and his own parents. The Soviets were ensconced in Pisarowice and Osiek, but for the most part overlooked Half-Village and its inhabitants, since they already seemed solid converts to the cause. The week the snow disappeared, the Pigeon and Pan Hetmański went off into the woods and had a Serious Discussion About Anielica, which lasted all of three minutes. After all, everything that needed to be decided had already been decided long ago.

30

Sylwester

O N T H E A F T E R N O O N of Sylwester, Pani Bożena and I are sipping tea in silence. I keep looking at the Eiffel Tower clock perched on top of the television set.

"You've already looked at that clock twenty times," she says. "Is it such torture for you to stay here?"

My face flushes. "I'm sorry. Stash is having a party tonight. I have to go home and change first, and then help him to do a few more things."

She looks over at me. She seems to age a little more every day.

"You're welcome to come if you want," I say. "I'm sure Stash would be pleased to see you again."

"Please. If you wanted to invite me, you'd have done it before. No one wants the company of an old woman on New Year's Eve."

"I like your company."

"I pay you."

"Honest, I like your company."

"Yes? Then why do you stay out every morning for two hours and come back with ready meals that took you ten minutes to purchase?"

"I'm sorry. I didn't think . . ." I don't know what to say. I take another sip of tea.

"Oh, go on," Pani Bożena finally says. "Get out of here."

"But I want to stay. Really."

"Go. Just go."

I go back home to change. Irena is still sitting on the love seat in her house clothes, her hair unwashed, one of the kittens that she's rescued from the snowy yard hissing softly in her hands.

"Stop it. Stop it," she chides him, dangling him in the air by the scruff of his neck as he paddles his legs. Her hand is already webbed with scratches. The water in the bathroom is running.

"She started getting ready at two," Irena says to me, then increases her volume so that Magda can hear. "That's longer than it took the Germans to take Paris."

"Why aren't you getting ready, Irena?"

Irena reaches for a thin slice of ham from a plate on the coffee table and tears off a corner. She forces it between the kitten's jaws, and he devours it with greedy smacks and growls, like a small black panther.

"There you go, Benito," Irena coos. "You stubborn little *skurwysyn*."

"Irena, why aren't you getting ready?"

"I can't leave Benito home alone tonight. He's sick."

Magda emerges from the bathroom. She looks stunning. She's wearing the black pants from Żaba that she says show off her *dupa* and a red, low-cut blouse with ruffles along the neckline. Her hair is sleek and glossy next to her face, and she's done something to her eyes that makes her look like Bette Davis. She comes over and holds her hand out to the kitten.

"Hey, Benito . . . *ch–ch–ch–ch–ch–ch–ch.*"

He reaches out and scratches her hand.

"Ow! He probably gave me cat AIDS." Magda pouts, bringing her hand to her mouth.

"Don't be silly, it's probably *him* who caught something from *you*."

"Come on, Irena, hup, hup. We're going to be late," I say. "Magda, tell your mother to get ready for the party."

"You're surprised she's not going?"

"Irena."

"Honest. I planned on going. If only little Benito weren't sick."

Magda tugs at her ear. "I didn't hear that. If only you weren't scared to see Stash?"

Irena reaches out to slap Magda on the backside, but she sidesteps the blow. "Very funny. Go on now. Go to your party. Tell Stash I'm sorry I couldn't make it."

"But, Irena, you don't understand. He's made all these preparations."

"I'm sure he didn't do it all for me. Anyway, what can I do? I have a sick kitten. He'll understand. Tell him I'll stop by another night."

"Please, Irena."

"Go on, now. Have a good time. Magda, you behave."

When I tell Stash she's not coming, his face falls, and he looks around at the room and down at his shirt and tie as if they have all betrayed him, as if all the work has been for nothing.

"I'm sorry," I say weakly. "I really thought she would come."

"That's okay. I'm sure you did the best you could. What was her excuse this time?"

"She had an emergency. Something important to attend to."

"She's sitting at home, isn't she?"

"With the cats," Magda adds.

"That woman. I remember when you had to tie her to a chair to keep her home," he says, and he forces a smile.

"Mama?"

"Oh, you don't know your mother at all."

But other people are already arriving, and he's swept off by a wave of high-pitched voices and kisses — left, right, left. Kinga arrives, dressed all in black, her hair swept off her face.

"Happy New Year," she says, and kisses us on the cheeks.

We have all been strictly forbidden to go behind the bar tonight because Stash wants us to have a good time, so we sit down at one of the tables and Stash brings us orange juice and vodka.

Magda raises her glass. *"Na zdrowie."* To your health.

"Za zdrowie," I answer. For your health. It's an old joke, but we all smile.

Stash stands up on one of the bar stools with his trumpet, his face turning a deep red as he holds the opening note as long as he can, and for the rest of the night, the music unrolls in one continuous ribbon, with people stepping on and off the stage as they please, picking up whichever instrument is handy and passing it to the next person when they're through. Whoever happens not to be playing at the moment goes back and mans the bar.

We watch Stash cycle through his trumpet, a trombone, and a clarinet, and he seems a different person with each one. I think about Tadeusz and how he's missing this. I think about him, with his orange juice and his sisters, and wonder if he would be shocked to see me now—Kinga, Magda, and I getting drunk as Russians. The drinks we carry back from the bar become paler, our cheeks, more flushed. The flames splash in their cups in the centers of the tables and the conversations flow all around us.

"I'll be right back," Magda says.

"Where's she going?"

"Probably to *flirtować* with some of the boys."

But when she comes back a few minutes later, she's carrying the video camera. My video camera. The one that Tadeusz gave me.

"Is that *mine?*"

"I thought we could show *mama* what she's missing."

"You went into my room?"

"You're always welcome to go into my room," Magda says, and I've had too many drinks to know if I'm offended.

She fumbles with the lens cap and the buttons.

"Give it here. You're going to break it."

Surprisingly, it feels natural in my hands, and I start to film the whole party—the stage, the bar, the knots of friends around the room, the boys Magda wants me to zoom in on.

"Make sure you get Stash," Magda says, and I find Stash behind the bar, smiling, his tie loosened.

"See, *mamo,*" Magda says, "see what you're missing?"

I turn the camera on Magda and Kinga. Magda sweeps her hair up with one arm and pouts and preens like the models in *Kobieta*. She gets up and cat-walks to the bar.

"I'm filming your *dupa*," I call after her, and Magda puts both hands on her hips and does a little shimmy, then cat-walks back. Kinga is laughing so hard, she forgets to hide her teeth. We play around a little more with the camera, and then we get bored. Kinga gets up to go to the bathroom.

"Ah." Magda sighs. "I wish I had a boyfriend again."

When Kinga returns, she has three saucers and a tall glass of water from the bar.

"Is Stash finally cutting us off?" I ask.

"No. We're going to read our fortunes."

"I haven't done this since I was ten," Magda says.

"Well, come on, *dawaj*. You go first."

Kinga sloshes some water into a saucer and places it in front of me. I loosen the candle from its teacup and hand it to Magda. She closes her eyes and tips it over on its side. The wax droplets fall, flattening as soon as they hit the water.

"Okay."

Magda opens her eyes. She turns the saucer around, ninety degrees at a time.

"Well, it's definitely a profile of somebody," Kinga says, "don't you think?"

I lean over the table. "Well, from this angle, it looks like General Jaruzelski."

"Maybe you're going to have his love child," Kinga offers.

"Is he still alive?"

"I think so."

Magda squints hard. "No. That is the face of Żaba. For sure."

"Żaba?"

"Who's Żaba?"

"Żaba, her ex, who ran off with Ruda Zdzira," I explain to Kinga.

"There's a girl named Ruda Zdzira? That's worse than Baba Yaga."

"Yes, but it's her fault. She named herself."

Magda retells the entire story to Kinga, and Kinga's face contorts in shock and sympathy.

"Maybe he's going to come back," Kinga says. "Maybe he's going to get down on his knees and tell you what a horrible mistake he's made and beg you to come back to him."

Magda smooths her bangs with her fingertips and tucks her hair behind her ears. I can tell that hearing it pleases her.

"Maybe he will become jealous once he finds out that you're having General Jaruzelski's love child," I say.

"You're disgusting." Magda laughs. "For that, you're next."

I take the candle in my hand and close my eyes. I keep my hand steady and hold my breath. I open my eyes. I examine the saucer. Kinga looks at it. Magda looks at it.

"I don't know," Magda says. "I hate to say this, but it looks just like . . ."

"Pigeon shit," Kinga says, and laughs.

Magda shrugs. "Sorry."

"That was actually my grandfather's nickname."

"Pigeon shit?"

"Pigeon."

"Because of his feet or the size of his pecker?" Kinga asks.

"I don't know. Ask your grandmother."

"Don't you talk about my grandmother like that!"

The three of us are drunk, drunk, drunk, and once again drunk, and we can't stop laughing. I can't believe I have gone my whole life without having girlfriends. The only kids my age in Half-Village and Pisarowice were boys, and by the time I went to *liceum* in Osiek, the other girls already had their friends, and I had Nela. I remember watching them pass notes in class or link arms down the street or in the bus shelters, giggling and whispering. They seemed to inhabit an entirely different plane, like government officials and mothers.

"My turn! My turn!" Kinga bangs her tiny hands on the table.

There's no debating what shape Kinga's wax takes. I swear on my Nela's grave that it falls exactly in the shape of England, with the narrow bit on the top, the wide southern coastline, the western shore throwing its hip out to bump Ireland into the Atlantic Ocean.

"*Boże,*" Kinga says.

"It's England."

"You see it too?"

"No question," Magda agrees. "It's England."

"Oh my God," Kinga says again. She's still holding the candle in her hand, and her face glows as if she's just swallowed the flame. "It's England!" She jumps up from the table. "I'm going to England!"

But Magda already has her by the arm and is steering her toward the door. "Come on. It's already ten to twelve. We have to hurry!"

"I'm going to England!"

"Now you're going to the Rynek."

I grab the camera and my coat, and Magda produces an old army helmet from somewhere. Kinga is still jumping up and down, and

Magda throws her coat over her shoulders. Several other people from the party are headed for the Rynek too. We run like madwomen, me with my camera and Magda with the army helmet gripped in her hand, and Kinga continues to shout.

"I'm going to England! I'm going to England!"

"Go on then," someone shouts from behind us. "Traitor."

"I don't care!" Kinga shouts. "I'm going to England!"

It has started to snow, the flakes sticking together in the air. There are hardly any cars on the road, and the few we see stop or steer around us. I grip the camera in my glove, and run, faster and faster, as I used to run as a child, flailing my arms, hanging on to the camera for dear life. I leave Magda and Kinga behind me, and I hear them shouting after me, laughing at me. The side streets and shops and parked cars blur by me. The cold air slashes at my face and lungs until they're numb, and then goes to work on my hands and feet. I see the clock tower and the steeples of St. Mary's rising in the distance, and I keep running toward them. I have the green light crossing Podwale, and only when my feet touch the cobblestones of Shoemaker's Street, I stop.

"Hey, you could flail for the Olympics," a boy says as a group passes by. I recognize him from Stash's as one of the ones Magda points out sometimes. He's tall and usually wears one of the navy peacoats that the entrepreneurial sailors have begun selling off now that the People's Republic of Poland is now just the Republic of Poland. Whenever I've seen him at Stash's, he always seems to be leaning against something—door frames, chairs, walls, railings—like the Roman statues whose limbs and torsos sprout tree trunks and rocks.

Kinga and Magda finally catch up, and we walk the rest of the way to the Rynek. "What the hell was that?" Magda asks, and she imitates me, her arms flapping.

"You're the one carrying the army helmet," I say.

"Better that than a traumatic brain injury." She fishes a shoestring out of her pocket and ties the helmet onto her head. "Didn't you hear about that girl in Wrocław last year who got hit in the head by a bottle and ended up a vegetable?"

Kinga and I look at each other and laugh.

The trumpeter begins to play the *hejnał* just as we reach the bluestone. There are so many people swarmed around the statue of Adaś, it looks like a warm afternoon during the summer, but the crowd remains silent, reverent, until the clip in the song—the point where legend says the trumpeter was shot in the throat by a Tatar arrow. Then the cheering begins. Bottles fly in wide rainbows across the night sky, splintering against the bluestone, and I look over to see Magda, shouting with the rest of the crowd, the army helmet tied tightly to her head. My own head feels naked in the air, but my fingers and my ears are strangely warm. Everyone around me is hugging and kissing, and I feel my body being pressed against other bodies, my face wet with snow and the kisses of strangers.

"Wszyskiego najlepszego," but most are so drunk, they can only manage *"Wszystki, wszystki."*

I remember the camera and Irena, and I break free from the crowd and stand up on one of the ledges of the Sukiennice. I have to cup my hand into an awning over the lens to keep the snow from falling on it. I don't see Magda or Kinga anywhere. I pan over the dark, milling crowd.

"Hey." Kinga appears at my side and pulls herself up onto the ledge. "Where's Magda?"

"I don't know."

We finally spot her off to the side, her army helmet falling over her eyes, her feet frozen in place.

"Magda! Magda! Over here," Kinga calls, but she doesn't seem to hear. She's standing in front of a couple, the boy wearing a black warm-up jacket, the girl with long red hair falling over her shoulders, a knit cap pulled down to her eyes.

"Cholera," I say. "I think it's Żaba and Ruda Zdzira."

"The one who named herself?" Kinga asks.

"Here. Hold this." And I give her the camera.

I spot the boy in the peacoat a few arches down on the Sukiennice.

"Please," I say, "I need a favor."

He leans against the archway as he listens to me, then shrugs off the stones. In just a few steps, he's at Magda's side, putting his arm around her and kissing her on the cheek, leading her back to me.

"Oh my God," Magda says. "Oh my God. Oh my God. I think I'm hyperventilating. I think I'm going to pass out."

"That was Żaba?" I ask.

"Oh my God. I think I'm going to pass out," she says again, and her face does look gray.

"You'll be fine." The boy in the peacoat takes over. He leads her to the ledge and sits her down. The initial barrage of bottles has subsided, and now there are only solitary explosions against the bluestone and lone voices calling out to friends to head back to bars or parties in friends' flats. The boy unties the string and removes Magda's army helmet. He pushes her head between her knees, pulls the cork off a brown bottle he is carrying, and holds it under her nose.

"Are you a doctor or something?" I ask.

"Or something," he says. "Now, just breathe. In . . . out . . . in . . . out . . ."

Kinga stands off to the side, shivering and stamping her feet. She lights a cigarette and we stand there watching Magda's back rising and falling. After a minute, she sits up.

"Better?" the boy asks.

She nods.

"Do you want us to walk you back to the club?" He's with another guy from the party, shorter and stockier, with short, gelled hair.

"That's okay," I say. "I think we're going home."

"Pity," the boy says, and he introduces himself and his friend. Sebastian is his name, and his friend, Tomek. Sebastian is the perfect gentleman, and he introduces Tomek exactly like you're supposed to introduce someone, giving a pinch of information out, tinder for a conversation. They're roommates with a flat in Kazimierz, the old Jewish quarter. Sebastian is from a village near Bielsko-Biała and Tomek from Warsaw. I tell them that I'm from a village in the Tatras, and they talk about a ski trip they're planning to Zakopane, but I don't tell them that I'm from the sheep-and-hut side and not the ski-and-cable-car side.

"And you're a bar girl at the club, aren't you?" he asks, turning up the collar of his peacoat.

"We all are."

Kinga gives a little wave, the red-orange end of her cigarette flitting in the darkness.

"Well, really I'm a law aspirant," Magda says, "but I'm taking a break."

Tomek mumbles something about a party, but Sebastian hesitates, his hands in his pockets, his dark hair falling in his eyes. "So, are you sure we can't walk you home?"

"Thanks. We'll be okay."

"Here," he says, handing the brown bottle to me. "Take this at least."

I smell it. *Wiśniówka.*

"I have a friend who makes it back in the village."

"Thanks," I say.

"Be careful," he says.

"Na razie."

They head in the direction of Wawel, Magda and I head home, and Kinga angles off toward her grandparents' flat. The trams have long stopped running for the night.

"Thank you," Magda says as soon as we are on the other side of the Sukiennice. She grabs my hand and squeezes it hard. "Thank you, thank you, thank you. Oh, you should have seen Żaba's face when Sebastian put his arm around me. And Ruda Zdzira's. She was so jealous!"

"I'm glad."

"Imagine! The best-looking guy on the Rynek."

"Do you think?"

"Do I *think?* Are you *blind?*"

She takes the bottle of *wiśniówka* from me and runs, and I chase her across Podwale, past the German drugstore. The snow has softened the corners and the edges of the street, swallowing the distant sounds of cars and voices. It reminds me a little of the white sheets of the Cabaret, the feeling that we are somehow tucked away in time and the world will stop and wait for us. We run a little way up Karmelicka and stop to catch our breath on the ledge of one of the shops. I rest the camera in my lap and Magda wedges the army helmet beneath her. The shop is a photographer's, and we examine the old sepia prints in the display window. Brides and grooms, graduates and babies. People coming and going.

"Shit," Magda says. "I can't believe I ran into them." She pops the cork out of the bottle and offers it to me. I wipe the lip on my sleeve and take a sip, and we pass it back and forth. It's already more than half-empty.

"Shit. I just can't believe it. The last time I saw either of them was on the landing at Ruda Zdzira's the day I put it all together."

"I thought you said you went to tell him off."

Magda takes another swig of the *wiśniówka*. "I lied. The truth is I lost my nerve."

"You?"

"I know," she says. "I couldn't believe it either. I was all ready. I knew exactly what I was going to say, and then . . . I just lost my nerve."

I smile.

"What?"

"I didn't tell Tadeusz off either."

"You didn't?"

"I got to the door of his flat. An hour and a half on the bus. An hour and a half all the way to Huta. All I had to do was knock on his door, and I couldn't do it."

Magda starts laughing. We pass the bottle back and forth, and a little of the *wiśniówka* dribbles down my chin, which makes her laugh even harder. I'm so drunk, I have airplanes in my head.

Magda picks up the camera from my lap and turns it around in her hands.

"You know what I wanted to be when I was little?" she says.

"An infantryman?"

"Seriously," she says.

"Artillery?"

"I wanted to be a dancer."

"*Stryptiz?*"

"Stop it." She hits me on the arm. "A ballet dancer. I wanted to be Isadora Duncan and dance at the Bolshoi and marry Mikhail Baryshnikov." She laughs and passes me the bottle. I hold it with two hands and take another mouthful. I can feel the warmth pooling in my stomach.

"And you?" she asks.

"A geographer." I laugh. "Definitely a geographer."

"You know, you don't have to take the exam just because my mother wants you to."

"No, your mother is right. I'm going to be twenty-three soon. What else am I going to do?"

"Anything you want," she says. "After all, anything is possible in the New Poland."

I laugh and take another drink. "That's *bzdury* and you know it."

"I know."

We sit for a little while longer on the ledge, passing the bottle back and forth. It must be at least ten degrees below because my thigh muscles are hard against my hand and my nostrils stick closed when I breathe in. The snowflakes are collecting in Magda's hair. Still, neither of us moves.

"Being a geographer can't be that bad," I say. "It's got to be better than selling plumbing parts in the market."

"Ej?"

"That's what I did right after *liceum*. That whole summer."

"I thought you worked at a cinema."

"That was after."

"You're kidding, right?"

"Nope."

"You mean flushers?" She starts to laugh. "And pipes and . . . God, I don't *know* any other plumbing parts."

"Well, there are pea traps and reducer bushings and float valves . . ."

"Shit, that's depressing." But she starts laughing so hard that she slips off the ledge. The army helmet clatters to the icy sidewalk and bounces a few times before coming to a rest.

"Ow," she moans, and I laugh.

The bottle has amazingly survived the fall, and she finishes it while sitting on the frozen sidewalk.

"Come on," I say, pulling her to her feet. "We're going to freeze to death out here." She takes the empty bottle and tries to balance it on a mailbox hanging on a nearby wall, but it falls and breaks on the sidewalk, leaving red spatters in the snow.

"It's a bomb! Run!" she shouts, and she grabs my hand, pulling me along behind her. I'm so drunk, I can't feel my feet making contact, but I can hear the crunch every time they hit the snow. I swing the camera by the strap and concentrate on the sound as Magda pulls me along.

Crunch, crunch, crunch, crunch. Crunch, crunch.

She stops suddenly at the tram stop at Urzędnicza and flops down on the bench, breathing hard.

"You know," she says, "she likes you better."

"Who?"

"My mother."

"What are you talking about?"

"I mean, if she had to choose, she would choose you."

"Don't be ridiculous."

"It's okay," she says, slurring, patting my hand, reassuring me as if I am a child. "Really. It's okay."

Suddenly, I feel the *wiśniówka* churning in my stomach and creeping up my throat. I wrench my hand away from her, jump up from the bench, and throw up behind the nearest tree. Magda is behind me in an instant, patting my back and handing me a handful of clean snow.

"Here," she says. "Suck on this."

We are quiet the rest of the way up Królewska, past the computer store and the twenty-four-hour store, all the way up the stairwell. There was no light in the window as we were walking along the Street of Kazimierz the Great, so I turn the key as quietly as I can. The flat is dark, but the living room door is open, and I can't see Irena's figure on the love seat.

"Mamo?"

"Irena?"

"Oh my God, she's been kidnapped," Magda says. "We should call the police."

"She's not kidnapped, you *głupek*. She went to the party. After we left. She and Stash are probably making out in his office as we speak."

"She went to the *party?* You really think so?"

"Think about it."

"Oh my God, she went to the party! Maybe she won't even come home at all tonight!"

But I don't have a chance to answer. The toilet flushes and Irena emerges from the bathroom in her pajamas. *"Głupie panienki,"* she says. "I'm right here." But there's a sly smile on her face that makes me think she's not entirely unhappy with what she overheard.

31

Onward Toward the Bright Future

THAT SUMMER, the call to the cities came, and the roads filled with people just as they had during the initial panic. This time, though, the exodus had the atmosphere of the last day of school, of leaving the contents of another year flung round the room, of leaping headlong into a vast, sun-drenched swath of time. They knew, of course, that the freedom was temporary, and that somewhere in the distance, Responsibility, Hardship, and Authority waited to catch them under the arms and set them back into their grooves. But for now, there was only unfettered joy, an absence of walls and bombs. The rules and restrictions that awaited them remained for now only a faintly glimpsed phantom on the other side, smirking in amusement at the present abandon.

It all happened immediately. Flirtations that had lasted the entire war bloomed overnight into requited love. Grand plans were drawn with the sweep of a hand. Decisions that at any other time would have been debated and thrashed about for months were made in a matter of hours. The Pigeon and Anielica announced their engagement; Władysław Jagiełło and Marysia decided to go along with them as they heeded the call to Krakow to rebuild; Marysia's parents made up their minds to sign up with the Red Cross for emigration to they didn't know where. Anywhere but here. And one of the Pigeon's sisters had fallen in love with a resourceful officer in the Home

Army who had looked after them during the war and who had been able to *załatwić* moving both of their families to London and possibly even America, provided that they left immediately. The Pigeon's mother, who had been fiercely loyal to their postage stamp of land all her life, wrote it off in the course of an afternoon.

"And what do *you* think about going to London or America?" the Pigeon asked Anielica on one of their walks through the woods.

She stopped suddenly and looked up at him. She hadn't even considered leaving Poland. Krakow seemed like the end of the world, and she could not imagine beyond it.

"Me neither," the Pigeon said, kissing her on the forehead. "I cannot leave Poland to struggle on her own. I would feel like a traitor. Though I would like to visit that America one day. That New York and that California."

Anielica was relieved, both that she wouldn't have to consider it and that this was yet another thing on which they agreed so completely. She tightened her grip on the crook of his arm.

"And what about Jakub?" she asked. For Jakub had refused to emigrate with his parents and sisters. "Should we take him with us to Krakow? He will be all alone in the village."

The Pigeon had not even considered taking him. Jakub had lived up at the old sheep camp for the duration of the war. He rarely appeared in the villages anymore, and once all the sheep had been slaughtered, no one had a reason to make their way up the hill. In the beginning, Anielica had occasionally made the trip to bring him food or supplies, but after the Night of the Barszcz, she had stopped. And so they were both surprised that he was not happier to see them approaching up Old Baldy Hill, walking hand in hand through the tall grass. In fact, they could have sworn that when Jakub saw them coming, he had turned around and disappeared into the hut.

"Jakub! Jakub! It's me," the Pigeon called. He went to the hut and knocked on the rough wooden door, which swung loosely on its hinges. The hut was no bigger than one of the side rooms of the Hetmański house, built by a lesser carpenter than the Pigeon thirty or forty years before. The outer boards, darkened by rot, clung to the frame like the teeth in a witch's mouth, the cracks and holes stuffed with bits of wool.

They could hear the buzzing of Jakub's voice through the walls, the steady monologue that ceased only when he slept, and as they stepped inside the hut, the volume increased, but his back was turned and it was hard to tell at first if he was actually talking to them.

". . . The berries will be ripe soon, so I can pick the berries, and then there are the pheasants, I have to check the traps today, the Germans are gone from the woods for now, but who knows when they will be back, and when they come back, maybe they will try to take me for Baudienst, or the army or the camps . . ."

"Jakub, the war is over," the Pigeon said. "The Germans are gone."

". . . and I noticed there is no bombing anymore, but it can't be over, it is impossible that it's over, and I will still have to haul the water and chop the wood and clean my clothes, and I haven't prepared dinner for visitors, and I don't have time to, don't have time for visitors today, don't have time . . ."

"Jakub, we brought you dinner. And we only came to tell you that we are engaged and to ask you if you wanted to go to Krakow with us. There has been a call to the cities to rebuild."

". . . and how should I have known that you would come to visit, since no one came for such a long time, everyone was too busy to visit me, and now everyone comes and says that they are leaving, *mama, tata,* Julia and her officer, and only Anielica came to see me during the war, only Anielica brought me medicine for the sheep, only Anielica, only Anielica, ONLY Anielica."

Anielica and the Pigeon looked at each other. Anielica's eyes told him to leave the hut, and he did, reluctantly, but Jakub only seemed to clench his teeth more tightly, increasing the speed and volume of his words.

". . . and you remember that time when you came up to see ME, and you brought ME the medicine for the sheep from Zakopane, and MY BROTHER came and saw you, but I was the one who told HIM about YOU, I was the one, I WAS THE ONE, and NOW you are marrying HIM, and leaving with HIM, and Krakow is VERY FAR, I have never been to Krakow, but it is VERY FAR, and you are going there with HIM and you will marry HIM and I was the one who told HIM about YOU, I WAS THE ONE, I WAS THE ONE . . ."

Anielica reached out and touched his arm, and for the first time that anyone could remember, he stopped buzzing. For a moment, she feared he might have suffered a stroke or a heart attack.

"Jakub? Jakub, are you okay?"

He looked at her strangely.

"Jakub, your brother and I, we are in love. But that doesn't mean that we don't love you too. We are going to Krakow with my brother and Marysia, and I think it would be good for you to come with us."

There was silence for a moment, then a faint vibration that increased and broke apart into words. " . . . and do you remember when you came to visit me and you brought me the sheep medicine, and it was in a little paper sack, and you brought me dinner, *bigos* and *kompot* and hard-boiled eggs, and you were wearing your green skirt and your white blouse with the blue flowers and your hair was on top of your head, and it was clipped with that brown clip you have, and it will never be like that, it will never be the same, you are moving far away, and with my brother, and I was the one who told him about you, if I hadn't kept talking to you that day, you would have left and he never would have seen you, if I would have stopped talking, if I would have stopped talking . . ."

"But Jakub, when the Pigeon and I are married, you and I will be brother and sister, and we will go to Krakow and have so much fun there. You know, they say that the city is paved in gold, that the women are all princesses riding around in carriages, that a dragon guards the castle . . ."

" . . . I have to check the traps, I don't have time for visitors, I don't have time to go to Krakow, I have to check the traps and pick the berries and wash the clothes and fix the roof, I don't have time, you have to leave, and take him with you, I don't have time . . ."

"Think about it, Jakub," Anielica said quietly. "We are not leaving until next week."

She leaned over and kissed him on the cheek before she left, and once again, he was silent, rooted to the spot where he stood on the rotted floor. He could not bear to come out and say goodbye to his brother, though he did pull the wool from one of the cracks and watch them as they walked back down the hill hand in hand.

32

Oh, I Happy. I Much Happy.

WINTER IN THE CITY is much worse than in the mountains. In the mountains, we just put on another sweater, feed some more branches into the stove, and add a splash of warm vodka to the tea. In the city, the cold is debilitating. The midday sun bouncing off the flat sheets of ice blinds everyone with a permanent squint, and each *mróz,* or freeze, creates a metropolis of simpletons, their hats pulled over their eyes, cursing softly to themselves. Metal seats and railings freeze hands and backsides with one touch, and gusts of wind, sharpened on the corners of the buildings, herd crowds of hunchbacks down the street at knifepoint.

Herding us into exactly what, we don't know. The new year brings many things the falling wax didn't predict.

For one, Stash starts to phone the flat for Irena. The first time it happens is a Sunday afternoon as we are clearing up from *obiad.* Irena answers, and when she hears his voice on the other end, she drops the receiver against the corner of the dresser, and it bounces onto the floor.

"Hang it up!" Irena hisses at me as she backs away.

"I'm not going to hang up on him," I whisper back. "It's Stash!"

"Then pick it up. Tell him I'm not home."

"He already heard your voice."

I can hear Stash laughing softly through the receiver, which is still lying on the rug.

"*Słucham,*" I answer.

"*Cześć,* Baba Yaga, do you think I could talk to Irena now?"

I look up at Irena, who is violently shaking her head and mouthing words at me.

"Um . . . I'm sorry, but she's not home?"

Stash laughs. "Baba Yaga, I know she's there. She just answered the phone. I hear her whispering."

"She says she's not."

Irena slaps me on the arm.

Stash chuckles. "All right then, do you know what would be a good time to call back?"

"Surprise her."

And she slaps me again, but there's something in her face that is reaching out to take the phone, even if her hands don't.

I try to get her to watch the videotape of New Year's, but she says she doesn't need to, that she has been to plenty of New Year's parties and knows what goes on at them. I leave the camera out on the table in my bedroom anyway, cued to the beginning, and though she never mentions it, a few days later, it has shifted just slightly from its place, and the tape is not rewound to the same spot.

"Irena?"

"Yes?"

"You never told me what happened with Stash."

"Maybe because it's none of your business."

"But you said you would tell me."

"When did I say that?"

"The day you took me around the Bermuda Triangle."

"No, I didn't."

"You have *skleroza*. You don't remember."

She furrows her eyebrows at me. "I don't even know why you're interested."

"I just am."

"You always want to hear the happy stories, don't you? Your grandmother spoiled you."

I don't answer. My grandmother used to say that sometimes silence is the best grease.

Irena smiles. "All right, then. I'll give you one happy story, and one happy story only. This isn't America after all. And you must promise never to tell Stash I told you."

"I promise."

"Or Magda."

"Never."

"Never."

I nod.

"Dobrze." She smiles. "It was ten years after I married Wiktor. June of 'eighty-two. Wiktor was passed out all that year, Magda was ten, my mother was living with us, and I had just resigned from the company of the troublemakers and started working at the cafeteria. But Stash somehow convinced me, and I went out with them. Early, because of the curfew, and at about seven I told everyone I was going home. And Stash, always the gentleman, Stash said he would *odprowadzić* me home safely—I don't know if your grandmother told you, but in the cities there were armored vehicles and *milicja* in the streets then. So we flagged down a private car, and what do you know but that it turned out to be one of our old school friends driving. He and his family were very wealthy."

"How?"

She shrugs. "I don't know. You didn't ask in those days. Anyway, he and Stash started talking about the music festival in Opole, which happened to be going on that week, and about all the singers who were performing. And he—Paweł was his name—had been watching it on television that evening, and there were rumors that the singers were going to organize something to protest Martial Law. And the three of us kept talking and talking about how great it would be to go there, and on and on, and—can you imagine?—by the time we came to my street, Stash had convinced Paweł to drive us to Opole. Can you imagine? All the way to Opole."

"How far was it?"

"Almost three hours in his Little Fiat and with the roads in the condition they were. If we had broken down . . . but we didn't. And when we got there, the concerts were over for the day, but there were parties in the hotel all night long. And in those days, there was no such thing as celebrity. No stars. So we ended up at a party with all the singers who had performed that day. And there were no rooms left, but at the end of the night, someone offered us their floor. That was just how it was in those days. So we slept for a few hours and then stayed for the concerts the entire next day. And we saw everybody. *Everybody*. Czesław Niemen, Beata Kozidrak, Krzysztof Krawczyk."

She is beaming.

"Oh, it was magic! And at the end of the next day, we drove all the way back to Krakow, just making the curfew at ten. And I had to be at work at six in the morning, and somehow *załatwić* a doctor's note saying that I had been sick the day before. Oh, I remember being so tired that day. I had just started working in the cafeteria then, doing inventory, and I had to redo all my work the following day. But I was so happy, I didn't care."

"And was there a protest?"

"Oh, yes. Jan Pietrzak sang 'So That Poland Will Be Poland,' and everyone stood up and cried. And of course there was the tree."

"The tree?"

"Yes, on the stage. There was no set. Nothing. Only one, lone, barren, windblown tree."

"That was a protest?"

"That was a protest. That and continuing with the festival, going where we wanted to go, as if the soldiers and Jaruzelski and Moscow simply didn't matter. We ignored them out of existence. 'Act as if,' we used to say."

"And your mother?"

Irena smiles. "She was furious. *Furious.* She'd had to lie to one of my coworkers and to Magda. We had no phone yet, so I couldn't call her, and by the time we got to Opole the first night, it was too late to call the neighbors. And the next day, well, I was so selfish, I didn't want her to tell me to come home. She nearly tore my ear off when I walked in the door. She thought I'd been arrested." She smiles again. "But Jezus Maria, it was exhilarating. When we were in that Little Fiat . . . just to pass right by my flat and go all the way to Opole . . ."

"And you and Stash? What happened?"

"Nothing."

"Nothing?"

A slow smile creeps across her face. "One night of nothing."

. . .

The other thing the wax didn't predict is the afternoon when Pani Bożena hands me my pay packet and tells me that she won't be needing me anymore.

"I'm sorry," I say.

"For what?"

"For not telling you I was buying packaged food from the supermarket."

"It has nothing to do with that."

"Is it the makeup or the *Dynasty* plots?"

"What are you talking about?"

"Never mind."

I guess once you find out you're not a grande dame, there's simply no point to having an audience anymore. To say the truth, I'm actually a little relieved. With both jobs, the stack of American dollars under my mattress was growing alarmingly thick, and for the first time I had the choice to leave the flat on Bytomska and move out on my own.

It's always easier to have things decided for you.

So I spend my time studying diligently for the geography exam. Magda makes me a schedule of what I need to study for the history portion of the exam, and she shares her books with me. Most mornings, thanks to an old student ID, I end up at the university library, sitting at one of the long wooden tables under the green glow of the banker's lamps, surrounded by books. It's nice, actually. It reminds me of Nela.

After my mother got sick and my father built the wall, I moved to Nela's side of the house, and for the next fifteen years, we spent nearly all our evenings in front of the stove, blankets wrapped around our shoulders, a little bench under our feet. We would either talk while Nela did her sewing, or we would read. When I was little, I read fairy tales and stories about little boys and girls saving entire collective farms by ratting out their parents or sticking their small fingers into the works of a jammed harvester. By ten or eleven, I was reading *The Adventures of Huck, Tomek Sawyer,* and *Ania of the Green Roof.*

I was nowhere near as voracious a reader as Nela was, though, so when I got bored, I would just watch her read, her lips puckered out like an old man's, her eyelids drooped, a deep line gathered between her eyebrows. It was the only time that she looked like an ordinary person instead of a starlet. She would become so absorbed in her novels that she could block out the sounds of my father on the other side of the wall, so absorbed that she wouldn't even notice when I got up from my chair and wandered around, poking into places that were normally off-limits to me.

"Nela? Did you know that there are books hidden in a secret compartment in the bottom of the wardrobe? And that some of them have the wrong covers?"

She was suddenly startled out of her reverie. Her face remolded itself into the shape of a starlet, and she put a manicured finger to her lips. "Beata, you must never tell anyone."

"Why?"

"You mustn't."

"But why?"

"Promise."

I promised, and she sat me down in front of the iron stove and told me a story better than any that I had ever read. She started with Günter Grass and Émile Zola, went on to George Orwell, Henry Miller, and Sławomir Mrożek, and ended up at an electrician named Lech Wałęsa. My grandmother had never talked about politics to me before because there were so many sad endings in politics, but she must have believed that there was a happy ending somewhere out there because this time, she glowed with excitement as she told me about the protests and the strikes in the shipyards and steel mills in Gdańsk and Katowice. There was freedom just around the corner, Nela promised me, and she wanted to live to see it. Until then she would have to be satisfied with reading about it.

"But the books that are not on the *indeks*? Where do they come from?"

"I have already told you more than I should. Hold it in like a mouthful of water."

I nodded gravely, and Nela replaced the books in the bottom of the wardrobe and put the panel back.

She seemed relieved to share the secret with someone, and from that day on, she stopped hiding them from me. When I was at the post office with her, I watched them arrive in the mail sack a few at a time, in plain brown packages with no return addresses. I helped her hide them in the tired boxes at the bottom of the storage closet, and after the post office closed for the evening, we would rewrap them, tie them with twine, and mark them up with canceled stamps and fake addresses. Once every few weeks, someone I did not recognize would come in, drop off a postcard of the Tatras, and leave with one or two of the packages.

Over the years, though, she hoarded the French authors. Proust, Zola, Dumas, Camus, Voltaire, Maupassant, Balzac, Flaubert, Hugo, Céline, Lamartine. They all found their way to the secret compartment in the wardrobe, and Nela made me promise at least once a week that I would never give them away, that I would take them all with me when I went to Krakow. I think for her, the French always made her think of freedom, if not for her, then for me.

As it happened, Nela read about freedom for several more years before the books could be handed over the counter openly. But by the time Poland became free, her weak heart had already imprisoned her. She died in her bed, exactly as she would have had the communists still been in power. When I went to Krakow, I kept *Germinal*, which was her favorite, and left the rest of the French in hiding in the bottom of the wardrobe. Everything else, I boxed up neatly and left in the house for Uncle Jakub to look in on from time to time.

"Hey," Magda says, and she takes off her coat and drapes it over a bar stool.

"Hey."

As of the middle of January, Magda no longer officially works at Stash's. The wine bar is becoming more popular, and her boss asked her to work six nights a week, which she agreed to since we've all known for a while that Stash doesn't actually need three bar girls. As it is, it's so slow lately that Kinga spends practically all night at the Englishmen's table, and I *still* have too much time to daydream about silly things like Tadeusz suddenly appearing in the doorway, telling me that I was right and the army was all a mistake. Sometimes I try to picture him sitting on his foot locker, telling vulgar jokes with the rest of the nineteen-year-old boys. I try to picture him playing cards or digging ditches or pulling triggers with the fingers that could once coax a woman's voice from a reed, and it makes me ache, maybe not for him but for something else.

Magda still comes by almost every night after the wine bar, but

I'm not sure if she's coming to hang out with Kinga and me or to see if Sebastian has reappeared. He has been strangely absent since New Year's, vanished into thin air, and Magda isn't interested in any of the other boys anymore. Most nights, we just quiz each other on history and watch Kinga trying to speak English to the Englishmen. The fat red-haired one has the most patience for her, and she concentrates hard, her face contorting as her mouth spits out the language that will always sound to me like someone eating rocks.

It's the middle of the third set one night when she comes back to the bar, pulling the red-haired Englishman along by the arm. Kinga weaves through the scattered chair backs easily, but he has difficulty squeezing through the narrow path she's cut, and he excuses himself in his booming voice and his jagged language.

"Ronan says he has a job for me in England. Can you imagine? A job in England!"

"Doing what?"

"Something about a farm. Magda, can you translate? Please? I want all the details."

I listen as Magda and the Englishman talk back and forth. I recognize a few of the words from the tourists, but most of the tourists were American or German or Scandinavian, with straight up-and-down accents, and Ronan's lists horribly to the side. Kinga nods gravely through the entire exchange, but as soon as Magda explains everything in Polish, her thin lips stretch into a grin.

Ronan, as it happens, owns a farm in Ireland and returns every summer to manage it. He's in the habit of bringing some of his students from the Agricultural Institute to work on the farm, and in exchange, they receive room and board and three hundred pounds a month.

"And a chance to practice my English," Kinga says.

"But *you*, Kinga, on a farm?" I ask. "Have you ever even *seen* a cow?"

"I have."

"I mean, not on a plate."

"I asked him about that," Magda says. "But he insists that there is even work for skinny girls who hate dirt." Magda and Kinga laugh, and Ronan smiles, though he doesn't know at what.

"But, Kinga," I continue, "how are you going to learn English if you're going with a group of Polish people? Won't you be speaking Polish all the time?"

"I'm sure there will be *someone* there to practice with," Magda says.

"And three hundred pounds. That's probably nothing compared to the prices there."

"I'm sure it will be fine," Magda says.

"Oh, I happy," Kinga says in English. She throws her arms around the mountain of a man and gives him a kiss on the cheek. "I much happy."

Ronan blushes a deep red, says something else to Magda and hurries back to the table.

"Oh, I happy," Kinga says over and over. "I much happy."

"I *am* happy," I correct her. "Even *I* know that much."

"I *am* happy," she says. "Am, am, am, am, am." It's true. I have never seen her happier. She completely forgets to cover her teeth when she smiles, and her two front teeth twist outward, ready for flight. She works behind the bar for the rest of the night, all the while chatting about her plans for the money, trying to decide whether she will stay in Ireland and work on the black after the summer is over, or return with all the English she has learned and work for a tourist agency in Krakow. Perhaps, she thinks, she can even take the entrance exam for the English philology department at Jagiellonian. Her grandparents, she says, would be so happy if she had a degree.

"I can't believe I'm going to England," she sings to the tune of the national anthem, and maybe it should be our new national anthem.

"It's *Ireland*."

"Okay, Pani Geographer. Ireland. Close enough."

That night, as we walk back home together, Magda and I are silent nearly the whole way. It's only as we come to the twenty-four-hour store that she turns to me.

"That's great news for Kinga," she says.

"Yes," I say. "Good for her."

There's a group of teenagers sitting on the curb in front of the store and two other boys coming out, swearing at each other, carrying bottles of beer.

"Magda?"

"Yes?"

"Aren't you just a *little* bit jealous?"

"Of her going to Ireland?"

"Of her getting exactly what she wants."

"Of course not," she says. "What kind of friend would I be then?"

We continue to the corner, past the tram stop and the post office, past the signs for the computer firm.

"I'm jealous as hell," I finally say.

"Me too," Magda says quickly, and we both laugh.

33

From There to Here

THEY LEFT FOR KRAKOW at dawn on a Monday. The business of preparation was so consuming that there was little room left for grief or goodbyes. The men made two trips down the mountain to Pisarowice with the bags, and they waited at the side of the river for Pan Romanenko to wake up and pole them across. From there, they grafted together the sections of road with whatever transport they could arrange. There were seven in the party, including Marysia's parents, and though it would have been easier to travel in a smaller group, they refused to split up.

Pan Stefanów took them as far as Biały Dunajec in his cart, where they found another willing cart to take them to Szaflary. After a few hours' wait, they found seven spaces on a bus to Nowy Targ. By the time they got to Nowy Targ, it was already suppertime, and the rest of the group waited outside while Anielica and the Pigeon went in to check the board. The station was packed with people sitting around, children sleeping in nests of clothes, adults playing cards or sharing homemade meals off their luggage. Anielica and the Pigeon threaded a path through the crowd, gripping each other tightly so they would not be separated. They got as close as they could to the departures board.

"Can you see what that says?"

There were pieces of paper taped here and there on the board, last-minute changes made to boarding lanes and times. There were only two buses left going to Krakow—19:15 and 22:05.

"But how can that be? Half these people are probably going to Krakow." They scanned the crowd in the station. There were students and soldiers, grandmothers and families, Russians, Gypsies, even a small group of French civilians. The three lines at the counter were twenty deep, except for the middle one, which people were shifting out of as the argument between a man and the agent became more heated.

"Come on," the Pigeon said. "We'll have better luck outside."

They found the right bus in the corner of the yard, the driver smoking off to the side.

"Wait here," he told Anielica.

Before he could even ask, the driver answered. "The nineteen-fifteen is already full. Been sold out since three this afternoon."

"But we are trying to get to Krakow. We have a small child with us and a grandmother and grandfather. If we take the twenty-two-five, we will arrive in Krakow at midnight and have to stay in the station."

"The twenty-two-five is already sold out too, but you're better off staying the night here than in the station in Krakow anyway. Fewer thieves."

The Pigeon looked back at Anielica. Her face was still hopeful; she couldn't hear the conversation over the noise of the buses idling in the yard.

"Please, sir."

"I can't help you."

"We can pay."

He shook his head and set his jaw. "The New Poland cannot be built on corruption and preferential treatment. We must all work fairly and honestly if there is to be a bright future."

"Right." The Pigeon walked back toward Anielica.

"Wait," the driver called. He put his cigarette out on his shoe and hurried to catch up with them. "Anielica. Anielica of Half-Village. I would never forget that face."

Anielica blushed, and the Pigeon scowled at him.

"At the beginning of the war. I had dinner at your house. With your parents. Stayed a night in your father's barn. I was with my friend Marek."

"I am the Pigeon. I sent Marek."

"*You* are the *Pigeon?*"

He managed to fit them all on the nineteen-fifteen, though they had to sit on their bags in the aisle. Still, no one hassled or jostled them or gave them sharp looks as they would have before the war. They were all in this together now, all with the same itinerary, all dreaming the same dream. All but the bus, which broke down just past Jawornik.

They filed off, the aisle-squatters first, and huddled around in small groups, deciding what to do next. The Pigeon joined the driver. He took off his coat, rolled up his sleeves, and stood up on the bumper to peer into the engine.

"What do you think?"

"Radiator. Definitely radiator."

It turned out to be a blown gasket, and not even the Pigeon's golden hands could fashion a new one. It was dark by then, and small groups of people had drifted up the road, dragging their luggage in the dirt. The optimists headed north toward Krakow, like windup toys that could not be stopped. The pessimists returned south to find lodging overnight in Krzeczów, the last town they had passed. After going around and around about the gasket, the Pigeon, the driver, and Władysław Jagiełło finally gave up.

"You should go," the driver said. "Try to find someplace to stay before it is too late."

"No, no," Anielica said. "You have been so kind. We cannot leave you here. We will wait with you."

"Another bus will be by soon," Marysia agreed. "For sure. We will wait."

There were a few Soviet transports, which seemed to steer intentionally for the side of the road, inflating the loose dirt into clouds of dust that engulfed them all. There were a few Good Samaritans who stopped by to peer under the hood, shake their heads, recheck what the Pigeon and the driver had already checked, and come to the same conclusion they had come to.

"Why don't you take Irenka into the bus and prepare a place for her to sleep?" the Pigeon said to Anielica.

"No, no, you should go," the driver said. "I have to wait here, but you should go."

The Pigeon looked up and down the road. It was a selfless offer made by the driver. And utterly meaningless. The other passengers had long ago been swallowed by the darkness, and there were only lone flickers of light on the horizon. Even if they found a willing house, it could not take the seven of them together.

"Here," the driver said, digging into his pocket. "There is a large manor house just east of here, controlled by two guys I knew from the Home Army. Tell them you are the Pigeon, and show them this." He gave him half a holy card of St. Sebastian.

"A manor house?"

"Abandoned by the owners."

As soon as the card was in his hand, there was no question in the Pigeon's mind that they would go. There was only the customary insisting and counter-insisting to go through before the party could troop off down the road.

"Oh, but we cannot just leave you here."

"I will be fine. The twenty-two-five should be coming by in an hour or so."

"Are you sure?"

"Sure."

This was the abridged version because the Pigeon was anxious to get his family on the road. That was how he thought of them now, his family, which now included three Jews and a little Gypsy girl. His family, and he would do anything for them.

The manor house was only a kilometer away, and most of that was on a private dirt road. The men carried the packs and bundles, and little Irena, who was half-asleep, was passed back and forth among the women. The house was impressive in the distance. The gates were twice a man's height, the bars branching and twisting into iron vines and leaves that spiraled just above the handles, forming what looked like the eyes of a grand hoot owl, scrutinizing their arrival. The house itself was set far back, but in the moonlight, they could just make out the arching lane, the grand colonnade, the rows of windows lined up in formation like maids and footmen under inspection.

"Who goes there?" The man appeared from nowhere, a shadow fleshing out some of the iron bars.

"I am the Pigeon. We were sent by Stepanek."

"Stepanek who?"

"He said he knew you."

"I don't know any Stepanek."

"He gave us this." The Pigeon fed the half-card of St. Sebastian through the iron bars. The shadow on the other side snatched it. The great eyes of the gate continued to watch them.

"How many of you are there?" he asked gruffly.

"Seven. Three men, three women, and a little one."

"And how long do you plan on staying?"

"Just the night. We are on our way to Krakow. The bus broke down."

They all held their breath, and for a moment, it seemed the only thing that separated them from the sprawling house and a good night's rest was the heavy breath of the man on the other side of the bars.

"Very well," he said, and they could hear the jangle of keys, the springing open of the padlock, the squealing of the old hinges. He held the gate open just wide enough for them to fit through, and as they followed the circling carriage lane, the house loomed larger, drawing them in, the front door opening just as their feet touched the steps.

"The *Pigeon!* Well, I'll be damned." The man at the front door hugged him warmly, thumping him on the back. "Word was that you were caught right between the Nazis and the Soviets, and your whole village was burned."

"Well, I am still here. In fact, we are on our way to Krakow."

"And you've brought half the village with you, I see." The man laughed. "Come in, come in."

"I feel like a princess," Marysia whispered to Anielica. Anielica nodded, but her heart was beating wildly. She knew, probably better than Marysia, that there were those who wanted the Jews out as badly as they wanted the Nazis gone. That it was likely that even this man, with his congeniality, was one of them, that if they had arrived in the clear daylight or if Anielica, the Pigeon, and Władysław Jagiełło hadn't entered first, they might have very well been turned away. And indeed, as Marysia and her parents came in, Anielica thought she could see a twitch of disapproval in the face of the man who had greeted the first three with such joviality.

"So, do you remember the time we were in that bunker with Krzysiek at Mała Dolina?" the Pigeon said, clapping his hand on the man's shoulder, and the man very quickly regained his cheeriness, taking two of the bags and leading the entire party up the stairs.

The house had already been stripped of its furnishings and fixtures, but they could still wonder at the plaster medallions and the beautiful patterns of parquet that were left. The man showed them to a large room, which they were to have all to themselves. It was at the end of one wing, and whatever sounds of activity they could hear through the walls and the speaking tubes, a thick, warm sleep quickly muffled. For five of them anyway. The Pigeon and Anielica could not sleep for the excitement, and they lay awake under their coats and sweaters, whispering about the city they saw in their dreams, the city that the very next day they would call home.

"They say that the streets are paved in gold, and all the women look like princesses and are drawn about town in silver carriages," Anielica said quietly.

"Well then, you will fit right in."

When they woke up the next morning, the dawn had peeled away the darkness in long, unforgiving strips. The shadows on the walls in the shape of foliage turned out to be yellowed water stains, and in the corner of the room, there was a large bare spot where the parquet had been pulled up and used as kindling. The medallions on the ceiling flaked plaster, and the grand colonnade outside, upon closer examination, was riddled with bullet holes. The entire manor should have been carted off to a field hospital. Or a Party rally, to be held up as a metaphor for Old Poland.

Marysia said the house had character, as if she were speaking of an ugly but beloved child, but the others had no such loyalties, showing openly their will to leave as soon as possible, to escape the rotting, decomposing flesh of the building, the disrepair that did not match up with their dreams, the desperation that had no place in the New Poland they were trying to build. Two of the men from the manor helped them with their belongings. They were clearly ex-partisans, both showing the signs of neglect of a man without a woman: the missing buttons, the stains on their shirts, the reticence broken only by pragmatic, utilitarian instructions to the other of where to go and what to carry. When they reached the road, they hardly recognized it in the light. Both the driver and the bus were gone, the only evidence, the long grass pressed down along the side of the road. They sat on their bags and let the warm air and the silence of the two men settle around them.

After about half an hour, one of the men stood up with his hands in his pockets, searching the horizon like a dog who can feel the secret rumblings of the earth. And indeed, a bus appeared on the crest of the far hill, stretched to its full length as it sped downward, disappeared into the valley, and reappeared suddenly like a great monster, rumbling and squealing, kicking up the dust before settling to a tame stop.

The card in the front window said Krakow, and there was only a brief glance from the driver to the men before he dismounted and helped load the bags. And in another minute, the seven from Half-Village were again sitting snugly in the aisle, headed for the golden city.

34

The Nazis, Soviets, Russians, Tatars, Ottomans, Turks, Cossacks, Prussians, and Swedes

S TASH KEEPS CALLING the house, and Irena keeps not picking up the phone. If it's ringing and Magda or I don't answer it, she just lets it ring and ring and ring. Which is why I think I'm imagining things when I'm walking to Stash's one day at the beginning of February and I see Irena on the other side of Aleje, walking toward the Square of the Invalids. I try to shout to her, but she doesn't hear me over the traffic.

"You're early," Stash says when I come in.

"Stash, why did I just see Irena on the street? She never comes along this way."

He only smiles.

"She was here, wasn't she?"

"I'm not allowed to say. And if you think you saw something, you're not allowed to say."

"Not even to Magda?"

"Especially not to Magda."

"Why not?"

He smiles. "I'm not allowed to say."

• • •

236

Magda comes by after the wine bar, and it's all I can do to talk about history and not Irena and Stash.

"I'm telling you," Magda insists from the bar stool. "August the Third was *not* the last king of the dynasty. It was Jan the Second Kazimierz Waza. From 1654 to 1665. Ask Kinga."

Kinga shrugs. "You think I remember any of that stuff?"

"Actually, it was 1648 to 1668," a voice behind us says.

It's Sebastian. It's been a month since he rescued Magda from Żaba and Ruda Zdzira, but he acts like we're all old friends, kissing each one of us on the cheeks, one, two, three. He moves with the grace of one of the businessmen coming in and out of the phone center on Wielopole Street, even in his soft, worn jeans and his peacoat.

He was in America for a few weeks, he explains, pushing the question mark of dark hair out of his eyes, visiting a family friend in New York.

"Ah, Nowy Jork," Magda and I echo, filling the words with reverence.

"Yes, the Duże Apple," he says, and we all laugh, Magda much louder and longer than necessary.

"Are you drunk?" I ask her after he takes his beer and sits down at a table with some of the other boys.

"On him."

I take the dishtowel and snap it at her. "Hey, hey. Think about your exams. Think about your future."

"Maybe he is my future."

I laugh. "You're always so dramatic."

"Come on, don't you think it's strange that I saw Żaba in the wax that night, and then I ran into him on the Rynek—the first time I've seen him since we broke up?"

"Everyone was on the Rynek that night."

"And then Sebastian appears out of nowhere and pretends to be my boyfriend?"

"But I *asked* him to go over and pretend to be your boyfriend."

"And then he leaves for almost a month and the night he comes back, I happen to be here?"

"You're *always* here."

She shrugs. "That's how fate works."

"It's true," says Kinga, who has become an expert on fate since finding out about the farm job.

"I thought you said you were too busy studying, too focused on the exam to bother with boys."

"With boys, yes." She smiles and looks at me from under her eyebrows like she used to do when she asked her mother for money. "But maybe I will have to make an exception for destiny."

My destiny, it seems, is geography. Irena gave me a list of all the topics on the exam, courtesy of her friend at the university, and it makes my head spin to look at it. I try to read in the mornings and hold the facts in my head all day long, repeating them over and over, stopping up the leaks in my mind to keep all the kings, battles, invasions, and executions straight. Old Poland keeps me company all day and becomes the background chatter for all my activities. I walk to the library with Vladimir the Great, eat at a milk bar with Boleslaus the Wry-Mouthed, arrive at Stash's with Sigismund the Old, flip over the chairs with King Władysław Jagiełło, and light the candles with Tadeusz Kościuszko. On Fridays, I go to Mikro with Nicolaus Copernicus.

"That *skurwysyn*. That fat *skurwysyn*."

Kinga throws her bag on the floor behind the bar and pours herself a shot of the best vodka Stash stocks. She drinks it down, still standing there in her coat.

"Who?" I ask.

"Kinga, is that you?" Stash calls from the office, but he doesn't come out.

"That *pieprzony* bastard sonofabitch pile of shit," Kinga says. "Fucking Ronan the fucking Englishman."

"Irishman."

"Jackass."

"It *is* you," Stash calls again from the office.

"What happened?" I ask.

"What happened?" Kinga lowers her voice. "I'll tell you what happened. He said he had a job for me all right, but that I didn't even have to go to England for it. He said he'd give me a hundred pounds right here in Krakow, and all I had to do was sleep with him. With that old, fat, greasy, mayonnaise-colored *skurwysyn*."

"Are you sure you understood him right?"

"Ha!" she says. "It turns out that propositioning young girls is the *only* thing he can do fluently in Polish."

"And what did you say?"

"What do you mean what did I say? I said no!" she hisses.

"That's not what I meant. How did you say it?"

"That's just the thing." She takes off her coat and drapes it over the back of a bar stool, then boosts herself up onto it. "After no, I couldn't say *anything*. I was so shocked, I just sat there for a minute and then left. We were at the café in the cellar of the Ratusz. We met there for coffee, and then he said it, and then I just said no. I couldn't think of anything else to say. Not even in Polish, much less in English." She pours herself another shot. "And I just know he's going to show up tonight with that stupid smile on his face, that fat old *skurwysyn*, and I *still* don't know what I'll say to him when I see him. Ugh. I just wish I could have told him what a jackass he is." She rests her head against the palm of her hand.

"I know," I say. "I'm the same. And then I always kick myself later. But you know who's good at things like that? Magda."

"Fat lot of good that does me now."

"But she'll think of something, and the next time you see him, you'll be ready."

Magda is incensed when we tell her. "What do you mean, what do you say? Tell him it's more than a hundred pounds if you have to go on a *pieprzona* spelunking expedition for it. Tell him he's a fat old goat, an *alfons*, a *kretyn*, a *pajac*, a *szmata*, a *buc*. Tell him he's such a sad, sad *skurwysyn* that he gets turned down even when he tries to pay for it." She pulls up a stool next to the bar and keeps at it, her words thickening Kinga's vitriol, whipping it into peaks of anger.

"You're right. You're right," Kinga seethes. "Just let him try to show up here. Let me at him. I'll tell him where to go this time."

But he doesn't come. In fact, none of the Englishmen do. The young girls they usually buy drinks for flit around aimlessly and begin sizing up the table of Sebastian's friends.

"That *skurwysyn*," Magda says. "If he's too much of a coward to show his face here, we'll go find him."

"Find him?"

"Find him."

"Just go to every single bar and café in Krakow until we find him?" I ask.

"Exactly."

"I hope you're kidding."

"He's a foreigner," Magda says. "He probably found Stash's through a fluke. Other than here, he probably only knows the bars on the Rynek. How many are there? Ten? Fifteen?"

"I don't know, Magda," Kinga says. "How will that go? 'Excuse me, I know I couldn't think of anything to say back to you this afternoon, but if you could just sit there a minute while I tell you what a dog testicle you are. In Polish. Which you don't even understand.'"

"He might understand the word *testicle*."

"Baba Yaga, tell her," Magda insists.

"I don't know, Magda. If she doesn't want to . . .'"

But Magda is not stopping. I see that glint in her eye. It's Magda the Prosecutor out to seek justice. "*What?* What's the matter with you two? 'I don't know'? *No.* We are *not* letting this one go. What's he going to do next? He's going to go right out and proposition the next girl. *No.* This is not about Kinga anymore. This is about Poland. Not even. This is about all women everywhere exploited by *skurwysyn* expats everywhere. If not for Kinga, then for them."

Kinga and I can't help but smile, but Magda is completely serious.

We clean up while the band is still playing and stop serving drinks at quarter to eleven. As soon as Stash plays the final note, we begin collecting glasses, practically standing over people as they drink. Most of them are headed out to catch their buses anyway.

"Someone is up to mischief," Stash says, wiping the sweat from his forehead back through his hair. "I'll close up. Just don't do anything stupid."

We go to all the bars and cafés that we know the foreigners frequent. First we check the cellars—Old Pub, Free Pub, the Garden, Black Gallery, Ritmo Latino, Bunker, and Dym. Then the cafés—Behemot, Mozaika, Out of Africa, and a few others, which are all closed or empty. We even try Maska, the new actors' bar, where it is easy to scan the room because the entire room scans you as soon as you walk through the door.

"Maybe he didn't go out tonight," I say. We are standing on Grodzka Street, deciding what to do next.

"He's out," Magda says. "I can feel it."

It's a particularly cold night, even for the beginning of February. The cold creeps beneath my clothes, settling in the folds so that when I move, a new wave of chills ripples up my skin.

"Maybe we should quit for tonight," I say. "Do this another day. Or wait until he comes back to Stash's."

"She's right," Kinga says. "We don't have to do this tonight."

Magda doesn't answer. She just keeps walking. Maybe she's too busy rehearsing what she's going to say, stoking the fire inside her. Maybe to her, it's so obvious we can't stop that she doesn't even bother to answer.

So we keep going, crisscrossing the Rynek, running out of bars, when Magda suddenly remembers another one, a cellar that serves as a hangout for both the security service and a group of skinheads, though she says they let anyone in who manages to find it. There's no sign. You just have to know which passageway to walk through, which stairs to descend, which door to open.

All the other bars on the Rynek have a gimmick—aluminum poles and electric-blue drinks in Black Gallery, American film posters and flags in Free Pub, red lights and steamy music in Ritmo Latino—but in this one, there are no gimmicks. The bar and the tables are nailed together from rough boards, and it looks very nearly like the old sheep hut up on Old Baldy Hill. I follow Magda in and hold the door for Kinga. I don't know what time it is, but even the skinheads must be tired, because there they are, a group of foreigners in full view, hardly garnering a glance.

"For God's sake, shut the door," someone shouts. "It's cold out there."

I turn. Kinga is frozen in the doorway.

"Come on," I say. I pull her into the room. Kinga's hand is stiff and cold through the knit of our gloves.

"I can't, I'm too embarrassed," Kinga says, and she goes back outside to wait in the passageway. I want to leave with her. My nerves have suddenly got the best of me. But Magda is already striding across the room toward the table of the Englishmen, and I can't leave her here by herself.

"Jezus Maria, would you shut the door?" someone shouts. "In or out."

There's an entire winter's worth of cellar smoke swirling behind Magda as she walks. I pull the door shut from the grip of the wind and stay a few steps behind. Ronan is sitting at the head of the table, a broad smile on his face, his booming voice welcoming her, perhaps offering to buy us a beer. I can only salvage a few words from the pile of English accumulating between them, but I understand what is happening by watching the ruddy faces of the rest of the Englishmen, who only turn to each other and snicker, roll their eyes, and take another sip of beer. Ronan's expression slowly spreads into a smirk. My face flushes with embarrassment for her and for me.

But Magda isn't self-conscious at all. She doesn't seem to care that we are the only women in this bar, that she is yelling in English and no one is even listening to her anymore. And watching her and the table of Englishmen, thinking about Kinga shivering outside in the cold, something happens inside me. I feel the flush of shame slowly condensing into rivulets of resentment. Kinga's, Tadeusz's, Magda's, mine. It's the resentment of an entire country, the muddied expectations of a whole generation collecting in the great cavern in my belly, seething, simmering, bubbling.

"Why you anger, little girl?" One small Englishman at the end of the table speaks up in broken Polish. "If you Polish girls no want proposition, tell friends stop accept our offers."

"*Co?*"

Magda and the table of Englishmen turn to look at me. The small one shrugs and continues. "Every girl have price. Only difference if we say enough high. You. You and friend here have price too."

Everything rushes into my head at once, including Irena's cats. "You smug *skurwysyn*. You shithead, frog-face, devil, sonofabitch, villain, hooligan, tyrant. You think you can have any Polish girl you want? You think you can take advantage of us because you have pounds and we have złote?"

There are twenty or so Polish men in the bar, all of them looking our way now. The Englishmen are quiet.

"Well, we are *not* all *zdzira*s. My friend Kinga didn't have her price. *We* don't have our price." Magda is staring at me with her mouth open. "Learn history. We Poles have fought against the oppressor again and again. For *centuries*. And now that we have our

242

freedom, we are not going to be turned into prostitutes by a bunch of pickle-faced *skurwysyn*s ..."

The men at the bar are coming off their stools. They are stocky and tall, clean-shaven and mustachioed, young and old.

"We fought against Napoleon. We fought against the Nazis. We fought against the Ottomans, the Turks, the Soviets, the Russians before they were Soviets, the Cossacks before they were Russians ..."

I glance sideways at Magda.

"The Tatars," she whispers.

"The Tatars!"

"The Prussians," she whispers.

"And the Prussians!"

"The Swedes."

"The Swedes?"

She nods.

"The Swedes!"

"Young lady." The bartender interrupts me. He's built like a barrel, his head shaved clean. "Young lady," he repeats. "I think we understand the scenario now. I think we will take it from here."

A few of the Englishmen grab their coats, but their path is blocked. One of the men leads Magda and me out.

"Have a nice evening, girls," he calls after us, as if we are stepping out after the theater. The door thuds shut behind us and we hear the iron bar slide into place.

Kinga is sitting on the ledge in the passageway. The smoke hangs in a cloud around her face, and the end of the cigarette glows bright red as she takes a final drag.

"Well?" she says.

Magda grabs her by the elbow. "Come on."

Kinga scrapes the end of the cigarette against the wall and puts the butt in her pocket. We hurry through the passageway, and the distant shouts and the scraping of chairs follow us.

"What happened? What happened?"

Magda tells her everything she said, word for word. "And then Baba Yaga started. *Cholera*, you should have seen her! She went all the way back to the Cossacks!"

"The Cossacks?" Kinga laughs.

"And then the men in the bar got up and told us that they would finish it for us. Oh, it was great! I wish you could have seen their faces when they realized they were going to have the next generation of Englishmen beaten out of them!"

"Really?" Kinga is jumping up and down, her hands bouncing in her coat pockets. "Really?"

"I swear. You should have seen it."

Magda and Kinga grab each other's shoulders and jump up and down like schoolgirls, laughing. The few figures on the street turn and look.

"Come on. Let's go celebrate," Magda says.

"Let's!" Kinga is smiling so widely, she's nearly biting a hole in her lip from happiness.

"I'm going home," I say.

"You're *what?*"

"I'm going home."

"You can't go home!"

"Yes, don't go home!"

"I'm tired."

"Oh, come on!"

"We need to celebrate!"

But for me, there is nothing to celebrate. I thought telling the Englishmen off would be cathartic, but the anger and resentment have not dissipated. There is no Happy End. After everything is finished tonight, I'm still only a village girl, a *góralka* with a strange name who can't remember her history, and the three of us are all just bar girls, our futures looming large in front of us and then abruptly falling away. I think about our dismal chances for admission to Jagiellonian, about Kinga's dream of fleeing the country, about the Polish girls flitting around the empty table at Stash's, lost without the Englishmen. I think about the video camera sitting on the shelf above my bed at Irena's, its little glass eye boring through me every time I walk into the room. And I already know that none of us will make films or argue a case in court or go abroad or become the next great *klarnecista*. Not now, not ever.

"Come on, Baba Yaga. Just one drink."

But I leave Magda and Kinga protesting in the street, and make my way home alone.

35

Work Just Like Stalin Taught You

ANIELICA HAD CAREFULLY constructed the moment of their arrival in her mind. Under the glass globe of her imagination, she had laid miniature stones for the Rynek and constructed tiny versions of the cloth merchants' hall, the city tower, and St. Mary's Church. She had set well-dressed women to walking, their long legs stretching out in front of them as if testing the water, she had created families feeding pigeons, merchants opening shops, and school groups holding hands in long chains, undulating across the expanse of bluestone. Under her glass globe, the tiny Wawel Dragon yawned smoke and flames, the Lajkonik galloped haltingly, and St. Jadwiga walked around barefoot, the coolness from the stones seeping through the soles of her feet.

But the scene in front of her when they got off the bus looked nothing like the scene in her mind. Buses choked and sputtered to a stop. The humid air stank of petrol fumes, unfiltered cigarettes, and human stench. Grimy hands groped for their lumpy bags and struggled to drag them out of the way. Pigeons turned around in helpless circles, pecking at crumbs. Anielica stood on her tiptoes and squinted across the depot, half expecting someone to appear out of the mass and greet them, welcome them, acknowledge the glow she felt radiating from her skin, the luminosity that marked them as special, that singled out that morning as something momentous.

But they were met only by gray, mediocre indifference. Indifference that they had left their loyal Tatras and their beloved families for this, indifference that they had sacrificed so much for Mother Poland, had taken the biggest risk of their lives, which would surely end in triumph.

Wouldn't it?

As they stood off to the side and looked around, the truth sank in that they were hardly extraordinary. Nearly everyone else milling about the depot had also left a real life behind for an imagined one in Krakow. They had all left their villages alone, had all arrived alone, and now they would all have to find their way in the city alone.

Unlike Anielica, the Pigeon seemed neither surprised nor disappointed. He had never built a glass globe of the city. He had one ideal, and that was Anielica, one goal, and that was her future comfort. He immediately stepped off the bus and went to work, stacking their packs and their suitcases, one atop the other, beneath the overhang of the depot. There were similar nests of luggage piled all along the edge of the building, and similar clusters of relatives gathered around nervously, for they too had only thought this far, or perhaps as far as the Rynek, and nothing more.

"What next?"

"What are we to do?"

"Where should we go?"

"What's going to happen to us?"

"Maybe we shouldn't have come."

In the end, the Pigeon took charge, vanquishing the fear and indecision that threatened to nibble away at them. "I'll go and see what I can see. You stay here."

So the rest of them settled in to wait. They were spine straight and alert at first, scanning the figures entering through the gate of the yard, trying to pick out the Pigeon's awkward gait, the way his toes kissed and his heels kicked out slightly to the side. Half an hour passed. An hour. Still he did not return. Their posture slumped, the women sat down, the sharp circle of the sun smeared across the afternoon sky, and the pile of luggage spread, leaking a hat here, a crust of bread there, a soft potato, a book, a handkerchief, as the time stretched and their needs surfaced. The buses came and went, and little Irenka stared in wonder at the hulking metal shells, reaching her hand out to touch their sides even though she was not allowed to leave the sidewalk.

If they had come sixty years later, the exact spot they were sitting on would be inside a megamall, and they could have occupied a few hours wandering from Timberland to Swatch to H&M, drinking cappuccinos, text messaging back to the village, and debating about whether the Twins would still be in office after the elections. But as it was, there was nothing to do but sit and wait. When Irenka grew bored of the buses, she began running in circles on the sidewalk, grasping wildly for the pigeons, who calmly stepped out of her path. Anielica grew more nervous, sitting and standing and sitting again, chewing on the inside of her mouth, contorting her Cupid's-bow lips into a scowl.

"It has been too long," she finally said. "Władysław Jagiełło, go after him."

Her brother laughed nervously. "You act like it is the village, Nela, like I can go into the woods and shout his name and he will hear me. In the city, he could be anywhere, and if I start calling after him, they will only look at me as if I am insane."

"He's right," Marysia's father said.

There had been stories recently of men abandoning their families, of being so overwhelmed with endings and beginnings and being caught in the middle that the only solution was to get away. Anielica chewed more vigorously on the inside of her mouth.

"I'm sure he's fine," Władysław Jagiełło reassured her. "I was in the woods with him for five years, and there was never anything he couldn't manage. We just need to wait a little while longer, and I'm sure he will be back any time now." But the words coming from his mouth were too abundant to be reassuring. Reassuring words were tall, sparse, stoic. "Don't be silly." "He's fine." "Trust me." But Anielica did not press. She knew that her brother was worried too. She had noticed the furrows in his forehead deepening, his eyebrows slowly creeping upward for the past hour.

The Pigeon finally returned in the late afternoon with a broad smile and a paper cup of ice cream that made Anielica feel silly for ever worrying. He gave the ice cream to Irenka, and the birds clustered around her on the sidewalk, just as the five adults gathered around the Pigeon. There were thousands of people out there, he explained. Thousands. Soldiers and civilians, Russians and Poles, Krakowians and villagers, some just passing through, others there for good. The Pigeon had spent the first hour or so running to and fro, asking each person this or that, trying to catch the tails of fleeting rumors and follow them to their source. It was a frustrating way to get all the information he needed, one scrap at a time, and eventually he had realized that all he had to do was stand in the middle of the street, listening to the conversations passing by, tuning in to them like competing radio frequencies, and piecing them together. After an hour of standing in the middle of the newly named Battle of Lenin Street, he had found out where they could find beds and meals, where to apply for their partisan legitimizations, how Marysia's parents could register with the Red Cross, what the likelihood of emigration was, and how long the backlog for weddings.

"Let's go," he said. "Lots to do. No time to waste." Tall, sparse, stoic, reassuring words. Anielica smiled and added their wedding day to the scene under the glass globe.

At first they had to stay in the temporary barracks, the women separated from the men, meeting up to take their meals either in the army canteen or one of the Red Cross tents. But each week there was progress, each week they gained a footing in the muddy future. By the end of the first week, Marysia's parents were registered with the Red Cross. By the end of the second week, the Pigeon and Władysław Jagiełło had their legitimizations that they had officially fought for the communist People's Army and not the Polish Home Army, their first lesson in rewriting history to make it more palatable. By the end of the third week, they were already working, building state flats as fast as people could occupy them, and by the end of the fourth, Marysia and Anielica had jobs in a small sewing concern, and Irenka was playing with her classmates in one of the newly opened preschools.

Life in the city moved blindingly fast. There was no time for leisure. The men held down their state construction jobs during the day and did private repairs and *remont* at night. Anielica and Marysia sewed uniforms: police uniforms, custodian uniforms, bus-driver uniforms, scout uniforms. In the New Poland, everyone had to have a uniform, and the women hunched over their machines for twelve hours a day to keep up, leaving only at suppertime for another job working on the black at the Old Theater, replacing the costumes that had been destroyed or stolen or used for emergency clothing during the war.

Work, work, work, and once again work. They all lived in a state of constant soreness and sleep deprivation, and the few hours that were not taken up by work were spent perfecting the art of *załatwić:* cobbling together favors, friends of friends, bribes, gifts, and access. Anything was possible if you knew the right people, and thanks to their connections in the Resistance, the Pigeon and Władysław Jagiełło were more successful than most. By the end of July, Marysia's parents were able to emigrate to a Scandinavian town with the *o*'s slashed out of the name as if they were mistakes. And by mid-August, their connections had managed to move the remaining five Half-Villagers up through the housing list and into a small but sunny communal flat overlooking Bishop Square.

The only time they surfaced was on Sunday mornings, when they would wake up late enough to see the parapets of the *kamienice* across the street glinting in the sunlight. It became the Pigeon and Anielica's habit to take Irenka for long walks on Sunday mornings so Marysia and Władysław Jagiełło could squander an hour or so of privacy in bed. The Pigeon and Anielica found their privacy then too, in the crowds of young families wandering the shaded Planty hand in hand, the children lagging behind and running ahead, always drawn back by invisible apron strings. In a crowd, who could know that they weren't married? Who could say that the dark girl between them had not been infused with a recessive gene from the subterranean roots of their family tree? So many wedding rings had been sold or lost in the war that even their naked fingers did not draw any attention. Who could know that Anielica still retained her father's surname? Or that at night the Pigeon still slept on the floor next to Anielica's mattress? Who could see the questions that hung over Anielica as they walked, the darkest one being why the Pigeon seemed utterly unhurried to seal their life together?

As they walked through the park next to the Square of the Invalids one Sunday morning, Anielica tried to distract herself by looking at the trees, at the makeshift kiosks along Aleje, at the toddlers squatting around the fountain, at the locked hands of the other couples. But instead of calming her, they only agitated her, the little chil-

dren an accusation of her barrenness, the other couples an indictment of her non-marriage with the Pigeon. Suddenly, she began
walking faster, and little Irenka had to double skip to keep up. The
Pigeon's grip tightened around her hand.

"Hey, hey, slow down. What's the hurry?"

She turned to him, and tears welled up in her eyes.

"What's the matter? Anielica? What's the matter?"

The bells of a nearby church began to peal, slowly and methodically. Anielica squeezed back her tears and swallowed the lump in
her throat.

"We're going to be late for Mass."

"I thought we'd go to a different church today."

"And Marysia and my brother? They'll be worried sick when they
can't find us at St. Mary's."

"We'll meet them afterward."

"I don't want to meet them afterward. I want to meet them now."

He stopped in the middle of the sidewalk and held her hand to
his chest. She set her muscles stiff against him. The other church was
half a block away, and as the bells grew louder and more insistent,
they blocked out everything else. Irenka broke away from them and
ran up ahead. The Pigeon mouthed Anielica's name again.

"Mamo!" she heard between the bells.

She turned to see her brother and Marysia standing on the steps
of the church with a bouquet of lilies and a picnic basket. Irenka
was pulling at Marysia's hand, stretching out her arm, testing if her
mother could support her weight.

"But . . . what are you doing here? How did you know we would
be here?"

"Anielica," the Pigeon said. "We're finally getting married today."

"On a Sunday?" was all she could think of to say.

"We have a special dispensation. I tried to arrange a ceremony just
for us, but there's such a backlog, it would have taken months."

"Today?"

"Right now."

It was a communal ceremony with nine other couples, and when
they exited the church, the handfuls of coins produced a deafening
metallic storm. Coins that people had saved from before the war,
coins that were worth next to nothing now, except in the number of

children they foretold. The other couples squatted on the sidewalk, scooping up as many as they could, and later, on, when they tried to have children, Anielica would blame herself for not doing the same. Instead, the Pigeon and Anielica stood there, clinging to each other in the middle of the chaos, like two halves of a countersign.

"You see? Everything is going to be okay," the Pigeon said, leaning down to have a look at her. She caught his lips with hers and kissed him in a way that would have sent Pani Plotka's tongue wagging, and she held on to him for a long time afterward, examining his face as if she had not seen him since before the war.

There was no money for a proper *wesele*, but from the church, the Pigeon and Anielica walked hand in hand to the Błonia. It was an immense, open cow pasture at the edge of the city, and on a sunny day in 1979, in an event that barely garnered a mention on the state-controlled television news, two million people would gather there to celebrate Mass with the newly installed pope. Some would even call that day the true end of the war.

But that afternoon in 1945, instead of two million, there were only the two of them, celebrating their own private communion. Marysia had helped the Pigeon pack the basket full of bread, sausage, plums, a bottle of Hungarian wine, and a volume of French poetry. They had no special dishes at home, and so the Pigeon and Marysia had borrowed from the theater a yellow damask tablecloth, two settings of china, and crystal glasses from the upcoming production of *Pan Tadeusz*. The Pigeon led Anielica all the way to the middle of the vast field, and there they spent the afternoon stretched out on the yellow damask, eating, drinking, and kissing, reading from the volume of poetry and lying flat on their backs, looking up into the immense sky. They stayed there through the afternoon, until the sun set over the Kościuszko Mound and the stars began to prick the darkness. No work to be done, no sheep to tend to, and no gossip to follow them, for they were now husband and wife.

36

Śmigus Dyngus

RONAN AND THE ENGLISHMEN don't come back to Stash's, and after the initial euphoria of telling them off, Kinga slumps into a depression, smiling less and slouching more, as if she's cupping her tiny body into a windbreak for her heart.

"Are you still going to try to go to England?" I ask. "Through your friend in London?"

"Why would I want to go to *Pieprzona* England now? I don't even want to learn English anymore. They're probably all perverts. Why would I want to talk to a whole island full of perverts?"

"Well, are you going to try to go abroad some other way?" I ask her. "To someplace other than *Pieprzona* England?"

"What's the point?"

"So, what are you going to do then?" Magda prods.

"What do you mean, what am I going to do? I'm going to be a bar girl, of course." She props her chin on her hand, staring vacantly out at the tables. "Just like I always have been."

After that, Magda and I don't say anything more to her about it, and with our silence, it feels as if we're leaving her for dead.

To say the truth, ever since the Night of the Cossacks, as Magda refers to it, sometimes I feel as hopeless as Kinga. Maybe it's only the dark, empty streets of late winter, but it starts to feel like my entire life is a television retrospective, nothing to look forward to, all the people I was once close to parading by, stuck on one of those moving walkways like they have in Warsaw now. My parents. Nela. My classmates from *liceum*. My neighbors. Tadeusz. Even Irena, now that she is going out all the time and seeing Stash on the sly. And I think that's why I keep studying like crazy for the stupid geography exam, why I try to be optimistic and hopeful when I'm around Magda. So she won't leave me for dead too.

She still comes to Stash's after work almost every night. Sebastian appears only once every couple of weeks, but even when he's not there, I can still see his effect on her. Some girls turn to wet flour when they fall for someone, their thoughts always coating the boy in question, their words flaccid and vague. But when Magda decides on Sebastian, it ignites something in her eyes, so they light up not only when she talks about him, but when she talks about everything else too. She speaks with confidence about next year, when — not if — we will both be at Jagiellonian, meeting after class, sharing the same group of friends. Nela used to say that routine can stick to your boots, and that's what the end of the winter feels like for me, each step its own individual struggle. But Magda uses her routines to pick up momentum, as if she's on sleigh runners, slipping easily through the grooves, the wind filling her nostrils and clearing her eyes. Everything that happens to her, good and bad, is part of her destiny, and she doesn't seem surprised at all when one night, Sebastian leans over the bar on his way out and invites us to a party.

"What kind of party?" Magda asks, as if there is something to be considered.

"A Śmigus Dyngus party."

"Śmigus Dyngus? Who in the world has a Śmigus Dyngus party?"

"We do. Can you come?"

"We?"

"My roommate and I. You remember. Tomek."

"I don't know," Magda says coquettishly. "We will just have to see how many *other* Śmigus Dyngus parties we get invited to before we commit to just one."

Sebastian smiles at her. He has a great smile, bone white and straight, like the American movie stars, and for a split second, I'm jealous that it's Magda who has coaxed it out of him. He writes down the address on a paper napkin.

"Hope you can make it," he says, and I secretly wish that I'd claimed him before Magda.

I take the tram to and from the university library on Easter Monday in order to avoid the gangs of little boys patrolling the streets with their buckets and milk bags. By the time I come back home, Magda is already locked in the bathroom.

"You'll have to wash out of the kitchen sink," Irena says. "That door's been locked for longer than the Berlin Blockade."

There's a towel draped over the coffee table, and Irena is ironing a light green blouse.

"Are you going out with Stash tonight?"

"That's none of your business."

"*Mamo*, it's not like it's a secret anymore." Magda emerges from the bathroom, damp and pink and smelling of spring. She's wearing a black strapless dress and strappy heels, both premature for the season. "You're wearing jeans?" she asks me.

"At least someone knows how to cover her *dupa*," Irena says.

"This *dupa*?" Magda arches her back and thrusts her hip out.

Irena looks up from her ironing. "You could serve tea off that *dupa* you've got it stuck out so far."

"That's not all it's useful for." She leans into the mirror in the hall and puts on her mascara.

Irena rolls her eyes. "Just don't let her shake any bushes tonight, Baba Yaga."

"Why Magda?" I ask. "Aren't you worried about me shaking any bushes?"

"Phooh," Irena says. She holds the blouse up to the light. "If a boy brought you to the bushes, you'd probably start talking about botany, or some film you saw once with a bush in it."

"I would not."

"But this one . . ."

"I heard that, *mamo*."

"Then stop eavesdropping."

"I'm not eavesdropping. You didn't even bother to say it behind my back."

"Turn around then."

"You act like I'm completely irresponsible. Name one irresponsible thing I've done," Magda says. "Besides failing out of university."

Irena takes off her shirt and changes into the blouse. "Just because I don't know about it doesn't mean you haven't done it."

"Just because you imagine it doesn't mean it's true."

"Well, Baba Yaga will be my insurance. Just in case."

Magda and I take the number 13 tram down to Kazimierz, taking care to sit near the driver's cage for protection. Magda checks the address on the napkin, and we get off at Joseph Street. It's only eight o'clock or so, and any other day, there would be shoppers and late-night workers filling and emptying the trams. On Easter Monday, though, most of the shops are closed, and the streets are deserted save a few, brave, mostly middle-aged women.

We walk down the middle of Joseph Street, swapping Śmigus Dyngus stories on the way. Magda tells me about the full-out water wars in Park Jordana when she was in elementary school, and I tell her about how Nela and I would sleep with a watering can next to our bed and try to be the first one up in the morning.

"Who won?"

"Most years she did. I'd wake up and she'd already be standing over me with the watering can." Magda laughs. "But the year my mother died, she pretended to be asleep, and she let me get up first and soak her."

We turn onto a cobblestone street, and Magda takes the crook of my arm and steps carefully in her heels.

"You really miss her, don't you?" Magda asks. "Nela, is it?"

"Yes."

"How did she die?"

"Heart failure. I was working at the cinema in Osiek by then. And I came home one day and she was gone."

"You were the one who found her?"

"No. My Uncle Jakub. The one who's not quite right in the head. He went and got Pani Wzwolenska, our neighbor, and she waited for me to come home. All the neighbors knew before I did. I was the last to know."

"You were working."

I can feel the slight warmth on my scalp as we pass below each streetlamp. I remember coming through the door, ready to tell Nela all about the film, and instead Pani Wzwolenska was sitting up waiting for me, her hands flat and still, resting on the big larch table. Just waiting. As soon as I came in the door, I knew.

"Baba Yaga? Are you okay?"

I've stopped in the middle of the street. I look her square in the face. "I wasn't working."

"What do you mean? You just said . . ."

"I lied. I was there watching a film. Just because. Just for fun. I told everyone else I was working that night. Only Nela knew I wasn't."

I start to cry right there in the middle of the street. Magda puts her arms around me, and I can feel her shivering in her thin dress and coat.

"You didn't know that would be the day. You didn't know."

"I should have."

"She probably wouldn't have wanted you there anyway."

"I still should have been there. Whether she wanted it or not." I feel Magda's arms tighten around me, and I wonder at how close we've become.

There's a noise behind us, and we both turn around. There are three of them, not more than eleven or twelve years old. They have an entire arsenal of plastic soda bottles, buckets, watering cans, and milk bags refilled with water, the tops pinched shut.

"Get out of here, you little jerks," Magda growls. "Can't you see now is not the time for your stupid little games?"

One of the milk bags lands at our feet, splashing the water up to our calves.

"Shit."

"Run!"

I run for several blocks, the wet bottoms of my jeans stiffening, the tears cold on my cheeks, the sound of Magda's heels clicking behind me. On Sylwester, I felt as if I was running toward something, but now I am running away. I run and I run until my lungs no longer hurt, until the salt dries and stings my cheeks, until I have the sensation of breathing through my skin. Magda's footsteps and her voice echo far behind, and I stop. The street is peaceful, the windows in the flats above rubbed warm with light.

"I think we lost them," Magda says, when she catches up. She is soaking wet and breathing heavily.

"They really got you."

"Are you okay?" she asks.

I nod.

"Do you want to go home?"

"I'll be fine."

"Are you sure?"

"I'm sure."

I think she's relieved. We find the right address. We're both a mess, me wiping my cheeks and nose with the back of my glove, Magda trying to clean up her makeup and fluff her hair, which is already clumping into dark icicles.

Sebastian opens the door before we even knock, as if he's been watching through the window.

"Śmigus Dyngus," he says.

"Śmigus Dyngus."

"Looks like someone got *śmigus-dyngus*ed on the way over." And he laughs.

We are painfully early. The flat is empty except for a few voices in the other room, and Sebastian shows us to the bathroom and offers us plush towels from a rack mounted on the wall. It's a Western bathroom — the toilet, sink, and bathtub all in one room — huge and freshly *remont*ed in creamy tile and chrome.

We clean up a little, and I feel relaxed and a little tired after crying. Sebastian comes back with drinks and takes us around the rest of the flat. It's twice the size of the flat on Bytomska, and I can tell that it impresses Magda too, that she's trying to quash her amazement as we walk through the rooms and see the glowing parquet floors, the Western beds, the light Swedish furniture, and the computer.

"What's that?" I ask, pointing to the machine next to the computer.

"It's a fax machine. You just put a piece of paper in here, dial a number, and it comes out in another fax machine anywhere in the world."

"*Niesamowite.*"

"Really. It's true." He smiles.

"Have you ever in your life seen anything like that?" I ask Magda. After working myself up on the street, I can now feel the relief washing through me, disentangling my nerves so that everything that reaches them seems light and simple and carefree.

"Of course," Magda says, but I know she's lying.

"It's my roommate's."

"Tomek?"

"Uh-huh."

"What does he do?"

"He's a *biznesmen*."

"What kind of business?"

Sebastian shrugs and laughs. "Nothing interesting enough to talk about."

The kitchen is also newly *remont*ed, with a big island in the middle. Sebastian introduces us to a few girls who are sitting on stools at the counter, and one of the girls scowls at Magda and me.

"And you remember Tomek from New Year's."

Tomek is in a chair off to the side, with a girl sitting in his lap. They are staring into each other's eyes, perfectly still.

"Clothed tantric positions," Sebastian says. "Ignore them."

Magda raises her eyebrows.

"I know," he says. "Try *living* here."

"Sebastian, honey," one of the girls calls from the island. She's a brunette with beady eyes and a pointy nose. "I need another drink."

"Certainly, Pani," he says, and he bows as he takes her glass.

"Do you think that brunette in the kitchen was his girlfriend?" Magda whispers. It's nearing midnight, and we're sitting on the Western bed in one of the bedrooms. I feel relaxed and awake after a few drinks, but Magda is sullen. Most of the others at the party are from Jagiellonian or the Academy of Metallurgy and Mining, and they all seem to know each other. The flat has filled up since we came, and Sebastian has been in constant motion, pouring drinks and fetching fresh towels for the ones who arrive sopping wet.

"No. Definitely not. Did you see the way he looked at her? 'Certainly, Pani.' You wouldn't say that to a girlfriend. Not one you liked anyway."

Magda fingers her crinkled hair. "Do I look okay?"

"You look great," I tell her. But really, she looks terribly out of place in her dress and heels. Everyone else at the party is wearing jeans and the bulky sweaters and thick, rubber-soled shoes that have been popular all winter.

"Are you sure?"

"Sure."

"But he hasn't looked at me twice all evening."

"He's just busy. I'm sure he'll be around."

When he eventually reappears, Magda sits up, and all trace of self-consciousness is gone.

"Enjoying the party?" He sits down on the edge of the bed next to Magda.

"It just got better," Magda says, and she turns to face him.

"And you?" He looks over at me. He has the most beautiful eyes, the color of wood buffed and polished over the years with stain and wax.

"I can't believe how many people are here."

"You didn't have parties like this in the village?"

"Did you?"

He laughs. "The only parties we ever had were Darek Wesołowski and I hiding behind the church drinking *bimber*."

"You were that boy."

"I was that boy."

And we start to talk about our villages. His is filled with coal miners instead of *górale*, but as we talk, we discover that there is a Pan Cywilski in Sebastian's village too. An Uncle Jakub. A Pani Wzwolenska. A Pan Romek. And it's comforting to talk about them, as if they and Nela are once again gathered all around me.

Magda stares at me as I talk. I can tell she's getting impatient, crossing and recrossing her legs. I stand up.

"I think I'm going to visit the bathroom."

"Visit the bathroom?" He looks at me strangely.

"Is that okay?"

"Sure. I'll come with you."

"I'm sure I'll find it on my own."

"I'll just show you."

"It's really not necessary."

I can feel Magda seething, and I don't want to turn around to see her face. Sebastian leads me out into the hallway. He bangs on the bathroom door and shouts for whoever is in there to open up. He pulls me in and shuts the door behind, and I'm shocked for a split second, until it dawns on me that there are five other people in there, sitting on the edge of the tub and the lid of the toilet, and then I'm shocked all over again. The air is sweet and greasy, and it takes me a minute to realize what's going on.

"This *is* what you meant, right?"

I nod. I can't bring myself to tell him that I really just wanted to go to the bathroom. I feel his warmth as he towers over me. I look around and see the others staring at me, and I remember what Irena said, that *głupstwa są najpiękniesze,* and I wonder if this is one of the stupid things I will look back on one day and smile about. One of the girls sharing the lid of the toilet begins laughing hilariously as if she's just read my mind.

Sebastian leans over so his face is only a few centimeters from mine. I can smell his cologne mixing with the smoke, and he smells like a real *chłopisko,* like he's just finished splitting logs or carrying a child across a stream. "You have smoked before?"

"Of course."

Sebastian makes a clicking noise with his tongue, and two boys on the edge of the tub get up. We sit down, and he pulls a pipe out of his pocket and fills it generously with *trawa,* pressing it down with his thumb. He puckers his lips around the stem, lights it, and takes several short, quick pulls. It's a beautiful pipe, meticulously carved, and the bowl glows a deep orange. He covers the stem with his thumb and hands it to me.

I can hardly feel the smoke going down, and it lands softly in my lungs. After a few puffs, I can feel it lifting me up and out from the inside, and I find myself concentrating harder and harder, as if my thoughts are the only thing holding gravity in place.

"Good, isn't it? Strong."

I nod. He sounds like one of the television commercials, and I laugh.

"What?" He gives my side a little pinch. He smokes a little too, then passes it back to me. One of the boys on the floor is telling a story that loops around and around with no ending in sight, and the others keep interrupting him. The two girls sharing the toilet lid look at me and whisper.

I lean in so my mouth is a few centimeters from Sebastian's ear, so close I can feel the narrow isthmus of air between us collapsing and falling into the sea. "Do you want to know the truth?"

"Yes."

"This is the most beautiful bathroom I have ever seen in my entire life."

He laughs. "Me too."

"Can I tell you something else?"

"Yes," he whispers. He leans closer, and I can feel his thigh pressing against mine, his hair brushing against mine.

"I just wanted to go to the bathroom."

We laugh so hard that I nearly slip back into the tub. He catches me with his arm, and when we stand up, it's still around my shoulders, and I have to keep my own arm from floating up to catch his waist.

"You should have said so. There are public toilets in the courtyard for that."

"I must remind you terribly of why you left the village," I say.

His arm cinches around me. "Maybe what I miss."

He smiles down at me, and for a moment, I think he might try to kiss me. But I think of Magda, and I duck out from under his arm.

"Do you want me to take you out to the courtyard?"

I shake my head. The *trawa* is bubbling through my veins, lifting my body, and I'm struggling to pin myself back down to the earth. "I'll find it. Just check on Magda for me, okay?"

The public toilets off the courtyard are dim and unheated, and I can see my breath. The mirror above the sink is streaked, the silver eaten away along the edges, and I stand in front of it for a long time, watching the puffs of breath escape my mouth. I start a contest with myself, trying to make each puff bigger than the last until I notice that I'm out of breath, panting at my own reflection. I laugh, and the girl in the mirror laughs back. But she seems only vaguely familiar, and I try to pull my own face back from wherever it is, lost behind the mirror. I scrunch my features together and frown so I look more like the Baba Yaga of the fairy tales. I turn my head to the side, tip my chin down and pout my lips like a Hollywood starlet. I look into the old mirror and try to see the little girl Nela saw. I try to see what Tadeusz saw. What Irena sees. Magda. And what about Sebastian? Why is he even interested in me? Why is he interested in me and not Magda, not the brunette in the kitchen, not any other girl at the party? And is he even interested in me, or do I just remind him of the village, or is he just high? And why do I feel this for him? Would I like him the same if Magda didn't swoon over him? Am I a bad friend, or do these things just happen? How did I get from there to here? I struggle to pull my thoughts free from the net of *trawa* cast over me. Am I supposed to be the witch or the starlet, the hero or the villain, the star or the sidekick?

I don't know how long I stand in the bathroom.

"Where have you been?" Magda asks. She's sulking on one of the sofas in the living room, watching a boy do some sort of Russian or Jewish kicking dance at the other end of the room. Tomek and his girlfriend are on the sofa opposite with a box of matches, lighting them one by one and extinguishing them with their fingertips.

"To the bathroom. I told Sebastian to come and check on you."

"Well, he didn't."

"He didn't?"

"Come on," she says. "I'm done. Let's go."

"But what about Sebastian?"

She waves her hand dismissively. "I barely talked to him all night. If we leave, it will at least be a good excuse to find him and say good-bye."

We look for him for a long time, but he seems to have vanished back into the bathroom, so finally, we just leave. We walk home the way we came, down Joseph Street and Starowiślna, the streets and sidewalks abandoned, the little boys and their buckets safe inside until next year. The streetlights are already off, the trams have stopped running, and Magda is shivering in her dress and heels.

"What a complete waste," she says, and the end of her cigarette lights up the darkness.

When we get home, Magda goes straight to bed. I knock on the translucent panel of the living-room door to say good night to Irena.

"*Chodź*," she calls. She's on the phone, her stocking feet propped up on the coffee table. She's wearing her dark green wool skirt with the light green silk blouse, and with her makeup, she looks at least five years younger.

"Can you believe that he left her for Zofia?" she says. "And that she came to the party anyway . . . I know, but could you ever . . . three children, can you imagine?"

She looks up at me and smiles. It's still strange to hear her gossip. I'm used to her talking about pensions and poverty, about communists and former communists and the *pieprzone* capitalists.

"Basia, I have to go. It's so late already . . . yes, yes, next week . . . okay, see you then."

She hands the receiver to me, and I untangle the cord and hang it up for her.

"Where's Magda?"

"She went straight to bed."

"Drunk?"

"On a boy."

"She didn't shake any bushes, did she?"

"No, nothing like that."

"Why do you smell like *trawa*?"

"There was some at the party."

"Did Magda smoke it?"

"No."

"You swear?"

"I swear."

Irena reaches for her tea and takes a sip. "That was my friend, Basia," she says. "We went to a Buddhist party tonight out in Wieliczka."

"Buddhists?"

"You know," she says, clasping her hands in front of her, rolling her eyes back into her head. "Hiya humyay, hiya humyay, bah bah bumyay, bah bah bumyay . . ."

"I know, I know. In Wieliczka, though?"

Irena shrugs. "It's a new world. Anyway, Basia says she knows someone at the pedagogical institute for you if geography doesn't work out."

"Thanks."

"You don't sound very excited."

"I'm just tired." I smile. "Too much *głupstwa* tonight."

She laughs. "Baba Yaga, if anyone could use a little more *głupstwa*, it's you."

37

The Last Sprout on the Potato

I N THE MAIN ROOM of the communal flat on Bishop Square
lived two brothers from Bielsko-Biała and their wives. The older
brother's wife was the prettier of the two. Her name was Bożena, and
she was from the rubble that used to be Warsaw, so she was only too
grateful for a stove to cook on and a husband whose head was so full
of love and loyalty for her that there wasn't room for much else. The
five Half-Villagers got along well with the older brother and Bożena,
and their interactions were full of the small kindnesses and consider-
ations required to live nine people to a toilet. The younger brother,
on the other hand, was bald and pushy, and his wife, a small, pointy-
nosed woman named Gosia, felt it her marital duty to transfer his
pushiness to the rest of the world.

At first, Gosia tried to establish her authority in the flat by passing
herself off to the Half-Villagers as a grande dame of Krakow, with
her proclamations of how it used to be before the war, before the
Germans and the Soviets and the swarms of refugees had taken over.
But one day, as she was in the middle of a story about Jan Matejko
and Stanisław Wyspiański and the mural at Jama Michalika, Bożena
innocently exclaimed that she had never known her sister-in-law
had lived in Krakow before, and Gosia was forced to sheepishly admit that she had been born and raised in a modest village outside
Bielsko-Biała. For a week afterward, she tried to pass herself off as

landed gentry, the land tragically and unfairly ripped from the family, in the manner of nineteenth-century novels, but her maiden name and her manners did not support the plot, and it was not long before she herself ran out of momentum for telling the story. As each day passed, as even her imagined superiority over her flatmates dribbled away and the other three women grew closer, she began grasping for anything, at first trying to leverage her connections — impossible when you had the Pigeon on your side — then her attractiveness — laughable next to a true beauty like Anielica — then her intelligence and wit, which her shallow reservoirs could not support for long.

In the end, there was only one thing left to use. It seeped out slowly, almost imperceptibly at first, tucked into the conversations with the other two women while Marysia was outside with Irenka. First, there were only sighs and clucking, then reactive grumblings, then more audible mutterings of "some people." How *some people* didn't discipline their children, how *some people* didn't pull their weight around the flat, how *some people* used *other people's* soap, pilfering their way straight to the devil, how *some people* did not clean their hairbrushes or brush their teeth or change their sheets often enough. How *some people* should marry other *some people* and *other people* should marry other *other people*. It was clear that she was talking about Marysia, but Marysia, always seeing the best in people, never noticed, even when she was in the room. And Anielica did not tell her.

She did not tell Marysia that Irenka had asked why her grandparents had killed Jesus, or that she had caught Gosia on the shared balcony, peeping in the window as Władysław Jagiełło was dressing. She did not tell her that Gosia's *some people* were also Hitler's *some people*, the same six million *some people* who had been gassed and incinerated, torn sibling from sibling, forced into cellars with the rats, and finally and magnanimously allowed to leave their homelands for countries with the *o*'s crossed out.

But in protecting her sister-in-law, Anielica had to bear the brunt of the attack every day, and so she reverted to the strategy they had used against the Germans. Act as if. Act as if you didn't see them, and they didn't exist. Act as if you didn't understand their language, and they were rendered babbling idiots. Act as if you couldn't feel

Hauptmann Schwein or his lackey on top of you as you made love to your husband, and the images shriveled up immediately. Didn't they? And so Anielica persevered in her silence, which she saw as diplomacy necessary for survival, but which pointy-nosed Gosia wrongly extrapolated into acquiescence and even agreement. As the summer wore on, Gosia began to speak even more directly, sharpening her words on the stone of her ill will, for it turned out in the end that she was looking to replace the Half-Villagers with another couple they knew from Bielsko-Biała.

"It's a wonder how *some people* get placed so quickly by the Housing Authority. It must be nearly impossible if you are not even married. And how can you be married in God's eyes if you are of the race who killed His son? We know a couple who has been waiting for five or six months, pure Polish on both sides. Not a crumb of challah between them, and they arrived in March and are still doing odd jobs, still sleeping on cots like Gypsies, all because *some people* keep cutting ahead of them in line."

Anielica eventually talked to the Pigeon about it in one of their whispered conversations late into the night, and after going around and around, they finally agreed that it was all talk, that the Pigeon had better connections than they did, that Bożena and the older brother were still sympathetic to them, and that it was easier to ignore the other two than *załatwić* another space on the housing list. And so it continued.

"*Some people* don't know their place."

"*Some people* try to jump higher than their heads."

"*Some people* should consider themselves lucky to still be alive."

Some people, indeed.

Going to the Old Theater every night to sew costumes was the best part of Anielica's day. It was only a short walk from Bishop Square, and she and Marysia had time to stop home for a quick supper and to tuck Irenka in. They arrived just after the show ended each night, as the actors were leaving for Jama Michalika. Backstage among the props and scenery, they would work in peace for three or four hours on two old Singer sewing machines.

When they left the flat each night, it was obvious that Bożena wanted to go with them, that she was tired of spending the late evenings with her sister-in-law. She had no sewing skills to speak of, but they offered her a few złote of their pay to press and steam the costumes, their least favorite chore, and she happily agreed.

Anielica would always talk fondly of those nights backstage at the theater, laughing and talking. Bożena would stand at the ironing board, singing songs from Old Poland at the request of the other two women. Anielica would listen, hunched over her work, and try to imagine the people who had raided the wardrobe closet during the war, walking the streets in corsets and knee boots and knickerbockers, confirming the Germans' notion of the Poles as primitive and backward.

Over the months, the songs Bożena sang became weighted with meaning as more and more of them were banned by the communists—subversiveness they called it—and the night the actor who played Iago in *Othello* returned through the back door to retrieve a hat, they nearly fainted from the shock.

"Which one of you was that just singing?" he asked, appearing suddenly from behind a rack of costumes. "Someone was just singing 'Flow, Wisła, Flow.'" The three women froze, and Bożena looked to the other two before answering.

"It was me," she said in a voice that was barely audible.

They held their breath, waiting for him to denounce her, but instead, he began to praise her voice, calling it the chirp of a songbird, the flutter of an angel's wings, and other platitudes that sounded odd coming from a man they had only heard reciting Shakespeare. Nevertheless, the following week, Bożena found herself singing for a small audience of other actors who had stayed back from the café, and there was talk of incorporating her into a new cabaret that was forming.

Gosia always made sure she was cleaning something when they came home at night, as if to make the point that they had been out merely gallivanting and she had been tightening the slack in the rope for the rest of them. She was envious enough when they told her about the job sewing costumes, and she grew downright jealous whenever they talked of seeing this or that actor, but hearing that Bożena had been invited to sing in front of an audience was too much, and new wrinkles stitched themselves into her forehead and around her lips.

"She was singing for the actors?"

"Yes, isn't it wonderful?" Marysia gushed, actually expecting Gosia to be happy for Bożena.

"Subversive songs?"

"Well, who says they are subversive?" Anielica protested. "There has been no official decree."

Gosia's face reddened, and in that moment, it was hard to see what even her husband, ugly little man that he was, saw in her.

"*This,*" she said. "*This* is the last sprout on the potato. I have been diplomatic. I have treated you as members of my own family, but I will not tolerate *this*. I will not allow them to make my sister-in-law an enemy of the state. It is one thing for *some people* to scandalize themselves, but when they begin to corrupt *other people*, that is a different story indeed. You think we don't know who you are? That your husbands are mercenaries? You think we don't know that *she* is Jewish? Where will it end? Who will keep them in line now?"

She would have slammed a door if it had been possible, but in a communal flat, it is difficult to find a door to slam, a dramatic exit to make, unless you want to be locked out. Instead, Gosia sat down on her mattress and crossed her arms defiantly.

The other three women looked at each other. All of them, even Marysia, had finished Gosia's sentence in their minds. *Now.* Now that Hitler was only a mass of black, sticky ash and his ideas swept under the rug of history. Now that the camps were closed and the *Kommandanten* were being hunted down and marched to Nuremberg.

They all went to bed uneasy that night, and even when the men returned and the sun came up, the greasy film of Gosia's words clung to everything in the flat. They could not eat or clean or wash up without being reminded, and the film seemed to spread, coating the lightbulbs and the windows of the flat, so that each day, the sun seemed to rise a little later and set a little earlier, the shadows of the inhabitants lengthened, and the dark circles under their eyes grew more pronounced.

38

The Bermuda Triangle

SPRING COMES IN THE form of progress. A McDonald's opens up at the end of Floriańska Street. A new bar called X-Ray appears beneath the DentAmerica office — the first bar to stay open past two in the morning. The new, bubble-shaped Little Fiat is introduced, making all the old Little Fiats on the streets look boxy. The Japanese cultural center along the Wisła has its grand opening, and people begin murmuring about sushi and ramen and other exotic foods. Word of each development is disseminated quickly throughout the city and monopolizes the small talk once the weather levels out and becomes dull.

I like the *frytki* at McDonald's. I think the new Fiat, the Japanese cultural center, and the yellow phone booths all look nice. Clean. Modern. Western. But as time moves forward, I'm still reluctant, still dragging my feet. I can already feel the dull rumblings of the geography exam from months ahead, and whenever I think about it, I have a feeling of inevitability and finality. Either I will pass it and become a geographer, whatever that is, or I will fail it and fall off into the unknown. I wonder what Nela would say. I wonder if the geography exam is what she imagined for me or if she is looking down at me, smiling grimly in resignation and disappointment. It's been a year since she died. When I first arrived, I felt her with me every day, guiding me through the streets we had talked about so many times. But now that the streets are changing, my memory of her is breaking apart too. In order to remember her face now, I have to conjure up each feature individually and press them together to make a whole, which lasts only a few fleeting seconds. I try to take out the copy of *Germinal* and hear her voice reading the words to me, but there is only a dull monotone, like the one speaker who dubs all the voices on the foreign television programs.

But of course, once you have come this far, you can't go back. The bright future is waiting at the curb, blasting American rap music and European techno from the stereo, and everyone around me seems to have already been seduced. Magda starts talking about when she can earn a salary, buy her own flat, and move out. Stash is thinking about remodeling the club. Irena starts going to cafés as if it is nothing. Even Kinga has moved on, though she is still bitter about England, as if the entire country has left her for a younger woman. Her new friend is Polish, at least twice our age, with a handlebar mustache and a flap of purplish black hair swept over the top of his head like a tarpaulin.

"Who is he?" I ask her.

"Just a friend." She crinkles her nose, and her pale skin streaks light pink, but she never explains. Sometimes he sits at the bar watching her for hours without saying a word, but he always waits for her at the end of the night, and they always leave together.

"Who is he?" I ask Magda one Sunday afternoon as we wait for Irena to finish making dinner.

"Whatever you do, don't ask her."

"I already did."

"You already did?"

"Why?"

Magda laughs. "*Why?* He's her sponsor, that's why."

"Her sponsor?"

Magda raises her eyebrows knowingly.

"*Who* has a sponsor?" Irena demands from the kitchen.

"I do," Magda calls back.

"Well, my daughter, be sure and tell your sponsor we need a

new television. The old one is shot to hell. Cable too. Don't forget the cable."

As the weather warms, the foundations of the city shift and melt beneath me, and I become nostalgic for the frozen ground that held everything in hibernation. I long for the smoky cellars and heavy drapes that all winter long managed to trap both inertia and camaraderie; once the cold releases its grip, people flee their homes and their regular cellar bars and scatter.

I blame it on this reshuffling that Sebastian stops coming to Stash's and starts appearing everywhere else—the bookstore on Pigeon Street, Kino Mikro, the park, the Rynek. Each time I feel guilty, as if I have somehow conjured him up myself, and it's the guilt that makes me pretend not to see him, that makes me hurry up and glance at my wrist as if I have a watch and a place to be. When he calls my name across the square, it's the guilt that makes me act surprised, as if I haven't spent at least part of each day since the Śmigus Dyngus party in his imagined company, as if he doesn't occupy a corner table in my mind.

"Are you sure he hasn't been by Stash's?" Magda asks.

I shake my head. "Although I saw him on the street the other day."

"Where? Why didn't you tell me? How come you get to see him and I don't?"

"I didn't know you were still interested in him."

"Well, I'm not going to give up on fate that easily. Even if she is cruel. Where was he exactly?"

"On the Rynek. Right by Plac Szczepański."

I start to report everything back to her, and the guilt abates. I begin to tell her the particulars of each meeting, and she gobbles them up greedily like one of the pigeons on the market square. I tell her when I see him and where, what he is wearing, what he says, how he looks. The only things I hold back are the smallest, most insignificant details—the fluttering in my stomach as we stand a few feet apart, my nervous smile as we talk, my secret pleasure at the sight of him.

There are a handful of days in my life that I want to erase or throw away or back up and take a running leap over as easily as I used to hurdle the runoff gutters down the mountain to Pisarowice. One of them comes disguised as an ordinary Monday in the middle of May. I'm sitting in the Pink Elephant reading, biding my time until I'm supposed to meet Magda on the Rynek to study. The Pink Elephant is packed; the afternoon lectures have just let out, and I'm at one of the long tables at the back, where already ten people have sat down and gotten up without distracting me from my reading.

"So, I just heard a good joke." I look up. Sebastian clanks his cup and saucer down on the table across from me. He flips the chair backward and sits down on it as if he's mounting a horse. Without even the usual pleasantries, he begins. "So, there's a Polish navy boat cruising around the Baltic, and they get a submarine on their radar."

"You know, I *am* trying to study."

"And the captain sends the young recruit Leszek down to see what type of submarine it is. So Leszek dives down and comes back up, and he says, 'It's an American submarine, sir.' 'Well, how can you tell?' the captain asks, and Leszek says, 'Because there was an American flag on the side and the loudspeakers were playing the American anthem.'"

"I'm serious, Sebastian. I'm going to fail my entrance exam and it's going to be your fault."

He smiles. "You don't want to study geography anyway . . . so, they keep cruising and come into contact with another submarine, and they send poor Leszek down again, and he comes up and says, 'It's a Norwegian submarine.' 'How do you know?' 'Because they were playing the Norwegian anthem and there was a big Norwegian flag painted on the side.'"

I smile. He is so earnest and animated, scooping at the air with his hands each time Leszek dives down and comes back up.

"And they keep cruising until they come into contact with *another* submarine. So they tell poor Leszek to dive down again, and Leszek dives down and comes back up, and he says, 'Sir, it's a Soviet submarine.' 'Let me guess—because they had the Soviet flag on the side and played the Soviet anthem?'"

Sebastian is wearing a denim jacket over a hooded sweatshirt, and with his perfect teeth, he almost looks American. "'No.'" His eyes are illuminated, and his lips spread into a wide smile. "'Because I knocked on the door and they opened it.'"

That's how the afternoon starts, with a joke.

"I'll be right back," he says, and dismounts the chair. "Don't move."

I try to concentrate on the history book again, but when he returns, I'm still on the same paragraph, rereading it, trying to make the words line up in some sort of order.

"Now it's not just an accidental meeting," he says.

He's used his book as a tray, and he unloads another cup of coffee, the cream pitcher, and the sugar bowl, which he's nicked from the counter. "I didn't know how many spoonfuls you take. You like coffee, don't you?"

"This is bribery, you know."

"I know." He smiles, waits for me to spoon some sugar into my cup, and takes it back to the bar. When he comes back, he turns the chair around and sits down. He reaches over and closes my book.

"I was reading that."

"Well then, it's hopeless, because you're still on the same page as when I went to get the coffee."

My face feels hot. "I suppose you never study for your classes."

He shrugs, then reaches over and gently tips up the spine of my book, glancing at the title. "I'm not exactly a student. Officially."

"What do you mean?"

"It's a long story. Basically, I just go and sit in on the lectures, get the reading lists, that sort of thing."

"What do you do then, if you're not a student?"

"Work for Tomek."

"What kind of work?"

He grins. "I guess that's how it is in the New Poland, eh? Always, what do you do? How much do you make? Do you have a VCR?"

"I didn't mean it like that."

"I'm only teasing."

"Because you don't feel like answering the question."

"You got me." He takes a sip of his coffee.

"Why did you say I don't want to be a geographer?"

He shrugs. "It's obvious. You never talk about it. Your friend, Magda, well, you can tell that she really wants to be a prosecutor, but you . . ."

"Speaking of Magda, I'm supposed to meet her in ten minutes."

"Where?"

274

"At Adaś."

Sebastian looks at his watch. "You can stay another fifteen. She has to give you the *kwadrans akademicki*."

I hesitate. And that's how it ends, with my hesitation.

"Do you want to hear another Russian joke?"

Instead of jokes, we talk about how we came to the city. I tell him about appearing on Irena's doorstep clutching her letter. How she didn't ask me any questions about what I planned to do or how long I planned to stay; she simply took my bags and put the kettle on for tea. He tells me about arriving on the late train from Bielsko-Biała and having to spend his first night in the station.

"My parents still don't understand why I would ever want to leave the village," Sebastian says.

"They don't?"

"My father firmly believes that people from big places and people from small places can never completely understand each other."

"Do you think that's true?" I ask.

"Do you?"

"Sometimes."

"Sometimes I feel it here too. Always in New York. My God, you should see New York. New York is Krakow times ten. Times one thousand. I've been there five times already, and each time I go, even though I can see it right in front of me, I still can't even *imagine* how big it is, how fast. Do you know what I mean?"

"That's how I felt standing on Aleje the first time. It took me ten minutes to work up the nerve to cross."

He laughs, and it rumbles right through me. When I think of the other boys my age, they seem large but unformed, their bodies full of the boyish putty that one day might shape itself into a man. But with Sebastian, there's already a hardness in his muscles, a sureness in the way he moves. He holds his gaze straight and steady across the table, and my mind slowly and quietly liquefies. The two girls at the end of the table look over. They've been sneaking glances at us the entire time, and I know that they're jealous of me, of what they think I have.

"I mean, New York is almost like watching a cartoon where the drawings suddenly pop out at you. You'll be crossing the street, and you'll almost get hit by one of those yellow taxis because you don't actually believe that it's real, that it's made of glass and steel. Because the back of your mind keeps telling you that it's only an image from a film. And you just walk around with a stupid grin on your face, shaking your head all day long because it's funny. It's *really* funny. Every time someone says something like 'Okay' or 'Wow!' or 'Have a nice day!' you think they are just saying it to entertain you, just because you are a tourist and that's what you expect them to say. God, I would love to see your face the first time you look up at the skyscrapers there."

I blush.

He smiles. Each time he smiles, it's like he's opening the door a little bit wider, nudging me through.

"*Cholera.* I completely forgot." I stand up and pitch the book into my rucksack. "I have to go. She's going to kill me."

He doesn't move. "Just tell her you were with me. She'll understand."

"I have to go."

He gets up. "I'll go with you. And if she's not still waiting, I'll help you with your history."

He puts his hand firmly on my back, and as we step out onto the street, a gust of wind whips against my cheek as a rebuke. We walk through the Planty, past the university. The light over the tops of the buildings is shifting toward twilight, and the Rynek is in the same state of suspension that it goes through each evening. Half the stores have their gates down; every other flat has the blinds drawn. The flower vendors are nearly packed up, trundling their carts back and forth to the Sukiennice. Two carriage drivers smoke and wait for the truck to take away the horses.

"Wait here. I'll go and check the statue." I cross through the Sukiennice to Adaś. To say the truth, I pray that she's not still waiting for me. I scan the faces. She's not there. As I walk back to the other side of the square, I hold my breath, hoping I will not hear her calling my name. Sebastian is leaning against the stairs of the Ratusz, waiting patiently for me.

"No Magda?"

"No." I try to sound disappointed.

"Wait here," he says, and he disappears into a corner shop. He reappears with a paper sack.

"Vodka?"

He opens the bag a little and lets me peek in. Pepsi.

"Come on. Time to work on your history."

"Where are we going?"

"It's a surprise."

We walk right past Jama Michalika to the end of Floriańska Street, where the shadows of the teenagers dart in and out of the fluorescent light cast by the McDonald's. It's so clean, so bright, it's as if they've managed to find a way to package the daylight, to tag it with a price, and sell it alongside the *frytki*. Sebastian stops in to buy two hamburgers, and I wait for him on the sidewalk with the teenagers.

When he comes back out, he's grinning, and the teenage girls stop their conversation for a moment to look at him.

"Where are we going?"

"You'll see."

He takes my hand and we walk along the city wall until we come to a set of stone steps that have long been chained off. He glances to see if there are any police around.

"Quick," he says. He holds the bags in one hand and helps me over the chain with the other. My heart is racing. A grandmother walking by looks at us disapprovingly but doesn't say anything. We scramble up the stairs and hide in the shadows under the wooden eaves, laughing, and I try to picture Sebastian back in his village, mucking around with his friends. We lean against the rough stone wall, our knees curled up to our chests, just as the king's soldiers and the queen's maids five centuries before. We pass the Pepsi back and forth and eat the hamburgers with the paper wrapped tightly around them, and Sebastian tells me about the city wall and the Czartoryski family. The orange light fades from the sky, the stones turn cold, and still we talk, stopping our conversation only when we see a policeman or a particularly grumpy-looking grandmother or grandfather passing by below.

It isn't as if I haven't considered Magda. She's been on my mind all afternoon — her dark eyebrows like crossed swords, her hands on her hips, her lips thinning their disapproval. But as I reason and justify and dither in my mind, as I minimize the situation and make excuses and concoct lies, time is rushing ahead. Sebastian and I are rushing ahead. He pulls me against him and I settle into his side. His long arms wrap around me, he slides his hands up my arms to my shoulders and tickles the baby hairs at the nape of my neck. He turns me toward him and cradles my cheek with one large palm. And then he kisses me.

I shudder.

"Is everything okay?"

I nod. He leans in to kiss me again, and our lips soften and stiffen, push and pull at each other while his long fingers trace my cheekbones, my jaw, my collarbone. I should stop it. I should tell him about Magda. I should tell him that I have to go. I should tell him something, anything, because then we would be talking and not kissing, and you can't betray your friend by just talking. But something pulls me forward, just like when I was a child climbing trees and I could feel the wavering crown, the thin, weak branches at the top beckoning to me even as the ones below started to give way beneath my feet. I feel his chest thumping, hear his breath thickening in his throat. And then I realize that it's my chest too. My breath.

"Who gives you the right?" a man's voice yells, and I start. "You. Up there on the wall."

Sebastian and I disentangle ourselves and jump up, snatching the hamburger papers and the empty bottle of Pepsi.

"This way," Sebastian says, and we scurry along the wall to the stairs, run down, and jump the chain. He grabs my hand, and we duck into a passageway on St. John's Street. We lean back against the wall, our lungs taking in as much air as they can, our hearts beating through to the stone.

"You know what?" Sebastian says between breaths. "I don't think that was even the police. I think it was only a grandfather."

We laugh, and our voices weave together and echo down the empty passageway. He grabs me and pulls me to him, and we fit together again so easily, as if our hands and our lips remember their places from a previous life. But all of a sudden, it feels like Magda is there with us in the passageway, scowling, her arms folded across her chest.

"I really have to go," I say.

"No you don't," he says, and kisses me again.

"I do."

I pull away, and he reaches over to straighten my collar and brush the hair out of my eyes. We walk to the tram stop next to the Lot Airlines office under the cover of darkness. We stand next to the shelter with our hands in our pockets as shy as if we'd never touched, as if the invisible barrier between us remains, still waiting to be broken.

"You know, we're having another party this weekend. For Juvenalia. On Thursday."

I can already hear the tram scraping along the tracks, the wire crackling overhead. "I have to work on Thursday."

"You can come afterward."

"Okay." My mind is spinning, thinking about what I will tell Magda. We do everything together, and if I go without her, she'll know I'm hiding something.

"Just okay?" He smiles down at me, amused. The tram stops behind me, and I can hear the doors slamming open, footfalls going down and up the metal steps. Just as I turn to get on, he pulls me toward him and kisses me one last time, a kiss that makes me stand on my toes.

"Thursday," he says as I get on the tram. The doors close, the bell clangs, and the wheels start to turn. I think about Tadeusz, and it all seems silly now—holding hands and drinking orange juice, watching movies, talking about dreams and pecking on the lips. None of it real. Out the back window, I watch Sebastian standing there on the curb, getting smaller, and my body buzzes and crackles along with the tram lines overhead, Thursday, Thursday, Thursday, all the way home.

Magda is sitting cross-legged on her bed, her back against the wall, a stack of books at her side supporting an ashtray and a cup of tea.

"I'm sorry, Magda."

She glares at me.

"I'm sorry. I was studying and then I just lost track of time. And then the *kwadrans akademicki* had already passed . . ."

"I waited for half an hour."

"I'm sorry. When I realized what time it was, I went there and looked for you, but you weren't there anymore."

She raises her eyebrows at me. Then, as if she can read my guilt, she asks, "So, did you run into Sebastian today?"

My heart stops. I worry that maybe she or even one of her friends saw us stepping out of the Pink Elephant, or holding hands outside the McDonald's, or kissing on the city wall. We must have passed hundreds of people on our way.

"As a matter of fact, I ran into him at the tram stop. As I was heading home." I try to keep my voice from lurching.

"Did you now?" She puts her book down and looks up at me coldly, suspiciously.

It's amazing how easily the rest of it flows off my tongue, smoothly, reassuringly, and I wonder when I became such a good liar. "He said he's having a party on Thursday night. For Juvenalia. He told me to make sure that I invited you. I told him that we both had to work, but he insisted that we come afterward."

"He mentioned me specifically?"

I nod. "He says he's sorry he hasn't been by Stash's much lately."

"Really?"

"Uh-huh."

"He really said to make sure you invited me."

"Uh-huh."

She jumps up from the bed and grabs me by the shoulders. I stiffen. For the entire afternoon, Sebastian and I were so close it's impossible to believe that he left no trace, that she's unable to smell him on me, to feel the imprints of his fingers on my shoulders, to see his reflection in my face.

"Oh my God," she says. "Thursday! I have so much to do before then. I have to paint my nails. I have to trim my bangs. I have to get a new outfit."

"Why don't you just wear the dress you wore to the Śmigus Dyngus party? It'll look different when it's dry." It comes out sounding harsher than I want it to, and Magda gives me a strange look. I pick up one of her books and riffle the pages. I fake a yawn and pat it away.

"Sorry. I'm just tired. Too much studying. I think I'm going to bed."

"Okay." Another strange look, and I hurry to the safety of my own room.

When Irena comes home, I'm sitting up in bed, rereading the

same pages I was reading that afternoon at the Pink Elephant. I hear her toss her keys on the hall table.

"Magda, you put out that cigarette right now. I can smell it from the corridor."

"That's what you get for going out to parties and leaving your children unsupervised. They start to smoke cigarettes."

"It amazes me that you go to the doctor every other week for one test or another, but you still insist on getting lung cancer. It smells positively *revolting* in here. At least open your window."

Irena pokes her head into my room.

"Still up?"

"Just going to bed."

"Well, good night then."

"Good night."

She stops in the doorway. "What's the matter?"

"Nothing. I'm just tired."

"You're a terrible liar." She comes in and sits down on the bed. She smells a little of smoke too. Smoke and perfume. She's wearing a pair of gray pants and a black top with an open neckline that shows her collarbone.

"Did you go out with Stash tonight?"

"Yes."

"Did you have a good time?"

"Don't change the subject. What's the matter?"

"You're the one changing the subject."

"What is it? The exams? A boy?" She stops suddenly. A slow smile creeps across her face. "That's it, isn't it? It *is* a boy. Did you get a letter from Tadeusz?"

"No."

"*Another* boy then?"

I want to tell her everything, every last detail: the wave of dark hair that falls across his forehead, the way people look at us as we pass them on the street, the touch of his long, flat-tipped fingers, the way he kisses, so *not* like an assassin. I want to feel his name rolling around in my mouth, repeat our conversation verbatim, explain how when I'm with him, I can be both a village girl and a Krakowianka. In the city, but not of it.

I smile, unable to control it.

"I knew it!" she says triumphantly. "You would *never* survive behind enemy lines."

"Thanks."

"And does he know?"

"Know what?"

"Know that you can't help but smile like that when you even *think* about him?"

I feel a sudden chill, and I pull the covers up to my shoulders like they do in all the American films after they've had sex. "Enough, Irena. Good night."

"Tell him," she says. "If you keep your feelings to yourself, you'll get cancer. Emotional sepsis. Almost as bad as smoking."

"I'm glad you're such an expert now. I'll be sure to thank Stash."

She stands up and smooths the front of her pants. "We're talking about you now. Tell him."

"He already knows, I think."

"I think, I think. Life's too short for 'I think' . . . tell him."

What am I supposed to say? That he knows, that I know, that the only one who's still in the dark is Magda? Irena stands in the doorway and smiles sympathetically, but I know that for all her sympathy for me, for all her complaining about Magda, for all the sarcasm that still passes between them, a daughter is still a daughter, and a cousin from the village, only that.

"I will," I promise, but I say it only so she will leave.

"I know you're only saying that to make me leave. Tell him."

39

The Knock in the Middle of the Day

S HE KNEW. Somewhere inside her body, she knew that they would come. They had been in the city for just over a year, and Anielica was almost three months pregnant, home alone with morning sickness. Everyone said it would let up soon, that she should be happy because it meant that it was probably a boy, but Anielica was growing weary, both of her body's constant rebellion against her and the reciprocal revulsion she felt for her body. She felt disgusted with herself before the Knock even came.

People who have never heard the Knock, who have never felt the Knock echoing against their temples or ricocheting around their insides always tell about it happening in the middle of the night, but the truth is that the middle of the night is only a euphemism for when you least expect it, and honestly, you never quite expect it. Anielica did not think twice that morning when she flung open the door, her mouth full of acid, her heart racing, her eyes bleary, like a wild animal under attack, looking for either relief or someone to blame. And certainly the man on the other side of the door did not look threatening in the least. He was only about ten years older, with creased leather shoes and an ill-fitting brown jacket.

"I am here to see Czesław Mrożek."

"He's at work," Anielica mumbled, and began to shut the door. She could feel her stomach churning again.

"You may be able to help me then."

"I don't want to buy anything. Whatever it is, we can't afford it."

"I am not selling anything. I only want to verify some information with you."

"I would feel better if you came by when my husband was at home."

She tried to shut the door again, but his shoe blocked it. "I just need to verify some information with you, Anielica."

When he said her name, she took a step back, and he took the opportunity to step into the flat.

"As I believe you have just confirmed, you are Anielica Hetmańska, now Anielica Mrożek, married to one Czesław Mrożek, also known as the Pigeon. You were married at the Church of the Holy Sepulcher here in Krakow, about four months ago."

She felt the breath being sucked out of her.

"You live here with your brother . . . by the name of . . . Władysław Jagiełło?" He raised an eyebrow but continued reading from his notebook. ". . . who is married to Marysia Holcman, an ethnic Jew, though she doesn't practice, or at least not that we know of. Her parents are Jonasz and Judyta Holcman, currently residents of Rømø, Denmark . . ."

"Who is *we?*"

"Your brother and sister-in-law have one child, Irenka, five years old, who attends Żłobek Number Two on First of May Street. You are pregnant with your first . . ." He looked up at her. "Congratulations."

She did not reply. Her head was reeling, and her stomach followed.

"Your mother is Maria Hetmańska, formerly Maria Kukla, born December 11, 1902, married to Franciszek Hetmański on April 4, 1919. They live in the village of . . . Half-Village . . . approximately ten kilometers south of Osiek in the Nowosądeckie region . . ."

The room began to close in on her. She felt her skin grow hot and the saliva fill her mouth.

". . . where, on January 22, 1945, one Russian soldier, there to liberate the village, was mysteriously shot by partisans believed to be fighting for the Home Army. There are currently fifteen residents in

Half-Village: one Pani Lubicz, widowed recently, one Pani Epler, also widowed recently . . ."

The back of her throat convulsed. She ran to the bathroom and slammed the door behind her, lurching for the toilet. She didn't make it, and she threw up on the rim and on the floor. She sat on the edge of the bathtub, exhausted, and cupped her hand under the water, rinsing the acrid taste from her mouth, splashing the cool water on her face, holding her wrists under the stream. When she turned the water off, she could hear him walking around the flat, the parquet creaking under his feet. This man she had never seen before was suddenly making himself at home in their lives, in their present and in their past. It was up to her to prevent him from skulking into their future.

She stood up and stared at her reflection in the small piece of mirror the Pigeon had mounted for her on the wall. She didn't want to recognize herself. She had been disgusted with her body for the past month, its softening and bloating and cramping, and the face staring back at her was ugly, blotchy, with pale lips, her damp hair sticking to her forehead. She knew what she must do, and she began, marching through it as she had marched through so many other things in the past six years. She took the rag from under the bathtub and cleaned up the mess, rinsing it down the drain, and when she was done with the floor, she went to work on herself with the same detachment, the same mechanical movements as any other distasteful chore. She brushed her teeth and pulled her hair back, powdered her face and put on lipstick, pulled her housedress tight and retied it. She stared one last time into the mirror, and what looked back at her was someone else's face, not hers, not the one her mother had borne, her father had named, her brother had teased, certainly not the one the Pigeon had fallen in love with.

She went back out into the main room, into the room occupied by the two couples from Bielsko-Biała. He was staring out the window, his back to her, and when he turned around and saw her transformation, she could see it registering in his eyes.

"I apologize," she said sweetly. "I am, as you say, pregnant." She brought it up, thinking that in this situation it might be a selling point, especially for a married man.

His eyes drifted over her, resting wherever they pleased.

"And forgive me for my rudeness earlier. I just don't understand why a man of your . . . your clear authority would even want to be bothered with us."

"Maybe your husband would be better able to answer that. He doesn't seem to tell you much."

She looked at the man's hands, still gripping the composition notebook he had read from. He wore an aluminum wedding ring, bent and chinked in places, and she tried to imagine the wife who had placed it on his finger. She saw a meek little woman, a woman who picked out his clothes and always had his dinner ready when he came home in the afternoon.

"Surely there must be something we can do."

"I'm not sure that there is."

But the way his eye had flickered made her ask again. "Surely there must be *something*."

"Nothing, I'm afraid," he said. "Unless the notes are lost. Terrible makeshift system we have at the moment. If this notebook and the file back at the station are both lost . . ."

He moved toward her, and everything that had only moments before been cloaked in vagaries and bundled in euphemism suddenly lay bare. She couldn't bear to bring him into the second room—their room—and so she led him to the bed Gosia and the younger brother shared. It was better that way. The revulsion she felt lying on their sheets, saturated by their odors and oils helped her to crawl into the inner recesses of herself, so that his motions on top of her seemed as distant as the noises from the flat above. He thrust awkwardly, groaning like an animal, not caring at all what he sounded like, and her thoughts suddenly went to the meek wife waiting for him at home. She pushed the image away, ashamed. The grunts came more deeply, more quickly, and he tried to suppress them by pressing his lips to hers, but she turned her head violently away, and he stopped suddenly and chuckled before resuming. She concentrated her gaze on the brown jacket on the floor, the shoes that had been stepped out of and left with the heels touching. The coat was even shabbier, the shoes even more worn up close.

There was no blood this time. No howling, no clinging to the leg of a table. No dramatic rescue, no rage. Only a simple transaction. A choice. A choice between Scylla and Charybdis, between the devil and Beelzebub, but nonetheless, a choice. One of the millions like it that would be made in the next fifty years, the secret negotiations taking place in the privacy of souls, never a win-win solution, only a not-lose. In the New Poland, there was survival for the ones who could stuff themselves down into the deepest part of themselves, who could lock the room of their conscience behind them.

When he left, the notebook remained, and Anielica held it with both hands, as if it were something precious and fragile. It was a small composition notebook, the kind that schoolchildren carry, and she marveled that somewhere there was a factory turning them out so soon after the war. She carefully turned the pages with her fingertips. Everything, everyone she loved was named: their parents, the church in Pisarowice, Irenka's nursery, their neighbors in Half-Village, the small town in England where the Pigeon's family was temporarily living before they got their papers to America, the boss at the uniform factory, the foreman at the Pigeon's job.

It was almost beautiful, really, to have the entirety of one's life contained within neat edges, within straight, even lines and thick, durable covers. But now the stench of that morning emanated from it, overpowering the entire record of life it contained. It had to be destroyed. Completely. Immediately. She brought the notebook into the bathroom, opened it and pinched the covers back between her fingers like one of those paper Christmas trees that decorated the table for a month and was folded neatly away. She stuck the corner of a single page into the open mouth of the water heater, where the pilot light glistened like a small blue tongue, licking at the edge. At first, she fed the flame slowly, twisting her wrist to control the ebb and flare. She wanted to watch the flames spread from one page to the next, to look over each name, each place, each date, and then watch the fire consume it completely, but the orange flames grew quickly out of control. She dropped the composition book into the tub, and it landed flat on its covers, the white pages in between bursting into a fireball, sending off tiny black flags of surrender into the air.

When it burned itself out, all that remained was the dampened cover, and Anielica carried it over to the trash bucket and simply threw it out. She paced back and forth, fearful of sitting on any of the beds, which seemed infested with her deed. She tried to forget the notebook, but it nagged at her from the trash bucket, and she could not think about anything else. Finally she went over and retrieved it, pinching it cautiously between two fingers, as if it were the corpse of a small animal or a bird. She carried it over to the window. She swung it open with her free hand and climbed over the sill and onto the balcony. She had hung up the washing that morning, and it was nearly dry in the warm September sun. She ducked under the Pigeon's work shirts, under her own skirts and blouses, under little Irenka's underpants, and she held the cover of the notebook over the railing for a moment before letting go.

For a split second, she actually thought it might spread its wings, glide gently across Bishop Square, and ride a breeze over the rooftops, disappearing behind the chimneys, drifting to the ground in a land far, far away. Instead, it dropped like a stone to the sidewalk just below the window, and Anielica stared down at it, watching the pedestrians divert around it or nudge it out of the way with their feet.

No one ever found out. Anielica washed the ashes from the tub and drew a bath. The blackened cover was gone from the sidewalk by the evening. Gosia and her husband slept in the sheets for the rest of the week, rolling around and marinating in the evil. She could never prove it of course, but it seemed that when Gosia returned from her job at the milk bar that night, she was surprised and perplexed to find the Half-Villagers still there.

Whether she did it to spite Gosia, to hide it from the Pigeon, or deny it to herself, Anielica somehow managed to stuff that morning so far inside herself that not even her memory could reach it. Only her body knew. Before Gosia had even changed the sheets on the bed, Anielica miscarried, and before they were able to move out of the flat on Bishop Square, she miscarried twice more, as if her womb were trying to expel an unwelcome stranger that would not leave.

In the spring of 1947, the five Half-Villagers finally moved into a newly built *garsoniera* on Rydla Street, which the Pigeon and Władysław Jagiełło had been able to *załatwić* through their connections. It was a big improvement since they did not have to share it with anyone, but Anielica was still not used to being stacked like firewood on top of her neighbors. There was always someone knocking on someone's door or pounding meat or beating a rug or listening to the radio or yelling at their children.

There was always someone watching you.

She never saw the man with the brown jacket and the creased shoes again, but plenty of others came and went at all times of the day and night. Sometimes someone was home; other times they would ransack the flat while they were gone or merely leave one item out of place as a calling card. The Pigeon would be picked up at work or on his way home, and Anielica would have to wait up into the wee hours for the click of the entrance door downstairs that signaled his return.

"Don't worry," her brother whispered to her. "He will be back by the morning. Just like last time. Try to get some sleep."

The volume of his reassurances calmed her. In the New Poland, the truths were separated from the untruths by decibels. The untruths were now proclaimed loudly with a brass band, relentless marching, and waving banners. Toward the Bright Future. All Power to the Workers. Life Has Become Better, Comrades; Life Has Become More Cheerful. The Soviets Will Keep You Warm. Meanwhile, everything real was whispered, passed softly and meticulously from one person to the next. For the next fifty years, this is how it would be. The quietest sounds would be the most important ones. And so, when she heard the click of the entrance door downstairs and the quiet scratching of the key in the lock, when she saw his silhouette and felt him gently slip into bed beside her, when she whispered his name, and he whispered back that everything would be okay, she believed him.

"Nothing happened," he said. "And nothing will happen. They only want to inconvenience me, nothing more. They will leave me alone after the elections."

"I just don't understand why they are still after you," Anielica whispered. "Why have they stopped coming after Władysław Jagiełło, but they are still after you?"

"Because they are fools," he whispered back. "Because they are fools."

Anielica was too scared to ask if this was a reaffirmation of his own innocence or an indictment of her brother, but she eventually learned to live around it. She lived around the doubt, the intruders, the disarray, the neighbors looking through their peepholes, the empty spot on the bed next to her some nights, the not-knowing. She got used to it, just as everyone else did. And as soon as she learned to live with it, her body dropped its guard, and one of her pregnancies finally stuck.

40

Juvenalia

I MAKE IT to the Rynek in time for the end of the opening ceremony. The mayor is shouting into the screeching microphone,
circling toward some kind of conclusion. ". . . and so, for the next
four days, the city will be in the care of our esteemed students." A
few bottles splinter on the other side of the stage. "Take good care
of our city. Leave it in better condition than you found it." There
are more shouts and bottles breaking. "And remember that it is *Juvenalia* and not *Bacchanalia*." The mayor chuckles nervously, but he
is drowned out by the din engulfing the Rynek, and the president
of the student association quickly steps forward and takes the key
to the city.

The parade starts immediately—a steady stream of students from
Jagiellonian and all the academies and institutes circling the Rynek.
Each has its own costume. The law students are dressed in black
robes with mop heads as wigs; the geographers bat inflated globes
in the air; the architecture students have mounted their final projects on their heads, creating a miniature, snow-white city of skyscrapers, museums, and houses bobbing along the parade route. The
Agriculture Institute follows on tractors, and the rest of the institutes on trucks, wagons, even a troop transport. The students from
AGH carry hammers and wear helmets, and one couple have painted

themselves copper-green and dressed up like the statues of the miner and the factory worker that they say will walk off their pedestals at the front of the school if a virgin ever graduates. A wave of cheers follows them, as it does every time someone passes dressed as Jaruzelski or Lenin or Stalin or the farm girl clutching a sickle and reaching up toward the bright future. Each Lenin or Stalin or Jaruzelski makes some irreverent gesture—devil horns or the middle finger—and we all laugh. The grim, knowing laugh of survivors. The laugh that no one our age really has a right to. After all, when the country was suffering most, we were all just kids, and the Soviets were only cartoon characters on our classroom walls.

"Ah, youth," a grandmother standing in front of me says to her friend, but it isn't clear whether she means this longingly or disparagingly.

I go home to change before heading to Stash's. Magda is hurrying out the other side of the courtyard carrying a small overnight case and a bag with her dress, the black cats scurrying out of her path.

"Magda!" I call. "Magda!"

She turns around. Her face is cinched tight. She waits for me, and I go over to her.

"What's the matter?"

"Take a guess."

"Was it bad?"

"Horrible. Yelling, door slamming, everything."

"I'm sorry."

"I mean, she's *impossible.* For almost the whole year, she's said that it's my life, blah, blah, blah, I have to make my own choices, blah, blah, blah, and now, all of a sudden, she's on my head about going out again. Like she's one to talk! She goes out more than I do! The last time I went out was that Śmigus Dyngus party, and what did I do? I sat around and had a few drinks."

"Did you tell her that?"

"Yes, but you know her. When she has it in her head not to listen, she doesn't listen."

"Do you think you should still go to the party?"

"I'm sure not staying home."

"True."

"Listen, I'm already late," she says. "I'm going to have to get dressed at work. Can you meet me over there?"

"Yeah, sure. See you later."

"*Pa.*"

When I go upstairs, Irena is still seething. She has a pair of scissors in her hand and is attacking the tags on a new dress with such violence that I worry she will cut the dress.

"Are you going out with Stash?"

She frowns at me. "I know you already talked to her in the courtyard."

"Irena, don't you think you're being just a little unreasonable? It's the first time she's been out in a month."

"That's not true. Stash says she's there almost every night."

"For an hour. On her way home from work. And we usually talk about history anyway."

She sits down on the edge of the love seat, pulls her pantyhose on, and immediately puts a rip in them.

"*Cholera jasna,*" she mutters.

"Irena, someone once told me that if you don't stop worrying, you'll get cancer."

"If you don't share your *feelings,* you get cancer. If you don't stop *worrying,* you get lupus."

"Well, either way, give Magda a little credit. She's too smart to do anything to jeopardize her chances now."

Irena raises one eyebrow. "I was smarter than that too. And nine months later . . ."

"Well, if it makes you feel better, the guy she's interested in doesn't exactly like her back."

"Boys who don't like you get you pregnant too."

"Nothing's going to happen."

"You don't know that."

"It's just a party."

Stash is in a bad mood tonight too, grumbling about the new outdoor cafés on the Rynek taking all his business. The club is only half full and the band plays sluggishly. He can tell that I'm anxious to leave.

"Oh, go on," he finally says. "Everybody else has gone to the Rynek. Go sit in a wicker chair and buy yourself an overpriced beer. You too, Kinga. With the way I've been playing tonight, I might as well be tending bar."

But Kinga, her chin propped in the palm of her hand, doesn't move. Ever since the man with the handlebar mustache started appearing, I've watched the hope slowly drain out of her face, her features growing fainter and fainter.

"Do you want to come, Kinga? I'm meeting Magda at the wine bar and then we're going to a party."

Kinga stares out at the man with the handlebar mustache, who is sitting at a table in the corner alone. "Juvenalia is for students," she says. "Not bar girls."

By the time I get to the Corner of St. Thomas the Disbeliever, Magda is already in the back room changing. The wine bar is empty except for one foreign couple, and the girls Magda works with—a Kasia and two Agnieszkas—take turns standing at attention in their lace aprons while the other two slouch behind the bar and gossip. Magda has evidently told them that this is The Night, the night she is going to make it clear to Sebastian what her feelings for him are. Kasia and the Agnieszkas question me about Sebastian almost as intensely as Magda, so that when she finally emerges from the back room, she has to clear her throat to get our attention.

"Oh, Magda, you look *beautiful*." Kasia and the Agnieszkas and I all whistle and clap, and the couple drinking their wine smile and squeeze hands across the table, whispering to each other in their own language.

"Absolutely stunning."

She is. But as I look at her standing in her dress and heels, instead of jealousy, I feel pity.

"He'd be a fool not to fall for you," Kasia says, and she reaches over and smooths Magda's eyebrows. One of the Agnieszkas finds some pins and secures the dress so the straps of her bra won't peek out.

"Don't worry. If you have to take it off quickly, it all comes off in one piece," she says, and I laugh right along with them, a traitor of the worst kind.

Manager Agnieszka offers to open a bottle of wine to celebrate, but Magda is impatient to get to the party.

"My destiny awaits," she says, twirling around. "And hopefully, my destiny is wearing those jeans that make his *dupa* look . . ." She smacks at the air with her lips and we all laugh again.

It's nearly eleven by the time we ring Tomek and Sebastian's *domofon*. No one comes to the door, though we can hear the voices and the music. We ring again, and it takes a few more minutes before a girl and a boy, pickled drunk, open the door.

"Who are you?"

"What do you mean?"

The girl giggles. "Who are you? Who do you know?"

"Sebastian and Tomek. Isn't this their place?"

The boy buries his head in Magda's shoulder, and she shrugs him off.

"Get off me!"

"They don't smell like *policja*," he says, and the girl yanks my arm and pulls me in.

The flat is packed to the windows with people, most of them already stumbling around, a few staring vacantly past us as we walk down the hall. Some of the architecture students still have their building models strapped to their heads, and I recognize the farm girl from the parade, wearing a low-cut blouse now, her forearms and face still painted copper-green.

"There are a lot of people here tonight."

"Mmm," Magda says.

She's not listening to me. She's only staring over my head with an insipid smile on her face, poised for the exact moment when Sebastian will appear to greet us. We thread our way through the crowd and stop at a bottleneck at the kitchen door, the architecture students trying to make it through the doorway two at a time. Magda is determined to find him, and just as she disappears ahead of me into the white city, a hand slips around my waist and pulls me off to the side, into a little nook next to a gigantic wardrobe in the hallway. "You look beautiful," Sebastian says. "No gangs of twelve-year-old boys this time?"

He kisses me, and it ripples straight through me.

"Not here," I say, "not in public."

He smiles. "You can take the girl out of the village . . ."

"But you can't promise her a *dzientelmen*?"

He flashes a smile. "I can promise I will be a *dzientelmen* for now. I can't promise anything about later on."

Something surges inside me at the thought, but I twist away from him until his hand falls away from my waist.

"I brought Magda."

"Well, we should probably go and protect her from those architecture guys. They're all *babiarze*, every one." He leads me into the kitchen. I put my hand on his back and feel the muscles tighten like ropes beneath his shirt. Magda is leaning against one of the counters, talking to a boy who has a copycat version of the new Japanese cultural center on his head. It's obvious that her eye is still roving for Sebastian, though, and when she spots him, her face softens.

"There you are," she says to me, then tilts her head down and looks up at Sebastian from underneath her dark eyebrows. "Se-bas-tian." She draws his name out.

"Magda, I'm glad you could make it," he says, and he kisses her on the cheek—one, two, three. There's nothing in it, to be sure. It's the same kiss we gave our classmates every morning in primary school, the same kiss we gave the grandmothers in the village after church on Sunday. But I can tell from how she smiles at me that she will make more of it when we talk about it later.

The architecture student Magda was talking to wanders off without even a thought to excusing himself, and Magda doesn't notice. She has flipped a switch, and she's suddenly entirely focused on Sebastian, animated and engaging as the two of them chat about the party, about Magda's exams, about the wine bar and the new Japanese cultural center.

"So, tell me, Sebastian," Magda says, "how come Baba Yaga is the only one lucky enough to keep running into you?" She cocks her head to the side and touches his arm. Sebastian gives me a strange look.

"Excuse me, will you?" he says, nodding to someone behind us. "I have to go attend to something. Help yourself to some drinks. I'll be right back."

As soon as he's out of sight, Magda gives a little squeal of pleasure. "Did you see that? Did you see how he was looking at me? And how he put his hand on my waist as he kissed me? I'm telling you, Baba Yaga. I feel it. It's going to happen tonight. I can just feel it."

"I'll be right back."

"Where are you going?"

"I have to go to the bathroom."

I go out to the courtyard, and I sit on the crumbling concrete steps for a long time, just looking up at the sky, which in the city never turns completely black no matter how many drops of dye night adds. If I say something, she will hate me. She will refuse to talk to me ever again, she will tell the story to Monika and Kasia and the Agnieszkas as an urban cautionary tale, and I will end up with the name Blondynka Zdzira or Village Zdzira or maybe even Baba Zdzira. If I say something, she will tell Irena, Irena will make the choice that I always secretly dreaded, and I will end up renting a room from a *babcia* in Huta. If I say something, Magda will stalk out of the party, walk defiantly toward the taxi stand on Starowiślna, and leave me to wallow in my own shame. I rehearse the scene over and over, but in every ending, I am selfish. I am a traitor. I am a coward. I look up into the sky and secretly wish for it to pull me into its darkness, to race me along some secret portal and dump me out into the clearing of the village. But I am on my own now, and there is no one left there to catch me.

When I go back in, I can't find Magda or Sebastian, so I wander around for a while, then sit down on one of the sofas in the living room. Tomek and his girlfriend are entwined on the sofa opposite, and through the crowd of people, I watch as they take turns stroking the flat of a large meat knife across each other's throats, attracting no attention at all. The girl sitting next to me turns as if she has something pressing to say, but only stares at me.

"Good party, no?" I say.

She's silent, still looking at me. She's probably just high. She probably sat on the edge of the tub in the bathroom all night, staring at people until they made her leave. To me, though, her stare is an accusation, and I rush out of the living room and into the hallway.

Magda is there, fighting her way out of the kitchen. I can see her eyes glistening in the dim light.

"Oh, Magda." I'm surprised when she lets me put my arm around her shoulders and lead her into the courtyard. We go and sit on the far steps, and she tries to wipe away the tears as quickly as they form in the corners of her eyes.

"I'm so sorry," I blurt out, but she only takes a crumpled tissue out of her purse and blows her nose into it. She leans her head on my shoulder, and I can tell by the weight of it that she's stone drunk.

"Oh, God, I'm such a *głupia panienka*. Such a stupid, stupid girl."

"What happened?" I ask quietly, and I hold my breath.

"I tried to fucking kiss him, that's what happened," she says. "I got fucking drunk, and I tried to fucking kiss him. Oh God." She begins to cry again, and a couple sitting on the steps across the courtyard look over at us.

"And what did he say?" I ask anxiously.

She dabs at her eyes and begins to laugh. Not a true laugh, but the leftovers of frustration and exhaustion. "That's the thing. He was a complete *dzientelmen*. He said that he was sorry, but there was some-one else. He said there was someone else, and then I felt like a *dupa*, and then that's pretty much it."

"Who is it?" I ask, trying to hold my voice down at the edges.

"How the *kurwa* do I know? I didn't exactly stick around and make small talk about her. Hopefully, it's some *zdzira* with syphilis."

I have never felt so free. She doesn't know. She doesn't know, and I resolve right then to end it with Sebastian. I will end it, and we will never come back here, and she will never find out. I feel as if I've just woken up from a nightmare to the comfort of my own walls, as if I've been given a second chance, and I snatch it as quickly as I can.

"Yeah," I say, "I'll bet she's a real *zdzira*."

"And fat too."

"Fat or flat?" I ask, and she laughs.

"And dumb."

We sit out there on the steps until we have listed every imaginable flaw of this imaginary girl, and then we start in on Sebastian. Sud-denly Magda stops laughing, and her eyes begin to well up again.

"Phooh!" I wave my hand and squint my eyes, a perfect imitation of her mother. "*Srał go pies.*"

Magda smiles weakly before answering: "And the puppy too."

We sit there for a little while longer, staring up at the perfect square of blue-black sky, die cut by the walls of the courtyard.

"Come on," I finally say, "let's get you home."

But she scowls at me. "Home?" she says. "Home?" She stands up unsteadily and grips the railing, balancing herself on the steps. Her mouth curls up at the corners, and she puts her hands on her hips. "Cousin, I spent two hundred thousand złotych on this dress. I'm going to get my money's worth." She turns on her heels, flips her hair, and struts across the courtyard to the bathroom. She has never called me *cousin* before, and while she's in the bathroom, I make another silent vow to the sky.

The architecture student with the copycat Japanese cultural center on his head is waiting for Magda as we come in the door, and he sweeps her off to the kitchen to get another drink. Sebastian is busy being the host, always whispering to someone or being whispered to or showing people in and out of the bathroom, which stays closed all night. I hear murmurs of *trawa, amfa, spid,* and *koks,* and it finally all makes sense. Tomek. Sebastian. The flat. The *remont.* The bathroom. The parties. Hanging around the university. The people whispering in his ear all the time. The fax machine. Maybe even the family friend in New York. I just want the night to be over, the whole thing to be over. I want to go home and sit in the living room, ask Irena about her night, to hear her tell Magda *srał go pies,* to wake up in the morning and have breakfast while Magda sleeps it off, to call back and forth to each other through the flat the entire day.

I avoid Sebastian for the rest of the night, and I'm standing in the doorway of one of the bedrooms, listening to one of the architecture students pontificate about somebody called Walter Gropius, when Magda reappears out of the crowd.

"Are you ready to go?" I ask.

She grips my arm tightly in response, and there's something pulsing in her eyes which I at first mistake for anger.

"What is it?" I ask, and I hold my breath, praying that she has not somehow found out that I am the flat, fat, syphilis-ridden, dumb-goose *zdzira* that we picked apart in the courtyard.

"I can't breathe," she says.

"What?"

"I can't breathe."

I laugh. "Well, you *are* talking. I think that means you can breathe."

She shakes her head vigorously. "My throat feels like this," and she clenches her fist in my face.

"Come on, you just need some air." I grip her hand tightly, like a child who has just been found, half in annoyance, half in relief. I lead her through the hallway of people. "Did you smoke some *trawa* or something?"

"*Koks*," she says.

"*Koks?* Are you crazy?"

"Marcin said he would make sure I was okay . . . but I can't find him now."

"You're crazy, Magda, you know that? *Crazy.* I know what your mother means now."

"Please . . . don't tell her . . . please."

"I'm not going to tell her. I'd be in as much trouble as you." I lead her outside. The cool breeze feels good. Magda can't stop moving, and I sit on the steps while she paces tight circles in the courtyard. Her face is white and waxy, and she's sweating profusely.

"Calm down. Don't breathe so hard. You're going to hyperventilate and pass out."

"Oh Jezus . . . I swear to God . . . I will never take drugs again . . . I will never drink . . . I will never have sex . . . I will stop smoking . . . I will join a convent . . . I will be nice to my mother."

I laugh. "I'll believe it when I see it."

"Baba Yaga . . . promise you'll . . . tell my mother . . . I'm sorry."

"I'm sure it's not that serious, Magda. You're just nervous. Take some deep breaths. Here, sit down." She sits down, but she's still taking quick, shallow breaths, like a dog in the heat.

"Maybe . . . we should go . . . to the hospital."

"And are *you* going to explain that to your mother or am I?"

"Baba Yaga." Her voice is whittled down to a thin reed.

"Yes?"

"Maybe . . . get Sebastian."

So *that's* it. *That's* what this is all about. "Sebastian?" I say, annoyed. "What's he going to do? Here, put your head between your knees. Do you want me to get you some water?"

"Don't leave." Her voice is muffled by her dress.

She's silent for a moment, and then goes limp. At first I think she's just being dramatic, so I call her name and shake her by the shoulders. She falls to one side.

"Shit. Sebastian!" I yell. His flat is on the ground floor, and I run inside and push my way through the crowd. "Sebastian!" Everyone turns to stare at me, a hundred pairs of bloodshot eyes, the white buildings of the architecture students suddenly still.

He comes from the direction of the kitchen. "Baba Yaga," he says, and some people turn and laugh at my name. He reaches out for me. "Where have you been?"

"There's no time," I say, and I grip his arm and pull.

"Someone likes it rough." He chuckles. Laughter erupts around us, and his head swivels to acknowledge it.

"It's Magda. She's passed out on the steps."

"Had a little too much vodka, eh?"

"She said she had some *koks*." His face goes slack, and he rushes ahead of me and out to the courtyard. Magda is still in the same position on the stairs, but the slumped figure doesn't even resemble her anymore.

"Oh Jezus," Sebastian says. He picks her up over his shoulder, and her arms and legs hang limp.

"I'll call an ambulance."

He shakes his head. "No ambulance. Absolutely not."

He opens the front door of the flat and yells inside for anyone with a car. A set of keys lands at his feet, and he runs to an old red Little Fiat parked in the street. Magda's head and arms bounce up and down as he runs. Her hair is in clumps, and she's drooling onto his back. All I can think of is how she's going to kill me when she wakes up for letting him see her this way.

He opens the door of the Little Fiat and slings her headfirst into the backseat. I climb over her and balance her head in my lap. Sebastian slams the driver's seat into position and gets in.

"Shit, there was nothing wrong with that stuff. You've got to believe me. There was nothing in there."

I hold Magda's head in place so it won't loll around in my lap on the curves or bounce when we hit the potholes. I comb my fingers through her hair, pieces of it still stiff with hair spray. Her dark eyebrows part smoothly away from each other, and she seems strangely at peace.

"We're still okay, right?" Sebastian calls to me from the front seat.

"What?"

"You and me, we're still friends, right?" His voice is insistent, and it strikes me as a strange thing to say with Magda's head flopping from side to side in my lap.

At the hospital, he jumps out and throws the keys on the floor of the car. He lifts Magda out and cradles her in his arms. He leans hard on the night bell with his elbow, and someone buzzes us in. The woman on night duty starts to shuffle some papers, but when she sees Magda, she jumps up from her desk and yells down the long corridor to the right. Two men appear with a gurney.

"We're still friends, right?" Sebastian reaches for my hand and squeezes it as they load Magda onto the gurney, nothing more than a load, a mass, a burden.

"Of course," I say absentmindedly as I watch them roll Magda down the bright white fluorescent corridor.

The front desk nurse leads me to a chair. She asks for Magda's name and a few other things.

"I'm just going to park the car," Sebastian says, leaning over me, kissing me on the cheek. "I'll be right back."

41

The End to End All Ends

ONE NIGHT, THE PIGEON did not come home. Anielica lay awake in their bed, listening to the faint sounds that were drowned out during the day: the electric meter scraping against itself as softly as a grasshopper's legs, the faint creaking of the parquet as one of the neighbors tried to walk off his insomnia, the shifting of her brother and his wife in the bed opposite, and even her own breathing, which seemed strangely detached from herself. The silence murmured the awful, honest-to-God truth.

"Did he say anything to you yesterday?" Anielica whispered to her brother when he awoke in the pink predawn. "Anything at all?"

"Nothing about this. To you?"

"No."

They sat quietly together until the sun fully rose, and when Marysia and Irenka opened their eyes and saw them both awake, they were disoriented, unsure whether the sun had properly set and risen or had hung in the sky all night long, dimming only slightly in the wee hours.

"I'm sure he'll be fine," Marysia said cheerfully. "It's like he always says, they only want to scare him. He'll be back tonight, I'm sure."

Anielica nodded, but Marysia's words were too plentiful, her voice too loud to be true.

They had to go to work that day. If they did not, people would be suspicious, and they might all be doomed. Anielica had seen it happen to another girl at the uniform shop. She was from a village near Zamość, and her husband had been taken away for Resistance activities. The morning after, in her distress, the girl had spoken of it to the woman who sat at the machine next to hers. By the break everyone knew, and when she went over to chat with her coworkers, they scattered like a flock of birds. Anielica and Marysia had wanted to reassure the girl, but they knew they couldn't. Subversion was considered contagious. Eventually, the whole situation had depressed even the supervisors, and they had to let her go.

So on they worked and did the shopping and went to church, but the Pigeon did not return. Three days. A week. Two. A month. His absence became obvious to all the neighbors, but even Irenka, who was only seven, knew not to speak of it, not even to her little playmates in the park.

At night, the three adults would sit up and scratch out strategies, carefully keeping their voices beneath the sound of the electric meter.

"We need to find another flat."

"Find another flat? But where?"

"I don't know where. But clearly there is someone in this building who has it out for us. They will be back for me, and maybe you too."

"Don't be silly. No one is coming for us. We haven't done anything. The Pigeon will be back. Just you wait."

"I really think it's better if we move. There is a guy at work I can talk to."

"And if the Pigeon comes back, and there is no one here? How will he know where to find us?"

"*When* he comes back."

"He will find us. If he can live in bunkers and barns for five years, if he can blow up German transports and hold off whole platoons of Russians, he can surely find us."

"He told me he was running newspapers."

"Well, that too."

"Jezus Maria." And she made the sign of the cross.

Anielica's only consolation was that as the emptiness ate away inside her, a baby grew to fill it. She held off on making any absolute

304

decisions as long as she could, but when it became too much of a scandal for her to spend late nights at the theater, when her stomach became too big to fit under her machine during the day, she allowed her brother to buy her a ticket back to Osiek on the train, which, like everything else, was once again running on a regular and efficient schedule.

That was the whole problem, really. By the spring of 1947, everything *was* moving Toward the Bright Future. The construction and reconstruction was happening so rapidly that the streets from one day to the next became unrecognizable, and the names were being changed as fast as the communist heroes could be cultivated and the signs hammered out. There were even plans to build a new steel factory and its own bedroom suburb to the east. Nowa Huta it was to be called. Everything was *nowa* in the Nowa Poland. New storefronts sprang up like mushrooms, connected by new streets and sidewalks, and supplied with new customers living in the new *osiedla*. The women's wardrobes bloomed again after years of lying fallow, fresh teals and pinks appearing on the streets as fast as they could be churned out of the factories. Everyone was shedding the deprivation and tragedy of the war. Everyone was moving on except the Pigeon who, wherever he was, was being left behind. And as Anielica watched the fashions and the façades change, as she watched even her own body transform, it felt a little like betrayal, like she was leaving him for dead.

She knew, of course, that she could not escape change simply by returning to Half-Village. In her letters, her mother had told her that the schools were running again, and the communists had built a post office in Pisarowice right next to the church. But at least there, the changes were happening more slowly than in the city, and at least there, the Pigeon's legacy still remained on everyone's lips. Here, even her own brother avoided saying the Pigeon's name as much as he could, and he tried to change the topic whenever Anielica brought him up.

"You will keep looking for the Pigeon while I am gone?" she asked the night before she was to leave. They ate their last meal together as they had every other one in the *garsoniera*, their plates balanced on their knees.

"Little sister . . ." her brother began. He did not bother to finish the sentence — they all knew how it ended — and by then even Marysia did not contradict him.

Anielica slept fitfully that night, waking up several times and patting the space beside her, as if the Pigeon had been playing a trick the entire time and would give up the game at the last minute. Standing on the train platform the next morning, she glanced over whenever something moved in her peripheral vision, and Marysia and Bożena took turns trying to soothe her nerves.

"It will not be long. As soon as the baby is old enough, you can come back and live with us," Marysia offered.

"And I talked to Małgosia at the theater," Bożena added, "and she said she could arrange some work for you if you could somehow *załatwić* a machine back in the village."

Anielica nodded and strained a smile, and there was a last round of kisses, which were more consoling to the three who were staying. The train pulled alongside the platform, its wheels squealing, the passengers from Warsaw looking sleepily through the square windows. Anielica took one last look up and down the platform, half expecting to see the Pigeon running toward her, yelling about the terrible misunderstanding, the terrible time he'd had getting back to her. But he didn't, and for the first time, the thought flashed across her mind that he never would, that he was gone forever.

42

The End to End All Ends

IN THE MORNING, it's as if night never fell, the sun never rose, as if the dawn that hangs in the courtyard outside is merely the bleached remnants of the previous evening's dusk. The waiting was bearable enough through the night hours, when the whole world waited with me with tangled limbs and even breath. But as soon as the birds begin to chirp and I hear Pani Kulikowska's twig broom rasping against the concrete slabs of the courtyard, I know that time has begun its cruel march forward, and that from now on, I'm waiting alone.

I wander from room to room. My body feels like a strange collection of parts, none of them synchronized. My arms and legs resist my movements, and the shapes of my thoughts don't match the words that run through my head. Every nerve stands alert, raw against my skin, but if there's something to feel, they pass nothing along. I don't get thirsty. I don't get tired or bored. I don't even cry. The only way I know I'm still alive is from the awful scraping inside my chest, hollowing me out like a gourd.

The night nurse at the hospital told me that it was a heart attack, that she must have been walking around since birth with a tear in her heart as small as the moon on a fingernail. The only legacy from her father. Maybe all those times she went to the doctor, maybe somehow she knew.

Sebastian never came back, and it finally occurred to me that in the car he had been begging for my silence and not my friendship. About an hour later, the nurse told me that Irena had arrived, and that I could leave. That was exactly how she put it, that I could leave.

"I don't want to leave," I said. "I told you. I want to see Magda. I want to see her mother."

"I can call you a taxi if you want."

"I'm not leaving." I think she could tell that I was serious because she didn't say it again, but she kept a close eye on me in the waiting room.

It was Stash who finally came and convinced me that it was better if I went home for a while.

"Where's Irena?"

"She's in the back. She's been talking with the doctors."

"Does she think it's my fault?"

"If anything, I think she blames herself."

"Then why won't she come and talk to me?"

"Just give her a little time."

I wait at home all morning, but Irena doesn't come, doesn't call. I walk the path from the phone to the door until I imagine I can see the wear in the carpet, and then I shift my path—the kitchen to the television, the bathroom to the balcony door. To say the truth, I stay away from Magda's room out of fear and revulsion, as if just inside the door lies her slumped body, her clumped hair, her slack jaw.

It's well into the afternoon before the telephone rings.

"*Słucham.*"

"Is Magda there?"

It's Kasia from the wine bar.

"Baba Yaga, is that you?"

"Yes."

"Is Magda there? I mean, she *did* come home last night, didn't she?"

Magda has told me stories about Kasia, that she is a terrible gossip.

"Baba Yaga, did I wake you?"

"No."

"Well, do you know when she'll be back?"

"She won't."

There's a heavy silence on the other end. "Well . . . I'll call later then?"

I hang up. I sit on the floor next to the phone for the rest of the day, as inanimate as the love seat or the lamp, an object casting shadows. The light sifts through the net curtains, yellow, then pink, then gray. Finally, the phone rings again, and I pick it up without a word and press it gingerly to my ear, as if it's a magic shell I've picked up off some faraway beach.

"Baba Yaga?" There's a pause. "Baba Yaga, it's Stash."

"I know."

"Irena asked me to call you. She doesn't . . . she doesn't think it's a good idea for you to stay at the flat tonight."

"Okay."

"She doesn't think it's a good idea for you to stay at the flat anymore," he corrects himself, as if the first sentence was merely to pick up momentum. "I've called Bożena," he continues. "She's expecting you. She said you can have one of the other flats in her building, and you can stay as long as you like."

"And Magda?" But I already know.

"I'm sorry," he says softly. My head feels like it's filling up, and everything else he says sounds like it's underwater. Something about coming to pick me up, something about the bar, something about Irena.

As soon as I hang up, I start to pack. Immediately, mechanically. I have been expecting some version of this ever since the nurse told me I could go home, and my mind stumbles on the word *home*. I pack my rucksack and two shopping bags without feeling anything pass through my hands, and I walk to the tram, my feet feeling for the ground that isn't there.

It's already evening, the far end of rush hour on a Friday, and the stragglers are returning home with bags of vegetables and their pay packets stuffed into their shoes. The tram toward the old town is only half full, but I stand at the end of the car, leaning my forehead against the window. I watch the tracks rushing beneath my feet, the shop windows passing by, the kiosks still lit up with business. It's a strange feeling to leap over a day that others have lived, and my mind compensates by repeating the night before over and over again, a piece of film flapping in the projector, a phonograph record at the end of its groove.

"Can I see your ticket, Pani?"

I lean back slightly, and in the window pools the reflection of a man in a shabby jacket flashing an ID.

"I don't have one."

"Well then, you must pay the fine."

I look at his face in the reflection, at his stern eyes accusing me.

"You are riding on the black," he says. "You must pay the fine." He takes out his notebook and flips to a clean page. "Name and address."

I turn around to face him and start to cry. I can't help it. It's been sitting on the surface all day. I reach out and grab him by the lapels, lean into him to keep from falling. I sob uncontrollably into his shabby jacket, biting off huge gulps of air and forcing them into my lungs.

"All right, all right," he says. "That's enough." He pats me on the back as if he's burping a baby, as if he has never consoled another human being in his entire life. I can feel the other passengers staring at me, but I don't care.

"Where are you getting off, Pani?"

I can't answer. I can't let go of his jacket. I can't stop crying.

"I said, where are you getting off, Pani?"

I don't remember giving the address, but there's a conference carried out above my head, and somehow my bags and I pass from one strong arm to another until I'm standing in front of Pani Bożena's building. I hear the *domofon* chirp, the muffled discussion through the intercom, the distant clank of locks in succession, the kindness in the voice of the stranger who has led me there.

"Thank you," Pani Bożena says. "Thank you. She's had a hard day."

"So it seems," the woman's voice next to me says.

Later, I hear the bass of Stash's voice through the floor, talking to Pani Bożena. I listen hard for Irena's voice, but it's not there, and even Stash doesn't come upstairs.

43

Years Don't Go Back; the River Doesn't Flow Backward

P AN AND PANI HETMAŃSKA met Anielica at the train station in Osiek. They rode the bus together to Pisarowice, where Pan Stefanów was waiting with his empty cart. Anielica had only been away for two years, and they had exchanged letters nearly every week, but her parents seemed much older than when she'd left. Her mother had grown thicker, her gray hair more prolific, and her father struggled with her luggage now.

When the baby was born, there was not the fanfare that had accompanied Irenka's birth, partly because Anielica had been away for so long, and partly because she was a single mother, and if the *górale* did not show at least some restraint, single mothers would soon be running rampant through the mountains, and they couldn't have that now, could they? Still, there were a few visitors bearing gifts. Pan Cywilski brought a new radio he had built from the leftover parts of the last war. The Romantowski boy brought his fiddle to play. Jakub brought a whole menagerie of wooden animals he had carved in his solitude on Old Baldy Hill.

"... They are for Baby Ania, for Baby Ania and for you, do you remember, I brought a wooden bear for Irenka, but I wasn't very good then, and it looked like a cat, but now I am better at it, and you see there is a bear, and a better bear, and a goat, and a sheep, and a boar . . ."

He was still the same Jakub, and Anielica, even though she was tired, still had patience for him. She held each figure lightly and turned it around in her hands, noting its eyes or its nose or whichever part she felt the most exquisite.

". . . and a worm, and a dog, and a chicken, and a whale, and a bird . . ."

She knew by now that he was dead. Her father would still talk about when the Pigeon would return, and her mother would reassure her that she would be back in Krakow before Sylwester, but Anielica knew in her gut already that he was gone, that her own life would end in Half-Village, and the next forty or fifty years—God willing—would be merely living out the means. After all, if he was still alive, there would be more visits by men in brown suits. If he was still alive, people wouldn't act like they did toward her, condolences in their handshakes, their eyes, their grim smiles. If he was still alive, all of Half-Village would not be imbued with his spirit and his likeness. She could feel his presence everywhere. Every stone, every board, every peg, every rope, every tree. Sometimes she would rub her hand against the wardrobe or twist her fingertip in the indentations of the pegs in the floor and imagine that she could feel the imprints of his fingers against her own, that she could see his reflection in the wood grain and release his scent with her touch.

She knew he was dead, but there is a difference between knowing something and being able to speak about it, and it was easier to carry little Ania down the mountain every day to the post office in Pisarowice than to admit it to anyone. Pani Plotka had finally found her own little throne in her own little realm of the empire, as Postmistress for the People's Republic of Poland, Station 43, Nowosądeckie region. If there was any post for Anielica, it would be waiting on the counter for her, and she would tear open the envelopes eagerly and raggedly as Pani Plotka watched. But the first line of Marysia's letters would always be about Irenka's school or her brother's job, or the progress in the city, and Anielica would feel a cavern opening up to swallow her from the inside out. Pani Plotka would stare at her from behind the counter as she read, clucking in pity, hoping that the gesture of empathy would entitle her to a scrap of information. But Anielica was too preoccupied to notice, and with a quick wave, she would hurry back home as fast as she could. She would go straight to the side room she and Ania shared and grope under her pillow for the small framed photograph she kept there, desperate to prove to herself that he had once existed.

It was the only photograph she had of him. It had been taken by one of his friends in the Home Army toward the end of the war. He was leaning against a tree wearing his jodhpurs, boots, and the jacket that she herself had sewn. He was squinting, a cocky smile on his face, the crook of his nose jutting out defiantly, refusing to reside in the shadow of his cap. She could sit and stare at it for hours, one hand corralling Ania's pudgy thigh into her lap, the other gripping the frame of the photograph. She let herself drift back to the moment in the woods when it was taken. Even though she hadn't been there, by now she probably knew that moment, that tree, that patch of growth better than the Pigeon himself had. It was her only escape from the village now, and she lingered there as long as she could, until at last Ania squirmed in her lap or her parents came to see why she was holed up in her room again.

44

Life As If

NIGHTTIME IS THE WORST. Sometimes it's hard to tell if I'm awake or asleep. The walls of the bedroom are blue, not the clear blue of the sea or a newborn's eyes, but the dense turquoise of institutions, and all night long, the flashing ribbons of color cast by the passing headlights mock me in my sleeplessness. When I doze off, I wake up confused. My head is at the wrong end of the bed, the light is coming from the opposite side of the room, and a shapeless but profound dread is squatting on my chest. I check off my thoughts, one by one, trying to find the source, and then it hits me that Magda is dead, and the guilt and longing begin to pick and tear at me all over again.

The first few days, I can't bear waking up to this, so I avoid falling asleep at all. I wander all night from the blue room to the brown room and back, or I sit on the window ledge, both sets of panes flung open into the heat like all the others on the block. I watch the prostitutes on the corner, dressed in only threads of clothing because of the heat, slouching and joking as they wait. When a car pulls up, the tallest one approaches, bending at the waist, leaning her forearm on the car window to talk to the driver. They turn down more cars in the summer than in the wintertime, laughing after them as they sheepishly creep away. They seem so free from where I sit, a condemned prisoner in a tower, only myself to blame.

And then, as it shifts toward morning, I listen to the sounds of the day switching on—the clanking of kettles, the blare of the morning television programs, the cars dropping off the girls from the night before and speeding away. And as each successive day gets turned over and the sand starts to trickle again, it seems impossible to me that the world has gone on eating and watching television and cheating on their wives, that the people on the street don't stop even for a split second to acknowledge the gaping hole where Magda used to be. To everyone else, she is nothing more than an anonymous, black-and-white death notice on a wall, ready at any time to be papered over by the next layer.

It must be toward the end of the first week that I awake in the middle of the night. There's a sickening floral smell in the air, like two months of spring compressed into a day. It takes a minute for me to place the smell, to recognize the glint of her hair, the weight at the foot of the bed that does not belong to me.

"Magda," I whisper.

Her hand reaches out and holds my left leg, just below the knee, lingering there long enough for me to feel the warmth passing from her hand to my calf. I wait for her to offer some relief, some resolution, some comfort to relax my paralyzed body, each muscle becoming more rigid and more isolated from the others with every moment that passes.

"How could you?" she whispers instead.

"I'm sorry, Magda. I'm so sorry. Forgive me." But there, alone in the dark, my own voice disturbing the silence is the most frightening thing imaginable.

"Forgive me," I say again out loud, but my voice echoes back to me just as it did the first time.

The bedsprings let out a squeal, and the gentle pressure around my leg releases. But the last thing I see as the silhouette dissipates into the darkness is not the glint of Magda's hair, but the curve of Nela's cheekbones.

I don't leave the *kamienica* for the rest of May and all of June. I don't go out to Hipermarket Europa, I don't go to Stash's, I don't go to the library, I don't go to Mikro. I don't even go out on the balcony. After all, how can you betray your cousin, let her die in the backseat of a

Little Fiat, and then go out and meet the world with the sun on your face? How can you go back and live among the shopkeepers and the tourists, the grandparents and the little children and not make an Act of Contrition to everyone you meet? How can you let your grandmother be discovered by your half-wit uncle because you are off watching a film, and continue to eat plum cake and tell jokes and kiss and listen to jazz and go to the cinema like nothing ever happened?

Pani Bożena does everything herself now. She's already up at dawn moving around downstairs, running the water and banging the dishes. She has a key to my flat, and she comes up every morning and coaxes me to wash up and do my hair in front of the scrap of mirror hanging in the bathroom. She makes me breakfast. She does the dishes. She goes to the market. She wrestles with the washing machine. She doesn't complain. She doesn't swoon. Liz Taylor and Katharine Hepburn, the grande dame, the cabaret star, and her *skleroza* are all gone. Her depression that winter seems to have burned all of it away, and now what's left sitting in the ashes is the real Pani Bożena, who turns out to be a very patient and sympathetic person.

"Don't worry, *kochana*," she tells me every day. "I will take care of you."

And she does. I spend my days in her flat, sitting on her chaise, flipping through the television channels, drifting in and out of sleep.

Sometime during the second week, Stash comes by.

"*Co słychać?*" he asks, ruffling my hair.

"Nothing."

He's carrying a plastic shopping bag. "Irena asked me to give you this. Some things you left behind."

He puts it on the end of the chaise, and I sit up. I open the bag cautiously and touch the things inside like I'm checking a pot of water on the stove. It's a jumbled mess, everything tangled together, as if saving them for me was an afterthought.

"How is she?"

"Same as you."

"Is she ever going to talk to me?"

"It's not you. She just needs time."

I had been sustaining a small shaft of hope, but the shopping bag sitting at the end of the chaise is the final stone on the cellar door.

There is no longer anything left open between Irena and me, nothing unfinished, not even a few personal items left consciously or unconsciously or subconsciously in a drawer.

"Hang in there," Stash says. "I'll come by again soon."

Pani Bożena brings the bag upstairs for me, and that night, I stow it in the darkest corner of the wardrobe.

The day of the law exam and the geography exam pass like any other except for the dull ache in my chest. I think about the students hunched over their papers, the blank table space with my name card. I think of the law-school aspirants and their parents standing around the archway on Pigeon Street waiting for the list to be posted. I try to imagine Irena across town, sitting on the love seat. I try to pose Magda against the door frame of the living room, smiling and fluffing her hair, bantering with her mother. But I can't. All I can picture is her body slung over Sebastian's shoulder, her head in my lap in the car, the bumps under the white sheet on the gurney being wheeled down the stark white hallway.

45

He Who Does Not Work Does Not Eat

ANIELICA EVENTUALLY TOOK a job teaching at the grammar school in Osiek. A few of the children who had come to her house during the war were there, and this made it somehow easier to abide by the slogans and the new textbooks, even the beady Georgian eyes staring down at her. What she could not abide by in the end was the removal of the crosses. The Soviets had not yet learned to skip the discussion step when it came to the highlanders, and so it was talked about for weeks before it actually happened, and the action was ordered weeks before the inspectors were to arrive.

"I just cannot bring myself to do it, Pani Rita," Anielica whispered one day after school. Pani Rita taught the fifth class and Anielica taught the fourth. "I would feel as if I myself were participating in the crucifixion."

"They will fire us if we don't. Or worse."

"I cannot do it."

"Think of the children. Think of who they will get to teach them if you leave." In a matter of a few years, there was already a They. An omniscient, omnipresent, menacing They that had to be whispered about and never quite articulated.

Anielica went home and prayed to the Virgin Mary, and when she came back in the morning, the cross was gone.

"Thank you," she said when she saw Pani Rita.

The crucifix had hung on the wall of the classroom for so long that it left an imprint of sunny yellow paint against a background of ocher, as if Christ had indeed risen and left his nimbus behind.

"Now it will be a reminder of the Resurrection," Pani Rita said.

And it did bring hope for a few short weeks, hope that even when something is gone, it is not *really* gone. The inspectors came and nodded and checked off and went, and all the teachers in the school breathed a sigh of relief. But after the next long holiday, they came back to find the walls whitewashed, the dual portraits of Grandfather Lenin and Uncle Stalin flanking the spot where the crucifix had been, places previously reserved for the two thieves.

Anielica couldn't bear the whitewashing. She quit at the end of the week.

But He Who Does Not Work Does Not Eat, and so when Pani Plotka retired from the post office shortly thereafter, Anielica took over. It was a small post office, serving only Half-Village and Pisarowice, and most people stopped in only once or twice a week. The post office in Osiek would have sufficed, and it was generally agreed upon that they had only really built it for the construction jobs it provided and for another wall to hang the portraits on. But Anielica took pride in keeping the little office running—waiting on customers, sorting the mail, and distributing the relief packages.

The year Uncle Stalin died, the year Ania turned six, they started to arrive. They were full to bursting with pity from American, Canadian, and English schoolchildren, and Anielica, as postmistress, had the responsibility of distributing their pity evenly to the surrounding families. They were anonymous, addressed to post codes and not people, and filled with things that must have been rumored to be lacking in the countries behind the Żelazna Kurtyna, or the Iron Curtain, as it had come to be called. Left shoes. Blue jeans. Lipstick. Pictures of Tony Bennett. No currency, or it would be confiscated. No books that were not on the *indeks*. All correspondence would be monitored, although the notes from the West were usually so trite and naive that they were hardly worth translating.

It was the best part of her job, distributing the relief packages. There were usually at least a few things that could be used or traded, and the family that received them would be joyful for a week. Some shook their heads in amazement that Anielica did not keep the packages all for herself, or at least use them to *załatwić* other things. In the New Poland, you took what you could get, whether you needed it or not, and eventually you would figure out how it benefited you. But to Anielica, the benefit was to see the excitement on her neighbors' faces as they opened the boxes, to visit the next time and notice the colorful cans and bottles turned into vases, the crayon drawings from the Western children nailed to the walls of the huts. It was a little like being Święty Mikołaj all year-round.

But one day a package arrived, with the same post code, but addressed to Half-Village and not Pisarowice, and though the handwriting was in the same uniform script that everyone else had, there was something rebellious about the *f*'s that made Anielica keep the package for herself.

She waited until closing time and locked the door. She set the package on the counter, grabbed one end of the brown tape, and pulled. Inside, there were wads of colored comic pages, six yards of wool bouclé wrapped carefully in paper and string, three books, ten bars of chocolate, a carton of cigarettes, and a large tin of coffee with a bright red label. Underneath it all, there was a tiny slip of paper. In her own handwriting.

I AM MISSING MY SECOND MOLAR
ON THE LEFT SIDE, BOTTOM.

46

Where the Devil Says Good Night

"B
A-BA YA-GA! Ba-ba Ya-ga!" It's Pani Bożena, coming to call me downstairs, but this particular morning there's something more insistent about her voice, like the women's voices in the main room the morning my mother died. I've been lying awake for a while already, and I stand up when I hear her coming up the stairs. She always looks acutely disappointed if I'm still in bed, as if she has failed me and I have failed her, and it's this and only this that swings my feet to the floor each day.

She usually stays just until I've picked out fresh clothes and turned on the water, until she's sure that I have sufficient momentum to carry me downstairs, but today she stands outside the bathroom door, asking several times if I'm finished yet, and would I hurry up before the entire day gets away. She goes down the stairs first, looking back at me every few steps to make sure that I'm behind her, and when she opens the door of her flat, she announces in a high-pitched voice: "Here she is!" For a moment I worry that this is some kind of scene, that she's back to how she used to be, and this morning I was actually roused by Ingrid Bergman or Vivian Leigh or Sophia Loren.

But when I turn the corner, there's a man sitting at the table, a man I have never seen before. He's sitting in Pani Bożena's living room as if he belongs there, his legs stretched out in front of him and crossed at the ankle, a cup of tea on the table next to him. He doesn't look much different from the tourists at Irena's in his tan pants and trainers, but when he turns his head to look at me, I see my mother's drooping eyelids and the crook in my own nose. I feel something inside give way like a trapdoor. It's *him*. From the photo. One hundred percent.

"Beata? Is it really you?" He stands up and smooths the front of his pants. Beata. It's the name of my baptism, the name on all my official documents, the name they called into the woods the day my mother died, the name on Nela's death notices under the words *survived by*.

"Baba Yaga," I say cautiously. "Everyone calls me Baba Yaga now."

"Beata," he insists. "Beata." He looks at me in the same way Nela used to look at me, searching my face for Nela's features just as Nela used to search for his.

"Beata," he says again, but this time, his voice cracks and his eyes well up. "I'm sorry," he says, "I'm sorry, but I look at you, and . . ." He draws a folded white handkerchief from his back pocket and wipes his nose.

I want to comfort him, but I don't know how. He's a fictional character, a figment of my imagination. It's the same as if someone would ask me to have tea with the real Baba Yaga or the Wawel Dragon or Pinocchio and carry on a conversation. He asks me questions, and I try to answer them. He speaks the Polish of fifty years ago, the words from the newsreels in the retrospectives.

Pani Bożena pours more tea and puts a *drożdżówka* on a plate for me, but I have no appetite. She and my grandfather banter back and forth using each other's first names, and I piece together that just after the war, eight of them shared a communal flat across Bishop Square with a mean little woman named Gosia, who doesn't even merit a "God rest her soul" after her name. I listen as Pani Bożena asks him about America, and he tells her that he owns a construction company in Nowy Jork now, that he has been trying to get off the blacklist ever since the communists were voted out, and only received word a week ago that he was finally allowed to return. All of his sisters are now in America, and he has twenty-two nephews and nieces, though he has never in his life remarried. Never in his life. That's exactly how he says it.

"Nela never remarried either," I say, and they both look over at me. The words seem so sparse, so meager. They can't begin to describe the vacancy in her eyes as she sat in front of the iron stove, touching the fur collar at her neck. Or the bleak acceptance of all the men in the surrounding villages who worshipped her but knew they could never overcome the respectful distance she maintained with them—a trim, proprietary hedge around her heart.

"Baba Yaga," Pani Bożena says. "Your grandfather will want to see a little of the city. You will take him around of course."

"When?"

"Well, today of course. As soon as you have finished your tea."

And this is how a stranger from America rescues me from the turquoise-blue walls in the third-floor flat of Pani Bożena's *kamienica*. And from my grief. Over the week Czesław is in Krakow, we go everywhere. We eat at Wierzynek, where a salad alone costs fifty thousand złotych and I'm scared to dirty the napkins. We go to Jama Michalika, and the waiters fall all over themselves bringing us trays of sweets and tea. We sit in the red booths at Maska and eat towers of ice cream with wafer scaffolding. We take the tour of Wawel Castle and the salt mines in Wieliczka. We drive out to Huta and the Church of the Ark in Czesław's rental car and sit in the coolness under the enormous crucifix and the ceiling that looks like the bottom of a boat. We go to the opera and the Cabaret, browse the boutiques and the antique shops, and watch a film at Mikro.

It is the closest my grandmother ever came to her fairy tale.

Two nights before Czesław is to return to America, we lie down in the middle of the Błonia after dark, hardly a soul around.

"I used to come here when I wanted to get away from the city," he says.

"Me too."

"You know, your grandmother and I had a picnic here after our wedding."

"She told me."

The grass bristles under my hand, and the crickets are scraping and chafing in the darkness. All the crickets in the city must congregate here at night.

"You know, my only regret is that I didn't marry her sooner. During the war. In the cellar if I had to. Maybe things would have been different then."

We lie side by side, silently, staring into the sky. When the streetlights go off at midnight, the stars are almost as bright as in the mountains.

"Beata?"

"Yes?"

"Irena told me that you were preparing for the entrance exam for Jagiellonian."

"I was."

"For geography?"

"Uh-huh."

"And why didn't you take it?"

"I don't know."

"And Bożena told me that before this week, you hadn't left the house in over a month."

"Yes."

"Because you think you are to blame for Irenka's daughter?"

"Yes," I say, barely audible above the noise of the crickets.

"Don't you think you should call her?"

"She doesn't want to talk to me."

"Only because you remind her of what's missing. But it would be better for both of you, I think."

I am silent. To say the truth, there is a part of me that never wants to see Irena again, that wants to let the memory of her and Magda fade and dissipate. Because sometimes it's easier to move on than to keep walking around the same hole in the floor. Sometimes it's easier to make new friends than to keep returning to family. But this I say only to the stars.

"Beata," he says. "Will you go with me back to the village tomorrow?"

"I think you will be disappointed," I say. "There's not much there anymore." It's true. When I left last year, there were only four inhabitants in Half-Village, including Uncle Jakub, who had moved into the old Lubicz house once there were no more sheep to mind.

"There was not much there when I left either." And he smiles in the darkness, the same cocky, sepia smile of the photograph.

We set out the next morning with a sack full of sandwiches that Pani Bożena made for us. Czesław seems nervous, and I can tell he doesn't feel like talking. I settle back into my seat. It's a nice rental car, with a sliding roof and leather seats, and the German engineering packs an unnatural silence around us.

I try to imagine Czesław's car in America. His life in America. I try to picture him among the skyscrapers and the yellow taxis or in an office somewhere, running his construction business. I try to imagine him celebrating the birthdays of his nieces and nephews with giant cakes and mountains of presents like I have seen in the films.

It seems like no time at all, and we are out of the city. I watch his eyes dart around, trying to take in the new reality. The freshly built houses and the satellite dishes, the new Little Fiats, the grandmothers on bicycles, the billboards selling country homes, tires, and yogurt. Even out here, where, as they used to say, the devil says good night, the billboards are everywhere.

I wonder how much change a person can take in one lifetime.

The fields give way to woods. The air-conditioning blows softly through the vents, and pockets of sunlight flash through the sliding roof. It takes only an hour and a half to get to Nowy Targ. From Nowy Targ, it will be only another half-hour to Pisarowice. I think of all the times Nela talked about Krakow like it was an entirely different cosmos. Even on the bus when I first came, it seemed so far. Two hours. That's all. And in fifty years she never went back. Not even to visit.

We come to the last stop sign before the river, and the car whirrs quietly beneath us, the turn signal clicking patiently as Czesław decides which way to go. Finally he turns left.

"Does Pan Romanenko still man the barge?"

"Pan Romek?"

"I guess being Ukrainian was not so easy after the war."

But when we get to the river, there is no barge and no Pan Romek. There's only a concrete slab in its place. Even at this, Czesław only shrugs his shoulders and drives right over. It's not until we reach Pisarowice that he stops the car.

"I'll be damned," he says. He looks up at the road to Half-Village and shakes his head. He cannot speak. He drives slowly up the hill as if the road is only a mirage, and at the top, he turns the car off and leans on the steering wheel, gathering his strength.

"Ready?" I ask.

He nods.

We get out, and the doors thump softly behind us. Outside, the midday heat is smothering, and the screeching of insects overpowers every other sound. We walk through the tall grass, through the clearing, past the boulder that marks the Epler boy's grave. We stop first by the old Lubicz house to see if Uncle Jakub is home.

"Uncle Jakub," I call, and knock on his door. "Uncle Jakub."

There's no answer, and I go right in, just as I used to when I lived here. And I think I'm in the wrong house at first, or that someone else has moved in. My eyes try to make sense of everything in front of me.

"*Niesamowite*," I say.

"Unbelievable," Czesław echoes over my shoulder.

In front of us are all of Nela's things. Not boxed up as I left them, but laid out like when she was alive. The table is set for four with her dishes and silverware, and her slippers and shoes are lined up next to the door. Her clothes, coats, and purses are hung up like paintings all around the room, and he has even arranged the skirts and sweaters into outfits that she used to wear. Her hairbrush, comb, perfume, and powder are neatly arranged on a table next to the bed, and her lipstick stands open and ready on the dresser. Some of the books are there, lined up neatly on the mantel, and there's a book of Miłosz lying facedown on a chair in front of the fireplace.

Czesław runs his finger along the spines on the mantel, examining the titles. He walks around the room, touching this and that: the hems of her dresses and the tines of her comb. Uncle Jakub has left his whittling on the table along with a half-cup of tea and the shell of an egg, so I know that he has only stepped out and will be back soon. I worry about what to say if he walks in on us, but how can I hurry Czesław along? She was his *wife*, after all. He should be angry. Something.

"We can go," he says calmly. He absentmindedly picks up one of the forks on the table and examines the tines, then puts it back in exactly the same place that he found it.

"I'm sorry," I say. "I left all her things in our house. Packed away. He said he would look after them. I'm sure if I ask him, you can take them back with you to America."

But he's not listening. His gaze is focused across the clearing to our house. As we come closer, he flinches. Nela and I had a hard time keeping it up by ourselves, and after a year of abandonment, it is even worse than when I left. The roof is rusted through in places, a few windows broken. Czesław instinctively clears the path to the door, stamping on loose stones, pulling weeds, tossing twigs and branches toward the woods.

"I'm sorry," I say. "Nela told me that you built almost everything here, and now . . . look at it."

"No sorries," he says. "It's only a house." But I can tell he's disappointed.

He opens the carved door, and it hangs loosely on the hinge. We both step into the living room. Inside, the stone wall has sprouted weeds in the chinking and has collapsed in one place, leaving a gaping hole to the other side.

"What is *that?*"

"My father built that. When *mama* got sick, he and Nela fought all the time. About his drinking. About *mama*. About me. One day, he ripped down the garden wall and rebuilt it here. Straight down the middle of the room. It was probably for the best. When *mama* got worse, I got to move in with Nela on her side."

The Pigeon lets his eyes roam up and down the wall, then shakes his head. "And then?"

"And then after *mama* died and my father left, I don't think Nela wanted to go over to the other side at all anymore. Neither of us did. So we just left it standing."

He looks like he wants to sit down, but there's nowhere to sit. All our furniture except for the giant wardrobe is at Uncle Jakub's now. Czesław runs his hand along the side of the wardrobe, just as Nela used to do, and I wonder if any traces of her lotion or her fingerprints remain. He wanders around, examining the walls and the windows, then steps through the crumbled section of the wall to the other side. I follow him, and he goes straight to the old *barszcz* stain in the middle of the floor. He stoops down to touch it, and he suddenly looks very old. He rubs his hand across the stain and looks at his palm.

"Were you there?" I ask. "Were you there the day Ciocia Marysia spilled the pot of *barszcz*?"

He looks up at me, confused, and suddenly he's going down, down, down to the floor. I think for a minute that he's had a heart attack or a stroke, but his movements are graceful and lucid. He stretches out on the floor, his cheek and the palm of his hand pressed against the stain.

"Czesław? Are you okay? Czesław?"

He's crying, weeping, and I don't know what to do. It's only a *barszcz* stain, and why would anyone cry over spilled *barszcz*?

"Are you okay?" I ask again. "Czesław? Czesław? Pigeon?"

But he doesn't answer, and finally, it dawns on me that this must be one of those stories with the sad endings that Nela never told me. I crouch down next to him, this man who has my nose, my mother's eyelids, and my grandmother's heart. This man I have only met this week. I pat his back. I touch his white hair. But it's not enough.

"I should have been here," he says, choking on the words. "I should have been here. I told her I would be here. And I was late that morning. I was running late. I was *too* late. And now. Too late."

And all of a sudden I am crying too. For the ending that I held in my lap in the backseat of a Little Fiat. For the ending that happened while I was away at the cinema in Osiek. For the ending of the *barszcz* story that I don't even know.

I lie down with him on the *barszcz* stain and put my hand on his, my face only a board's width from his. I stare into his milky eyes and feel the slight warmth of his breath, and he stares right back at me. Neither of us tries to stop the tears or reassure the other one. Neither of us wishes to soften the hardness of the wooden floor or bleach the stain away. We only lie here, restless, staring at each other, our eyes searching for plain acceptance of what we have said. Of what we have done. Of what we have failed to do.

We lie on the stain for a long time. The stain that has been here forever and will outlast the both of us. Our bodies settle and our breath becomes deep and even. He pulls his handkerchief from his pocket and doesn't think twice about handing it to me, and I don't think twice about taking it from him. Because we're together now, and we are family, and he and I and Irena are the only ones left.

And I guess that's why we decide to move the wall back to where it belongs, because we know that no one after us will do it, will even know where it once stood, protecting my grandmother and her family from the advance of the outside world. We throw the stones out of the house and kick them with our feet into a rough perimeter. I hand them to him one by one, and he carefully fits them into place, wiggling them a little until they lock together. Pani Wzwolenska comes out of the house and shakes her head as if we're crazy, but she goes back inside and comes out with two glasses of apple juice. In the end, it takes us three or four hours, and the whole time, I worry that it will be too much for him, that the day is too hot and the stones are too heavy. But there's a lot of strength left in him, in this seventy-year-old man, and I wonder if he always had this strength in America or if he came back and reclaimed it here.

We talk as we work, and now it seems like there's nothing we can't say. He tells me about being a partisan during the war and then resisting against the communists in Krakow, how they came for him first in the middle of the night, and finally and frighteningly in the light of day. How they gave him two options: the first one death for him and danger for his family and friends; the other, a One-Way Ticket. He tells it all simply, plainly, bluntly. There are no fairy tales, no missing endings, and no *barszcz* stains. Only when he comes to the part where they put him on the train does he suddenly fall silent, as if nothing important happened after that.

"But if you were in America all this time, why didn't you try to contact her?"

He stops and straightens up. He looks at me, confused. "But I was in constant contact with your grandmother."

"You were?"

"She never told you?"

"She told everyone you were dead."

He sits down on a section of the wall. "We passed letters through the post office, through the relief packages, and a few of her sewing clients who were not under suspicion. And I tried to get back. Many times. But I was on the list and in the files, and once you're on the list, you're there forever. I tried to get her to leave too. I had papers made and bought the tickets. Once in 1956, then 1968, then 1984."

"She could have left?"

"It would have been difficult, but she could have left."

"Why didn't she?"

"What do you mean, why? Because of you and your mother. She would have had to leave you alone. To leave you behind."

We go back to work, but in silence now, each of us retreating to our own thoughts, the only sound the clomping of the stones as they stack up one on top of the other. When we finish, the wall is sturdy and even. Pani Wzwolenska invites us inside for supper, but we want to stay outside to watch the sun go down, so she goes in and brings back sandwiches and more apple juice. The treetops are just piercing the setting sun, and we ask Pani Wzwolenska to join us, but she just shakes her head and laughs because she can see the sun set like this any night of the week.

We sit on the wall for a long time, eating our sandwiches and listening to the crickets until the sun is only a few glittering scraps of gold at the base of the trees. I know we are both waiting for Uncle Jakub to return. It would be a shame for us to have come here and missed him, but maybe it's better this way. Maybe he would be too embarrassed if he knew we had seen his shrine to another man's wife, to a woman who had only ever let him watch her sheep, turn over her garden, and chop her wood.

And it's as I'm turning this over in my mind that I hear the old Trabant roaring up into the clearing, drowning out the crickets for a moment until he kills the engine. I hear him get out and slam the door, the constant monologue that has kept him company all these years buzzing from his lips. The door of his house opens and shuts, opens and shuts, and I look over nervously at Czesław, who only pats my knee and smiles.

The houses in the village form a perfect horseshoe around the boulder in the middle, the road to Pisarowice filling the opening, and if you loop behind the houses, you can pass through all the yards. This is apparently what Uncle Jakub does, and it's not long before we see him coming around the corner of Pani Wzwolenska's house.

". . . I saw the car, and Baba Yaga, I cannot believe it, Baba Yaga, you are back and I have been thinking about you a lot lately, and you have not written in a while, and you put back the wall, but how ..."

He suddenly falls silent. Czesław stands up and holds his palms out in front of him.

"It's me, Jakub," he says. "It's me."

Uncle Jakub inches toward him.

"... It is you, it is really you, and I didn't know you were coming, I would invite you in if my house was not such a mess, did Baba Yaga tell you I am living in the old Lubicz house, and it is too bad I cannot ask you to come in, why didn't you tell me you were coming, oh, I cannot believe it, my house is such a mess, I would be so ashamed ..."

I wait for Czesław to interrupt him, to tell him that we've already been to the house, and to ask him for Nela's things to take back with him to America. But Uncle Jakub goes on and on, and I slowly realize that Czesław is not going to say anything about it. We sit on the wall for another hour, our backsides melding with the stones. We talk through the darkness and the swarms of mosquitoes, none of us suggesting that we go inside. When we are ready to leave, Czesław hands Uncle Jakub two envelopes, one filled with photos, the other with dollars.

"You didn't say anything," I say as we walk to the car in the clearing.

"He's my brother."

"But she was your wife."

"She was many things to many people," he says softly. "Besides, I can't get those years back by taking back her dresses."

But I don't want him to come all the way out here and leave with nothing. "Wait. I think there's still something of hers. In the wardrobe."

We go back inside, and they are still there, hidden in the secret compartment in the bottom of the wardrobe. The French. Proust, Zola, Dumas, Camus, Voltaire, Maupassant, Balzac, Flaubert, Hugo, Céline, Lamartine.

"She made me promise to take them with me to Krakow," I say, "but I couldn't manage. Maybe you want to take them back to America? At least a few of them?"

He picks up one of the books and turns it over in his hands.

"The French ones were always her favorite," I say. "I did take a copy of *Germinal.* She used to read it to me all the time . . ."

But he doesn't seem to be listening. All of his attention is focused on the book in his hands. He opens the back cover and furrows his eyebrows. He pulls out a pocketknife and unfolds the blade.

"Czesław?"

He holds the front cover steady against his body and inserts the blade beneath the end page, pulling it swiftly away from himself. He separates the end page from the cover, and two crisp hundred-dollar bills fall out.

"*Boże.*"

He smiles.

"Did she know?"

"Of course. Here. They're yours now," he says, handing them to me. I have never held a hundred-dollar bill before. They're heavier than I thought. I feel like I'm holding the entirety of Nela's life, all of her opportunities and possibilities, which she denied herself and squirreled away for me.

Czesław is not finished. He spreads the front and back covers of the book like wings and pokes the tip of the knife down inside the spine until a tiny bit of paper pokes out from the other end. He wiggles the paper like a loose tooth until it comes out, a tight roll about ten centimeters long. He hands it to me.

"Go on."

It takes me a minute to unfold, and even then, it wants to curl back into itself. There's writing on both sides, tiny, like squashed insects. The paper has been folded and unfolded so many times, it feels as soft as flannel.

"Every book?"

"Every book."

At first, I can barely make out the words in the moonlight, but by the time I finish, I understand completely why Nela never remarried, why she kept his photograph under her pillow all those years, why she didn't even need to amplify the tiny lettering with her voice or speak about what she already knew in her heart.

There are about eighty books hidden in the bottom of the wardrobe. When we are finished, we put all of them back under the false bottom except for two. The stack of letters leaves the little house flattened between the pages of Maupassant, the money tucked into Dumas.

There's nothing more to say on the way home. I sneak sideways glances at Czesław, his serious expressions breaking into secret smiles from time to time. I think about how much Nela gave up for my mother and me. Every day, for years and years, without ever complaining. I wonder if she ever resented us or regretted the choice she made. I think of the others in their generation going quietly about their business even after their world flipped on its head. Twice. I think about Stash in the basement of the police station on Mogilskie Street, the families of the striking factory workers throwing food over the walls, the protestors on the Rynek being sprayed with fire hoses, the thousands of knocks in the middle of the night. I think about Irena and how she sacrificed for Magda just as Nela did for me.

When we arrive back in Krakow, it's an ordinary summer night, and people are everywhere, walking hand in hand, laughing, shouting to each other down the street. But inside the German rental car, all the sounds are muffled, as if we've somehow preserved the quiet of the village and brought it back with us.

"Beata?"

"Yes?"

"Beata, I want you to think about coming back to America with me."

It's an enormous question, and I want to answer with a long list of why I can't go, why I must stay here. But to say the truth, now, without Nela, without Magda and Irena, without so much as a flat or a boyfriend or a course of study, what's really here for me? Streets? *Kamienice?* The Rynek? The Błonia? Even those are more Nela's than mine.

"I need to think about it."

"I expect you do."

Pani Bożena gave me a key when I moved in upstairs, but this week is the first time I've actually used it. It's late, and her flat is already dark, so I go straight upstairs and dig in the wardrobe for the shopping bag Stash brought over. I carry it to the bed and dump the contents out into the valleys of the *pierzyna*. If someone had asked me to guess what I'd left behind, I would have been able to name a few things. The video camera, my ticket to Krakow, a pair of old sandals, the copy of *Germinal*, the photograph of the Pigeon. And Nela's fur collar.

I snatch it up from the pile and bring it to my face, and the smell is a perfect blend of Nela's perfume and the cigarette smoke and cooked onion of Irena's flat. I run my hand over it, and the fur ripples like water over a rocky riverbed. I let my fingers linger over one spot on the seam, a sharp point poking out, spewing a length of thread. As soon as he said it, I knew exactly where to look. My fingers had always stopped on it, worried over it, like a loose tooth or a mole or a rough spot on the inside of my cheek. I give the hanging thread a little tug, and instead of being held fast by the backstitch, it gives way immediately. There were always shortages, and Nela would use whatever she could find to stiffen her collars: a piece of composition book or a folded Christmas card or an old Party flyer. I pull the first one out and unfold it, then work the other two through the hole. It's exactly as he said. 1956. 1968. 1984. Airline tickets to New York, rubbing up against her neck all those years.

I try to picture America and what it would be like. I remember the noisy, clattering language of Irena's tourists and what Sebastian used to say about New York, about the taxicabs and the skyscrapers and the "Have a nice day." I think back to all of the American films I've seen, with the inevitable Happy End. I see the old Kinga jumping up and down and asking me if I am *crazy*, telling me that *of course* I should go. Why *wouldn't* I? The steely question mark tugs like a fish hook at the back of my mind. But as I hold the tickets, my hands start to shake, and a different plan begins to form somewhere else, in the place that still remembers how to stack rocks and climb a tree, how to see far and wide and run as if my life depended on it.

47

Solidarność

I DON'T SLEEP VERY WELL, anticipating the morning. I wake up early and walk over to meet Czesław at his hotel. The German rental car is already sitting out front, and the doorman bows and calls me Pani Beata. I sit in the shiny lobby and wait for him to come down.

"And?" he says when he sees me, his eyes searching my face for the answer.

"I'm sorry," I say. But if I'm sorry, it's only for him. I do not want to go to America. I do not want to live in a film with yellow taxis jumping out of the screen and skyscrapers rising from the ground like in "Jack and the Bean Plant." I do not want to live in the shadow of a certain Happy End. Or a pretend one constructed from boxes of someone else's old things. I do not want to speak someone else's language and live someone else's destiny. Not even Nela's.

"No sorries," he says. "Are you sure?"

"I'm sure."

It's the hardest goodbye I've ever had to say. It feels final, like he is indeed taking Nela across the ocean with him, and I'm finally saying good-bye to her too. He drives me back to Pani Bożena's, and we stand on the sidewalk in front of the old *kamienica*. He gives me three kisses for the Polish way and a hug for the American. I've only known him for a week, but our movements seem so natural that anyone watching would think that we have been grandfather and grand-daughter all our lives.

"You know you can visit whenever you want," he says.

"I know."

"And you can always change your mind about America."

"I know."

"And I'll be back to visit as soon as I can."

"I know."

I stare after the car as he drives away, and for the first time since I set foot on Bishop's Square, two of the prostitutes getting dropped off from the night before look over at me and nod in acknowledgment. It's a moment of pure solidarity on a bright summer morning. We are sisters here, and even though we have not yet put in our three generations of squatting, we have all suffered enough in this city to say that we are from here.

I go upstairs and wrap the camera in the dishtowel, tying the corners until it makes a tight package. I stow it in the bottom of my rucksack with a few other things, I go out onto Bishop Square, and I start to walk. Not toward the Rynek and the tourists, but in the other direction, where instead of grand *kamienice,* there are concrete *osiedla,* instead of cafés, milk bars, and instead of boutiques with names in French or Italian, there are squat stores and kiosks still named in the communist way: Vegetables. Fruit. Shoes. Women's Clothing. I walk past the kiosks, the *lombardy,* and the secondhand stores. I end up in Huta, near People's Square. There used to be a giant statue of Lenin here, one of the first and most dramatic to be pulled down. I go into an ordinary milk bar a little ahead of the lunch crowd. I pick out a table with two grandmothers and a grandfather and sit down in the empty seat.

"Excuse me." I turn to one of the women. "Would Pani mind if I interviewed Pani?"

The woman pretends not to hear me. The other draws back, wary. "For what?"

"For a film."

"Are you from a television program?"

"No."

"Are you from the police?"

"No."

"The secret police?"

"No."

"The tax police?"

"No." We Poles are not known for trusting strangers.

"How many questions?"

"Just a few."

"About what?"

"About Pani's life."

She laughs. "About my *life?* About *my* life? You would be bored to tears in a moment, *kochana*."

"It's probably more interesting than Pani thinks."

"Dear"— she leans toward me and whispers conspiratorially— "look around. We are in a milk bar in Huta with a bunch of pensioners, and what's more, this is the highlight of my day." She smiles and shakes her head stiffly. The other one only looks into her soup.

"I'll answer your questions," the grandfather finally says. "I spent six years fighting in the war and eleven in a camp in Siberia. I'm not afraid of anything." He has two silver teeth, and his hair is white and thick as weeds.

I unwrap the camera carefully, take the lens cap off, and focus until I can see him in the little screen to the side. My hands are shaking, and suddenly, it all seems like a bad idea.

"It's ready," I say.

"I'm ready," he answers.

"Well, first of all, I was wondering . . . you see, wondering if . . . well, if Pan could tell me a little about Pan's life."

So he tells me about the war, about Huta when it was first built in the fifties, about conditions in the steelworks and the strikes in the seventies and eighties. The two grandmothers listen and fill in the dates and the street names when he can't remember. When he finishes, he looks up at me as if he's expecting to receive a grade.

"Anything else?"

"They were very good stories," I say timidly, "but what about Pan's family?"

"What do you mean?"

There are about fifteen tables in the milk bar, and everyone is watching us now except the woman behind the counter, who I suspect could continue ladling soup and ringing up plates through an

337

air raid or a hurricane. My heart is pounding, and my armpits are damp. I try to think of Magda, how she walked right up to the table of Englishmen in the security services bar. And then it dawns on me. I was right there next to her. I told the Englishmen off too.

"Your family," I say, this time a little louder.

"My family?"

"Yes."

"I don't have a family. My parents both died early in the war."

"Any brothers or sisters?"

"I was an only child."

"Children?"

"No."

"A wife?"

"Never married."

"A sweetheart then?"

If I had been watching him with my naked eye, if I hadn't been looking at the screen, I might have missed it. I might never have seen his forehead ripple, his eyes recede. He looks away from the camera and gets up from the table. "Look, I don't think I can help you with your school project. I think you're looking for someone else, someone unhappy. My life has been a fine one. A fine one."

I hear the murmurs around me, and I feel my face flush. The grandmothers also leave, and I'm sitting at the table alone, even though the crowd is growing. I think about what Irena told me once, that there's a big difference between knowing something and being able to talk about it. I feel the disapproving eyes on me as I spread out the dishtowel and wrap up the camera, knotting the corners. I feel someone hovering over my shoulder.

"I'm leaving," I say. "You can have the table. I'm leaving."

"That's too bad."

I look up at her. She's a very modern-looking grandmother with reading glasses nestled in her short gray hair, muted lipstick, and stylish pants. You hardly ever see a grandmother wearing pants, even in the New Poland.

"Who are you interviewing?"

"Just average Krakowians."

She puts her bowl of soup down on the table. "Well, I'm not from Krakow. But you can still interview me."

My fingers begin tugging apart the knots in the dishtowel. "So where is Pani from?"

"The village."

"So am I. Which one?"

"No one ever asks which one."

"I know."

"Cold Water. It's in the east, in Bieszczady."

"Never heard of it."

"And you?"

"Half-Village. Not far from Osiek."

"Never heard of it," she says. We both laugh. She has a laugh that's right on the surface, a bubble that bursts as soon as the air finds it.

"Can I turn the camera on?"

"Go right ahead. Not that anyone wants to look at me at my age."

"Not at all. I think Pani is very stylish."

"Thank you, *kochana*," she says, and she tips her glasses so they rest on her nose. "I can't see anything anymore," she explains. "Not even my soup." She picks up the aluminum spoon, and her head bobs in and out of the frame as she eats.

"And how did Pani's eyes get so bad?" I ask.

"Reading," she says. "That damn literacy." She laughs again. One of the other grandmothers watching clucks in disapproval at her language.

"Only from reading?"

"Oh yes, I used to read all the time when I was a child. All the time. They couldn't keep me in books."

Two students sit down at the table with us and begin to eat.

"I used to hide away in the *stodoła* when I was a girl. I made a little hidden cave for myself out of the hay."

I nod.

"I had to hide because my mother didn't want me to read. She thought I would be less likely to follow the Church if I got too smart. So I would be in the *stodoła* and I would hear my mother yelling, 'Han-ka! Han-ka!' I would hear her, but I would pretend I didn't." She smiles secretly at me as if we are accomplices for something that happened fifty years ago.

"So where did Pani get the books from?" I ask.

"Well, of course, we had no books at home," she says. "Only the

Bible. Because of how my mother was. But you see, the teachers at school liked me a lot and they understood, so they loaned me books to read. There was one teacher in particular. Pani Anita. And when I finished all of the books at school, she took out books from the library and gave them to me. Or at least she told me they were from the library. Later, I realized that most of them were not on the *indeks*, so I think she got them from other places. I remember one time I was reading Émile Zola . . ."

"Émile Zola?"

"Émile Zola. You have read?"

"He was one of my grandmother's favorites. She loved the French."

"Yes, so you know then, he was a complete shock, especially back then. A complete shock. And my mother found me with it in the *stodoła*. The worst possible book she could have found. And she only had to read a few sentences before she was ranting about *niemoralny* and Sodom and Gomorrah and the Pharisees." The two students at our table are listening with rapt attention. The woman puts down her spoon and lifts her hand to her head. "*Oj!* And then . . . oh, it was *awful* . . . she made me watch her throw it into the stove to burn. Oh, it was *awful.* And then when it had burned, she took a scoop of ashes from the stove and wrapped them in paper, and she made me take them back to the teacher at school who had given the book to me. Oh, I was so ashamed," she says. "So ashamed."

"And did the teacher stop giving Pani books?" I ask.

"Oh no," she says. "She continued. She was not afraid of my mother. In fact, after that, I think she tried to find the most controversial books she could . . . you know, out of spite. She wasn't afraid. Pani Anita. She was really something."

"And then?"

She pauses and looks away, and for a moment, I worry that she won't continue. Really, she's only savoring the ending herself, turning it over one last time within her own mind before sharing it with someone. "And then I went to university and became a professor. French philology. Not here. In Lublin."

The two students hold a quick conference and pick up their soup plates.

"Thank you."

"Thank you," we reply, but I don't take my eyes off the little screen.

The woman looks at her watch. "I have to be going too," she says. "But good luck." She grasps my hand for just a moment, and I can feel her warmth.

Once again, my table is empty. I'm scared to look up and see all the eyes watching me, but I picture Magda in my head, all those days we spent worrying over kings and queens and battles and invasions, and I stay in my seat, my heart beating wildly.

"I will answer your questions. Are you paying?"

The woman is disheveled, with no front teeth and a long, dirty sheepskin coat even though it is July.

"No."

She shrugs and sits down anyway.

I fumble with the camera. "Okay. Ready."

"Where is the microphone?" the woman lisps through the gap in her teeth, and she holds out her hand.

"No, no. It's right here." I point out the square of silver mesh no larger than a button.

"That's the microphone?"

"Yes, Pani."

"And the picture?"

I flip the screen around so she can see.

"Matko Boska," she says, and her lips begin to quiver slightly. The woman watches with wild eyes as if she's witnessing the woodland fairies themselves dancing across the screen.

After her, two more grandmothers sit down. One tells me she was an executive secretary for a chemical company. She has raspberry-colored hair and she wiggles on her chair to straighten her back.

"For thirty-two years. And you know what I have to show for it? A pension that's not enough to feed a cat and the worry of being raped by some hooligan as I walk down the street. The damn capitalists and their shock therapy, congratulating themselves because the shops are filled, but who can afford anything? And to add insult to injury, every time I turn on the television, I either have to watch commercials for junk I can't buy or see that damn Wałęsa kissing Reagan's *dupa* in a different quadrant each time."

"Clinton."

"What?"

"Clinton's *dupa*."

The woman shrugs. "Same cabbage, different meal."

"Oh, don't listen to her," the friend says, "she is always talking about politics, this one. Politics, politics, politics."

Several people around us start to argue about capitalism, and even the woman behind the counter looks up from her register.

"And what about Pani?" I ask. "What did Pani do?"

"I worked in the opera house."

"As a singer?"

"In the ticket booth. But I could have been a singer. I had a beautiful voice when I was young. I even got a scholarship to study in Berlin. And working in the ticket office, I got to know all the famous singers and musicians and conductors at the opera, and they all knew me. In fact, when I retired, they had a party for me, and they asked me to sing, and Jadwiga Romańska told me that I had a beautiful voice. Can you imagine? Jadwiga Romańska."

"And the scholarship in Berlin?"

"What about it?"

"Why didn't you go?"

"I got married. To Sławek. Oh, he was so handsome! And he was a very good dancer."

"A *very* good dancer," the friend with the raspberry hair says.

"Yes, and she always used to flirt with him." The woman points at her friend.

"I did not!"

"You did too. Anyway, I did not go to Berlin. I stayed here, married Sławek, and we had three lovely children."

"Well, two lovely children and one with no common sense," the friend interjects.

"Do I say that about your children?"

"My children are not like that."

As I walk home, the sun on my face, I start to think about these two women and how they bantered back and forth the way Magda and Irena and I used to. I think about all the stories and secrets I have heard from the strangers in the milk bar while Irena remains silent clear on the other side of town. When I get to Pani Bożena's, I walk right past her door and down to the teachers' dormitory at the end of the street. I'm shaking with adrenaline. The receptionist nods at me, and I close myself in the little booth. I pick up the receiver and slide the card in. My fingers know the number by heart. I wait. My breath catches on each pause, and my heart flings itself against its cage in vain. The phone rings on the other end, the long beeps and pauses sending out my plea in Morse code.

No answer. I sit in the booth and stare at the phone for a long time afterward.

For the next three weeks, I spend every day filming, either in milk bars or in parks away from the center. As it turns out, my *góralka* hands, the ones that Irena used to joke were good for plucking chickens and shearing sheep, are also good for digging inside people, pulling out family roots and scrabbling under the dust for memories. And my *góralka* eyes turn out to be good at picking out the glimmers of dreams and the pockmarks of regret.

Sometimes I draw suspicious glances, and sometimes the people approaching me on the paths change directions or veer off, but when they sit down, most of them are relieved to talk, to have someone to listen. They tell me about 1939, 1945, 1956, 1970, 1981, 1989, and all the years in between. They talk about the communists and the Resistance, Jaruzelski's culpability or his political acumen. Everyone has a memory about one of the pope's Masses on the Błonia. There are the tremendous, life-shaking stories — infidelities, children lost, visits by the SB in the middle of the night, miraculous visions, the War, the Trains, death, and the mortality of dreams. But I also hear about the mundane. I hear the recipes from the shortage years, strategies for waiting in lines, names of family pets, layouts of childhood flats, details of long-past vacations at the sea, spouses' quirks. Sometimes it feels like Magda is right there beside me, smoking a cigarette or carrying her army helmet under her arm or whispering jokes into my ear. As if we are on a treasure hunt for all the stories my grandmother left out. Beginnings, middles, and endings, happy and sad. I gather up as many as I can, protect them in black plastic, swaddle them in a plain dishtowel. Over the weeks, I'm surprised to find that the more stories I record and the longer I carry them around, the lighter they become. I find out that the difference between knowing something and being able to talk about it is that there are many hands now, and we all share the burden.

The last interviews I do are on the Feast of the Assumption. I spend the entire morning settled on a ledge along Grodzka Street, the sun beating down on me as the procession floats by. I remember the stories Irena told me about the protests, the fire hoses, and the blue dye, and some of the people I talk with tell the same stories.

It's almost the end of another summer and the beginning of another school year. I've already received four letters from Czesław, all the way from America, but nothing from Bytomska Street. I didn't have the nerve to call again, so I wrote instead. Four lines, each word carefully vetted. But nothing. The only reply I received was from Stash, who came by when I wasn't in and left a note with Pani Bożena. Six lonely words. *Be patient. I'm working on her.*

I thought I'd hear from her by now. I really did.

I walk back to the *kamienica* after the procession, and Pani Bożena calls to me from one of the empty flats on the first floor.

"In here!" She's wearing a housedress and a head scarf, and she's scrubbing down the painted woodwork. I've never seen any of the other flats, but this one looks like it belongs in a manor house. It's all in white, with windows stretching from the ceiling to the floor and a great plaster medallion in the center of the ceiling. I can't believe it's been locked up empty this entire time.

"Did you go to the procession this morning, *kochana*?"

"Uh-huh."

"And you did more of your interviews?"

"Yes. A few good ones. What are you up to?"

"Cleaning," she says. "A couple came by today. They will be moving in next week."

"It's a beautiful flat. I'll bet you can ask a lot for it."

"I think it will be nice just to have more people around."

I turn to go upstairs.

"Baba Yaga?"

"Yes?"

"You know that you can stay as long as you want. I'm not going to rent your flat to anyone else."

"Thank you." I start up the stairs again.

"Baba Yaga?" she calls after me again.

"Yes?"

"If you want, you can do one of your interviews on me."

Pani Bożena answers every question I ask her. We are at it for over an hour, and I have to go upstairs in the middle for a new tape. It is my ninety-eighth, and last, interview.

48

So That Poland Will Be Poland

A S THE SOVIETS used to say, "The years do not stop; the river does not flow backward." In the fall, I manage to get a job as an assistant at one of the new production studios opening in Huta. They do local television commercials mostly, but once in a while, there's a documentary or a retrospective. My boss is a woman named Zenka, who has short red hair and blue cat's-eye glasses, and who doesn't laugh when I tell her that I want to apply to go to Łódź next year. She even lets me stay and use the editing machines after everyone has gone home for the day, and the interviews I made in the summer are slowly piecing themselves together.

I move out of Pani Bożena's and into a *garsoniera* on Siemaszki, far from the center but close to the bus stop. It's nothing special — one room, a half-bathtub, a phone, a hot plate, and a refrigerator — but I scrub and polish it until it feels like home.

One night as I'm standing in the corridor, digging for my keys, I hear the phone. The ring is jarring, like a child banging pots. I drop my rucksack and the bag of groceries and jam my key into the lock, but I'm too late. It stops ringing as soon as I reach it, and when I press the receiver to my ear, the only thing I hear is the steady, mocking dial tone.

I check the time. It's eleven-thirty, well in violation of the understood rule that no one calls after ten except in cases of death or infidelity. It could be Czesław, calling from America. Or maybe something has happened to Pani Bożena. I stand over the phone for a few minutes, waiting for it to ring again, my heart beating and my hands trembling.

"Ring again, you little *skurwysyn*."

"Is everything all right?" It's the neighbor woman across the way, standing in the open door in her robe.

"I missed it," I say. "Sorry if it woke you. I don't know who might be calling so late."

"I hope everything is all right," she says. "It's rung a few times tonight already."

It doesn't ring again until two days later, so early in the morning that I'm still in bed.

"*Słucham.*"

There's a muffled "*Oj!*" on the other end, and the sound of the phone dropping to the ground.

"*Hallo?*" I say. "*Hallo?*"

"Baba Yaga?"

It's Irena. Jezus Maria, it's Irena.

"Yes? Irena? Is it you?"

"Baba Yaga, you will come to dinner on Sunday. Sunday at one." It's an order. Terse, forceful, efficient. Typically Irena. And then without waiting for an answer, she hangs up.

I lie back on the bed in my pajamas, laughing until the tears come to my eyes. She called. She called. Jezus Maria, she called.

I'm more nervous than I have ever been in my life. More nervous than before my first date with Tadeusz, more nervous than when I was sitting on the wall with Sebastian, more nervous than I was at the milk bar in Huta the first day I tried to film. I push the button on the *domofon* and wait.

"*Tak?*"

"It's Baba Yaga."

The door buzzes and I go in. The videotape and the bottle of Hungarian wine in my rucksack bump against my back. I walk up the stairwell, which seems so empty and sterile now. I ring the doorbell and listen to the scuffling and the voices behind the door as I wait. It's not Irena but Stash who finally opens the door. He kisses me on the cheek and smiles.

"You've cut your hair," I say. The ponytail is gone, his hair cropped so that the streaks of gray are now only a handful of metal shavings scattered along his temples.

Irena is sitting in the same place on the love seat as when I saw her for the last time before the Juvenalia party, but she looks much different. She's lightened her hair and is wearing a smaller pair of wire-rimmed glasses. She stands up and smooths the front of her pants.

"Welcome, Baba Yaga." She sounds stiff and mechanical, and we both stand there, not knowing what to do.

"Why don't you have a seat," Stash says. "Would you like anything to drink?"

"Tea, please," I say, but when he leaves the room to get it, there's an awkward silence, and I regret asking for anything.

"So," Irena says.

"So," I say.

"Did you hurt your leg?"

I shake my head. "Why?"

"Oh, I thought I saw you limping a little."

"No." I look around the room. The painting above the television is still the same, though she's added another one over the love seat.

"It must have been the rucksack," she says. "The weight of the rucksack."

"Yes."

Her eyes glance nervously around the room. "Pani Bożena said that you are making a film," she says. "And that you are working at a film studio in Huta now."

"Yes. I'm going to apply to Łódź for next year."

"I didn't realize there were film studios in Huta."

"Well, everybody's making television commercials now," I say. "It's mostly television commercials."

More silence. She looks like she wants to stand up and run away, but she forces herself to stay on the love seat.

"I like that painting a lot."

"It's an old one," she says.

"It's nice."

348

"I've started again."

"Painting?"

"Yes. Badly. Nothing I would put on the walls. But I've started again."

"That's good."

"It is."

Mercifully, Stash returns with the tea, and he begins to chat and fill in the awkwardness as best he can. He talks about the club mostly, about his plans for the *remont*, about the new bar girl, whom he doesn't think will last long. I listen for Kinga's and Tadeusz's names, but he doesn't say anything, and I don't want to ask.

Irena gets up to serve dinner, and Stash follows.

"Can I help?"

"Oh no, no," Irena says. "You are my guest."

That word.

We eat dinner from the coffee table like we used to, only today, it's draped in a lace tablecloth, and we use the good china. Irena asks politely if I've had enough *kotlet*, enough *surowka*, enough potatoes, enough *kompot*. We talk about Czesław's visit and what a surprise it was. After dinner, we drink tea. I ask how the tourist season is going, and she tells me about the idiots who have opened up the new youth hostel. Idiots, she says, nothing stronger, and I wonder if she's holding back because of Stash or because now I am the guest.

I excuse myself to go to the bathroom, and I steal a glance at the translucent plastic panel that used to lead to Magda's room. I half expect to see the smudges of light betraying some movement inside, or smell the cigarette smoke wafting from under the door, or hear Magda's voice calling to me. But everything is quiet.

I go back into the living room and we talk some more. Eventually, Stash runs out of things to make conversation about. I don't want to leave, but I can think of nothing more to say, and no one stops me when I stand up.

"Thank you for dinner," I say. "It was nice to see you again."

"You're very welcome. I'm glad you could come."

Stash gets my rucksack for me.

"Oh, I forgot. I brought you some wine." And Irena gushes for a minute about how it's her favorite.

I stand there, the door already open, and I rub the edge of the videotape through the material of the rucksack. We haven't said a word about Magda the entire afternoon. I look around at the flat one more time. If the doors are open, you can see into every room from the front hall, and in the end, it's the rooms and the things — the love seat, the dingy linoleum, the mirror in the front hall — that press me to remember, that plead with me not to leave just yet. And I know it too. I know that if I leave now, with our measured politeness intact, it's a certain end for us. The next time we speak, we will be forever doomed to the surface, vulnerable to any weak current or soft breeze.

"Irena, I copied this for you." I hand her the videotape. "It's of Magda."

There turned out to be seven and a half minutes of footage of Magda from Sylwester. It had seemed so long when I'd recorded it, but in the end it only turned out to be seven and a half minutes. It's all I can return to her from an entire lifetime.

She holds the videotape in both hands and looks at me, her eyes wide and watery behind her glasses.

"I'm sorry." My voice startles me, and I grab her with more violence than either of us is expecting. "Irena, I'm really sorry," I say, and this time, my voice does not echo back to me unmet, but is swallowed up by the warmth of her shoulder and the folds of her blouse.

She hugs me tightly, stroking my hair. My grandmother used to tell me that the most important things that are said are the ones that are barely audible, and Irena whispers to me what Magda could not, what Czesław could not, what Nela herself could not.

"It's not your fault," she says. "It never was."

I am not naive anymore. I know that it will never be the same as it was before Magda died. Everything will never be okay. The videotape will sit unwatched in the bottom drawer under the television where the letters used to be, and every time that Magda unexpectedly appears in the middle of an old story, it will turn sour in our mouths, and Irena or I will have to stop and change the subject. I know that when we banter back and forth, the third voice will always be noticeably missing, and when we hug, we will both be groping for a phantom limb. But I also know that if Irena holds on to any blame for me or for herself, she will try not to show it. Because family is family, and that is what you do for each other. And if I have doubts that someday I will go to film school in Łódź and become a director, I will never say it. Because I know, in my deepest deep, that we are all working for Magda's Big Life now, for Tadeusz's and Kinga's and Nela's and Poland's, and we are only at the beginning. I am not yet on the shelf. Irena's book is still open. And somewhere out there is an ending that even my grandmother could have told.

ACKNOWLEDGMENTS

Thank you to so many people:

Anna and Anita, who made me one of their own when I was just a *głupia panienka*. The late Susanna Zantop and the Brandenbusch family for sparking my love of travel and language. Steve Pergam and Angela Chan for first telling me about the golden streets of Krakow. Robert Binswanger for showing me the importance of taking risks. Dartmouth College for betting on those risks.

Gołębia 3, Andrzej Kowalczyk, Kornet, Kino Mikro and Pod Baranami for coffee, pigeons, Dixieland jazz, movies, and inspiration. Patrycja Stefanów and the Stefanów family of Krynica, the Kubas family of Half-Village/Pół-Wieś, Bartek and Dominika Kisielewski, Dave Murgio and Magda Samborska-Murgio, Luca Casati, Dave Lundberg, Zenka Toczkowska, Marzena, the Hessel family, Władysław Jagiełło, Gaetane, Katell, Marcin, Paweł, Peter, Ignacy, Adam, Baba Jaga and Johnny, the two Agnieszki, the *klarnecista,* and the girl from Long Island, wherever you all are, for happenstance and *głupstwa*.

The people of Krakow, for spontaneously telling me their stories at tram stops and milk bars from Rydla to Huta. And also for forgiving any errors I have committed with regard to their beloved city.

Tara Hardin-Burke, my first reader in writing and in life. Aleks and Barbara Kuźmińska for checking my Polish. Stephany Wisiol-

Albert, Bill Betz, and Damian Grivetti for helping Magda die a plausible death.

My father, for encouraging me at different times to become a reader, a baseball player, a wanderer, a woodworker, a cartoonist, a social worker, a teacher, a writer, and a forgiver. My mother, for telling me at a young age that I only had to do my best and never mind the rest. Mags and Clay, Matt and Aleks, Dan and Diana, I don't know what I would do without you. All my family, friends, students, teachers, and colleagues. I am constantly learning from you, whether you realize it or not.

My agent, Wendy Sherman, for helping me see far and wide. Michelle Brower, for rescuing the manuscript from the slush pile. My editor, Anjali Singh, for pushing me to be truer to myself and closer to my vision. Everyone from Houghton Mifflin Harcourt.

And finally, Marcel Łoziński, whom I have never had the good fortune to meet, but who, in a forty-minute film, set my standards for art and for life.